By NICKI BENNETT

Always a Bridesmaid
Evan's Heaven
Flight
Home for Christmas
New Traditions

DREAMSPUN DESIRES
#10 – The Cattle Baron's Bogus Boyfriend
#58 – Bad to the Bone

With Ariel Tachna
Under the Skin

ALL FOR LOVE
Checkmate
All for One
Stronghold

HOT CARGO STORIES
Hot Cargo
Something About Harry

EXPLORING LIMITS
Exploring Limits
No Limits

OUT AND ABOUT
Out of Bounds

Published by DREAMSPINNER PRESS
www.dreamspinnerpress.com

Published by DREAMSPINNER PRESS
www.dreamspinnerpress.com

NO LIMITS

NICKI BENNETT
ARIEL TACHNA

Published by
DREAMSPINNER PRESS

5032 Capital Circle SW, Suite 2, PMB# 279, Tallahassee, FL 32305-7886 USA
www.dreamspinnerpress.com

No Limits
© 2019 Nicki Bennett and Ariel Tachna

Cover Art
© 2019 Tiferet Design
http://www.tiferetdesign.com
Cover content is for illustrative purposes only and any person depicted on the cover is a model.

Trade Paperback ISBN: 978-1-64405-072-9
Digital ISBN: 978-1-64405-071-2
Library of Congress Control Number: 2018966307
Trade Paperback published August 2019
v. 1.0
Previously published as three novellas, Breaking Limits, Transcending Limits, and No Limits, by Dreamspinner Press, 2010.

Printed in the United States of America

This paper meets the requirements of
ANSI/NISO Z39.48-1992 (Permanence of Paper).

CHAPTER 1
NIGHT TERRORS

HE STRAINED wildly against the restraints, but the metal only cut into his wrists, adding a trickle of blood to the sweat that coated his clammy skin. The blindfold kept him from seeing, the ball gag kept him from crying out, but nothing could keep the walls from pressing down on him, crushing him beneath their relentless weight. He fought for a lungful of air, but he couldn't catch his breath, couldn't stop the trembling that shook him as the dark and the cold and the silence closed around him. He'd buried him here, and he'd never get out, never get away....

A hoarse cry broke the stillness of the late summer night. Devon Aldridge's arms flailed against empty air as he struggled, shivering when the warm breeze wafted over his sweaty skin. His arm struck something and he recoiled violently, pulling away with another raw sound.

Knocked out of a sound sleep by Devon's harsh cry and a glancing blow of his elbow, Kit Webster shook his head, trying to wake up enough for rational speech. "Devon?" he asked softly, not wanting to wake their third lover if Devon's cry had not already done so.

"Devon?" Jonathan Braedon muttered groggily, reaching for where his lover should have been lying curled against him. His eyes fluttered open when his hand met only empty space and cool sheets. "What's wrong, babe?"

Kit sighed. So much for not waking Jonathan. Since they were all awake anyway, he leaned over and switched on the lamp. His eyes widened when he saw Devon huddled in one corner of the bed, knees drawn up to his chest, shivering violently. Pushing back the covers, he knelt up, trying to catch Devon's eye. "What's wrong, luv?"

Devon blinked as the voices penetrated his nightmare—warm voices, caring voices—his lovers' voices. The sudden glare of the light revealed not the dank crawl space of his nightmare, but the familiar bedroom of Jonathan's rental house. Kit and Jonathan stared at him with worried expressions.

Jonathan couldn't imagine what might have disturbed Devon so much, but it didn't matter now; he had to do something to ease the panicked look in his lover's eyes. He slid over the sheets, reaching forward slowly to stroke Devon's leg, his touch as gentle as if he were calming Hengroen, the horse he rode in his role as Arthur in the *Camelot* miniseries that had brought them together. When Devon didn't pull away from his hand, he moved closer, drawing the shaking man into a loose embrace. "It's okay, babe," he murmured, his voice low and as soothing as he could make it. "Shhh, it's okay."

Devon allowed himself half a dozen heartbeats resting in Jonathan's strong arms before swinging his legs off the edge of the bed and sitting up. "Sorry about that," he muttered, trying to force his voice to sound lighthearted. "Probably shouldn't have eaten that leftover curry right before bed—bloody indigestion's giving me the heebie-jeebies!"

Kit frowned, looking to Jonathan for guidance. It seemed an awfully pat answer for what appeared to be more than just a simple nightmare. He wanted to push, to insist on a better explanation, but he wasn't sure that was the best path to follow.

Shrugging at Kit's questioning gaze, Jonathan returned his attention to the man beside him. He'd dealt with a preteen son long enough to recognize an attempt at distraction when he saw one. Drawing a calming breath, he moved next to Devon and put an arm around the bigger man's shoulders, relieved that at least they were no longer shaking. He tried to think of a clever response to draw Devon out, but he was too worried to be subtle. "Don't try to bullshit us, Devon. That wasn't something you ate giving you *agita*. What's going on?"

Kit scooted to Devon's other side, his arm going around Devon's waist, waiting for an answer.

Devon really didn't want to have this discussion, but he knew Jonathan wasn't going to let it drop that easily. Rubbing his hand through his hair, he sighed. "It was just a nightmare, Jon. Maybe a delayed reaction to the bloody helicopter ride or something."

"That was over a week ago, Devon!" Jonathan knew how much Devon hated flying, even though it had been the fastest way to rescue him and Kit from the mudslide that had trapped them on their way to location filming, but he couldn't believe that was still bothering him. He traced Devon's shoulders with his hands, feeling the tension in the set of the broad muscles. "At least tell us what the nightmare was about," he urged, kneading the tight deltoids with gentle pressure.

"My mum said talking about a nightmare took away its power," Kit added. "It always worked for me. It isn't as frightening when you think about it calmly."

Feeling like the world's biggest prat for making the two of them worry, Devon shook his head. He should have been stronger, should have been able to keep his reaction inside, but Robert's call had shaken him even more badly than he'd realized. "It was just... I was trapped. Underground. You might have noticed I don't do small spaces well." He swallowed hard, hoping at least part of the truth would be enough to convince his all-too-perceptive lovers that it was just a random bad dream.

Devon's answer was too calculatedly casual, but Jonathan didn't know what good it would serve to push any further. Obviously, Devon didn't intend to share whatever was troubling him. Trying his best not to feel shut out, Jonathan settled for pulling Devon back down beside him on the wide bed. Holding him close as Kit spooned against Devon's other side after flicking off the light, Jonathan ran his hand through the tousled golden hair. "Go back to sleep, babe," he whispered, too wide-awake himself to close his eyes. "We've got an early call."

Kit didn't know what was going on, but Devon had been off his game all day. His takes had gotten a little better as lunchtime neared, Lancelot's persona finally winning out over Devon's fatigue; but then, during lunch, Kit saw Devon on the phone, talking agitatedly, and it seemed he had never recovered. Concerned, Kit decided to see if he could catch Jonathan alone for a minute. Fortunately the director was finished with Lancelot, but he wanted to shoot an interaction between Arthur and Percival one more time, giving Kit the opportunity he sought as they walked back to the trailer once Niall was finished with them. "Did Devon seem to be acting odd to you?"

"I thought at first he was just tired," Jonathan agreed, rubbing his beard with the back of his knuckles. "Even after he fell back asleep last night, he was pretty restless. But he's pulled some all-nighters before this and never blown his lines the way he did today. He wasn't Lancelot, and that isn't like Devon at all."

Kit sighed, a mixture of relief and concern. At least he wasn't the only one who'd noticed. "He was doing better right up until he got a call at lunchtime," Kit added, not sure Jonathan had seen Devon on the phone. "Do you suppose it was his ex-wife calling and making problems over the divorce?" They had talked about Devon's divorce more than once. It was one of the few things that really seemed to tear Devon up.

"Maybe, but usually when he's dealing with Marcy or the lawyers he gets quiet. Today he seemed—" Jonathan searched for the right word. "—brittle, maybe, like he was angry but trying to hide it by joking around." He shook his head, frowning. "Whatever it is, he obviously doesn't want to talk about it."

"So you think we should just ignore it?" Kit asked, surprised. "I mean, he seemed really upset. I hate to see him like that." He hesitated, thinking for a moment. "You know what it reminds me of?"

"What?" Jonathan didn't want to just ignore something that was troubling Devon so deeply, but he wasn't sure what they could do to help if their stubborn lover wouldn't confide in them.

"The day we went to the beach house," Kit replied, "when Devon was in such a mood. You remember, he told us a little about his"—he looked around to make sure no one was within earshot—"past. It reminds me of the mood he was in that day."

Jonathan nodded slowly, considering Kit's insight. Not for the first time, he thought how much the people who only saw Kit's beauty and charm underestimated him. Kit had a sensitivity to the emotions of others that Jonathan envied. "But once we got him to the beach, he was fine. I thought we'd convinced him we didn't hold his past against him—in fact, I thought we'd made it pretty clear that under the right circumstances, we even enjoyed it." He couldn't hold back a small grin as he remembered just how much they'd all enjoyed Devon's dominance that weekend.

"So what changed?" Kit mused. "Could we have done something that triggered another memory? Or I could be miles off the mark, and it could be something totally different. I really think we should at least ask him." He paused outside the door to their trailer, wanting to be in agreement with Jonathan before they stepped inside and faced Devon.

"You're right," Jonathan agreed, "we have to ask. I'm just not sure that in the mood he's in, he won't think we're ganging up on him."

"Do you want to talk to him alone?" Kit suggested, seeing the sense in Jonathan's concern. "Or I could, if you'd prefer."

"Let's see how he's doing now that filming's done for the day first," Jonathan decided. Kit's idea made sense, but a part of him didn't want either of them to question Devon alone. As unlikely as it had seemed at the beginning, they'd managed to make their unconventional threesome work, and his gut told him whatever the problem was, they needed to solve it together.

Kit nodded and opened the door. Stacy and Carol, their makeup artists, were inside waiting for them, but there was no sign of Devon. Putting on his best face, Kit stepped into the trailer and smiled at the women. "Is Devon finished already?" he asked, playing up his surprise.

"He was here and gone in about fifteen minutes," Stacy confirmed. "He didn't say much, but I got the impression he was in a bit of a hurry."

"Yeah," Carol agreed, "he didn't even tease us about our plans for the night the way he usually does."

Jonathan met Kit's eyes over the pictures of his son that covered one corner of his makeup mirror. The fact that Devon hadn't waited for them worried Jonathan even more than his unusual edginess. Something was definitely wrong, and whether it upset Devon more or not, they needed to find out what it was.

Kit saw the determination on Jonathan's face and nodded slightly. They would finish up here and get home as quickly as possible so they could get to the bottom of this. Pasting on what he hoped was a passable smile, he looked at Carol. "So, what *are* your plans for the evening?"

Jonathan closed his eyes and let his mind drift as Stacy worked, only half listening to Kit's and Carol's chatter. He couldn't help but worry that confronting Devon would only serve to drive their prickly lover farther away. They had no choice but to try, though. They'd just have to make Devon see that they weren't trying to pry—their concern for him was based in love. He was startled when Stacy broke him out of his reverie with a nudge of his shoulder. "Go home and get some sleep in your own bed, Jonathan," she teased.

"Who says he'll be anywhere near his own bed?" Kit replied with an impish grin. "Last I heard, the king had plans for the evening."

"My only plans right now involve finding some food." Jonathan laughed, careful to keep his tone teasing. He picked up Excalibur from where it leaned against the side of their wardrobe closet, having gotten in the habit of taking it home with him when they left the set so he could practice his swordplay during their rare free time. "C'mon, Percival, let's see if we can hunt down the king's champion and see if he'll join us."

"I could eat." Kit levered himself out of his chair and headed toward the door. "See you tomorrow, ladies," he added as he stepped out into the cooling night air, shutting the door behind them after Jonathan joined him.

Inside the trailer, Stacy paused in putting away the cleansing supplies and straightening the counter. She met Carol's eyes speculatively. "You think…?" she asked.

Carol looked at the door, then back at Stacy. "Nah," they said in unison after a moment, returning to their work so they could get on with their own plans for the evening.

AFTER DEVON'S uncharacteristic behavior all day, Jonathan was relieved to see Devon's car parked in the drive as they pulled up behind it. He cocked an eyebrow at Kit, then shrugged. "Looks like the lion came back to his den after all," he muttered. "Let's see if we can find out what's got him so worked up."

Kit nodded and got out of the car, waiting for Jonathan before walking inside. They no longer knocked at one another's houses, having long since exchanged keys. Deciding to opt for humor, Kit chirped, "Hi, honey, we're home."

Devon grimaced, draining his tumbler of scotch and giving serious consideration to downing another before facing his lovers. At least they didn't seem to be irritated at him for leaving without a word. He should have tried to think up some plausible excuse, but he was still too shaken by the day's events to think of anything clever. Falling back on his experience that partial honesty was the best policy, he turned to greet them, rubbing the back of his head, which really did ache. "Sorry for leaving like that," he grumbled. "I've had the headache from hell all day, and when Niall cut me loose, all I could think of was getting home and taking something to get rid of it."

Kit crossed to where Devon was sitting on the couch, took the glass from his hand, and set it on the table. "If it's a headache that's bothering you, this isn't the cure. I'm sure Jonathan will get you a glass of water. Close your eyes and let me see if I can help you relax," he suggested, probing the tense muscles of Devon's neck with gentle fingers.

After carrying the tumbler and the half-empty whiskey bottle into the kitchen, Jonathan returned with a fresh glass of ice water and the bottle of aspirin he'd retrieved from Devon's kitchen cabinet. He set the water on the table, shook out two tablets, and handed them to Devon. With a comforting smile, he knelt at Devon's feet, pulled off his shoes and socks, and set them off to the side. Taking one of the strong, slender feet in his hands, he began to rub it soothingly, alternating long, gentle strokes with firmer pressure at the reflexology points on the instep and the base of the toes. "Just relax and let us take care of you, Devon," he urged, watching his lover's face as both he and Kit continued their ministrations.

Letting his eyelids fall closed, Devon arched his shoulders, trying to let go of his tension beneath the calming touches. *This is what's real*, he told himself. *This is what I need to concentrate on. The hell with what that bastard said.* The pounding ache that had inhabited his skull all day long was finally beginning to ease when the ring of the telephone sounded from the kitchen. His eyes snapping open, Devon jumped to his feet before either of the others could think to answer it.

"What the fuck?" Kit muttered, looking at Jonathan. He got up and started after Devon. He had no idea what was going on in Devon's head, but it was past time they found out.

Jonathan caught Kit's arm, preventing him from following Devon and pulling him back to wrap his arms around Kit's narrow hips. "Let him go, Kit-Kat," he urged, looking up from where he still knelt at the foot of the couch. "We'll find out what's bothering him, but he won't appreciate feeling like we're eavesdropping or spying on him."

"It just eats at me to see him so upset." Kit gestured helplessly toward the kitchen. "There's got to be something we can do for him. Something."

"Let's get him fed and take him to bed," Jonathan answered with a waggle of his eyebrows and a leering smile. "Between the two of us, I think we can find some way to clear up his bad mood." He rested his chin on Kit's hip bone, his expression sobering. "And after that, we'll talk."

His pulse slowing with relief, Devon couldn't help but smile when he walked back into the parlor to see his lovers embracing. "Starting without me again?" he growled playfully, hoping the teasing would distract them from the near panic with which he'd run for the phone. "That was Niall.

He wants me in early tomorrow for some reshoots of my scene with Guinevere with new and improved dialogue."

"We were just waiting for you." Kit grinned, relieved to see the black cloud lifted, at least for the moment. "How does dinner sound? I bet we could convince Jonathan to cook if we asked him nicely."

Jonathan glanced up at Devon with a smile. They'd keep it light and playful for now; Devon needed relaxation, not confrontation. "And after that, we'll see what else we can cook up," he drawled, reaching out to invite Devon to rejoin them.

COLD SWEAT trickled down his back as he fought to steady his breathing. He couldn't fail again, that was why he was here in the first place, but he could feel the walls closing in on him with each shuddering breath. He twisted against the cramp in his shoulder blade—he'd wrenched it during his struggles, and the cruel pull of the restraints behind his raw back made it worse. The movement sent a shower of damp earth falling over his face, and he couldn't hold back the moan of terror as his lungs seized and his limbs twitched in a futile need to break free, to claw his way out of here, to escape....

Devon's struggles and his sudden cry woke Jonathan with a start. His arms tightened instinctively around Devon's thrashing limbs, but that only made him fight harder, his elbow striking Jonathan in the chest. "Devon!" He let go and raised his hands instead to hold the shaggy blond head still. "Devon, wake up. It's okay. It's me, Jonathan," he murmured, trying to keep his own fear out of his voice.

Jonathan's cry woke Kit as well. *Shit!* he thought. *Here we go again.* He settled his hands on Devon's shoulders, kneading soothingly as he added his own soft murmurs to Jonathan's. He didn't know how to get Devon to open up to them, but this had to stop.

Devon's eyes snapped open to meet Jonathan's, his lover's gaze wide with love and concern in the darkened bedroom. He drew a ragged breath and shook his head, the warmth of Jonathan's hands at his temples and Kit's on his shoulders grounding him from the last remnants of the nightmare's terrors. He raised a palm to scrub at his face, horrified to discover his cheek damp with tears. "Fuck," he whispered, wiping at the other cheek in turn. "Fuck, I'm sorry."

"You don't have anything to apologize for," Jonathan insisted, pulling Devon forward to rest their foreheads together. "But you have to tell us what's doing this to you, babe. Let us help you."

Kit's hands drifted lower over Devon's back. "You're covered in sweat!" he observed, surprised. This wasn't just a bad dream. Devon was having night terrors! "Why don't you go with Jonathan and have a quick shower while I get us all a drink, and then we'll talk."

Still half caught in the submissive mind-set of the dream, Devon was unresisting as Jonathan helped him to his feet and led him toward the bathroom, murmuring soothing words and wrapping an arm around his trembling shoulders. "The water will make you feel better," Jonathan promised.

Jonathan's eyes met Kit's in concern before he and Devon disappeared into the bathroom. Kit scampered down the steps in search of the brandy and three glasses. He was putting them all on a tray to take back upstairs when the phone rang. Frowning as he glanced at the clock, he wondered who could be calling at such a late hour. Niall had phoned earlier, so surely it wasn't him. He picked up the receiver. "Hello?"

Silence stretched on the other end of the line as the caller processed the realization that Devon hadn't answered the phone. *So the big blond isn't spending his nights alone!* This could be even more intriguing than he'd hoped. "Have you worn Devon out?" he rumbled in amusement.

"Who is this?" Kit demanded, not recognizing the voice but taking offense at the insinuating tone.

"Tsk, tsk." The caller chuckled softly. "You haven't earned the right to ask any questions… yet." The voice hardened into a tone of command. "Tell Devon I'll be expecting an introduction." Not bothering to wait for a reply, he severed the connection, his groin tightening in anticipation. *Oh yes, this will be good, very good indeed.*

Kit frowned, looking down at the tray. Tea might well have been a better choice, but after that phone call, he needed a brandy. Picking up the platter, he headed back upstairs to see if Jonathan and Devon were finished and to join them if they were not.

CHAPTER 2
JUST BREATHE

DEVON STOOD beneath the cascading water, letting it wash away the taint of horror from his memories as its warmth soothed the chill of his clammy skin. Jonathan's hands, strong and gentle, eased his head back to dampen his hair, but he couldn't force himself to open his eyes. Not yet. He couldn't bear to see Jonathan's expression change to scorn for his weakness, or to pity, as he knew it would when the truth came out. He knew his lovers well enough to realize he'd have to give them a full explanation—but he still kept his eyes closed, delaying the inevitable a little longer.

Devon's continued silence and docility ate at Jonathan's studied calm. He wanted to push Devon against the wall of the shower and hold him there with his body, wanted to demand that Devon tell them what the hell was going on and why the fuck he was keeping it from them. But however much better that would make him feel, it was the last thing Devon needed, especially in the state he was in after the nightmare. He'd have to wait for Kit to return before starting the discussion anyway. Holding back a frustrated sigh, Jonathan poured some shampoo into his palms and began to work it through Devon's locks, trying to will away Devon's tension.

Kit set the tray down on the table next to the bed and walked into the bathroom, drawn by the sound of the running water. He pulled aside the curtain and stepped into the shower, immediately adding his hands to Jonathan's on Devon's body. "Feeling better, lover?" he asked.

"Mmmnn," Devon rumbled, but it was getting harder to keep his eyes closed with two sets of hands wandering over his body and stirring his cock to stiffness against his thigh.

"Somebody's waking up," Jonathan observed wryly, though he didn't move his hands toward Devon's erection and did his best to keep his touches soothing. His own answering arousal was making itself known, but as wonderful as they could make one another feel, it would only distract them from the need to talk.

"Good." Kit smiled, knowing what both his lovers were surely feeling, for he was feeling it too. His passion, though, was tempered by the chilling call he had received. "You got a rather strange telephone call while I was downstairs," he added, keeping the movement of his hands steady as he spoke.

Jerking upright from beneath the shower's spray so quickly that his head swam, Devon grasped Kit's shoulders and turned to face him. "You answered the phone?" he demanded fiercely. "Who was it? What did he say?"

"He wouldn't give his name when I asked," Kit replied, meeting Devon's eyes. He didn't want to add to Devon's panic, but he needed Devon to understand that he—they—were serious about finding out what was going on. "He said to tell you he was expecting an introduction."

Devon's muscles tensed at Kit's response. "That bastard!" Devon cursed, tightening his grip on Kit's shoulders, so enraged he didn't notice the wince of pain. "That bloody, mother-sodding bastard! I'll rip his head from his fucking body before I let him get anywhere near you!" He reached for the curtain, ready to charge out of the shower that very instant.

Clutching at Devon in turn, Jonathan hauled him back, and this time he *did* pin him against the wall. "You're not going anywhere until you tell us what the fuck is going on," he insisted, holding the fiery green gaze with his own implacable stare.

"I agree, but I think this might be a conversation better suited to the bedroom than to the shower stall. Right, Jonathan?" Kit said firmly, turning off the water. "I brought some brandy up for all of us. We'll go in, sit down, and talk. Then we can see about ripping someone's head off his body."

Devon met Jonathan's gaze a moment longer, then nodded, pushing a hand through his dripping hair. A tense silence held as each man dried off, with none of the teasing offers of assistance that would normally accompany the activity.

Wrapping a towel around his hips, Jonathan nodded for Devon to precede them into the bedroom, squeezing Kit's shoulder for reassurance as they followed.

Devon stood awkwardly in the center of the room, as if he were still considering bolting. "Sit," Jonathan insisted, pointing to the corner of the bed and taking a cross-legged position across from Devon.

Kit settled right next to where Devon flopped on the bed, spooning up behind him. Jonathan's intensity was so pointed, so focused, that Kit could only imagine how harried Devon was feeling. Deciding on a different tack, he wrapped his arms around Devon and nuzzled his neck. "Come on, Devon. Talk to us, please. We can't help you if we don't know what's wrong. At least tell us who was on the phone."

Taking a sudden interest in the crumpled burgundy sheets beneath his knees, Devon shook his head. "Robert," he said wearily, giving in to the inevitable with poor grace. "That were—that was Robert."

Shocked by Devon's defeated tone and the lapse into broad Yorkshire—a sign of how deeply he was shaken—Jonathan tried to let go of his own fear and frustration. He reached forward to close a hand around the one of Devon's that was picking nervously at the sheets. "He's the one you told us about at the beach house?" he asked, his voice quiet.

Jonathan's question brought back to Kit the conversation they'd had with Devon where he'd revealed a little of his past involvement with a hard-core BDSM scene. Kit had all but put it from his mind, despite the games they'd played since then. Devon wasn't like that, wasn't a heartless, unfeeling Dom. He was a tender, creative lover, even when he was being commanding or fucking Kit over a porch rail. As rough as things had gotten between them at times, ever since that one time he and Jonathan had scared Kit inadvertently, Devon had been the model lover. "Is he the one who's been calling you the last couple of days?"

"Aye," Devon admitted in answer to both questions. "He's the one. Bastard's been calling for the last week."

"You said—or at least, you implied—it was over between you," Jonathan protested. His stomach roiled at the thought of the man who had abused Devon, badly enough to have caused the terrifying dreams that had tormented him the last few nights, trying to make contact again.

"Hadn't seen or thought of the bastard in years," Devon rumbled, though only the first part of the statement was true.

"Then why would he start calling you now?"

"And why would he want to meet me?" Kit added. "You certainly made it sound like you didn't part on very good terms."

"He's here." Devon couldn't hide the shudder that shook him at the thought of even being on the same continent with his former master. "He's managed to get an invitation to visit the set. And there is no way in bloody hell I'm introducing you to him!"

"All right, wait a minute." Jonathan took both Devon's hands between his. "Even if he does manage to get on set, there's nothing he can do, Devon. Between the crew and the cast and security, there'll be dozens of people around. So you introduce us, we say hello"—*I manage not to knock his teeth down his throat for what he did to you*—"and then he's gone. Don't let it get to you this way."

"How'd he get permission to come on set?" Kit asked, rubbing his hands soothingly over Devon's back. "I thought Niall was being really careful about who he allowed around."

"Professional courtesy," Devon muttered, his voice dripping scorn. "He's been gloating about how much he's looking forward to it. He'd just better stay the fuck away from the two of you." He growled, balling his hands into fists beneath Jonathan's clasp.

Unclenching Devon's hands, Jonathan twined their fingers together and squeezed gently. "What exactly did he do to you, Devon?" he asked in a low voice. "Tell us about the dream."

"You know you can tell us anything, Devon," Kit added. "Just don't shut us out."

Drawing an unsteady breath, Devon tried to bring his anger under control, tried to find a dispassionate voice that would hide the shame he felt. "The first time I met him was on set," he began. "I was a bit in awe—eager to work with him, anxious to make a good impression." He snorted in disgust at the memory. "A bunch of us went out for drinks after the first week's shooting—just getting to know each other, like. You know how it is after everyone's been drinking for a while; the conversation started turning suggestive. I'd done a little experimenting with BDSM, not much really, but he made a comment, and I answered back, made it sound like I was more experienced than I was—trying to impress him, I suppose." Devon gave another scornful laugh. "He called my bluff—invited me back to his place. I couldn't back down, not if I didn't want to look like a fool."

Kit winced. He'd been in situations like that before. They never ended well. While he was glad for the insight into Devon's past, he didn't see how it related to the present. "And the dream?" he prompted. "What does that have to do with your nightmare?"

"That was when it started, that first night," Devon replied, his voice lowering as he let himself remember what he'd spent the years since then trying to forget. "He told me afterward that he'd gone easy on me, but now that he knew how well I could take it, he wouldn't hold back. Made me feel proud, strong. And at first it was good—more than good," he admitted. He flushed at the memory of how willingly he'd gone under, how hungry he'd been for the older man's approval. "I'd have done anything for him, and damn near did."

Devon's words sent a double chill down Kit's back, one for the thought of someone trying to break Devon, the other for how strongly the feelings Devon described resembled his own. Looking at Devon directly in front of him and Jonathan sitting there facing them, Kit knew that despite the surface similarities, this was different. Devon might give them orders from time to time, might push their limits, but he wasn't looking for a slave, wasn't trying to recreate them to fit his image of the perfect lover.

Remembering how incredibly aroused he'd been that weekend at the beach, Jonathan nodded. He could understand how tempting it might be to submit to someone you trusted—and how dangerous it could be if that trust was misplaced. "What went wrong?" he asked, afraid he already knew the answer.

"In the beginning, we stuck to pretty basic stuff—restraints, gagging…." Devon flushed again, his voice thickening. "Flogging. Then he—we—" He dropped his head, not wanting to see the expressions on Kit's and Jonathan's faces at his admission.

Inwardly flinching, Kit tightened his embrace, wanting Devon to feel his support. He could see how much these memories upset him, and a part of him wanted to stop, to tell Devon that it didn't matter, that he should just forget about it. He knew better, though. This was poisoning Devon from the inside, and if they didn't get it out in the open and dealt with, it would start poisoning their relationship too. Kit loved Devon too much to let that happen. "Then?" he said softly, his lips against Devon's nape as he spoke.

"He said he wanted us to try something different, that I was the first partner he trusted enough to share it with—and I was daft enough to believe him. We'd already—" Devon swallowed, just the memory enough to make it hard to breathe. "He'd already fucked me once cuffed to the bed—I was so far under I couldn't deny him anything. It was so good when he started, slow and more tender than he usually was. He was stroking my throat, wrapping his hands around my neck while he kissed me—he almost never kissed me—it was so good, so sweet, and when we both started to get close, he—he started to—to squeeze." He shook his head, blind to anything but the memory. "Maybe I could have stopped him then, but I never even thought to try. I was so fuckin' close, and all I could feel was him inside me, and my blood pounding in my ears, and it felt so fuckin' incredible…. I'd never come that hard before."

Jonathan hated this, hated hearing Devon talk about it, hated the thought of his being hurt, but most of all hated the idea that this bastard had made Devon like it. He wanted to lean forward and kiss Devon's neck, to wipe away the memory of the other man's hands, but he knew he shouldn't distract Devon from finishing his story. Tightening his grip on Devon's fingers, he willed his voice to calmness. "Was that what the nightmare was about?"

Kit bent his head, unable to meet either of their eyes as he struggled to deal with the myriad of emotions. Anger was starting to burn within him, low in his gut, at the thought of some freak doing these things to Devon, forcing him into such a situation. He knew Devon would say there had been no force, but Kit knew better, even if the force had not been physical. His resolve increased with the strength of his anger. This Robert—the name was a curse in his mind—would not be allowed to hurt Devon again.

Daring a glance up, Devon was caught by the intensity of Jonathan's gaze. In his eyes he saw unquestioning understanding and acceptance, not the condemnation he'd feared. A rush of emotion hit him so strongly that he blinked back sudden tears. "No." He shook his head, holding on to the comfort of Jonathan's gaze like a lifeline. "Not then; not at first. But every time after that, he'd start a little sooner, squeeze a little tighter— hold on after a little longer. One night—" He hesitated, but Jonathan's nod encouraged him to go on. "One night he was upset about something—I don't even remember what it was, something from the day's filming, maybe. Anyway, he'd told me he didn't want to hear anything out of me, warned me not to make a sound. He'd—"

Looking into Jonathan's eyes, feeling Kit's hands trembling on his shoulders, Devon couldn't tell them how he'd come so close to safewording after Robert had beaten him harder than he'd ever done before and then taken him while he still hung in the restraints; how Robert had throttled him until he was sure he was going to suffocate, taunting him the whole time, daring him to tell him to stop. Pride alone had kept him from struggling when the cruel hands closed around his throat, when Robert slammed into him without preparation and choked him until black waves obscured his sight. He would have cried out his safeword then, but he couldn't even draw enough air to speak. They both orgasmed together, and he couldn't hold back the gasp of pain when Robert's hands finally slackened enough to let him suck in an agonized breath.

"He—I—when he let me go, I gasped, and he—he said—he told me if I couldn't obey a simple order, he'd have to show me what being quiet meant." Devon shuddered as his breathing quickened in response to the memory. "He took me down, cuffed my hands behind my back, and he—there was a crawl space under the porch of his house, he put me into it and he—he—it was—"

The remembered horror in Devon's eyes cut into Jonathan's soul. Opening his arms, he pulled Devon into his embrace, kissing his temple, his ear, his neck. "'S okay," he whispered, tears rolling down his face unheeded as he rocked Devon in his arms. "It's okay, it's over. He can't touch you anymore."

"We won't let him," Kit agreed hoarsely, his eyes damp with his own unshed tears. He moved onto his knees, lining his body up with Devon's back, adding his lips, his caresses to Jonathan's. He moved his hands gently, sliding them over Devon's skin, seeking to wipe away the memory of any touch but theirs.

Feeling the dampness of Jonathan's tears against his throat, Devon lifted his lover's face, brushing away the moisture, and joined their lips together, the need to give comfort pulling him out of the memories of the past. He parted Jonathan's lips with his tongue, drinking in the taste of his mouth, banishing Robert from his thoughts, taking comfort in the presence of the men he loved. With his free hand, he reached back, captured Kit's arm, and pulled him closer, leaning into his strength.

Devon's taking control of the kiss told Jonathan more than any words could what he needed. Devon was strong; he'd walked away from this bastard once and he'd beat him again, but right now he needed reassurance of his own control, and Jonathan would give that to him. Lying back on the pile of pillows against the headboard, he pulled Devon down on top of him, spreading his legs to coax Devon to lie between them. He gently broke away from the kiss, giving in to his need to trail his mouth down the strong column of Devon's throat. "Make love to me, Devon," he whispered, the low rasp of his voice confirming his need.

"Yes," Devon husked, desire for his lover—for both his lovers—flaring in him. Twisting his shoulders, he drew Kit's mouth to his, conveying his own need with the urgent dance of his tongue. "Kit," he urged, "want you to make love to me." He needed both men's touch, both men's love, to wipe away the last traces of Robert's poisonous memory.

"Anytime," Kit replied fervently, love and lust mingling at the request. He shifted so that he knelt between Jonathan's outspread legs, pulling Devon between his own thighs, facing Jonathan. "Go ahead," he urged. "Touch him like he asked. You know what he likes." As he spoke, he stroked Devon's chest, tweaking his nipples.

Jonathan moaned as Devon's hands mirrored Kit's words, coasting over all the sensitive spots his lovers had discovered. He tangled his hands in Devon's tousled hair and pulled him back into a deep kiss, claiming Devon's mouth to demonstrate exactly how he wanted to be claimed in turn.

Kit watched Devon and Jonathan kiss, their passion turning him on immensely. There wasn't any danger of what they shared getting mixed up with Robert's twisted ideas, not if the other man had foregone the incredible pleasure of kissing Devon. Kit took advantage of that freedom every chance he got. That triggered an idea, so fleeting he almost dismissed it. Almost. Moving his hands to Devon's shoulders, he urged him to slide lower, sending Devon's lips skimming over Jonathan's collarbone on their way to his nipples. "Bite him," Kit urged. "You know how he likes it."

Devon let Kit guide him without even thinking about it. The suggestion coincided so well with his own desires that he never questioned the instruction. Kit's lips on his back, nipping and kissing, only added to the sensation, and to his surprise, he felt himself slipping under, not like he had with Robert, not out of pride or fear, but out of need and love. With a sigh of relief against Jonathan's skin, he gave himself over to Kit's direction, knowing without needing to be told that Kit would never abuse that trust.

Jonathan was surprised to hear Kit take control, a role Devon usually assumed regardless of his relative position in the pile of their bodies, but before he could question it, Devon relaxed against him, following Kit's instructions. Jonathan quit wondering and enjoyed the feel of Devon's teeth closing around his nipple.

A little surprised at Devon's easy acquiescence, Kit wondered how far his two lovers would let him take this. Not that he had any intention of turning it rough, but he wasn't usually the one giving directions, however tame they were. He sat back on his heels and tentatively closed his hands over Jonathan's, moving them from Devon's head to his chest. "Touch him," he directed Jonathan. "I want to hear him moan."

The delicious torment of Devon's mouth on his chest had Jonathan close to moaning himself. Kit's command only reinforced what he longed to do anyway. He ran his palms over the width of Devon's broad chest and then returned to rub circles over the pebbling nipples. When he'd coaxed them to firm peaks, he pinched them between his fingers, rolling and tugging the sensitive buds until he wrung a groan from deep in Devon's throat.

Biting his way toward Jonathan's other nipple, Devon didn't try to hold back his moan of pleasure, knowing it was what Kit wanted to hear. He arched his hips upward, opening himself further to Jonathan's touch and hoping to brush against Kit, missing the warmth against his back.

Kit brushed a gentle hand over Devon's arse. "Feeling greedy, are you?" he teased, letting his fingers drift into the cleft between the muscular buttocks. On impulse, he lowered his head and nipped sharply at the curve of one cheek.

Startled, Devon instinctively bit down harder on Jonathan's nipple, their cries echoing as they bucked against each other. "You know what we want," Devon gasped, licking a soothing swath over the swollen flesh beneath his mouth. He met Jonathan's eyes, their blue depths cloudy with desire. "What we all want."

Kit grinned. Yes, he knew what they wanted. He grabbed the lube from the bedside table, took one of Devon's hands, and squirted gel onto his fingers. "Get Jonathan ready," he said firmly.

His desire spiraling at Kit's commands, Devon saw a matching spark in Jonathan's eyes. He stroked lazily down Jonathan's cock and then lower, sliding his hand behind it to skim the dark crease. At the same time, the cool slickness of Kit's hand delved between his own legs, preparing him as he opened Jonathan, all their movements wordlessly synchronized in a loving dance.

"Lift your knees, Jonathan," Kit instructed. "Let Devon in." Even as he continued preparing Devon with one hand, he reached around and palmed Devon's hard cock with the other, slicking it and guiding it to Jonathan's entrance.

Acceding without question, Jonathan opened himself to his lovers. Hearing Kit direct Devon made him feel as if both of them were making love to him at the same time. Jonathan closed his hand over Kit's, raising his hips to draw Devon inside, a deep moan of pleasure escaping as the thick shaft filled him. He pulled Devon's head back down to his, breathing the sound into his parted lips.

Devon drank in Jonathan's heated breath, filling his lungs with the sweetness of his groan as he sank into the welcoming sheath of his body. Kit's breath was warm on his shoulders as he twisted his fingers inside him, stretching Devon for his own penetration. Gripped fiercely by desire, Devon knew it was safe to ask for what he needed, knew his lovers cared for his pleasure as much as their own. "Now," he pleaded, the head of his cock finding Jonathan's sweet spot in the same instant Kit's fingers rubbed against his. "Now, kitten, please...."

It was a plea Kit had no intention of resisting, the nickname Devon used so rarely betraying the force of his need. He withdrew his fingers and slid into Devon's willing depths, joining all three of them body and soul. He gasped anew at the sensation of heat and pressure on his erection. After the months they'd been together, he should have grown *accustomed* to it, as he should have grown accustomed to feeling his lovers inside him. While the sensation was now familiar, it had lost none of its power. He hoped it never would.

Pressed on each side by warm male flesh, Devon felt the last of the nightmare's terror melt away, powerless to stand against his love for the two men who accepted him and supported him without question. Kit's thrusts pushed him deeper into Jonathan; Jonathan's arms pulled them both closer, merging them into a single, loving being. Three sets of lips slid over any flesh they could reach. Three voices moaned and whispered words of need and desire as their bodies rocked together, climbing the pinnacle of ecstasy, moving faster and harder as they neared the peak. Devon fought to catch his breath as the pressure mounted inside him, panting at the sweet friction of filling and being filled. With a sudden gasp, he stiffened and cried out as his orgasm took him, leaving him shuddering between his two lovers, each aftershock triggering another ragged moan.

The flare of Devon's warmth spreading inside him pushed Jonathan nearly to the brink. He slid a hand between their bodies to finish himself, gasping as Kit's palm closed over his own to guide their strokes. The movement stirred Devon inside Jonathan's slick channel, triggering Jonathan's shattering climax.

The constrictions of Devon's body around him and the slippery heat of Jonathan's seed on his hand were enough to send Kit spiraling into release, his body jerking inside Devon's, filling his lover with his essence. He regained just enough awareness to keep from slumping bonelessly. To avoid crushing Jonathan, he rolled to one side, pulling Devon with him so he still lay enfolded between the two of them.

As his breathing slowly steadied, Devon drew comfort from the solid presence on either side. He'd thought he'd never know the pleasure of going under again, not after the way Robert had abused his trust, but giving in to Kit had been so easy, so good—the way it should be, had to be, for any kind of relationship to work. It seemed he had finally found a partner both strong enough and gentle enough to dominate him in all the right ways. *Partners*, Devon corrected himself, nestled between their warmth. He still had to face Robert, but the thought no longer had the power to terrify him, because he would not be facing him alone.

CHAPTER 3
BAD BLOOD

KIT WAITED impatiently in the trailer, having sent Stacy and Carol home early, promising he'd be able to provide any help Devon or Jonathan might need removing their makeup. Devon had spent the entire day ragging on him for one thing after another, and while it was all in fun, Kit didn't want an audience for what he had planned. After the tense few days they'd had with Devon's nightmares, Kit hardly begrudged Devon a little fun, but it was time to turn the tables. Hearing Jonathan's and Devon's voices outside, he positioned himself by the door, ready to tackle Devon as soon as he came inside.

"At least when we were at Camelot we didn't have to wear this bloody armor," Devon griped, looking back at Jonathan as he entered the trailer. "I can't wait to get out of—" His words were cut off as a body slammed against his, knocking him into Jonathan. Acting on instinct, he kicked out at his attacker's feet, throwing the body roughly to the floor before he realized who it was.

Kit gasped as he landed hard with Devon, still in full costume, crushing him. "Get off me, you wanker," he protested, laughing. "You're heavy."

Jonathan offered an arm to help Devon lever up off Kit's slighter frame. "I don't think you quite have the hang of it yet, Kit-Kat," he teased. "When you tackle somebody, you're supposed to end up on *top*."

"I would have if you hadn't been behind him to catch him," Kit groused good-naturedly. He gave Devon a once-over. "Get changed. When we get home, I'll give you a proper wrestling match."

Devon snickered, though the image of Kit's lissome body wrestling with his was enough to start him hardening under Lancelot's leathers. "We'll have to think of some kind of handicap to make it a proper match," he teased. "What do you think, Jon? Maybe I should tie one arm behind my back to make it even?"

"I don't need a handicap," Kit protested. "You just wait. I can take you in a fair fight."

"I can see I'm going to be stuck playing referee." Jonathan chuckled, stripping off his tunic. "Where are Carol and Stacy, anyway? I'm sure they'd enjoy watching the two of you go at it."

"I sent them home—I didn't think Devon would want an audience to see me pummel him." As much as the exhibitionist in Kit might get off on knowing someone was watching them, he doubted Devon, and more especially Jonathan, were ready to have them outed to the makeup team that way.

"In your dreams," Devon countered, losing no time peeling off the heavy layers of Lancelot's costume. He fleetingly considered a shower, but the thought of wrestling with Kit while Jonathan watched was becoming more and more enticing. He settled for a quick scrub of his face with one of the wipes kept on the counter, handing another to Jonathan before dressing in his own clothes.

Jonathan cleaned off his own makeup and, foregoing the constriction of boxers, stepped into his worn jeans and pulled his T-shirt over his head. He picked up the pieces of their costumes and hung them in the wardrobe closet. "There, now Stacy and Carol won't crab at us in the morning. C'mon, let's get home where I can grab a beer and the two of you can tussle all you want."

"What are we waiting for?" Devon challenged, heading toward the door. "May the best knight win!"

Kit grinned at Jonathan, recognizing the quote from an early episode's script. "Your delivery was better," he joked, following Devon outside.

"That's why I became king and he winds up being banished," Jonathan teased, though the reminder that Devon would not be needed on set while they filmed the episodes after Lancelot left Camelot made him fall into an uneasy silence. Knowing his tendency to overthink things, he'd tried to avoid looking too far ahead in the relationship, and he pushed the depressing thought from his mind for now. Time enough to deal with that later; right now he'd enjoy every minute they had with Devon. He picked up Excalibur, hoping to make time for some practice that evening, and followed his lovers out of the trailer.

As soon as they got inside Jonathan's house, Kit emptied his pockets and pulled off his belt and charms so they wouldn't hurt Devon or get tangled up. "Let's go, bad boy," he challenged again, rocking lightly on the balls of his feet. "Time to put your money where your mouth is."

Devon couldn't help but chuckle at Kit's attitude, but his arousal was as strong as his amusement. He winked at Jonathan before pulling his shirt over his head, then tucked his left arm into the back of his belt. "Big talk from a little knight," he teased, dropping into a crouch. "Bring it on, sunshine."

Kit circled Devon slowly, watching the way he moved, admiring his sleek grace but also looking for weaknesses. With one hand behind his back, Devon would be off-balance a little. Kit just had to figure out how to use that to his advantage. He lunged at Devon's side, pushing so he'd fall in the direction of his bound arm.

The strength of Kit's lunge caught Devon by surprise. He'd thought he'd learned to stop underestimating Kit by now. He let his torso absorb the blow, wishing Kit had removed his shirt, too, so he could feel their bare skin touching.

Jonathan could read Devon's thoughts on his face as the longing gaze swept over Kit's torso. "Take off your shirt, Kit-Kat," he suggested huskily, shifting on the couch to adjust his growing arousal.

Taking a step back to make sure Devon didn't attack him while his hands were tangled in his sleeves, Kit stripped the shirt off, leaving himself bare to the waist. As soon as it fell to the ground, he tackled Devon again, succeeding in taking him down this time.

Kit's weight settling on top of him had a definite effect on Devon's libido. He pushed off the floor with his free elbow, maintaining the press of their bodies as he flipped Kit over, landed on top of him, and ground his erection into Kit's hips. "Right where I want you," he growled. "Underneath me."

Kit bucked up against Devon, dislodging him enough to roll out from beneath him. He grabbed the strong arms and rolled again. "What if I want you beneath me?" he challenged.

The thrust of Kit's hips against Devon's, mimicking the action he hoped they'd soon be engaged in, goaded Devon into pushing back roughly. "Who said this was about what you want?" he countered, shifting suddenly and rolling atop Kit again.

Kit's moan at Devon's commanding tone turned to a yelp of pain when something sharp slit the skin of his upper arm.

"Fuck!" Jonathan cried out when he saw Kit roll into Excalibur. He leaped from the couch, grabbed the hilt of the sword, which he'd leaned against the wall, and moved it out of the way of the two struggling men. "Shit, I'm sorry, Kit! Are you okay?"

Kit pushed up with his uninjured limb. He reached around to where it hurt, and his hand came back red with blood. "Fuck, I'm bleeding! I didn't think they kept the swords sharp enough to cut. Thank God it isn't a real sword or I'd be minus an arm. Can you tell how bad it is?"

Jonathan crouched on the balls of his feet, peering over Kit's shoulder. He touched the cut hesitantly, frowning when his fingers were quickly covered with blood. The gash wasn't deep, but it was several inches long. "We'd better get a bandage on it quick." He frowned. "Devon, can you grab the first aid kit from the—Devon?"

Devon hadn't moved since Kit's first pained shout, Jonathan realized. He'd pulled his legs up to his chest and sat leaning on one elbow, staring blindly at Kit, a cold sheen of sweat breaking out on his brow. "Devon?" Jonathan repeated, his attention torn between his two lovers.

Kit grabbed his discarded T-shirt and wrapped it tightly around his arm, coming up on his knees to peer into Devon's face. "Devon?" he echoed, starting to reach out before realizing his hand was stained with blood.

Squeezing Kit's shoulder reassuringly, Jonathan raised his other hand slowly to Devon's cheek. "Devon?" he called again, his voice as gentle as his touch. "Babe, what is it?"

The tenderness of Jonathan's presence broke Devon free of the vision that had overwhelmed him at the sight of Kit's blood. He shuddered and rubbed his hand over his face, forcing himself from memories back to the present—a present where he had once again harmed his lover. "Fuck, I'm sorry, Kit." Devon groaned as Kit clutched his bloodstained shirt around his arm. "What the fuck am I doing to you? I can't do this anymore," he growled, pushing to his feet. "I won't do this again! Not to you!" He turned blindly toward the door, his only thought to get away before he could hurt either of them any further.

"Devon!" Kit shouted, jumping up after him, completely ignoring his injured arm. Yeah, it hurt, but losing Devon would hurt a whole lot more. "What the hell are you talking about?"

Jonathan rose and stood in front of Devon, blocking his path. "You're not running away from us, Devon," he insisted, taking him by the arm and guiding him back to the sofa. "You didn't hurt Kit—it was an accident. If it's anyone's fault, it's mine for not moving Excalibur when the two of you started to play." He cupped Devon's face, forcing him to meet his concerned gaze. "I'm going to take Kit into the bathroom and clean him up. Promise me you won't try to leave. We need to talk about this."

Devon ran his hand through his hair, still shaken from the emotional ferocity of the memories. "I'll stay," he muttered wearily. "I just— bollocks! I don't want…. I'll stay."

It was the best Jonathan could do for now. He dropped a kiss on the top of Devon's head, then turned and followed Kit into the bathroom.

Kit let Jonathan tend to his arm, but his thoughts remained focused on Devon's outburst. "What's going on with Devon?" he asked, needing some reassurance that everything would be all right. "Is it still…?" He didn't want to evoke the specter that had haunted them the past few days. He had thought, had hoped, they had banished that particular ghost.

"I think this bastard Robert has a lot more to answer for than we suspected," Jonathan said tightly. Setting his jaw, he unwrapped the bloody cloth from Kit's arm with gentle hands, relieved to see the cut was not as bad as he'd originally feared. "I think we can get by without stitches." He wiped away the blood that had already started to dry with a clean washcloth. "I don't know what's going on in Devon's head right now, but it seemed like seeing your blood is what set him off, and I'm willing to bet that prick had something to do with it." Jonathan fit a large bandage over Kit's cut, trying to get his anger under control before they returned to the parlor. He couldn't let Devon think his anger was directed toward him.

"I want to know who he is," Kit decided as Jonathan worked on his arm, his own anger bubbling beneath the surface, quelled only because having them all angry and upset could only end in catastrophe. "And I want him the hell away from Devon."

"Well, we already know Devon met him on one of his films." Jonathan smoothed the adhesive ends of the bandage into place. "Let's see what else Devon will tell us now, and then maybe I can do some checking. Especially since he's supposed to show up on set."

Kit nodded. "The more we know, the better we'll be able to deal with whatever else comes up. One way or another, though, I want the bastard kept away. He's hurt Devon too much already." He looked at his arm in the mirror, seeing no remaining trace of blood. "Am I all done?"

Jonathan wrapped his arms around Kit and turned him until they were facing each other, lowering his head to take his mouth in a slow, warm kiss. "I want to protect him as much as you do," Jonathan murmured. "We'll find a way to deal with this together."

Kit tightened his arms around Jonathan's waist, leaning into the kiss, drawing strength from it, strength he would need to face whatever demons haunted Devon. "Together," he agreed when their lips separated.

Devon looked up as Kit and Jonathan walked back into the parlor, his expression drawn with worry and guilt. "How bad is it?" he asked, his gaze flickering between the two. "Do we need to take him to hospital?"

"I'm fine," Kit insisted, keeping his tone deliberately light. "It was just a little scratch. See, Jonathan bandaged it up all nice and neat. Give me a day or two and you won't even know it happened."

"It shouldn't have happened at all," Devon insisted. "I had no business wrestling with you like that. I'm bigger than you, stronger—I should have known you'd wind up hurt."

"That's not the way I remember what was happening," Kit said. "Until I rolled into Jonathan's sword like an idiot, I thought I was doing a fine job of holding my own. Yes, you're bigger, but that doesn't mean you're automatically going to harm me. I know you'd never deliberately hurt me that way."

Devon flushed at Kit's words, his head dropping in shame. "But I did," he muttered thickly, his hands clenching into fists on his thighs. "I always do."

Jonathan moved next to Devon on the sofa as Kit sat on his opposite side, the two of them surrounding him with the warmth of their presence. "Something happened, didn't it, Devon?" Jonathan asked gently. "Something else that this reminded you of?"

Kit wrapped his arms around Devon from one side, while Jonathan's arms encircled him from the other, and waited for Devon's answer.

Taking a deep breath, Devon tried to relax, but he couldn't let go, not when every time he closed his eyes he saw that long-ago night—only this time the face of the young man beneath him was Kit's. As much as he wanted to forget the ugly incident, his reaction tonight proved that was impossible. Whatever happened as a result, his lovers deserved to know the truth.

"What I told you before," Devon started in a voice so low Jonathan could barely hear him. He cleared his throat and started again. "This is worse—I don't know if I can…. It's more than just admitting how weak I was. He made me—" Devon hesitated, shaking his head in denial. "No, I can't blame him. I was the one who—" He broke off again in frustration, trying to stand. "You shouldn't have to deal with this crap. I need to go."

Kit's arms tightened, keeping Devon in place. "You need to stop running from this," he corrected firmly. He had never been hurt the way Devon had been, but he knew what the weight of emotional baggage could do to a man. The only way to be free of the past was to face it and deal with it. "It will haunt you until you do. As for dealing with this crap, as you call it, I think we're the ones with the right to decide when it's too much. I don't recall complaining. Are you complaining, Jonathan?"

"Only because Devon keeps trying to leave." Jonathan placed a hand on Devon's thigh to keep him from standing. "There's nothing you can tell us that's going to change the way we feel about you, Devon. What happened years ago can't touch what we have now." He caught Devon's chin in his other hand, forcing him to meet his gaze. "Unless you let it."

Devon nodded slowly, some of the tension easing from his rigid muscles. He didn't know what he'd done to deserve the unconditional support of the two men who sat at his side, but he wouldn't let Robert— or even Robert's memory—drive them away.

When Devon relaxed, Kit leaned in and nipped lightly at his earlobe. "Can you tell us now?" he asked softly. He didn't want to pressure, but he also didn't want this to fester and lead to nightmares like the last time Devon tried to "protect" them from his past.

"I'll try," Devon agreed, his gaze falling. He would tell them—they had the right to know what he'd done—but he couldn't look in their eyes and admit it. "We'd been together for a while, and he—Robert—he said that I'd done so well with everything he asked, I was ready for the next step. That was when he brought in Blaine. He—they'd been together before, he said, and Blaine would be perfect for me to learn on—to learn to be a Dom."

"You're a wonderful Dom," Kit protested, remembering their time together at the beach house and how amazing Devon had made him feel. He had no idea what was on Devon's mind, but he didn't see how it could be as awful as Devon seemed to think.

Something teased at the edge of Jonathan's memory, but the abject tone in Devon's voice made him push aside any consideration but reassuring their lover. "He wanted you to learn to be a Dom? Why?"

"In some twisted way, I think it made him feel even more powerful," Devon admitted. "Like he wasn't pulling only the sub's strings, but mine too." He sighed, rubbing his eyes wearily. "I couldn't have done it if it wasn't so bloody obvious Blaine wanted it. We were both damn pathetic, looking back. We'd have done anything, taken anything, just to hear a word of praise from him."

Kit knew how that felt. Though he had no problem escaping that headspace most of the time, he remembered craving Devon's approval on the porch of their beach house. He would have done just about anything that afternoon too. "What did he make you do?"

Jonathan rubbed his free hand gently down Devon's back, unwilling to interrupt but wordlessly encouraging him to go on.

"Oh, he made sure to teach me everything," Devon said scornfully. "Everything he'd ever done to me, he taught me to do to my 'boy.' And God help me, I liked it—I liked hearing him tell me I'd done well, liked making my sub beg for what he wanted, bloody loved watching him get off when I finally gave him what he needed."

And that's the difference between you, Jonathan thought. Devon didn't get his enjoyment from power, from control—he wasn't describing what he took from his sub, but what he'd given to his partner. "So you both wanted it," Jonathan prompted when Devon fell silent again. "What happened to change that?"

"One night, he wanted me to shave Blaine," Devon said, closing his eyes as the scene replayed behind his lids. "I'd cuffed him to the bed so he couldn't move, and Robert had this bloody straight razor." Even now, Devon felt a throb of arousal at the thought of shaving Jonathan or Kit that way. "The thing was so damn sharp, I was going slow to be sure I didn't slip—and Robert laughed, told me that Blaine would like it if I cut him." Devon swallowed against the gorge that rose in his throat at the memory. "He told me to cut him, and I did—just a little nick, really. I'd gotten worse myself with a safety razor. And he told me—he told me to do it again. And again."

Kit gulped, both at the thought of being cut that way and at the understanding of how the injury on his arm must have affected Devon. "You didn't mean to cut me," Kit reminded him firmly, trying to hide the tremble still dancing along his nerves. "And you weren't doing anything Blaine didn't want, right? I mean, Robert wasn't lying to you, was he?" He couldn't imagine wanting to be cut, but that didn't mean someone else might not feel that way.

Devon shook his head, too ashamed to look up. "After the first time, I could tell Blaine was frightened, and the longer it went on, the worse he got. He kept looking from Robert, back to me, and I thought—I hoped—but he wouldn't use his safeword, even though by then I could tell he was terrified." He dropped his head into his hands, burying them in his hair. "When I realized he wasn't going to stop me, I felt sick. I couldn't do it anymore, no matter what Robert said. I started to back away, and he—he told me I was weak, that I needed to make my sub want it, to take control. He—he hit me, hit my arm, and the razor—it cut Blaine, deep, and there was so fuckin' much blood—"

Devon was all but talking to himself, Jonathan realized, lost in a memory only he could see. Lifting Devon's head gently, he combed the tangled hair back with his fingers. "It was an accident, Devon," he repeated, his voice quiet but insistent. "Just like with Kit. You didn't mean to hurt him that way."

"If I didn't mean to hurt him, I should have stopped as soon as I knew he was frightened, and I didn't. I didn't!" Devon's voice rose as he forced his way to his feet. "I knew he was fuckin' terrified, and I kept on anyway, so Robert wouldn't think I was fuckin' weak! What does that make me? How could you ever trust me now that you know?"

"Where is Robert now?" Kit rose to his feet as well and approached Devon slowly. "Is he still standing behind you, goading you on? He wasn't there when you claimed us at the beach. We were completely yours that weekend. You could have asked us to do just about anything, and we would probably have done it, just like you're saying you did for Robert. Think about what you asked, Devon. Think about what you did to us. You're the same man now that you were that weekend. And the fact that you still feel guilty about something that happened years ago is just more proof that *you are not Robert*." He drove his last words home hard, trying to break through Devon's self-imposed isolation.

Jonathan stood and held Devon by the shoulders, trying to convey all his love and trust through his touch. "Kit's right, Devon. The fact that it's still eating at you is proof that Robert didn't win—not then, and not now. Someday I'm going to show you just how much I trust you," he promised, his voice heavy with arousal at the thought. "But right now, I just want you to let us love you."

"Come upstairs with us," Kit seconded. "Let us show you how much we want you." *How much we'll always want you.*

Jonathan lowered his head to kiss the exposed skin of Devon's chest. "Want you, Devon," he urged, rubbing his stubbled cheek over the coating of golden hair. "Want to show you… how much…." He closed his lips around a peaked nipple, moaning at the taste of Devon's skin.

"You can bloody well wait until we get upstairs where we can get naked and be comfortable," Kit scolded, slapping lightly at Jonathan's hands. "Come on, Devon. The king can join us when he's got himself under control again."

The combination of Kit's teasing words and Jonathan's passionate kiss returned Devon's focus firmly to the here and now. "Getting naked sounds good to me," he admitted, grateful beyond words that his confession had not driven them away.

"Let's get upstairs, then." Jonathan grinned, giddy with relief that they'd managed to allay Devon's self-doubts. He jumped to his feet and bounded up the steps before either of the others could react, leaving a trail of clothes along the way.

Kit chuckled at Jonathan's enthusiasm. Not that he wasn't feeling the same way. It just amused him. "Shall we join him?" he asked, offering his hand to Devon.

Devon enclosed Kit's hand in his, reaching the other to hover over Kit's bandaged arm without touching it. "I'm sorry, Kit," he repeated quietly. "I never meant—"

Kit caught Devon's free hand and lifted it to his chest before leaning forward to kiss him tenderly. "I know. You wouldn't hurt me deliberately. Accidents happen. Now can we go upstairs and shag the king blind?" He was not trying to dismiss Devon's feelings, but they'd all had enough drama for the day. It was time to lighten the mood.

An enthusiastic "Fuck, yeah!" from upstairs shattered the last of Devon's awkwardness. Whether he deserved it or not, these two amazing men wanted him, and he was going to show them exactly what they meant to him in return. Giving a final squeeze to Kit's hand, he headed up the stairs two at a time, bursting into the bedroom to find Jonathan already naked on the bed.

"About time the both of you got here," Jonathan complained, stroking a hand over his already impressive erection. "It's a good thing I don't get jealous, or I'd think you two were starting without me again."

Laughing, Kit unbuttoned his jeans and pushed them down his legs. "If anyone started without the others, it was you," he pointed out archly. Stepping up behind Devon, he started working on the fastenings on his lover's trousers.

Devon kicked off his clothes impatiently and nudged Kit onto the bed, where he landed across Jonathan's legs. Kneeling beside him, Devon lowered his head for a gentle kiss, letting his hands wander over the smooth torso as his lips wordlessly offered his contrition.

"Oof!" Kit gasped as Jonathan's knees dug into his back. He pushed on Devon's shoulders, not to break the kiss, but to roll him over so he could lie more comfortably. When Devon lay on his back, Kit rose up on his knees, taking control, determined to show Devon that his revelations hadn't changed anything. He kissed his way down Devon's neck and chest, his destination clear even if he meant to take his time getting there.

Kit's lips tempted Devon to lie back and give up control, but he still needed to prove his repentance. Shifting to his side, he trailed gentle kisses across Kit's collarbone and down the shoulder of the injured arm, detouring to tease a honeyed nipple before moving lower. Shifting his legs, he aligned their bodies so that each of them could touch and kiss the other freely.

The sight of Kit and Devon pleasuring each other started a low heat building in Jonathan's belly, growing more intense as their attentions grew more intimate. When Devon shifted again to take Kit into his mouth, Jonathan couldn't resist molding himself against Devon's strong, graceful back, his arousal prodding the taut buttocks as he traced lips and teeth over Devon's shoulders.

Kit let Devon position him as he pleased. It didn't matter to him how they configured their bodies as long as he could still get his hands and lips on Devon. When Devon's mouth closed over the tip of his cock, Kit moaned, nudging one of Devon's thighs so he could reach the treasures hidden between them. As soon as they parted, he dipped his head, licking at the heavy sac.

Devon pressed back into the comfort of Jonathan's embrace, his purr of pleasure around Kit's shaft turning into a groan when Kit lapped wetly at his bollocks. At the same time, Jonathan's hands slid lower, his lips trailing a meandering path down Devon's spine as his fingers followed the contours of his splayed legs.

Reaching the upper curve of Devon's buttocks, Jonathan let one hand stray for a moment to brush over the top of Kit's head, lovingly ruffling the tousled hair. He glided his fingers down Kit's smooth cheek, lingering at the place where Kit's mouth met Devon's flesh, the link between the three of them so strong in that instant he felt awed by it. Sliding lower, Jonathan pressed his lips to the place his hand had been, overcome with love for them.

Kit shifted, his lips following Jonathan's for a moment. He knew they needed to make this encounter about Devon, knew Jonathan felt the same way though they had not discussed it, but the sense of rightness when Jonathan's mouth met his on Devon's body was too powerful to let go immediately. He tangled his tongue with Jonathan's as they teased the man between them.

The two sets of hands and lips moving over Devon, when his emotions had already been set on edge, were rapidly fraying his control. The two mouths meeting around his bollocks made him lift his head in shock, and the sight of Kit and Jonathan kissing with his flesh still between them was almost enough to send him off. He moved his free hand over their joined heads, caressing whatever skin he could reach until the pleasure became too intense to resist. "Too much," he gasped, arching back to try to pull away. "Too soon."

Kit disengaged from Jonathan's mouth at Devon's words, lifting his head to peer up at him. "No such thing." He skimmed his lips across Devon's thigh. "Let us love you."

Jonathan had relinquished Kit's mouth regretfully but found it equally alluring to nip his way up Devon's buttocks, spreading them with his hands to lave the crease between them. He teased his tongue at the entrance he shortly planned to claim, circling it until it pulsed against him before plunging as deeply as he could into the smoky depths.

A cry of pleasure tore from Devon's lips. He thrust into the contact, trying to draw the probing muscle even deeper, but it wasn't enough. "Please, Jon," he gasped, needing more of that searing fullness. "Ah, Jesus, fuck me!"

There was nothing Jonathan wanted more at that moment, but he ignored Devon's increasingly frantic pleading and spent another few delicious minutes stretching Devon's entrance with his tongue, adding a saliva-wet thumb to the clenching passage. He scrabbled blindly under the pillow until his hand closed on the tube of gel they'd learned to always keep within reach. He slicked some quickly over his eager cock, adding a generous dollop to his hand before pulling his mouth away and working his second thumb in its place, stretching the entrance between them. "Are you ready for me, Devon?" Jonathan asked hoarsely, resting his head on his lover's sweat-sheened back while he moved his hips into position. "Ready to feel me love you?"

Kit paused, watching Jonathan prepare Devon, the sight as powerfully arousing as if Jonathan's hands were on him instead. When Jonathan shifted and started to slide into Devon's tight arse, Kit moved as well, shifting lower on the bed so he could reach the place where his lovers joined. He flicked his tongue out to savor their combined tastes.

Devon panted as Jonathan thrust into him, filling him with the hot friction he craved. When Kit's tongue lapped over his overstretched flesh, his cock jumped against the smooth skin that pressed over it. "Good," he gasped, "so bloody fuckin' good… need more…." He closed his fist around Kit's length, pumping it as he swiped his tongue wetly over its tip, too lost in the haze of his impending orgasm to do any more than taste everywhere he could reach.

Jonathan spread his legs wider to let Kit's head settle between them, bending his knees to open as fully as he could to Kit's seductive mouth. His hips jutted in small, tight thrusts, the movement just enough to drag the head of his cock over Devon's sweet spot with every pulse. The rhythmic squeeze of Devon's muscle around him and the hot, wet lap of Kit's tongue at the base of his shaft were quickly bringing him to his own climax. He bit into the hard muscle of Devon's shoulder, trying to hold back until his lovers were ready to come with him.

Kit had no idea if Devon had anything in mind when he asked for more, but it planted an idea in his head. Sliding down toward Devon's feet so he could see what he was doing, he pressed a finger against the tight aperture that stretched to welcome Jonathan's cock. Moving that way took him out of the reach of Devon's mouth, but he didn't even care. Not if it meant giving Devon what he needed.

A sound that was almost a whimper escaped Devon when Kit's cock slid out of the reach of his tongue. He tried to keep stroking the slickened shaft through his fist, but his grasp weakened when a wet digit worked its way alongside Jonathan's cock, the added fullness stretching him to the breaking point. With a hoarse shout, Devon's muscles contracted around the insistent friction, his bollocks spasming as he came without his cock being touched.

Kit's finger pressing against Jonathan's sensitized shaft and Devon's passage convulsing around him brought Jonathan to his own fierce climax, filling Devon with the slickness of his release.

The incredible tightness that accompanied Devon's spasming around his finger and Jonathan's cock caught Kit off guard. He hadn't thought that far ahead, and he groaned with the thought of what Jonathan might have felt, of what it might feel like on his cock instead of his finger. He slid his finger free, licking at the traces of Jonathan's come on the slick digit. His cock throbbed like a toothache. He reached down to take himself in hand only to have his arm swatted away.

Devon wasn't about to let Kit see to himself after his two lovers had taken such good care of him. With a low growl, he replaced Kit's hand with his own, enjoying the way the beads of fluid from the tip allowed his hand to slide easily on the hard shaft.

Kit moaned when Devon started to stroke him. He was already so close from all that had come before. It wouldn't take much more for him to climax. When Jonathan reached over to join Devon in pleasuring Kit, that was all it took. Kit's back arched and his cock jerked in his lovers' hands, his seed spilling out over both fists as he shouted his release and collapsed onto the bed next to the men he loved with every beat of his heart.

Smiling at the strength of Kit's climax, Devon and Jonathan continued to stroke his skin gently until his eyes opened again and he smiled back at them.

"Turn around here," Devon urged, wanting to be able to hold Kit properly.

Kit scooted around on the bed until his head was facing the same direction as his lovers'. He moved willingly into Devon's open arms, while Jonathan's arms closed around both of them from behind.

"He can't touch us," Kit murmured, his grip tightening. "He has no power that we don't give him."

Devon wasn't sure that was completely true, but he didn't want to start another discussion tonight, didn't want to let any thought of Robert taint this moment. They were all tired from the long day and the emotional scene downstairs. He was caught between two of the most wonderful men in the world. He was not going to ruin that by dwelling on things he couldn't change. Tomorrow was soon enough for the worries that remained.

CHAPTER 4
PLAYING WITH FIRE

KIT WALKED past the door to the second bedroom that served as Jonathan's office, surprised to hear the clatter of the keyboard. None of them were technology junkies, and their computers rarely saw any use, given how little they were home. Glancing inside, he saw Jonathan hunched over the keys, a frown on his face. "Whatcha doing, Jon?" he asked, stepping inside the room.

Jonathan ran a hand through his hair, pushing it back from his face before swiveling the chair to look at Kit. "I thought I'd try to figure out who Robert is. We know Devon met him on a movie, so I thought...." He shrugged, his cheeks flushing a little. "I thought if I pulled up a list of Devon's movies in IMDB, I might be able to find one with Robert somebody in it...." He shrugged again. "Maybe it's a crazy idea, but it's all I could think of."

"Can I help?" Kit asked, thinking that was the most sensible idea Jonathan'd had since the last time he suggested having sex. "I don't know how it'll help us, but at least we'll know who's haunting him."

"The first step in preparing for battle is knowing your enemy," Jonathan countered. This might not be a war like the battles they were filming, but he was more than prepared to face down the man who had dealt so much pain—physical and emotional—to Devon. "I guess we just start looking through the cast lists of Devon's films." He clicked on a title at random, and a new page of publicity photos, plot summary, and cast credits appeared.

Kit nodded. He supposed this was a battle. A battle for Devon's mind and heart. "Well," he said when the page came up, "I guess we just have to go through each one until we find a costar named Robert."

"Devon said it was years ago. Let's just work our way backward." About a third of the way down the list, they hit pay dirt—Robert was the first name listed. Jonathan whistled softly and glanced over his shoulder at Kit. "This has to be him. No wonder Devon's still intimidated by him!"

Kit shivered, thinking about the other actor. Every photo of him Kit had ever seen oozed menace. Maybe some of that came from the kind of roles he often took, but even the candids had the same aura. Given what Devon had said about their relationship, Kit could understand his fear. "He also mentioned Blaine. Was there a Blaine on that set too?" he asked.

Jonathan scanned the list of cast names. "No," he said slowly, "but Devon said he'd been with Robert before him. Maybe Robert met him on another movie?" He clicked on Robert's name, pulling up an even lengthier list of films. "Let's see who he acted with before Devon." Jonathan clicked on the entry prior to Devon's film, his face twisting into a scowl. "Bingo! There's Blaine, all right." His expression softened as he read the next name on the cast list. "Well now, look at that! It's been too long since I talked to Mariselle." Looking up at Kit again, Jonathan smiled. "We worked together on *All the Right Reasons*. Let me see if I still have her number somewhere. I'll bet she'd be willing to tell us whatever she knows about Robert." The name came out sounding like a curse.

Kit smiled, Jonathan's enthusiasm rubbing off on him. Not for the first time, he was glad Jonathan had been around Hollywood for a while. It seemed those contacts were about to come in useful. He only hoped Jonathan had kept the actress's number.

It only took a few moments for Jonathan to pull out his phone and scroll through his contacts. He grinned at Kit, then checked the clock. "Good, it's not too early to call LA. Let's see if we can get in touch with her right now." He added the international access code before letting the phone dial the number, trying to keep from tapping his fingers impatiently as the connection worked its way across the Atlantic. Finally, the ringing stopped and a feminine voice answered. "Hello, Mari? It's Jonathan.... Yeah, it has!... You have? That's great to hear, thanks.... No, I'm still on location in England. Actually, I was calling to ask a favor."

Kit listened as Jonathan caught up with his friend and former costar. From the length of the conversation and the hardening of Jonathan's features, Kit surmised that the actress did indeed have things to tell them. When Jonathan hung up, Kit asked, "Well, what did she say?"

"She's definitely not a fan," Jonathan answered, rubbing the back of his neck. "The first thing she told me was not to get messed up with him, even before I could ask her anything specific. Apparently Robert makes a habit of picking out someone new on every film to latch on to. He dug his claws pretty deep into Blaine, from what Mariselle saw." He shook his head and reached for Kit, needing the reassuring warmth to counteract the chill that had settled over him as his friend described the atmosphere on the set. "I don't think there's any doubt that he's Devon's Robert."

Kit nodded, wrapping his arms around Jonathan to both give and receive comfort. "So what do we do now that we know?"

Jonathan sighed and pressed a kiss to Kit's temple. "I don't know, kitten, but at least we know what we're up against. I suppose we just try to make sure he doesn't get anywhere near Devon while he's here."

"That's easy enough. Devon's rarely alone anyway, and all we'd have to do is drop a word in the ears of the other knights and they'd help too," Kit responded with more calm than he was feeling. He was pretty much adrift here, but he knew one thing without a doubt. The Knights of the Round Table would look out for their own.

"I think we'd better handle it ourselves if we can," Jonathan said. "I don't think this is something Devon would want to get around, and anything we'd say to the others might open him up to questions he'd rather not answer."

Kit hadn't thought about that. "Well, you and I can still make sure he isn't alone. That way, if Robert does come on set and try anything, Devon will have at least one of us there with him."

"We'll have to be sure we're not too obvious about it," Jonathan cautioned. "He won't take it well if he thinks we're babysitting him."

Kit grinned at that. "Oh, I think we can convince him we're not just babysitting." He ran his hand down Jonathan's chest. "This doesn't feel like babysitting, does it?" He leaned over and nipped at Jonathan's lips. "Or this?"

Pulling Kit closer, Jonathan deepened the kiss. "This feels like something that will make us late for makeup," he murmured regretfully.

Kit couldn't argue with that, but he was still reluctant to pull away. "This is also what's going to keep Devon completely unaware that we're hounding his steps."

"TO ME it seemed exceedingly strange," Lancelot said. "Maybe it was only a test, but almost I should have said that she was tempting us."

Devon stared defiantly at the rest of the knights scattered around the Camelot set.

"Speak no evil of the bearer of the Holy Grail!" Kit protested in Percival's elegant tones. "We must undertake a quest for the holy relic. It must be found!"

Devon turned to face the younger knight, his gaze sweeping over the camera crew to gauge Niall's reaction to the scene. The director was chatting with a group of men who stood beside him watching the interchange, and Devon froze when he recognized one of the visitors.

Robert.

"I shall deny none of you the right to undertake this quest, my valorous knights." Jonathan imbued his line with all the sorrow Arthur felt at Merlin's prophecy that the Grail quest would lead to the dissolution of the Round Table. He waited a beat for the response Lancelot was supposed to make, vowing to undertake the search. When Devon didn't reply, he glanced at him cautiously, hoping to salvage the take. "Surely the most perfect knight in the realm shall succeed in this quest," he ad-libbed, trying to catch Devon's eye; but when Lancelot still didn't return with his line, Jonathan followed his gaze to the cluster of men talking with Niall, who was so absorbed he'd forgotten to stop the cameras. "Fuck," Jonathan muttered, glancing back at Devon. *He'd* come on set after all.

"Cut," Niall called when the missed line finally penetrated his awareness. "Let's try that again, shall we?"

Given a chance to come out of character for a moment, Kit glanced around the set, his gaze landing on the unfamiliar silhouette behind Niall. The man stepped forward a little and Kit tensed. His eyes went immediately to Devon. Seeing his distress, he reached for Devon's hand with no concern for any possible audience. "He can't touch us," he murmured, trying to remind Devon of their earlier conversation. "Not unless we let him."

Kit's touch and his quiet words broke the spell that had held Devon paralyzed. He squeezed Kit's hand for an instant, his gaze flashing to Jonathan's reassuring smile. Back in control of his emotions, he pulled Lancelot's courage around him like a cloak and focused on Arthur, waiting for Niall's cue to begin again. "I too swear to undertake this sacred quest," he carried on with his line. "I shall search every corner of the land to find this holy relic and return it to Camelot."

Jonathan answered with Arthur's lines, and the scene continued, but from the corner of his eye, he watched the group of men with Niall until they left the set.

Having resumed his mark, Kit waited for the scene to end. He had a few choice words to say to their unwanted guest. The next time he glanced over to where he had seen Robert, though, the other man was gone.

It was a good thing Lancelot was supposed to be on edge with eagerness to depart on the Grail quest in the afternoon's scenes, because Robert's appearance had left Devon badly shaken. He searched the set at each break in filming, but Niall wrapped for the day without the visitors making a reappearance. Devon knew his former lover wouldn't be satisfied with just surprising him on set. He dreaded seeing Robert waiting outside the makeup trailer or leaning against his car in the parking lot, even though he knew his fears weren't reasonable.

Once out of makeup, the three of them made it to Devon's house without incident, and Devon opted to try to rid himself of some of the day's tension with a shower while Kit and Jonathan picked up Chinese takeaway for dinner. He'd just finished drying and had wrapped a fresh towel around his waist when the shrill ring of the telephone cut along his nerve endings. Knowing who it would be before he answered, he clenched his jaw and picked up the receiver. "Aldridge," he snapped.

"You certainly haven't lost your fancy for pretty boys," Robert drawled. "Does he taste as sweet as he looks?"

"Stay the fuck away from him," Devon growled. "Whatever your game is, I'm the only one you'll play it with. Don't pollute him or the rest of the cast with your insinuations."

"You don't think he'd appreciate my attentions? I'm hurt," Robert replied, amused at the protectiveness the big blond was showing toward the pretty chit he'd seen on set that afternoon. "I bet he'd beg for it with the right encouragement."

Devon couldn't help but feel a flush of pride and arousal at remembering the times he'd made Kit beg—followed by an immediate wave of disgust so raw that for a moment he was afraid he was going to vomit. "You make me sick," Devon hissed. "Say what you're going to say and then fuck off."

Robert laughed. "Who's going to make me? You? You couldn't do it before, sneaking away in the middle of the night like a fucking coward instead of facing me like a man. I think I'll drop by one of these nights and put him through his paces, see if you've gotten any better at training them. You sure as hell couldn't get it right with Blaine."

"You come anywhere near him or anyone else on this set and you'll find out how much of a man I am," Devon snarled. "Don't tell me I hurt your feelings when I left—is that what this is about? I didn't think you cared so much."

"Tell me when and where," Robert answered. "We'll see if you still remember how to crawl."

Shouldering open the front door, his arms full of steaming cartons, Jonathan stopped in his tracks at the expression on Devon's face as he held the phone to his ear. *That bastard*, he realized, his rare temper flaring as he watched Devon's hand clench around the receiver. It must be that bastard Robert.

"Devon?" Kit called softly to get Devon's attention. He gestured for Devon to hang up.

"Is he there?" Robert asked, hearing another voice. "You're generous, giving him permission to call you by your name. Tell him I'm looking forward to meeting him. Soon." He set the receiver into the cradle and leaned back against the headboard of the bed in his hotel room, well satisfied with the way things were turning out.

Jonathan dropped the food on the table and pulled the phone from Devon's hand, squeezing his shoulder as he held the receiver to his ear. "Listen, you prick," he started, but only the hum of a dial tone answered him.

"Bastard hung up," he fumed, setting the handset back in its cradle and turning to Devon. "What did he say to you, babe?"

Offering silent support, Kit ran his hand up and down Devon's arm. "Whatever it is, you don't have to deal with him alone."

Devon leaned into Jonathan's embrace, shaking his head. "Just more of the same shite he's been spreading all week," he answered, unwilling to repeat the innuendos about Kit. "I shouldn't let him wind me up that way, but he still knows exactly how to set me off."

Nodding to Kit, Jonathan guided them to the couch, settling Devon between them. "Maybe so, but remember you beat him. You walked away," Jonathan insisted. "You don't owe him anything, least of all conversation. Just hang up the next time he calls."

"That's right," Kit agreed. "Whatever it was he did that drove you away, focus on that. He doesn't have a hold over you anymore."

"Kit's got the right idea." Jonathan rubbed soothingly over the tense muscles at the base of Devon's neck. "What made you leave him back then? Maybe remembering that will make it easier for you to turn your back on him again this time."

Devon sighed, twisting his head to work out the kinks as Jonathan's touch turned into a deeper massage. "Aren't you sick of listening to me blather?" His lovers had been nothing but accepting of everything he'd revealed to them about his past, but a part of him couldn't help but wonder when he would reach the limits of their acceptance.

"No," Kit declared. "This isn't a game, where we give up just because things get difficult. If something's bothering you, we want to know about it so we can help." Kit glanced at Jonathan as he spoke. It wasn't something they'd talked about, but Kit couldn't imagine Jonathan not feeling the same.

"Nothing you tell us is going to make us think any less of you," Jonathan insisted. "Especially anything that made you decide to leave that ba—" He bit off the epithet, knowing Devon needed support, not anger. He wished he dared to admit the truth of what he really felt, why the thought of Robert's abuse made him angrier than he could ever remember being in his life, but he wasn't sure how Devon would react, and his control was so precarious now that Jonathan couldn't risk a confession that might be unwelcome. "No matter what you tell us, we'll be here for you," he said instead.

Devon rested his elbows on his knees, dropping his head into his palms. "I thought the—the knife play—would have driven Blaine off, as badly as he'd been hurt, but it didn't." Devon shook his head, falling deeper into the memory. "Robert said since I'd already marked him, we ought to make it permanent, something he could never forget. And I wouldn't do it—I couldn't."

"More permanent?" Kit repeated with a shudder as he thought about the cutting Blaine had endured. "Like what? A tattoo?"

Devon tried in vain to think of some way to soften the confession. "A brand," he said flatly.

"That's sick!" Kit cried, his outrage getting the better of his self-control. "I'm glad you told the bastard to take his twisted ideas and shove them up his arse!"

Jonathan might have smiled at Kit's vehemence if he wasn't so shocked. He wasn't averse to the idea of tattoos—each of his own was linked to a special memory—but to brand someone like a horse, as a sign of ownership… no wonder it was more than Devon could bear. "So you left?" he asked quietly, squeezing Devon's hand.

"Aye, but it wasn't in any burst of righteousness," Devon muttered, dropping his eyes from Kit's. "I didn't confront him and tell him off; I didn't even fucking tell him I was leaving. When filming wrapped the next day, I just packed up and left. I hadn't seen either of them again—until today."

"You left," Kit repeated. "You knew he was wrong and you left. That's all that matters."

Jonathan suspected that not having faced Robert when he left was part of the reason he still haunted Devon now, but he wasn't going to let the sadistic fucker anywhere near his lover again, not if there was any way he could stop him. "I'm sick of talking about that cocksucker," he said crudely. He leaned forward and ran his tongue up the side of Devon's neck and around the shell of his ear. "I can think of a lot more pleasant ways to spend our time."

"I'll second that notion," Kit agreed, grabbing Devon's and Jonathan's hands and pulling them to their feet. "Let's go someplace more comfortable."

Devon reached over to turn off the phone's ringer before facing them. "Let him call now," he said with a twisted smile, wishing he could turn off the echo of Robert's voice in his head as easily.

They would never be able to truly relax with the tension still hanging in the air, Kit knew. Taking a deep breath, he looked at the other two men. "Race you!"

Jonathan met Kit's eyes in a silent message of approval before breaking into a wide grin. "Last one naked has to blow the other two," he challenged, already pulling his shirt over his head.

"Not fair, you're already halfway there," Devon protested, glancing at Jonathan's bare feet as he struggled to kick off his shoes and unbutton his slacks at the same time. "And I happen to know you're not wearing anything under those jeans."

Kit thought Jonathan's "punishment" sounded pretty damn appealing. He sprinted for the bedroom, determined to lose the race and win the challenge.

CHAPTER 5
BREAKING FREE

DEVON LEANED back against the headboard of the king-size bed, enjoying the view of Jonathan's lean arse wriggling out of his jeans. He cocked an eyebrow at Kit, still struggling with the buttons of his cargo trousers. "What's this, Percival? Can you not match the deeds of your king and your fellow knight?" he drawled in Lancelot's most prideful voice.

Kit's face broke into a wide grin. "I have not your years of experience," he pointed out, taking his time with his clothes as his gaze raked Devon's naked body and Jonathan's nearly naked one. "Of course, I shall reap the fruits of that experience."

"How so?" Jonathan answered in Arthur's deeper tones, kicking his jeans free and dropping onto the bed next to Devon, "when by the terms of our wager you must now serve our pleasure? I would say it is we who have the advantage of you." He winked at Devon, glad to see the lines of tension that had creased his forehead eased away by their banter.

"You do not think it will be my pleasure to serve you?" Kit asked smoothly, reaching out to stroke the two knights' swelling cocks. "I find myself rather eager, suddenly, to be of such service." He dropped to his knees. "May I see to you, my king?"

Unable to stay in character, Jonathan contorted in laughter. "Devon should really have the honor of your attentions, since he was the first one naked, but if I tell you to see to Lancelot first, one of us is going to wind up making that corny 'uses his lance a lot' joke," he said with a chuckle.

Kit laughed too. "Well, Devon," he asked, still grinning, "where do you want me?"

The touch of Kit's hand and the thought of that laughing mouth closing over his cock brought Devon to full, straining hardness. He slid forward, spreading his thighs to bracket Kit's shoulders. "Between my legs, of course," he answered cockily, leaning back on his palms.

"Of course," Kit repeated in a mocking voice, though his grin belied the tone of his words. He scooted forward a little more so he knelt at the foot of the bed between Devon's widespread thighs. He dipped his head and nuzzled the inside of one leg, nipping lightly at the skin. "Was that what you had in mind?"

Jonathan settled back against the headboard, his hand gliding gently over his own erection as he watched his lovers teasing each other. They were such opposites in so many ways—light and dark, north and south, rough and smooth—but they complemented each other perfectly. Once again he wondered how he'd ever gotten lucky enough to have not one, but two such incredible men in his life.

Devon drew a hissing breath, his cock jumping at each pinch of Kit's teeth on the sensitive skin of his inner thigh. "Take your time," he muttered, his voice deepened with arousal. "I'm sure you'll find it eventually."

Kit laughed again, darting his tongue to dampen Devon's bollocks before resuming his leisurely exploration of his lover's legs.

"You *have* done this before," Devon reminded Kit, arching his hips into the teasing flicker of Kit's tongue over his bollocks.

"And why is that a reason not to take my time and enjoy it this time?" Kit inquired, looking up at Devon.

"Because you have another lover waiting for his turn?" Jonathan chimed in, his voice playful. "Take your time. Just remember I expect at least as much attention when you get around to me."

Kit lifted his head and licked his lips. "I can't wait," he replied huskily. "Devon won, though, so he gets my undivided attention first. I'm sure you can figure out a way to keep yourself entertained while I see to him."

"Don't entertain yourself too well," Devon warned, threading a hand into Kit's curls to gently encourage him to return his mouth to where it belonged. "I want to watch him bring you off when we're done, my king."

Kit let himself be led, curving his lips around the breadth of Devon's cock, inhaling deeply the scent of the soap he had used in the shower and of the arousal that was so much a part of their lives. He worked his way slowly toward the head, then lowered his mouth over the tip and sucked in the entire length.

A deep moan rumbled in Devon's chest as the velvet softness of Kit's mouth enveloped him. Leaving his hand resting lightly on Kit's head, he trailed his free hand down his abdomen, his muscles trembling at the dual sensations.

The sounds from Devon's lips were music to Kit's ears. He smiled around the cock in his mouth and hummed deep in his throat, letting the vibrations add to the sensations already assailing Devon.

Devon's fingertips followed his pale treasure trail downward to the patch of hair that surrounded his cock. His hips arched upward involuntarily, pushing him deeper into the warm cavern that surrounded him. He played through the short curls, moving his fingers closer until they could brush against Kit's cheek.

Kit tipped his head into the tender caress. He looked up at Devon, letting all the love he felt show in his eyes. He could not say the words with his mouth full of Devon's erection, but he gave the emotions free rein on his face. It no longer seemed like a risk to open himself up that way, not when Devon touched him so lovingly.

The pressure in Devon's chest had nothing to do with the sensations Kit's mouth was creating and everything to do with the expression in his bottomless brown eyes. He wanted to speak the words that would tell Kit how much he'd come to feel for him—to love him—but he was too overcome by the strength of the emotion to find his voice. He settled for tracing his fingers over Kit's lips, the caress as close to a kiss as his current position would allow.

Jonathan's breath caught as he watched the look his lovers shared—a look that was clearly one of mutual love. A few months ago, he might have been devastated to see them gaze at each other that way, but his feelings for both of them had deepened so much, it gave him only joy to watch them sharing this moment. He knew they would welcome him if he moved to join them, but he was content to give them this time together, knowing he had his own place in both their hearts.

Kit's eyes fluttered shut when Devon's fingers traced his lips. He opened his mouth a little wider, catching the tip of one finger between his lips and Devon's cock, returning the kiss as best he could in his current position. Then he turned his attention to his lover's pleasure, bringing his hands into play, one on Devon's bollocks, the other farther back, ghosting across the tight pucker of flesh.

Devon's head fell back as Kit's hands joined his mouth, escalating the pleasure. He quivered as the slender hand drifted between his cheeks and over the muscle that clenched at each gentle touch. "Kitten," he gasped, the nickname all he could manage before another moan was wrenched from his throat.

Taking the diminutive and the moan for approval, Kit repeated his caress, the tip of one finger probing more deliberately at Devon's entrance as he continued to bob his head on the thick cock in his mouth. Without lube, he wasn't going to do more than tantalize, but he had no qualms whatsoever about teasing Devon to the limits of his endurance.

Spasms of need shook through Devon at each press of Kit's finger. He fought not to thrust wildly into his mouth, his hips rocking in between the wet suction on his cock and the penetration he craved. "Please," he groaned as the pressure inside him grew nearly unbearable, "need to, God, please."

Kit's eyes flicked to the tube lying on the bedside table, well out of his reach. If he'd been closer, he would have grabbed it so he could finish Devon off the way he so obviously wanted.

Devon's plea and Kit's sidelong glance drew Jonathan from his loving reverie. Retrieving the lube from the nightstand, he slid forward to place it at Kit's side, pausing to drop a kiss on Devon's stomach and another on Kit's cheek before leaning back against the headboard again, his hand settling around his growing erection.

Sending Jonathan a grateful look, Kit popped the top on the lube and coated his fingers quickly, then slid his index finger slowly but firmly inside Devon's body, crooking the tip to find his sweet spot. The yelp that escaped let him know he found it. Meeting Devon's eyes, he pressed again, sucking hard as he silently asked his lover to come for him.

Kit's long, slender finger pushing into him was all Devon needed to lose himself completely. Circling his hips to rub against the invading digit, he cried out hoarsely and gave in to his body's demand for release, clenching his fists in dark hair as he pulsed into Kit's insistent mouth.

Kit swallowed all Devon had to give him, relishing the tangy, slightly bitter flavor as he continued to work his prostate, prolonging the climax for as long as he could. Devon needed this release of tension after the day they'd had. They all needed it. He'd taken care of Devon. Jonathan was next.... Then he'd see about getting them to take care of him.

After bestowing a last loving lick on Devon's softening cock, Kit lifted his head and met Jonathan's eyes. "Well, my king?" he drawled.

Watching Devon come undone under Kit's loving ministrations had left Jonathan achingly aroused, but before he claimed his prize, he needed to kiss Kit. Opening his arms wide, he beckoned Kit to come to him where he leaned against the headboard.

Devon rolled to the side of the bed as his breath steadied and his pulse slowly calmed to a normal level. The tension that had wracked him for the past days was gone, and a warm smile spread across his face as he watched Kit crawl up the mattress and into Jonathan's waiting embrace. Jonathan immediately pulled Kit into a heated kiss, and Devon knew Jonathan was tasting his own release as his tongue plundered Kit's mouth.

Kit settled easily against the familiar warmth of Jonathan's body, giving his mouth willingly. Jonathan's tongue was a welcome invasion as it sought out every last taste of Devon's come. Kit had pushed his own desire to the side while he was taking care of Devon, but now, with Jonathan in charge, his self-control wavered, and he arched his hips forward, rubbing shamelessly against Jonathan's thigh.

Savoring the mingled flavors of saltiness and sweetness, Jonathan could have lost himself in feasting on Kit's kiss. The temptation to pull Kit's hips against his, to drag their swollen, leaking shafts together until they both found release, was nearly overpowering. But that wasn't what they'd wagered, and reluctantly he eased back from the kiss, trying to rein in his rampant emotions with a light response. "Don't think you can get out of the second half of your forfeit by distracting me this way," he teased, circling the base of his shaft in a tight grip as he willed back his all-too-eager reaction. "In fact, I think I deserve something special for my patience."

"Special?" Kit purred. "Did you have something particular in mind? You know how I like to please." He kept his gaze locked with Jonathan's as he lowered his mouth to swipe his tongue playfully across one peaked nipple before moving lower to nip at the tattoo that adorned Jonathan's lower belly.

Jonathan fought to keep his eyes from fluttering closed as Kit's lips and teeth worked their tantalizing way down his body. "Any time, any way you touch me is special," he murmured hoarsely, his eyes dampening with the power of his emotions. "Just… put your mouth on me, kitten."

He shivered as Kit lapped over the head of his cock, curling to catch the droplet of fluid that leaked from its tip.

Kit took no time at all in granting Jonathan's wish, closing his lips around the engorged head and sliding down the thick shaft. He consciously relaxed his throat and swallowed, letting the hard cock fill his mouth and throat until he had taken Jonathan in completely. Just as slowly, just as deliberately, he worked his way back up, until only the tip remained inside his mouth. He lapped teasingly across the slit, savoring Jonathan's unique flavor.

Tremors quavered through Jonathan's groin as the hot moistness of Kit's mouth settled over him like wet silk over steel. He called out wordlessly when the head of his cock bumped the back of Kit's throat, then dragged through the damp friction of lips curled over teeth until only the head felt the catlike rasp of Kit's tongue. "Gonna melt," he groaned, gripping his thighs to keep from clutching the bobbing brown curls. "So hot... so good."

Kit lifted his head, amusement getting the better of his passion for a moment. "Nothing's going soft down here, my liege," he pointed out as he stroked the hard shaft.

Devon had to chuckle at the bereft expression on Jonathan's face when Kit stopped his attentions to make his comment. "Here, mate," he called, tossing the tube of lubricant to Kit. "Our king looks like he's going to blow a few fuses if you don't get back to business."

Kit caught the tube with a grateful grin and popped the cap, returning his mouth to its previous occupation as he again coated his fingers with the slick gel. The eagerness with which Jonathan parted his legs would have made Kit smile if he could have around the mouthful and more that currently spread his lips. He accepted the silent invitation, trailing his fingers over Jonathan's sac and down to his entrance. He nudged at it gently, waiting for the muscle to relax and admit him.

Bending his knees to open himself completely to Kit's touch, Jonathan gasped when the first lube-slick digit slid into him. He thrust his hips upward, pushing his cock deeper into Kit's throat and impaling himself completely on the slim finger at the same time. "More," he moaned, the feeling of fullness only serving to whet his hunger even further.

Kit sucked harder, pulling on Jonathan's cock as strongly as he could. He added a second finger, sweeping the tips repeatedly across Jonathan's prostate.

"More," Jonathan demanded, rasping unevenly as he clenched around the probing fingers. He could feel his climax building, the muscles in his thighs and groin tightening as he chased it, but it remained just out of reach. He ached to be stretched further, filled deeper, sucked harder, purged of the last remnants of anger that still heated his blood. "More," he repeated, his voice breaking on the desperate plea.

Kit had no idea what was driving Jonathan's pleas. Usually by now Jonathan would have broken, but he gave him what he wanted, adding a third finger to the two already stretching Jonathan's sheath and letting his teeth drag up the cock in his mouth as he bobbed his head. His own desire thrummed loudly in his veins, but he ignored it in favor of Jonathan's pleasure.

Satiation danced just outside Jonathan's grasp. His head tossed blindly from side to side, his hands clenching and releasing as Kit's fingers fucked him. He opened his mouth to plead for more, but only a strangled moan escaped with his tortured breath.

Inspiration striking, Kit lifted his unoccupied hand to Jonathan's nipple, pinching it firmly, hoping that would be enough to push him over the precipice and into release.

Jonathan's entire body tensed as ecstasy exploded through him, firing through every nerve like a burst of lightning. His cock jerked and poured out its hot cream in pulse after pulse, his muscles jumping with each aftershock.

Kit swallowed rapidly, trying to keep up with Jonathan's release. He pulled back, panting for breath, before lowering his head and licking the king's cock the rest of the way clean. Aching now for his own relief, he rolled onto his side, fisting his engorged erection.

"Here, now," Devon protested, crawling forward to pull Kit's hand away and push him onto his back. "After the yeoman service you just provided, we can't make you take care of yourself too." With a wicked grin, he pinned Kit's shoulders to the bed and sucked the leaking cock into his mouth, his blond hair tickling Kit's stomach.

As worked up as Kit already was, it didn't take any more than that. With a hoarse shout, he came hard, filling Devon's mouth with creamy fluid. His panting continued, slowing finally as he regained control of himself.

Called back from the wave of orgasmic bliss he'd been floating on by Kit's shout, Jonathan rolled over on the crumpled bedding and captured his mouth, pouring all the love he felt for Kit into his kiss. He reached out to Devon, tugging him closer, urging him wordlessly to join them.

More than happy to comply, Devon swallowed the last of Kit's release and scooted upward, nudging Jonathan to join his mouth on Kit's, their tongues swirling in a three-way dance of unspoken love.

The sound of a phone ringing made all three of them tense, eyes darting to one another's faces in steely resolve before Kit started laughing. "That's my cell phone," he pointed out, pulling away to answer it. "There's no way the prick has my number. It's probably the Orkneys. They said something about wanting to go out tonight."

He reached for his pants and grabbed the phone, tapping a button when he saw Bevan's number on the display. "Hey, Bev, what's up?"

Kit nodded a couple of times as he listened to the invitation, then said, "Okay, see you there in about an hour." Ending the call, he turned back to his lovers. "It seems the Orkneys have organized a welcome for the new actors now that Éamon and Glynn have arrived. Everybody's meeting at the pub in about an hour."

Jonathan groaned quietly. "Can't we just stay here?" he muttered half teasingly. "I'm not sure I can even stand, let alone contend with a pack of drunken knights!"

"Come on, you homebody." Devon laughed, sitting up and stretching. He felt full of energy and ready to indulge in some harmless inebriation with his friends. "Besides, I'm looking forward to meeting your new big brother. I didn't get a chance to meet him when he was here to film the coronation." He slapped Jonathan on the flank as he bounded out of the bed. "Let's shower and reheat the food before we get going. I'll stand the first round for all of us."

As tempted as they all might have been to start something in the shower, Kit reminded them sternly that they had less than an hour to get dressed and eat before driving to the pub. Reluctantly, they limited themselves to quick kisses, teasing touches, and promises of what they would do to one another when they got back home. Just under an hour later, Jonathan pulled into the parking lot of the quiet local bar the Knights of the Round Table favored when they were more interested in drinking than dancing.

A chorus of welcomes arose as the three men entered the pub. The raucous shouts from the younger Orkneys, teasing them about arriving together, hinted to Devon that they had some catching up to do, so he waved to the table and headed straight toward the bar, thinking to order their first round of drinks before taking a seat at the crowded collection of pulled-together tables. He'd only taken a step or two when he froze in place, his head snapping back in a perfect double-take to stare at the figure seated in the middle of the chattering, laughing group.

There, sitting among the cast as casually as you please, was Robert, arms extended along the back of the chairs on either side of him, not quite around Colm and Rhodri, but definitely hinting that he could—and would, Devon knew—take advantage at any moment. Devon's face hardened as he called to Kit, asking for help at the bar.

Kit frowned, wondering why Devon suddenly needed help to carry three drinks, but he shrugged and went to join him anyway. "What's going on?" he asked as they approached the bar.

"He's here," Devon hissed, nodding toward the table with barely restrained rage. "Robert."

Kit's heart clenched. "Here? But Bevan said this was for the new cast members! What the hell is he doing here?"

Seeing Devon and Kit whispering together at the bar, Jonathan excused himself from Blythe's embrace and walked over to join them. "What's wrong?" he asked, following their gaze to the group at the other end of the table and recognizing Robert from earlier that day. "What the fuck is that prick doing here?" he spat, turning his back to hide his anger from the rest of the cast.

Despite the seriousness of the situation, Kit had to smother a laugh. "I just asked the same thing," he explained, the tension returning to his face and his voice as he glanced over his shoulder again. "Surely Niall didn't make a last-minute casting change."

Devon's face hardened at the thought. "If he did, then for the first time I'm looking forward to Lancelot being exiled," he rasped.

The bitter words sent a pang of pain through Jonathan's chest. Not being the type to dwell on what he couldn't change, he'd tried to forget the fact that Devon would be leaving the production before he and Kit, at least temporarily, but Devon's comment made the impending loss all too real. Unwilling to lose even a moment of the time they had left together to Robert's influence, Jonathan scowled. "He can't be one of the new actors,

Devon—what role could he possibly play? Besides, Niall's said all along he didn't want to cast the series with typical Hollywood stars."

"Look," Kit interrupted, "we're not going to figure anything out hiding here by the bar. Let's just go over and meet everyone. There will be an explanation for why he's here. And if we're wrong, and he's been cast for something, we'll deal with it. He is *not* going to get the better of us. If nothing else, somebody needs to warn the Orkneys."

"Remember, you're not alone, Devon," Jonathan added, his hand lingering for just a moment on Devon's as he took his beer from his grasp. If it had only been the familiar knights at the table, he might have given Devon a quick kiss, but he hadn't met the newest cast members yet, and he especially didn't want to give Robert any more ammunition to use against Devon.

Devon nodded once, his jaw clenching as he walked toward the table. He wasn't going to give Robert the satisfaction of letting him see how much his presence had unsettled him. "So, which one of you is our king's brother?" he asked, looking around at the new faces.

"I guess that would be me," a strawberry blond man spoke up, "as I'm playing Kay. I assume you're Lancelot, since your friend looks too young to have fathered a son yet. Éamon Driscoll," he added, extending his hand.

"And I'd be your son." A younger man stood and offered his hand as well. "Brodie Stewart, otherwise known as Galahad. Pleased to meet you, Dad!" he added with a grin.

Devon smiled broadly, taking Éamon's offered hand and clapping Brodie on the shoulder with his other. "Well met, my son!" he said, marveling again at Niall's casting acumen. Brodie's fair looks gave him a resemblance to a younger Devon, and the aura of innocence he conveyed despite their surroundings convinced Devon he would make a perfect Galahad. "Though I'll have you know Lancelot was a mere lad when he fathered this whelp," he retorted to Éamon.

Robert watched the exchange with barely veiled derision. Deciding to enjoy the opportunity Devon had handed him, albeit unwittingly, he turned to the boy he had seen at Devon's side earlier in the day. Brodie was attractive enough, but the brunet was the one who held Devon's—and therefore Robert's—interest. "If he decides to replace you, I'd be happy to finish training you properly, since I know he's made a mess of it." He deliberately pitched his voice so that only the kid could hear him.

Kit stiffened at the insinuation in the older man's words, but he knew enough from what Devon had told them not to rise to the bait. Instead, he ignored the comment and extended his hand to Éamon. "Kit Webster," he said by way of introduction. "Percival. Care to introduce the rest of the newcomers?"

Éamon grinned as he shook Kit's hand and nodded toward the large dark-haired man at his side. "This big drink of water is Glynn Aherne, Bors to you. And James Synclair, who'll play Mordred, ill-fated love child of our king and this lovely damsel." He gestured toward a fair-haired man about Kit's age who was speaking with Anwyn Davies, the actress cast as Morgause, mother of the Orkney knights as well as, though neither knew it yet, Arthur's half sister.

Waggling his eyebrows at Anwyn in a flirtatious leer, James chuckled. "I could almost wish I'd been cast as King Lot instead. Anwyn is far too young and beautiful to be my mother."

The slender blonde grinned at him pertly. "Flattery will get you anywhere, though not until after Morgause wears herself out mooning over Arthur," she countered, her gaze passing over the other new arrivals and stopping to linger on Jonathan. "You can see why I have no trouble with that," she added with an appreciative smile.

The group around the table chuckled. "You may not have any trouble," Colm joked, "but I'm not so sure Percival and Lancelot will care for that too much. They tend to be a little… possessive of our king."

Devon frowned and directed a quelling glance at the youngest Orkney. The three of them had become comfortable enough being open among the rest of the cast, but the last thing he needed was for Robert to set his filthy sights on Jonathan the way he already had them trained on Kit.

"So that's the way the wind blows, is it?" Glynn asked, speaking for the first time. "Nice to know it's a tolerant cast. Not every set is." As he spoke, he leaned back in his seat and draped his arm around the back of Éamon's chair.

Anwyn glanced across the table at Blythe and Elsinore, the dark-haired actress portraying Morgaine le Fay. "Why are all the good ones already taken?" She pouted even as she winked to Blythe and Ellie. "I have a feeling we're going to be kissing a lot of toads if we expect to find a prince on this set."

"There are so many lovelies in this cast, though," Robert drawled. "I wouldn't know where to begin if I had the choice." His gaze lingered on the three women present before moving to Kit and then on to Devon, an air of challenge on his face.

Kit's face tightened in anger. "Then I guess it's a good thing you don't have one."

Rhodri glanced up. "Have you met before?" he asked. "I know the get-together was supposed to be cast only, but when Robert stopped by to introduce himself on set, we asked him to join us. I mean, how often do you get the chance to drink with a legend?"

"His reputation precedes him," Kit told Rhodri, his expression hardening even more as he thought of all the suffering this man had put Devon through in the past week, and the however many years before that. Kit downed his shot and looked at Devon and Jonathan. "I need another drink. I'll be back."

"That sounds like an excellent idea," Robert declared, rising from his seat and heading toward the bar in the wake of Devon's intriguing sub. He hadn't had a new toy with so much spirit since he'd broken Devon. He would enjoy breaking this one in too. After he was finished putting his former sub back in his place.

Seeing Robert trail after Kit, Jonathan pushed his chair back roughly and followed, muttering a curse under his breath.

Several heads turned in surprise at their king's unusual behavior. Addison Nichols's bushy eyebrows rose as Devon caught up with Jonathan and gestured angrily toward the bar, but the older man shook his head when Rhodri started to follow them. Something was definitely going on between the four men, but the actor playing Merlin sensed that whatever it was, their friends needed to work it through in private.

Catching up with the young beauty as they neared the bar, Robert rested a heavy, claiming hand on the boy's shoulder. "I was right," he growled. "Devon still doesn't have the slightest idea how to train a sub. No boy of mine would dare act the way you have tonight. It's time you learned some manners."

Jonathan didn't arrive in time to hear what the other man said to Kit, but he saw the grimace of disgust that crossed his lover's face. "Get your fucking hands off him," he snarled, wedging himself between Robert and Kit. He wished for once he hadn't left Excalibur at Devon's—he'd like nothing better than to take this prick's hand off at the wrist for daring to touch Kit.

Robert arched a challenging eyebrow. He had expected Devon to object—after all, the boy was Devon's—but he hadn't expected a challenge from this quarter. Seeing Devon arrive, he turned his attention to his true quarry. "You know what they say about lending out your sub, don't you?" he asked conversationally. "You get him back, but he's never quite the same. Of course, since you've already made that mistake, I'll borrow him for the evening and teach him some manners for you. You sure as hell haven't taught him any."

Before Devon could respond, Jonathan knocked Robert's hand from Kit's shoulder and caught a handful of the older actor's shirt. "You filthy hyena," he rasped. "Aren't you man enough to find someone yourself? You've got no business with Devon anymore, and you're not welcome here. I suggest you leave—now."

"I'm not anybody's sub," Kit added, stepping up beside Jonathan. "I make my own decisions and answer to myself and myself alone. Devon and Jonathan are my *lovers*, not my Doms, not that a freak like you can understand that distinction."

"I should have known Devon wasn't man enough to satisfy a pretty thing like you," Robert drawled. "When my cock's buried down your throat, you won't be so mouthy."

Robert's sneering insults to both his lovers set the fuse to Jonathan's temper. Acting without thought, he smashed his fist into the actor's smirking face, knocking him into a barstool and sending him crashing to the floor. He'd bent over him to haul him up and deck him again when Devon grabbed his arm, holding him back.

Kit glared down at Robert. "I wouldn't fuck you if you were the last man alive," he snarled. "Devon and Jonathan are ten times the man you'll ever be."

"What would a prissy bottom like you know about real men?" Robert ground out, struggling to his feet.

Jonathan fought to shake off Devon's grip, more than ready to knock Robert's insults down his throat a second time. "Only an ignorant bastard like you would automatically assume he's the bottom. You'd never be able to understand what the three of us share, so just shut the fuck up and get out of here. We don't ever want to hear from you again."

"And who's going to make me?" Robert challenged, getting into Jonathan's face.

"I am," Devon retorted, tightening his grasp on Jonathan's arm to prevent his infuriated lover from throwing another punch. He stepped between the two, squeezing Jonathan's shoulder in reassurance before releasing him to face his former Dom. "I should have done this years ago," he growled. "Your idea of mastery makes me sick. It ends now."

Robert snorted. "You didn't stand up to me then. You won't do it now. You're still just a pansy boy with no balls." He reached for Devon's shoulder, intending to send him to his knees where he belonged.

Once Devon would have found it unthinkable to stand up to Robert's insults. Now, in his bone-deep assurance of his lovers' acceptance, his response was instinctive. His blow knocked Robert back against the bar, scattering stools in every direction and drawing the attention of the group sitting at the other side of the room.

"Do our friends need some help?" Glynn asked, looking around the table. As one, the knights rose to their feet and headed toward the four men at the bar.

"What are you doing?" Rhodri yelled as he approached the bar, though it was not at all clear whether he was addressing Robert or his fellow cast members.

Kit turned at hearing Rhodri's voice, trusting that Jonathan would not let Robert get the upper hand on Devon. "Old, unfinished business," he told the others. "Let Devon handle it." When he had confronted Robert, he hadn't thought about it, determined to defend Devon, but now, seeing Devon finally standing up to his former Dom, he realized that Devon needed to do this for himself, ending Robert's tyranny once and for all.

Devon pulled Robert upright until their faces were only inches apart. "You no longer have any place in my life. If you ever contact me or any of my friends ever again, I'll kick your sorry arse all the way back to LA."

"Big words from a little man," Robert goaded. "You wouldn't want word of your little fling to get out, though, now would you? Wouldn't help your career, and it would be a disaster for theirs."

Addison approached the bar, drawing the mantle of Merlin's dignity around himself like a cloak. "You may want to reconsider that threat," he said, the mild tone belying the steel beneath.

"What do you think you can do to me, you old queen?" Robert snarled.

"We queens have far more power than you might realize," Addison replied, turning to walk away, leaving the threat implied. He had no idea what had happened between the four men, and he would not do anything until he knew he would not hurt Jonathan, Devon, and Kit by his actions, but he would not stand by and watch his friends persecuted for their relationship.

Robert grabbed Addison's arm. "Listen, you—"

The rest of the words never left his lips. The four Orkneys surrounded Robert, glaring at him with clenched fists. "Our friends told you to leave," Rhodri said, his voice hard. "I used to admire you—if I'd had any idea what you were really like, I'd never have invited you to join us."

"You gonna get rid of me, pipsqueak?"

"You can't possibly take on all of us," Glynn pointed out, his calm, deep voice resonating with reason. "Why not leave before anyone gets hurt?"

Infuriated, Robert swung out blindly, not caring who he took down but determined not to let this group of posers get the better of him.

Devon caught his former master's arm, bearing it down with a strength honed by months of swordplay. "You forget, I know things that would be as damaging to your career as anything you could say about me."

"And plenty of your former castmates would be happy to corroborate Devon's word," Jonathan added, thinking of Mariselle, certain she wasn't the only one who had seen and abhorred Robert's behavior.

"You have no power here," Kit added. "Cut your losses while you still can."

Robert's scornful gaze swept over the assembled group, meeting a unified front of opposition in return. He snorted with laughter as he pulled free of Devon's grip. "Enjoy your little fantasy world while you can," he taunted. "You've already proven you can't make it in films if you've sunk to working on television. A year from now no one will even remember this ridiculous series, and you'll all be lucky to find work in dog food commercials."

He stalked to the door, turning to glare at Devon, who stood surrounded by the entire cast. "And if you expect this freaky little threesome you have is going to last, you're even stupider than I thought—which is pretty hard to imagine." He paused for a moment, but no one bothered to dignify his insults with a response. With a final sneer of laughter, he walked out, the swinging doors of the pub rocking behind him at the force of his exit.

CHAPTER 6
MAKING LOVE

A STUNNED silence had settled over the bar at Robert's words. Suddenly, as if his exit had released them from a spell, everyone began talking at once.

"Are you all right?"

"What was that all about?"

"What set him off, anyway?"

Ignoring the sudden chatter around them, Kit looked directly into Devon's eyes. "It's over," he said softly. "He can't bother you anymore."

Devon drew a deep breath and released it, feeling the last of Robert's influence flowing out of him with the exhalation. "Bloody straight," he affirmed just as softly, reaching out to take Kit's arm, turning just enough to clasp Jonathan's as well. "Don't know why I didn't do that years ago."

Jonathan hoped he knew the answer to that question, but this was not the time to go into it, nor was it his place to provide the answer. He settled for clasping Devon's forearm in return, a warrior's greeting to outsiders, his other hand settling on Kit's shoulder, completing the circle that was their strength. "What do you want to tell them?" he murmured, nodding to the group of concerned friends approaching them.

"Just some old, unfinished business." Devon answered the questions with a rueful grin. "Sorry to have thrown a spanner into the party atmosphere. Next round's on me, right?"

Glynn looked around the bar at the assembled cast. "I don't see any spanners, but if I'm not missing my count, I do see two Oscars, a dozen BAFTAs, and a knighthood among the cast. That prick has no idea what he's talking about. Another drink sounds perfect." He joined the three, clapping hands on Jonathan's and Kit's shoulders before treating Devon to the same. "We 'freaks' have to stand by each other."

"Are we really that obvious?" Kit asked with a grin, knowing their relationship was an open secret on the set. Nobody talked about it, not really, but everyone seemed to understand and accept it.

"Mate, I just met the three of you, and I can already feel the heat," Glynn answered. "I bet it sparks like hell on screen."

"It's wuv," Colm teased in his best *Princess Bride* imitation. "Twu wuv."

The words set the Orkneys howling, Rhodri and Bevan finding the comment particularly funny. Kit looked away with a pang, knowing that for him, it was indeed true love. If only Jonathan and Devon felt the same way, everything would be perfect, but even now, even after the intimacies of earlier that evening, he dared not speak the words that would commit him to his lovers, not because he doubted his feelings, but because he doubted his reception outside the heat of the moment, like when they'd made love in the beach house.

"All three of them? Really?" Éamon asked Addison, as if fascinated by the idea and sensing the older man would have the clearest insight into what actually went on around—and off—the set.

"You have a problem with that, mate?" Devon retorted, overhearing the question. He hadn't expected that reaction, since it was common knowledge in the industry that Éamon and Glynn were a couple, but just because Éamon was gay didn't mean he'd approve of a three-way relationship like theirs. Devon hoped he wasn't going to cause any trouble. The last thing they needed was friction between members of the principal cast.

"None at all," Éamon answered, "except maybe jealousy. I was wondering what a guy had to do to get that lucky."

"I still wonder the same thing," Jonathan answered honestly, relieved that Éamon's reaction was a positive one. He would have managed his scenes with the other man if it hadn't been—he was an actor, after all; that was what he was being paid for—but he was glad he wouldn't have to work with someone who actively disapproved of him and his choices. The thought made him pause, considering what it would mean if the relationship with Devon and Kit were to continue, to become known outside the fantasy world of this utterly atypical cast. Recognizing that he might not have anything to worry about if the relationship ended with filming was even harder to contemplate.

Devon's glare softened to a smile at his newest castmate. "Fortune favors the bold," he said in Lancelot's confident tone.

"How bold?" Glynn asked, eyes running over Devon, Kit, and Jonathan lasciviously.

Addison watched the interactions with a keen eye. This was the closest any of the three had come to talking, in his hearing, about their relationship. He caught a glimmer on Kit's face, then one on Jonathan's, that made him wonder. It was obvious to him—to anyone watching, really—how much the three men meant to one another, but he wondered if it was at all obvious to them.

"Let's just say they made me an offer I couldn't refuse," Jonathan said, surprising himself with his openness. But somehow it felt comfortable, right, not to hide the truth. He'd always trusted his instincts, and he sensed that the newest members of the cast could accept what the three of them shared.

Glancing over at Éamon, Glynn smiled. "I know the feeling," he murmured. Turning to Devon, he added, "So where's that round?"

Blythe, their Guinevere, slipped her arm through Devon's. "You all go sit back down," she told them. "I'll help Devon carry the drinks."

With a nod and much milling about, the group of actors moved back toward the table where they had been sitting before Robert provoked Kit. Jonathan hung back for a moment, listening to the Orkneys each vying to top the others in the stories they could tell the newest members of the cast about the three of them, before deciding this would be a good moment to visit the men's room. He wanted to wash the last taint of Robert's touch off his skin.

As he stood at the sink rinsing his hands, he couldn't help but smile at his reflection in the cracked and silvered mirror. "How the fuck *did* you get so lucky, old man?" he asked himself, his cock tightening in anticipation of returning home at the end of the evening, of the three of them loving one another without Robert's specter as an unwelcome fourth in their bed.

"It's a very good question," Addison agreed from the doorway, "not because you don't deserve it, but because most of us search our entire lives for one person to love us. To have found two, who love each other as much as they love you, is luck indeed!"

Jonathan's first impulse was denial, but as he considered Addison's words, he thought back to what he had felt when Robert had come on to Kit, to his rage at the man's treatment of Devon, to what he felt every time the three of them made love. It didn't matter who was on top, who made the decisions, who took whom—that was what they did, every time. They made love. Suddenly all his reasons for holding his feelings in check each time he was tempted to say the words seemed foolish. If their time together was destined to end when filming did, something he had always tried to avoid thinking about, all the more reason to make the most of the time they had now.

Addison watched the emotions play across the younger man's face, solidifying his belief that the three had not admitted their feelings to one another. "The time has come, I think, for the king to show his leadership once again," he observed softly. "They will follow where you lead."

"I hope you're right," Jonathan answered, though even if he was mistaken, if Kit and Devon didn't love him as deeply as he loved them, he wouldn't regret telling them how he felt. He was tired of hiding it.

"Trust an old wizard," Addison intoned in Merlin's gravest tones. "And if you can't trust him, trust an old queen."

"I do," Jonathan said, pulling his friend into a grateful hug. "Both of you."

Addison laughed and returned the hug. "Let's go. Your lovers are probably wondering if I've stolen you away."

"If anyone could, it would be you, Addison." Jonathan grinned.

"Don't tempt me," Addison scolded, stepping out of the restroom and back into the bar.

Jonathan followed, instinctively scanning the room until he spotted his two lovers. Devon was still leaning against the bar with Blythe, their heads almost touching. That didn't surprise him much. Fortunately for the chemistry required between their characters, Devon admired the elegant blonde who portrayed Guinevere, though judging by the expression on his lover's face, at the moment she was giving him an earful about something. He was more surprised to see Kit talking with Anwyn, just away from the table where the Orkneys had the newcomers in stitches with their tales. Though Jonathan hadn't filmed many scenes with her yet, he knew Anwyn had taken her role as mother to Gawain, Gaheris, Gareth, and Agravaine to heart, and by virtue of the actors' friendship had practically adopted Kit as another of her "sons," though Kit generally tried to avoid her mothering. Curiosity getting the better of him, Jonathan headed toward the bar, only to see Devon flush and straighten as soon as he spotted Jonathan approaching.

"Need a hand with those drinks?" he asked, wondering what Blythe could have been saying to garner such a reaction. "I'm sure the only reason the others aren't complaining by now is that the Orkneys are telling them all kinds of lies about us."

"Remember what I said, Devon," Blythe declared before turning her attention to Jonathan. "Here," she said, handing him several glasses and bottles. "We can get the rest."

With Jonathan's eyes on him, Devon couldn't help but feel a flush warming his cheekbones—the curse of being fair-skinned, though there weren't many things that could make him blush anymore. Blythe had just managed to find one of them, and she'd refused to be put off until she'd said her piece. Trying to divert attention from himself, Devon wrapped his hands around as many bottle necks as he could. "Thanks," he muttered, hoping Jonathan would think the words were for him as they headed toward the large table.

"About time!" Rhodri cheered when Blythe, Jonathan, and Devon arrived with the drinks. "Telling stories is thirsty work!"

"You don't need an excuse, Rhodri, especially when someone else is footing the bill," Devon retorted. He suspected telling the truth was thirsty work too, though he didn't plan to do more than nurse a beer or two for the rest of the night. If he was going to do this—and Blythe's argument had been very convincing—he wasn't going to rely on liquid courage to see him through it. He had just stood down Robert, for Christ's sake! How much harder could this be?

Kit and Anwyn returned to the table just then, Kit looking more than a little shell-shocked. He grabbed one of the shots of vodka and downed it in a single gulp, then reached for another, but Anwyn grabbed his hand. "That won't help," she scolded. "Just relax and trust me."

Kit didn't say "what if." He'd used all his excuses already, and Anwyn had shot down every single one. He knew she was right, but that didn't make him less nervous. He looked at Jonathan, then Devon, letting the sight of their beloved faces bolster his confidence. They wouldn't shoot him down, even if they didn't feel the same way. They weren't that kind of men.

Jonathan wasn't exactly sure, afterward, how he'd made it through the rest of the evening. He'd chatted with the others, even engaged in a fairly lengthy conversation with Éamon Driscoll, though he couldn't have said later what they'd talked about. All the while, his attention was drawn to his lovers, always aware of where they were and who they were speaking with, even when they weren't in his line of sight. A low but constant spark of arousal flickered inside him, like a fire damped down to embers, needing only a little fuel to burst into flame again.

When he judged enough time had passed that they could leave without appearing rude, Devon yawned loudly and rose to his feet, excusing himself to the rest of the table. "Early call tomorrow," he reminded them, nodding toward the newcomers. "Don't let us stop you, though—you haven't lived until you have to make a five o'clock makeup call after a night of partying with the Orkneys."

"Since we drove in with Devon, we'd better be going too," Jonathan added, knowing they weren't fooling anyone.

"Don't wear yourselves out too much," Colm teased as Kit rose as well. "We're fighting King Lot's army again tomorrow, and we need our knights at the top of their game."

"What's a small castle to the Knights of the Round Table?" Kit asked haughtily, staring down his nose at Colm.

"The doom of us all if Arthur can't defeat Lot," Colm retorted cheekily.

Kit shook his head. "Okay, you win. I promise, no exhausted king or knights tomorrow. Can we leave now?"

"Oh, very well," Colm agreed grudgingly, the expression spoiled by his twinkling eyes. "Have a good night, gentlemen."

"We will," Devon promised, his eyes softening as he smiled at the two men at his side.

Kit started toward the door, turning back to smirk at Colm over his shoulder as they left. It wasn't nice, but he couldn't help gloating silently that he was going to get laid tonight—spectacularly laid—and Colm would be going home alone. Unless he could persuade one of the local girls to go home with him. Even then, it couldn't possibly compare to Kit's own good luck.

GLANCING AT the alarm as he slipped under the cool sheets, Jonathan couldn't believe it had only been a few hours since they'd left Devon's bedroom. So much had happened in the interim, so many emotional swings that their loving interlude might have been a week ago for as much as he needed to reconnect with his lovers. He slid to one side of the bed, folding back the covers and leaning on an elbow as he watched his fair- and dark-haired companions undressing, offering a silent thanksgiving to any power that might be listening for bringing these men into his life.

Kit finished stripping off, folding his clothes, and setting them aside. His eyes flitted back and forth between Devon and Jonathan, his conversation with Anwyn echoing in his mind. He wanted to say something, wanted to tell them, but he couldn't seem to find the words. Seeing his own desire reflected back to him in their eyes, he let the concern go. He would say something later, after they'd made love and affirmed their relationship in that most primal of ways.

Despite both his lovers waiting for him, Devon undressed slowly, remembering Blythe's words. Jonathan was already in bed with the covers pulled back to reveal his bare chest, the small pink nipples that always seemed to be hard tempting Devon to take them between his teeth; Kit was leaning over to set his clothes on the dresser, providing a tantalizing view of smooth, tawny buttocks. He hungered for them both, not only for their obvious physical appeal, but for their unconditional support as he'd worked through the shock of Robert's reappearance. They hadn't been turned away by his past, and they'd stood by his side when he needed them, and even more, they'd sensed that he needed to face down his former Dom himself to extinguish the last of Robert's influence on his life. Devon knew intuitively that the nightmares were over—those caused by memories of his time with Robert, at least. Whether he would be able to leave these two when his part in the filming was over without spawning a new set of nightmares was a different question. Blythe was right; he couldn't let any more of the time they had left pass without taking action.

"Come to bed, Devon," Jonathan urged, holding out his free arm in welcome, knowing without having to look at Kit that they both wanted the blond between them. "I am so fucking proud of you, babe. You showed that bastard more class than I would have in your place."

Kit chuckled, having trouble imagining Jonathan not acting with class, but he didn't contradict him, moving instead to stand behind Devon and urge him toward the bed. Tonight wasn't about Jonathan anyway, but about celebrating Devon's newfound freedom. "Let us love you," he said instead. "Let us show you how proud of you we are."

Kit's words were the opening Devon needed, but before he could speak, Kit nudged him from behind, gently pushing him to his knees on the bed. Jonathan reached up to draw him closer, and Devon slid under the covers, tangling his legs with Jonathan's as Kit curled against his back and wrapped an arm around him to rest on Jonathan's hip.

The connection Jonathan felt with both his lovers at this moment was so strong that any lingering fears melted away in the warm glow of simply being with them. "I realized something tonight," he admitted, his knuckles tracing the curve of Devon's cheek while he interlaced the fingers of his other hand with Kit's. "Watching you stand up to Robert made me see that there was something I need to tell both of you, something I can't take the chance of waiting to say until filming is ready to end." He drew a breath, the strength of his emotion making it difficult for him to speak. "I love you," he said simply, knowing that no words he could find would give the declaration any more meaning. "Both of you. I don't know where we go from here, but I need you to know how very much you both mean to me."

Devon's heart felt as if it were going to swell right out of his chest. "Jon," he rasped, reaching up to cup his face, blinking away a sudden moistness as his gaze met a pair of equally swimming blue eyes. He rolled onto his back enough to touch Kit's face with the same gesture, seeing a matching glow in the ocher depths. "Kit… I never expected this to happen, but I love you both so much, so damn much."

"I know," Kit murmured, tightening his hand on Jonathan's fingers as he lifted his other hand to clasp Devon's. "I was going to tell you both tonight, after… both of you." He took a deep breath, not because he was afraid to say the words, not after his two lovers had already made their declarations, but because he had never said the words to anyone besides family. "I love you," he declared firmly.

"Who the fuck would have believed it?" Devon marveled, his voice thick with emotion. Kit's grip contracted around his hand, and Jonathan leaned forward until their foreheads touched, the back of his fingers still brushing over the light stubble of Devon's jawline. Devon squeezed his eyes shut, fighting a lifetime of conditioning that insisted men don't cry. "I don't want to leave you," he admitted, a tear slipping from beneath his tightly closed lid to trickle down a chiseled cheek. "Think Niall would notice if Lancelot hung around after he's banished?" he asked, trying for a lighter tone without much success.

"He might notice, but he wouldn't kick you off the set," Kit insisted, his embrace tightening at the thought of Devon leaving. The strength of their threesome had already carried him through some difficult moments in filming, but the most demanding shoots were still to come. Having to face that without both his lovers there was daunting. A part of him wanted to beg Devon to stay, but he understood that Devon had to settle his business with his ex-wife once and for all so he would be free to move forward with his life. With their life.

"We'll work it out somehow," Jonathan insisted, wishing he felt more confident than he sounded. "It's only temporary—Lancelot has to come back to rescue Guinevere." He didn't mention the separation they'd all face when filming ended, though his words applied to that as well. "Somehow, some way, we'll make it work." His lips met Devon's, pressing against them gently as his thumb brushed the moisture from his cheek. "We didn't let your past break us apart. We won't let distance beat us, either."

"Let us love you, Devon," Kit reiterated, propping up on one elbow to kiss Devon tenderly. "Let us *show* you how we feel."

Gently freeing his hand from Devon's clasp, Jonathan threaded his fingers into Kit's curls, pushing up enough to reach his lips. Their eyes meeting in wordless accord, Jonathan thought again how Kit always managed to sense just what he or Devon needed. "Love you, kitten," he whispered before easing back to claim Devon's lips, spreading his legs to welcome him between them. "Want you, Devon," he murmured when the kiss broke at last. "Want to feel you love me, the way you did the first time."

"Won't be like the first time," Devon answered, cupping Jonathan's buttocks to draw him even closer, moaning when their cocks throbbed against each other hotly. "Back then, I only wanted you. I'm going to make it so much better for you now." His palms roamed Jonathan's chest, rubbing his thumbs over the hardened nipples, catching them between his forefingers to roll and tug on them the way Jonathan liked best.

"We'll make it perfect for each other," Kit declared, curling along Devon's back, sliding his hands over hard muscle and bare skin. He spared an amused thought for Robert's mistaken belief that he was the bottom in the relationship, but only for a moment. He had far better things to occupy his thoughts, like driving his lovers absolutely out of their minds with pleasure. Knowing Devon's preferences now nearly as well as he knew his own, he nipped lightly at the curve of his shoulder before biting down hard, harder than he had ever dared before.

Devon groaned as Kit's teeth cut into his deltoid, making his cock jolt against Jonathan's where they were trapped between their bodies, winning an answering moan. "Fuck, Devon," Jonathan panted, grinding his hips hard against Devon's pelvis. He pulled Devon's head to his, kissing him fiercely, rocking in short, hard thrusts that dragged their cocks against each other, the motion growing smoother as they slickened with each other's precome. Jonathan skated his other hand down the curve of Devon's waist to where his own thighs wrapped around both Devon and Kit, then back up Kit's body where it molded to Devon's.

"Not tonight," Kit insisted, rocking firmly against Devon's arse. "Tonight we're making love."

"Always," Jonathan agreed when he could finally tear himself away from the intoxication of Devon's mouth. "Any way, every way we're together, it's love. We may not have really said the words before tonight, but that's always what it's been." He worked a hand between their bodies to circle Devon's cock, running up and down its length, gently easing back the foreskin to coax more fluid from its tip. "Please, babe," he entreated, inching himself upward until he could guide the shaft between his legs. "Need to feel you inside me."

Unable to resist the plea in Jonathan's voice, Devon thrust into the cleft between his buttocks, his precome lubricating the already sweat-damp crease, but that alone wasn't enough to let him continue. He knew Jonathan wouldn't protest, but tonight of all nights he refused to inflict any pain on either of his lovers. Scrabbling under the pillows, he found the tube of gel they'd left there earlier in the evening and squeezed a dollop onto his fingers, then reached over Jonathan's hips to work his way past the clenching entrance, determined to prep him completely. Jonathan's gasp as the first finger slid inside sent Devon's own need skyrocketing. "So good," he crooned, twisting the digit deeper until he could scrape the pad against Jonathan's sweet spot. "So hot, so tight. Open up for me, Jon. Gonna make it so good, so good for us both."

Kit pushed up on one elbow to watch as Devon prepared Jonathan. The sight of those strong fingers disappearing in Jonathan's firm arse made his own cock swell painfully. He looked around for the lube, snagged the tube, and covered his fingers with the slippery gel. Sliding them between the cheeks of Devon's backside, he probed gently, mirroring the caresses Devon was bestowing on Jonathan. "And you open for me," he husked.

"Always." Devon echoed Jonathan's response as he reacted to his wordless appeal for more. Working a second finger into the muscle that stretched and squeezed to draw him in deeper, he felt himself reacting the same way to Kit's touch. "Either of you—both of you." He gasped, the layered sensations of Jonathan stroking his cock as Kit scissored his fingers inside him stealing his breath. "Want you both—love you both—so much."

"Now, Devon," Jonathan insisted, feeling the heavy shaft swell with each curl of Kit's fingers. He needed that thickness filling him, uniting him with Devon and with Kit through him, an unbroken circle of desire and love. Hitching his hips until he could throw his top leg over Kit's thighs, he guided Devon's cock to his entrance, working it between the fingers that still filled him, wanting to take as much of Devon inside him as he could. "Love you so much—want all of you—always." A cry of pleasure broke from his throat as the slick head of Devon's erection entered him, the long fingers still surrounding it. "Oh God, babe," he panted, his hips lifting to seek even more of Devon's length. "More, want more, want you inside me forever."

"You have me," Devon promised, the burn of Kit's fingers making him jump inside Jonathan's hot sheath. "Always—no matter where we are—always—" His lips closed over Jonathan's, uniting them in yet another way, his emotions stronger than any words could describe.

Deciding Devon was stretched enough and wanting desperately to be a part of the joining already taking place on the bed, Kit slid his fingers out and slicked his shaft quickly, lined up and pressed inside, letting Devon's movements draw him in deeper with each stroke.

This moment was more than anything Devon had ever dreamed of—loving and knowing himself to be loved in return, not once but twice, without jealousy or weakness—strength building on strength, love building on love. Sheltered between his two lovers, giving and receiving pleasure in equal measure, a wellspring of joy overflowed inside him. His free hand caressed Jonathan's cock as Kit filled him, each thrust driving him deeper inside Jonathan. The sensations spiraled through him, as though he were feeling both his lovers' pleasure on top of his own. With a wordless shout of pure adoration, Devon spasmed inside

Jonathan, Kit's urgent pulses driving the intensity higher with each pump of his hips.

Kit bit his lip hard to stop himself from coming the minute Devon's climax started, squeezing his cock repeatedly, tightly. He wasn't ready to let go of this moment of communion, this instant of infinity. He knew, rationally, that they would find it again each time they made love, each time they whispered their love or shouted it to the heavens, but this was the first time, the moment they first made love openly, knowingly, intentionally rather than hiding their emotions behind the mask of physical sensation, and he was loath to have it end. He reached for Jonathan's hip, wanting the physical connection to both men that would mirror the emotional and spiritual one they had finally acknowledged.

Devon's hand on Jonathan's cock, his heat spilling inside him, were nearly enough to push Jonathan over the edge. Only one thing was missing, and as Devon's head fell to his chest in ecstatic release, Jonathan reached out for Kit, pulling his head down over Devon's shoulder to join their lips as his orgasm flared inside him like a thousand shooting stars.

Though their lips barely brushed as they met over Devon's body, Jonathan's kiss broke Kit's resolve, sending love and lust welling through his heart and body. His release sent him flying, higher than any plane, than any mountain, yet he felt only exhilaration, knowing his lovers were there with him, ready to catch him, to support him, comfort him, help him, love him. With them by his side, he could do anything. "I love you," he shouted hoarsely.

By the time the spasms of pleasure slowed, Devon was too drained to do more than collapse against Jonathan's chest, his breathing still rough and shaky. The warmth radiating from Jonathan beneath him and Kit behind him grounded him, imbuing him with a sense of peace and rightness. He could still feel Kit inside him, though not as deeply, as tightly, as when Kit had stretched to kiss Jonathan. He wasn't sure he'd ever felt a lover as deeply inside him as Kit had been in that moment. "Love you," he murmured, clasping each of his lovers' hands and raising them to his chest. "Love you both."

Jonathan squeezed Devon's hand, stretching his fingers until they could brush the back of Kit's, his other hand combing through Devon's rumpled hair. Maybe later he'd find the words to convey how much the two men beside him had come to fill his heart and his life; for now, lying joined with his lovers like this was enough, and everything he needed.

Coming down from the sensual high, Kit chuckled softly. "You know," he murmured, "I could almost be grateful to that bastard. His interference finally got us to admit our feelings."

Jonathan privately wasn't sure he could ever forgive that twisted piece of shit for abusing Devon's trust, but he wasn't going to let even the thought of him spoil this moment. "I owe Addison for convincing me to tell you," he mused, humming in contentment as Devon settled into a more comfortable position against his side. "He's right—I'd be lucky to have found only one of you. Loving you both is a gift beyond price."

"Blythe told me I was a coward," Devon admitted, curling around Jonathan as Kit's warmth pressed against his back. "Said I was using my failed marriages and the fact I was leaving as excuses to keep from facing what I really felt for you both." A yawn escaped as he spoke, making Jonathan chuckle when it ruffled the hair on his chest. "Dunno 'bout you, but I can't argue with Guinevere." His voice trailed off into a muffled murmur.

"Any more than I can argue with Morgause," Kit agreed. "Anwyn said pretty much the same thing to me, said I'd been mooning over you both and that it was time to stop being a kid and admit that I had found an adult relationship worth keeping." Stifling a yawn of his own, he shifted more comfortably against Devon's back.

"Sleep," Jonathan whispered as his lovers' breathing softened, letting his own eyes drift closed.

Following Jonathan's direction, Kit's eyes fell shut, his last thought before sleep claimed him that they would make the most of every day they had left together, free of Robert's taint and secure in one another's love, so that when filming ended, they would have such a wealth of shared loving between them that they would be able to endure even that.

CHAPTER 7
START ME UP

"Is it just me?" Kit asked Jonathan when they entered their trailer at the end of the day. "Or is Devon avoiding anything more than vanilla sex?"

Jonathan arched his back, vertebrae cracking as he worked out the tension of the day's filming before dropping into his makeup chair. "You noticed it too?" He stretched one arm, then the other before starting to unfasten the layers of chain mail and leather armor. "Not that I'd ever complain about any sex with either of you, but I haven't seen the toy box in weeks. Not since—"

"Since Robert showed up," Kit agreed. "I thought we banished his specter last week when Devon beat him up, but I guess I was wrong." He sank into his makeup chair, pulling his tunic free carelessly. Stacy and Carol would fuss, but he needed it off. Now. "Could he still be afraid that he'll treat us the way Robert treated him?"

It took several deep breaths before Jonathan could even consider Robert without a red haze of anger clouding his thoughts. "That bastard has so much to answer for," he muttered. "At least he'll have a harder time getting his sick kicks with anyone else. Addison told me he's put the word out with some of his friends—the 'gay grapevine,' he called it—that Robert is dangerous." He loosened his tunic enough to pull it over his head, draping it over the chair back. "It still burns me that after the hell he put Devon through, he walked away with nothing more than a sore jaw."

"I know," Kit agreed, "but I don't know what else we could have done. I'm more concerned about Devon, though. He was just getting comfortable as a Dom again when this happened. I wonder if it's time to confront him. As much as I love everything we do together, I'm not willing to just abandon the games we played, not when they brought us all such pleasure."

A surge of liquid heat spread through Jonathan's loins, his cock hardening at the memory of the fierce pleasure he had experienced at the beach cottage the first weekend Devon had acted as their Dom. That was an experience he definitely wanted to try again. "We'll just need to find a way to convince him," Jonathan murmured, his voice husky with desire.

Kit's grin widened. "Oh, I'm sure we can think of something," he assured his lover, lust pooling in his groin. "Do you suppose greeting him at the door in nothing but our cock rings, with the toy box and his leathers in hand, would do it?"

The swelling in Jonathan's groin surged into a full-fledged hard-on at the image of Devon poured into his skintight leathers. "It sure as hell does it for me," he admitted, standing up and dropping his leggings to pool on the floor. "C'mon, kitten—let's get ready so as soon as Carol and Stacy are through with us, we can head home to shower and get everything set before Devon gets back."

Kit chuckled as he waited for his naked king to dress in street clothes. He knew better than to think they'd get out of the bathroom without making love, but maybe it would take the edge off enough that they would have the patience to convince Devon to claim them again like he had at the beach.

DEVON TRUDGED up the walk to his rental house, rubbing at a kink in the back of his neck. Brodie and the Orkneys had tried to talk him into going out for drinks when they'd finally finished running through the scene of Lancelot preparing Galahad to be knighted, but he'd begged off. They'd accepted his excuse of wanting to read the new pages of dialogue Niall had distributed, but from the ribald glances they'd exchanged as he headed to his trailer to change out of costume, he knew they were convinced he was off for a wild night with his lovers. Lately, though, he'd lost his appetite for anything more than the most vanilla of lovemaking—if *anything* about their threesome could be considered vanilla, he supposed. But any thought of games inevitably reminded him of his time with Robert, and although he had finally driven his former master out of his life, it seemed he hadn't yet succeeded in freeing himself of the taint of his memory.

No sooner had Devon opened his front door than he found his arms full of energetic Kit. Jonathan closed the door behind him and slid his jacket from his shoulders, gently massaging the knots he found with strong fingers. It would have been a perfectly stereotypical welcome home—*if* both of them weren't stark naked and proudly sporting their cock rings around their nascent erections.

"Welcome home, Sir," Kit purred, nuzzling Devon's neck eagerly. It was more forward than a proper sub would have been, but until and unless Devon agreed to their plan, he wasn't really a sub. "How can we serve you tonight?"

"You've had a long day," Jonathan added, working around Kit's clinging embrace to unbutton Devon's shirt from behind him, letting his cock nudge between Devon's asscheeks in the process. As soon as he had the shirt halfway open, he burrowed a hand beneath it to find and tease the soft blond pelt coating Devon's chest. "Tell us how we can please you."

Not to be outdone, Kit lowered his head as soon as the skin of Devon's chest was revealed and nipped sharply at his collarbone, knowing how much Devon enjoyed that little bit of rough. "Tell us what you want," he added, looking up and meeting the glowing green gaze.

"Seems to me you're doing a fine job of conning that out on your own," Devon managed to comment before Kit's teeth closed on his shoulder and Jonathan's hands dipped lower to cup him as he worked open his trousers. The "own" turned into a moan when Jonathan conquered the zipper and slid his slacks down around his ankles, wrapping a callused palm around the quickly engorging flesh he'd uncovered.

"But think how much *better* we could do if you'd guide us," Kit replied, pulling back from the embrace enough to nip at Devon's nipples, first one, then the other. He glanced over his shoulder at the toy box and leathers sitting on the coffee table. "Everything you need's right there. Just tell us what you want us to do, Sir."

Jonathan could feel Devon tense in his arms when he saw what they'd laid out for him. "Not exactly a pipe and slippers, is it?" Devon grated, turning his head away to gaze somewhere in the direction of the kitchen linoleum. "I don't think I can go back to that again."

"We want it, Devon," Jonathan murmured against his ear, letting his lips trail down the strong column of Devon's throat. "We want to serve you, to give you pleasure."

"We love every part of you," Kit added, "including the Dom. And we've missed seeing that side recently." He pressed closer, letting his erection bump against Devon's. "Do you remember the weekend we spent at the beach? Do you remember how good it felt to take control and bend us to your will? All you have to do is ask and that can be yours again. Either of us, both of us, tied up, spread wide, however you want us, for your pleasure. And ours, luv. Don't ever think that we don't want this just as much as you do."

The fierce jump of Devon's cock at Kit's sinful words made it useless for him to deny exactly how well he remembered. "A man'd have to be dead not to want you—either of you—that way, but I can't…." He swallowed harshly, searching for the words to explain. "All of that, it's part of what I've finally put behind me. It took years, and both of you loving me, to break free of it… of him… and I still—" He rubbed his face, trying to make them see. "I can't even think of it without thinking of him, and I won't let him have one more moment of my life. I won't let him defile anything to do with either of you."

"Then don't let him steal this from you," Jonathan argued, pulling Devon back against his chest. "Don't let him rob you of something that all of us want. We trust you, Devon. We love you, and—" Letting Devon go, he slid to his knees, resting his forehead against his lover's bare thigh. Gently, he mouthed at the pale hair that gilded it, the same emotional vulnerability he'd felt that weekend at the beach beginning to suffuse him. His voice gentled as he nuzzled Devon's thigh. "We want to submit to you."

"Were you really thinking of him at the beach?" Kit added, dropping to his knees in front of Devon, mimicking Jonathan's pose. "Was he controlling your actions that weekend? His idea of being a Dom was sick and twisted, and you suffered for that, but that wasn't how you were with us. Yes, you controlled us. Yes, you mastered us—and we loved it, in case you don't remember—but you didn't hurt us. There was nothing of the rat bastard in what we shared then, and there won't be any of him in what we do now. Unless you keep letting him hold you back. Do you really want to put away your toys, your leathers, that side of you, and pretend it doesn't exist—that it never existed? I really hope the answer is no, because you promised to expand my horizons, and I don't think you've even really begun."

The tight knot that had been squeezing inside Devon's chest loosened at the sight of Kit and Jonathan voluntarily on their knees before him. He slid a palm under each man's chin, raising their heads to look deeply and searchingly into each of their eyes. Azure-blue and ocher-brown gazed back at him with total and unconditional love and trust. He caressed each cheek with a thumb, his heart swelling at the magnitude of the gift they were giving him. "What did I ever do to deserve the two of you?" He closed his eyes and vowed to banish Robert's memory from ever again touching what he shared with these two incredible men.

"It's hardly worth putting m'leathers on, is it?" Devon mused, letting go of their chins and stroking one hand slowly over his hardened cock. Jonathan's eyes had dropped immediately to the floor, but Kit continued to stare at him with a cheeky grin. "I'd only be taking them off again before very long, wouldn't I?"

"It's up to you, of course, Sir," Kit replied, "but we really hoped you'd wear them. For us?"

Devon's gaze turned to the butter-soft trousers and the toy box arranged on the low table before returning to the two men before him; he brushed aside a tendril of hair from Jonathan's cheek, finding it slightly damp to his touch. "You've already showered?" he asked, sorry to have missed the chance to relax his tired muscles under warm water. A guilty flush colored Jonathan's cheeks, and Devon hid his smile. He knew his lovers too well to expect they could have showered without making love. "Started without me again, did ye?" he growled, catching Jonathan's jaw in a firm grip and holding it still when he would have dropped his gaze again. "Which one of you fucked the other?"

"I did," Kit admitted in a small voice, everything in him reacting to Devon's show of dominance. "Let us make it up to you," he suggested meekly. "Let us help you shower."

Regardless of whether or not he topped, Kit was a damned bossy bottom, Devon thought. The suggestion was tempting, though. "I'd prefer a soak," he decided, tapping Kit on the shoulder. "Go and run it for me." He nudged Jonathan and nodded toward the kitchen. "Get me a drink, and bring it into the loo." He picked up his discarded clothing and strode toward the master bedroom, never doubting his instructions would be obeyed.

Kit hurried to the bathroom to draw Devon's bath. He turned the water on full, adjusting the temperature the way he already knew Devon liked it. Once that was in order, he leaned forward to put the plug in the drain so the tub would fill.

Entering the bathroom, Devon's first sight was Kit's arse facing him as he leaned over the tub. That was an invitation too blatant to resist.

Gripping Kit by a hip to steady him, Devon laid a firm slap across one smooth cheek. "That's for taking Jonathan without my permission," he rumbled, feeling a tremor run through Kit at the contact.

"I'm sorry," Kit apologized immediately, even as he pushed back against Devon's hand. "But you weren't here and he begged so sweetly...." He paused, realizing he was probably getting them both in even more trouble. Hiding a grin, he added impulsively, "How was I supposed to resist?"

"Mouthy." Devon *tsk*ed, striking a slightly harder blow on the other cheek. Kit had clearly been asking for more, and Devon was happy to oblige him.

Just the way you like me, Kit thought as he wriggled with the slight pain and growing warmth, but he didn't say anything aloud. There would be time for that later if the situation warranted.

Holding the tumbler of scotch carefully to keep it from spilling, Jonathan entered the bathroom just in time to see Devon smack Kit firmly. Kit's low moan and wiggle convinced him the blow was more arousing than painful, and Jonathan found his own cock tightening in response to the spanking. Moving gracefully to his knees, he held the drink out to Devon, his voice quiet as he said, "I hope this will suit, Sir."

Devon made note both of Kit's eager reaction—despite his continued challenging comments—and the hungry light in Jonathan's eyes as he'd watched the second blow. A scenario began to take shape in his mind as he dropped a hand to Kit's shoulder, pulling him back to sit on his heels. Devon stepped into the tub and lowered himself carefully, a sigh escaping as the warm water—just the right temperature, he noted with appreciation—covered his tired limbs. "I'll take that drink now." He extended a hand languidly to Jonathan, sighing again as the chilled liquor eased down his throat. A man could get used to this!

Not waiting for another order, Jonathan picked up the soap and began to lather Devon's feet where they rested on the edge of the tub, massaging the insteps with his thumbs. Devon's quiet groan sent a shiver of pride through him. He wanted to lean forward and press a kiss to the bend of his lover's ankle, but he was already acting without Devon's explicit permission and didn't want to go too far.

Seeing Jonathan's advances being accepted, Kit picked up a washcloth. "May I help you bathe, Sir?" he asked, not wanting to be accused of being cheeky too soon.

Setting down his drink, Devon leaned forward and allowed the two to wash him, letting the day's tension fall away at their soothing hands. Jonathan seemed content to wait when they had finished bathing him, but Devon could feel Kit's nervous energy despite the lad's best attempt to kneel quietly. Hiding another grin, he rose to his feet, standing for moment to let the water cascade from his body before motioning for a towel.

For the same moment, Jonathan let himself enjoy looking up at Devon's toned body, silvery droplets of water defining the strong limbs as they ran downward. Blinking to remind himself that he was supposed to be serving Devon's pleasure and not his own, he reached for a towel and held it open for Devon to step into, then tucked it around his waist.

"Would you like your leathers now, Sir?" Kit asked, needing something to do besides just wait. The tension in the air was palpable, and he was having trouble sitting still.

The air in the tiny bathroom was thick with more than just steam; Devon couldn't imagine struggling into his leathers in that charged atmosphere. "In the parlor." He gestured for them to precede him, then reached down to open the drain and adjust himself beneath the towel.

Kit hurried back into the main living area, eager for whatever Devon had in mind for them. Visions of the hours spent on the porch at the beach assailed him as he tried to imagine what their lover might demand of them this time.

Once both Kit and Jonathan were kneeling before him again, Devon dropped the towel and nodded at Kit; since he seemed to be the one most eager to see him in his leathers again, it seemed only fair to allow him to help. Especially since it was the last thing he'd be helping with for a while. "Give me a hand getting into these," he ordered.

"Yes, Sir," Kit answered eagerly, grabbing the leathers and holding them out for Devon to step into. Images of how Devon looked in the clinging black pants flitted through his mind, making his mouth water.

Gripping Kit's shoulder as he stepped into the supple garment, Devon let him ease the black leather up his legs, stopping him only when he would have pulled them over his hips. "Jonathan," he commanded their other lover, who was watching with a rapt expression, "get my cock ring from the toy box." He'd never be able to last through what he had planned without it.

Jonathan rummaged through the contents of the box, wondering with a twinge of excitement which of the toys Devon might choose to use on them, until he found the smooth leather ring. Kneeling before their master, he held it out on his palm, hoping he might be allowed the privilege of easing it onto Devon's growing erection.

"Put it on me," Devon murmured, running his hand through Jonathan's silky hair. His grip tightened as careful fingers coasted over his cock, guiding the band over his length until it encircled the base and then pulling it snug, making him thicken even more beneath the firm pressure. Taking a step back, Devon allowed Kit to carefully ease the snug pants the rest of the way up his hips. Carefully doing up the bottom two buttons, he left the rest free, the head of his shaft peeking out from the open vee. He liked these pants too much to risk staining them.

Knowing at least Kit's eyes were on him, Devon slid his palms down the clinging leather, over his hip bones, and back up his thighs, following the split of his fly. He consciously cleared his mind of the day's stress, of his lingering misgivings, of everything but the smoothness of the grain beneath his fingers and the sensations his own touch transmitted. A successful Dom needed to find the right headspace as much as his subs did, so Devon stilled his mind and just let himself feel, stroking over the planes of his abdomen unhurriedly, trusting Kit and Jonathan to find their own equilibrium as he slowly let himself become comfortable with the role he was about to resume.

Kit did his best to sit quietly at Devon's feet, awaiting the next order, the beginning of whatever scene their Dom would dictate, but he didn't understand the delay. Next to him, Jonathan seemed perfectly serene as he waited, but Kit couldn't stop his eager twitching. He managed, barely, to hold his silence, but he could not sit still, leaning forward finally to nuzzle at Devon's groin.

A touch that definitely didn't come from his own fingers snapped Devon out of his reverie. Glancing down, he hid a smile as Kit tried to bury his face between the open plackets of his leathers. "Did I give you permission to touch me?" he asked, his voice carrying a hint of steel beneath its silk.

Kit froze, caught in blatant disobedience. "No, Sir," he said in a small voice, not trying to justify his actions. If Devon wanted an explanation, he would ask.

"Jonathan," Devon purred, wondering whether the other man would balk at what he was about to command him to do to Kit, the way he had that first weekend.

Jonathan raised his eyes from their contemplation of the floor and met Devon's calmly. A detached part of his mind noted that Devon's gaze was sharp and decisive, without any of the hesitancy that had colored it the past few weeks, but he pushed the thought aside and answered quietly. "Yes, Sir?"

"Go back to the toy box and get the restraints, two sets. The suede ones."

Jonathan rose to his feet and gathered the requested items, returning to kneel at Devon's feet, breathing in and out slowly to calm the sudden surge of his pulse. The memory of being restrained on the porch of the beach house, of being claimed first by Kit and then by Devon, made his cock throb against the unrelenting ring. He held the flexible leather out silently, hoping he would be allowed to serve his lovers that way again.

"Kit." Devon hid a smile at Kit's eager expression.

"Yes, Sir?" Kit's heart pounded at the thought of being restrained, of being at Devon's mercy.

"On your feet. Move the toy box and lie down on the table." Devon registered the slightest slump of Jonathan's shoulders, promising himself he would be sure to make up for his other sub's disappointment. "Face up."

Kit swallowed forcefully, rising to his feet with as much grace as he could manage. He set the toy box on the floor, bending at the waist to give both his lovers an extra tempting view of his arse, though he doubted they needed tempting at this point, then lay back on the table as Devon had directed, trying to find a comfortable position. In the end, it probably didn't matter. Devon would position him as suited him best. He was just glad the house came furnished with a suitably sturdy table. He didn't relish having it collapse under him in the middle of their session.

Letting Kit's shimmy go unremarked—the lad really was incorrigible, and it wouldn't do to reinforce his behavior—Devon ran his hand lightly over Jonathan's now dry hair instead. "Secure him to the table, Jonathan, hands and feet. Tightly enough to keep him from squirming too much, hmm?"

Still on his knees, Jonathan turned to fasten the soft leather cuffs around Kit's ankles, then bind them securely to the legs of the coffee table. He could feel the slight tremor that shook through Kit's shins as he held them. Wishing he could reassure Kit, he gave the leg he was holding a gentle squeeze before crawling to the other end of the table and securing Kit's wrists. He couldn't resist interlacing their fingers for just a moment before straightening up, the length of the table—with Kit's body stretched across it—between him and Devon.

"Good boy," Devon praised, beckoning Jonathan to him. "Even though you've already had your fun for this evening"—Jonathan's heart dropped, fearing he wasn't going to be allowed to participate in whatever was to come—"I think you deserve a treat for obeying so readily." Devon picked up the toy box, strolled around the table, and set it at Jonathan's side. "Pick out a plug for yourself, and I'll put it in you."

Swallowing roughly, Jonathan whispered a quiet "Thank you" before looking down at the jumble of latex in the container, wondering if the plug would be all he was allowed to feel for the rest of the night. Knowing he was already stretched and still slippery from making love with Kit in the shower, he selected a wider plug than he had ever worn before, holding it out to Devon for his approval. "This one, Sir?"

Devon's eyebrows rose, but he said nothing, inclining his head and motioning Jonathan toward the couch. Jonathan rested his forearms on the cushions and leaned forward, lifting his hips to present himself to his master.

Bound to the table, Kit listened to the exchange in silence, his skin still tingling where Jonathan had touched him lightly while fastening the restraints. He hoped he had not gotten Jonathan—or himself—in trouble with Devon, but they hadn't been in the middle of a scene when they made love in the shower. Surely Devon could not intend to punish them for that! He scolded himself silently. Devon was *not* Robert, was not unreasonable. If pretending to be put out with them added to their play, he had no doubt Devon would do it, but not because he was truly upset. Letting that thought reassure him, Kit returned his focus to the physical sensation of being restrained. The width of the table left his arms and legs splayed wide, knees lifted, his body stretched out for his lovers' delectation, yet it seemed their attention was elsewhere. Reminding himself to be patient, that Devon had two subs to take care of, not just one, he tried to calm his breathing and his racing pulse as he wondered what they would do to him once they turned their attention to him.

After glancing back to reassure himself that Kit was waiting as patiently as could be expected—not that he could do much of anything else—Devon ran an admiring hand down the elegant plane of Jonathan's back, lingering on the curve of his buttock. Bending forward, he held the plug to Jonathan's lips, which opened automatically to admit the bulbous head. "Get it good and wet," Devon advised, watching appreciatively as Jonathan suckled the latex until it glistened with his saliva. Squeezing some lube onto his fingers, he explored the crease of Jonathan's arse with his other hand, teasing at the opening that would soon be stretched wide to accept the thick plug. The entrance opened to him easily, more proof that Kit had been there before him. Plunging two fingers inside, he coated the clinging channel with the gel, scissoring them to judge if his sub was ready to be claimed. When he felt Jonathan starting to quiver beneath him, he tugged the slick toy from his mouth and plunged it into him, corkscrewing it to ease the way, knowing from the groan Jonathan quickly bit off that the burn was as much pleasurable as it was painful.

Digging his fingernails into his palms to keep from bucking when the plug pushed into him, Jonathan groaned, his cock jerking against the rough fabric of the couch. Taking a few short, panting breaths, he tried not to clench around the intrusive toy, letting the burn wash over him and focusing instead on the stretch of his guardian muscle, the fullness that pressed against him, hinting at the pleasure he still hoped to earn. Devon's strong hand caressed his flank, soothing him, and he relaxed further, letting himself sag slightly as his muscles gave up their tension.

"That's good." Devon straightened with a final pat to Jonathan's hip. "Very good." He glanced at Kit again, judging by his eager gaze that he had enjoyed watching Jonathan's reward. "Feeling a bit neglected?" he asked Kit, sauntering back to the toy box and selecting a set of nipple clamps. "You shouldn't. I have an adornment in mind for you too."

Chapter 8
Feeling the Pinch

KIT'S GROIN tightened as he looked at the pieces of metal in Devon's hand. He had no idea what they were, but the expression on Devon's face assured him he'd be finding out soon. "What are they for?" he asked, hoping Devon would talk first and act second.

Devon raised an eyebrow, his glance clearly reminding Kit that he was once again overstepping his limits by speaking out of turn. "They're for expanding your horizons," he answered with a cocky smile, echoing Kit's comment of a few minutes earlier. Without warning, Devon bent over and grasped one of Kit's nipples between his thumb and forefinger. Tugging until it hardened, he twisted it slightly, his mouth twitching at the gasp Kit made no effort to hold in. *You haven't felt anything yet, lad*, Devon thought. He squeezed one of the clamps open, then closed it over the distended nub, careful to keep the tension from becoming too tight.

Devon's words both reassured and unnerved Kit. Then the clamp closed over one nipple, replacing the pressure of Devon's fingers, and sensation exploded outward. "Shit!" he cursed before he could consider how that response might affect Devon and Jonathan. "Oh fuck, that hurts!" He panted as the pain radiated out and then settled in, no longer unbearable, but a backdrop for whatever was to come. His whole body felt sensitized, as if the pressure on his nipple had somehow lit up every nerve.

Jonathan clenched his fingers into his thighs to keep from jumping up when Kit cried out in pain. *Trust Devon*, he told himself sharply, his gaze flickering from Kit's face to Devon's and back to Kit's again, reassured by what he saw there. *You said you trusted him—he knows Kit's limits by now. He won't go beyond what Kit can take.*

Devon watched Kit closely, recognizing the moment his body transcended the pain. He traced the dusky aureole gently with a long finger, avoiding the clamp itself. "All right, then?" he asked softly.

"Yeah," Kit husked, the tender touch as arousing as any more intimate caress. "*He* would never have asked, you know," he added, hoping he was not going too far.

The unspoken trust in Kit's assurance made Devon close his eyes for a moment, letting his confidence settle back over himself. He could do this. Breathing deeply, he opened his eyes and slid back into his role. "Still talking out of turn," he chided, though his voice was warm. "And I didn't hear you address me properly."

"Yes, Sir, I'm fine, Sir, thank you for asking, Sir," Kit parroted immediately, a cheeky smile on his face now that he knew his comment had not destroyed the mood of the evening. Memories of the two swats Devon had given him in the bathroom assailed him, the thought of feeling their like now, when his skin was so much more sensitive from the clamp, making his cock leak a little despite the constriction holding back his release.

"Brat." Devon laughed, bouncing the second clip in his palm. He tweaked Kit's other nipple a little more firmly, prepping it for the pinch before he fixed the remaining clamp around it. He glanced over his shoulder at Jonathan, still kneeling quietly behind him. "Come look at this, Jon," he invited. "Doesn't he look good in them?"

Shuffling forward, Jonathan moved to the side of the table opposite Devon, the plug that stretched him shifting inside with each movement. "Beautiful," he whispered. Now that he was close enough, he saw that the clamps were shaped like delicate tweezers, a silver ball threaded over the legs to adjust the tension, a cluster of crystal beads dangling from fine chains at the tip. The silver clasps glinted against the dark circles of Kit's nipples. He wondered whether Devon had bought them with Kit in mind. "They're beautiful, Sir. He's beautiful."

Jonathan's reaction made Kit's chest puff with pride. He wanted his lovers to find him beautiful, to desire him as strongly as he desired them, as he loved both of them. "Just for you," he murmured. "Sir," he added guiltily after a long enough pause to reveal his forgetfulness once again.

"There are chains," Devon said thoughtfully, trailing his finger from one clamp to the other, "that connect from here to here. They'd pull on the clamps when you move, and they'd look so good against your skin. Maybe next time you can earn those." His cock throbbed at the image, but it was more than Kit was ready for, he knew. He would save them for another session.

Kit felt the subtle reprimand as sharply as any harsh word. He bit his lip, holding back the comment that bubbled up of its own accord, his eyes sliding sideways to Jonathan's still, composed form. He envied Jonathan's easy acceptance of the sub mentality when they played their games. He had no illusions that Jonathan's submissiveness would carry over to other areas of their lives, yet Kit did not seem able to give up that last bit of control the way Jonathan did.

Jonathan bit back a moan at Devon's description, imagining the graceful sway of silver links as Kit walked, imagining Kit's face as Devon gently tugged on the chains. The mental picture was so vivid he almost didn't hear Devon's voice the first time he spoke.

"So, what should we do with our beautiful boy, Jonathan? What would you like to do to him?"

Breathing in deeply, Jonathan let go of his own need, settling in the place where all that mattered was his lovers—obeying Devon's commands, watching over Kit, giving them both pleasure through his yielding to them. His own arousal didn't disappear, but he was able to subdue it, knowing his reward would be all the sweeter for having seen to theirs first. "Whatever would please you most, Sir," Jonathan answered truthfully.

"Touch me," Kit pleaded immediately, every inch of his skin begging for attention. Turning to look at Devon, he continued, "Just let him touch me, Sir. Please."

"Would you like that, Jonathan?" Devon asked. The temptation to touch Kit himself was strong, but watching Jonathan would be almost as erotic, and the sub had been so obedient he deserved some reward. "Would you like to touch Kit?"

"Fuck, yes," Jonathan groaned. "Please, Sir, let me please you both."

Kit nodded enthusiastically, biting the inside of his cheek to keep from repeating his plea, not wanting Devon to refuse because he was being "cheeky."

Devon stretched onto the couch, leaning against the cushions and letting one hand tease the damp head of his cock. "Go ahead, then," he told Jonathan. "Show me how much you can please us both. Touch him anywhere, any way you like—except his cock," he added, almost as an afterthought. "Make him come that way, if you can, and then I'll fuck you."

Jonathan's muscles clenched around the plug at the promise in Devon's words. "Oh fuck, yeah," he murmured, already feeling Devon's thick cock reaming him instead of the lifeless toy. "Want that, Sir. Want you inside me." Pushing his weight off his heels, he shifted up, eager to lavish pleasure on Kit, even if he couldn't suck him the way he wanted to. Seeing the way Kit's cock already leaked against his stomach despite its constraint, he paused, glancing back at Devon. "Should I take off his ring, Sir?"

"Leave it on," Devon commanded. "Maybe it will remind him he's only to speak when he's given permission, since nothing else seems to."

"If you want me to be quiet," Kit replied cockily as his body thrummed with anticipation, "put something in my mouth." Hungrily, he eyed the cock Devon was stroking, hoping he might get a taste of it.

"Keep talking and you might be surprised what I put in your mouth," Devon answered. Kit was incorrigible, but he'd just given Devon the excuse he needed to put another of his toys to good use. He considered commanding Jonathan to retrieve it, but his sub was kneeling so patiently, albeit with the look of a starving man staring through a restaurant window, that he didn't have the heart to make him wait any longer. "See if you can shut him up, Jonathan," he ordered.

The permission he'd been silently pleading for granted, Jonathan nodded, mindful that Devon seemed disinclined to listen to chatter. As he crawled to the table, the plug was a constant reminder of the reward he would earn if he performed well. He didn't mind having to wait for his own fulfillment; giving pleasure to Kit, and by extension to Devon, was no hardship as far as he was concerned. Stopping when he reached the side of the table, he knelt again and studied Kit's face, reassured to see nothing but desire and an undercurrent of mischief in the wide brown eyes.

"Come on, Jonathan," Kit teased softly, hoping Devon wouldn't be able to hear him. "I know you can figure out some way to keep me quiet… or at least make me incapable of speech."

The part of Jonathan's head that had already embraced his submissive role was startled at such blatant disobedience, but Kit's impishness still couldn't help but make him smile—it was as natural as his charm and his beauty. Leaning forward, Jonathan dragged his thumb over Kit's lips, lingering while his fingers caressed his cheek. "Shhhh," he whispered almost soundlessly at Kit's mock pout. He wondered if he dared to kiss Kit into silence. He glanced up at Devon, sprawled in catlike elegance on the couch, watching them with an amused look in his eyes. Their Dom didn't say anything, and after all, he had given Jonathan permission to touch "anywhere, any way he liked." Giving in to his own longing, Jonathan placed a hand on either side of Kit's head and kissed him.

Kit turned immediately into the kiss, giving Jonathan complete control of his mouth and their interaction. Bound as he was, he had little choice, but that did not even figure in his thoughts. All he knew was the touch of firm lips against his, gentle hands on his face, a beginning of respite for the desire throbbing through him, centered in his clamped nipples and his bound cock. His cock would not be receiving any attention—Devon's orders—but perhaps Jonathan would touch the clamps, adding to the mixture of pleasure and pain that already had Kit so on edge.

Jonathan began the kiss gently, tenderly nibbling at Kit's lips, resisting the temptation to taste him at once deeply and hungrily. He would have to build Kit's arousal without touching his most sensitive flesh, and to do that he would take his time, layering sensation on sensation. He wound the fingers of one hand into Kit's hair, caressing his scalp, while the other followed the line of his jaw and the long, slim neck and throat. When Kit's head lifted to seek more contact, Jonathan let his tongue trace the outline of slender lips, accepting the unspoken invitation when they parted beneath him.

The kiss was so much what Kit needed and yet not at all what he had expected. Devon's words, the command he had given Jonathan, combined with the clamps, already had him fiercely aroused. It wouldn't have taken much, when Jonathan first knelt beside him, to make Kit come. A few tugs on the clamps, a couple of fingers in his arse, and cock ring or no, he would have climaxed. The kiss Jonathan was bestowing on him now had no connection to that level of tension. Jonathan's mouth, Jonathan's hands, soothed him, eased the passion riding him, brought him down from the shock of pain from the clamps and the surge of arousal at being bound at Devon and Jonathan's mercy. His heart swelled with love, as it did every time either of his lovers kissed him, amazement at how well they knew him, how easily they gave him exactly what he needed, warming him in a far more lasting way than any surge of lust.

Watching the two kiss slowly, almost languidly, surprised Devon at first. As keyed up as Kit had been, as long as he'd made Jonathan wait, he'd expected their first kiss to be explosive. He should have known better, reminding himself that he was not watching two near-strangers whose only interest was achieving physical release. These were lovers— *his* lovers—and watching them show their love in every touch of lips and fingers made him hungry to claim his share of the banquet. By the rules he had laid down, though, he could only do that once Jonathan made Kit come. It was time to step things along.

"Jonathan." Devon's voice sounded thick in his own ears. "Touch him. Touch the clamps."

Kit moaned into Jonathan's mouth at Devon's words, his passion surging to the fore again at the mere thought of what any contact with the clamps would do to him. Devon really did know him well.

Lifting his head from the kiss, Jonathan smiled at Kit's moan, equal parts protest and plea. Leaning forward onto his elbows, he swung a leg over Kit's prone body, straddling the slim hips. The move set the plug rocking deeper inside him as he scooted backward, sitting on his haunches. For just a moment he gazed down in appreciation at the elegant silver clips adorning each wide, dusky nipple; then he bent forward and lapped around them, wetting them, worshipping them, soothing the abused flesh even as he stimulated it.

"Oh God, Jonathan!" Kit gasped as even the soft touch of his lover's tongue set his flesh to throbbing again. Not painfully, but powerfully, his whole body jerking in reaction, pulling at the suede that held him in place.

Encouraged by Kit's response, Jonathan drew one of the clamps into his mouth, suckling it gently as his fingers toyed with the other, spreading his saliva over it, tracing the contours of the clasp gently enough to set it quivering. His cock leaked at the sounds Kit was making, at Kit undulating beneath him, bumping the plug's handle, arousing him even more.

Devon could see Jonathan's buttocks twitch as he clenched around the plug, and it was getting damned hard not to give in to the urge to pull it out of him and sink into that tight heat. "Soon," he promised Jonathan. "You want it, don't you? Want to feel me filling you? Kit wants it too, I warrant. Touch him there, Jon—rest your thumb on his hole. Don't put it in—just let him think about what you're feeling, what you're going to feel once you bring him off."

Jonathan couldn't hold back his own moan of anticipation at Devon's sultry promise. Lifting his head, he raised the thumb that had been teasing the second clamp to his mouth, wetting it before reaching behind himself and between Kit's legs. Taking the other nipple into his mouth, he traced the crease between Kit's cheeks blindly, spreading his fingers until he could press his saliva-damp thumb against the puckered opening.

Kit squirmed wildly within the extent of his bonds, curses falling volubly from his lips as Jonathan teased him at Devon's direction, touching but not penetrating, arousing without delivering, even as his mouth stimulated the other pinched nipple. "Please," he begged, trying to lift his hips just a little more, to gain a little more pressure. "Please, I need you inside me, need you to touch me."

As much as he could sympathize with Kit's need, there was no way Devon could let his vocalization go on unchecked. Mindful of the near-disaster that could have resulted from pushing Kit beyond his limits at the beginning of their relationship, he considered his next step, smiling when he hit on a solution that could give them all what they wanted. Pushing to his feet, he retrieved the toy he'd contemplated earlier and moved to the head of the table, looking down at the erotic tableau as Jonathan straddled Kit's hips, his mouth still closed over one of the clamps, his fingers buried between the cheeks of Kit's arse. He touched the back of Jonathan's head gently, his fingers sliding into the tawny hair.

Jonathan stiffened at Devon's touch, wondering if he'd done something wrong while at the same time longing to push up into his hand, to plead for more attention for himself. Raising his head, he looked up at Devon towering over them, up the long legs encased in skintight leather, the engorged head of his cock pushing through the open placket, up the toned planes of his abdomen and the muscled chest to meet glittering green eyes.

Seeing the trepidation in Jonathan's gaze, Devon tipped his chin upward with his other hand, the backs of his fingers ruffling the stubbled jaw. "You're doing fine, Jon," he reassured his lover, glancing down at Kit still writhing beneath him. "Take the clamps off now."

"No, leave them, please," Kit protested before he could think about how Devon might react to his comments. He didn't want the incredible pressure to go away, didn't want a lessening of the tension that held him in its grip. "I'm so close." If Jonathan stopped now, he'd lose that edge.

His free hand hovering above Kit's chest, Jonathan hesitated, waiting for Devon's response. His other hand stroked the damp length of Kit's crease, his thumb still pressing over the entrance as Devon had directed, hoping that might be enough to drive Kit over the top.

Kit squirmed beneath Jonathan, biting his lip as he caught sight of Devon's face. The thumb was driving him wild, almost as wild as the clamps on his nipples. Just a little bit more....

Trying to maintain a stern visage, Devon nodded at Jonathan, knowing better than either of his lovers what would happen as soon as the pressure of the clips was released. Behind his back, he gripped the smooth silicone toy as he waited for the inevitable. "Now, Jon."

Reluctantly, Jonathan reached for the clamp he'd been suckling, moving as gently as he could to slide the restraining bead upward enough to ease the clip from the reddened nipple. Greatly daring, he pressed a fraction harder against Kit's puckered entrance, not quite penetrating, but pushing the opening just a little wider with the pad of his thumb as the clip slid loose.

Kit had expected the clamp's removal to lessen the sensation assailing him. The opposite was true. The sudden cessation of pressure allowed his blood to rush back into the previously constricted flesh, a feeling not unlike having his cock ring removed. Combined with the increased thrust of Jonathan's thumb against his hole, it pushed Kit into the throes of a powerful orgasm, his cock twitching as if disgorging the contents of his painfully full sac, though only a dribble escaped the confines of the ring.

Jonathan's own cock throbbed against the leather strap of his ring as Kit thrashed below him, hitting the handle of the plug and pushing it hard against his prostate. Heat flared through him so fiercely that he bit his lip to keep from groaning, his fingers trembling as he fumbled to remove the second clip as quickly as he could.

The release of the second clamp, the renewed surge of desire, tore through Kit, a wordless shout issuing from his throat as he thrashed wildly on the table before collapsing back against it, replete and exhausted as he would never have believed possible only from having his nipples pinched and his entrance toyed with. Looking up at Devon again with hazy eyes, he murmured, "I didn't know."

"Just expanding your horizons, lad." Devon let the corners of his lips twitch for a moment before stretching out his hand to Jonathan to reclaim the silver clamps. "You've earned your reward," he assured him, knowing the effect that watching—and feeling—Kit climax below him must have had on Jonathan. "There's just one thing I have to care for first." Looking down at Kit, he brought his other hand forward, letting them both see the ball gag dangling from his fingers. "Since you can't seem to keep your mouth shut, Kit, we'll have to find another way to keep you quiet."

CHAPTER 9
GAG ORDER

"YOU DIDN'T keep my mouth busy," Kit retorted, knowing the gag was going in his mouth whether he spoke or was silent. "What was I supposed—"

With an indulgent smile, Devon bent forward and took Kit's mouth with his, silencing him by the most expeditious means possible. He let his tongue probe deeply, savoring the flavors of tea and clove and Kit, and even the hint of Jonathan he imagined he could taste from their earlier kisses. Kit met him with enthusiasm, as he did everything, sucking Devon's tongue deeper into his mouth and worrying it gently with his teeth. Devon let the kiss last a little longer than he should, knowing it would be some while before he could enjoy the pleasure again, but finally he pulled back, the gag still dangling from his fingers. "I much prefer my method of keeping you quiet," he admitted, "but I have other plans that involve my mouth, so I'm afraid it will have to be this for now." He eyed Kit from beneath a raised brow, wondering if he was going to fight him.

Kit considered protesting, but he really had no grounds for it. Devon had made it clear, the first time they had played like this, that he expected his subs only to speak when spoken to, and while Kit had only a passing idea of what other forms of discipline Devon might choose, a gag was surely the least of them. Nodding, he lifted his head and opened his mouth.

Somewhat surprised at Kit's immediate obedience, Devon ran a finger around the parted lips before popping the ball inside. He waited for Kit's attempts at positioning it to stop before adjusting the strap to a comfortable pressure. He could feel Jonathan's gaze from behind them as he bent to the toy box at the side of the table, straightening with nothing more threatening in his hand than a soft length of scarf. He trailed the ends over Kit's chest, earning a shiver before he placed it in the lad's right hand.

"If you need us to stop for any reason, drop the scarf," Devon instructed. He didn't plan anything that should come close to causing Kit to need to safeword, but he wasn't going to make any assumptions or take any chances at pushing Kit too far ever again, and trussed up as he was, Kit's back could spasm and he'd have no other way of telling them. He brushed Kit's cheek, trusting that he, and Jonathan too, would understand the gesture was a safeguard and not a threat.

Kit's eyebrows raised in surprise as he closed his fist around the scarf. Yes, they had talked about safewords, back when they first started out, but he had never even considered using his. Even so, the thought that Devon cared enough, as his lover and his Dom, to make sure he had a way out if he needed it, made him smile as best he could around the gag. He nodded to show his understanding, hoping Devon could read his gratitude and his love in his eyes.

Relieved at Kit's smile, Devon glanced back at Jonathan. He still straddled Kit at the lower end of the table, his erection standing stiff against his stomach, his eyes warm as they watched Kit. Seeing Devon's gaze shift to him, Jonathan dropped his eyes, waiting for the next command, hoping Devon would remember the bargain he'd made. Kit wouldn't have hesitated to remind their Dom already, Jonathan knew, but he was content to wait, certain anything Devon ordered him to do would lead to their mutual pleasure in the end.

Rising from the table, Devon stepped back, once more taking in the image of Kit's firm body spread open for their taking and of Jonathan straddling Kit's hips, his posture tight with anticipation and arousal. It was time he gave something to Jonathan, he knew, but something that kept Kit included as well. "Move to the end of the table, Jonathan," Devon ordered, dropping his hand to pop open another button on his leathers, easing some of the pressure on his engorged cock. "Kneel up, with your hips in the air."

Jonathan's shaft swelled at the sultry note in Devon's voice. The deep, thick accent became stronger during their games, the sound of Devon's commands arousing him as much as the actions Devon ordered him to perform. He positioned himself on his knees between Kit's spread legs at the edge of the table, grasping the sides with his hands, raising his hips to present himself to his Dom, his lover, hoping Devon was ready to take what he wanted so much to offer. He wished he could turn his head to look at Devon, to try to read his intentions in his eyes, but he kept his gaze focused downward at the almost as enticing view of Kit's groin, the circlet of his cock ring blending with the dark curls that framed his still-hard shaft.

Kit squirmed on the table, the pressure on his cock keeping his desire from fading despite his earlier orgasm. With the gag in his mouth, he couldn't keep his lovers' attention on him by speaking, so he lifted his hips as best he could, trying to remind the two men not to forget him in their quest for their own release.

"Insatiable," Devon grumbled to Jonathan, stifling a smile. He noticed Jonathan moistening his lips and added in a slow drawl, "What should we do with him, Jon?"

"Suck him," Jonathan whispered, raising his eyes just enough to meet Kit's, hungry for the taste Devon had denied him earlier. "Let me suck him this time, please, Sir."

The low rasp of Jonathan's voice fired an answering hunger in Devon's blood, but there was no reason to deny Jonathan what he asked for while Devon took his own pleasure. "Go ahead." He nodded his permission, using the moment when Jonathan's head dropped to gather another necessity from the quickly depleting toy box.

Lowering his head to nuzzle at Kit's abdomen, Jonathan breathed in the heady scent of his lover's musk. He teased at the dark nest of curls for a moment while the rosy column stiffened beneath his regard. When it stood at attention before him, he let his tongue trace its length, following the vein that pulsed beneath the silken skin down and back up again, swirling around the enrobed head before finally lapping the bead of fluid that was all the ring allowed to escape.

Kit's head tossed back and forth as Jonathan's tongue lavished attention on his rapidly reawakening cock. Were the gag not in the way, he would have already begun to beg. As it was, he had to settle for moaning low in his throat and pushing his hips up toward Jonathan's mouth. He kept his hand clenched tightly around the scrap of silk, determined not to let it slip accidentally from his fingers, ending the sensual torture Jonathan so lovingly imposed on him.

Encouraged by Kit's reaction, Jonathan opened his lips around the head of his cock, teasing his tongue around the shroud of foreskin, flicking over the veiled ridge, so intent on winning another groan of pleasure that it caught him by surprise when he felt Devon's hands grasping his ass, parting his cheeks. His own mouth as blocked as Kit's, he growled deeply when slick fingers wandered down his crease, teasing around his hole, skimming over the skin stretched so tightly around the plug that filled him. His muscle flexing involuntarily, Jonathan pushed backward, arching his hips, trying to follow the maddeningly elusive touch while taking Kit even deeper into his mouth.

Devon knew Jonathan probably couldn't help his body's reaction, but it was time he started to learn the discipline Devon expected from his subs. Drawing his hand back, he slapped the tightened globes firmly, surprising a muffled grunt from the kneeling man. "I didn't give you permission to move," he said sternly, watching as Jonathan immediately dropped his hips. "Your pleasure is my responsibility to administer, not yours to seek."

Shamed at needing to be admonished, Jonathan shrank back, trying to focus on what he was doing to Kit rather than what Devon was doing to him. Whatever it was, it would be good. He could trust Devon to see to that. Breathing in deeply, he slid his lips farther down Kit's shaft, exhaling slowly as the silken hardness filled him, emptying his mind of any concern but that of pleasuring his lover. A sense of freedom grew in him, letting him focus fully on just this moment, knowing that Devon would take care of him, would give him whatever he needed.

Another moan escaped around the gag in Kit's mouth as the smack Devon delivered forced Jonathan forward onto his cock. He tried to keep his hips from bucking up even more into the wet cavern, shivering in delight at the suction as Jonathan swallowed to keep from choking. He heard their Dom's words of warning to Jonathan, knew they should apply to him as well, but he was too far gone in pleasure to process them completely. Later, when he could think straight again, he'd think about them, try to make them apply to himself. For now, all he knew was how close he was to coming again, held back only by the constriction of the cock ring. He gripped the scarf until his knuckles turned white. Whatever happened, he did not want to drop it.

Watching Jonathan deep-throat Kit—hard to believe a few short months ago Jonathan had never had a cock in his mouth before!—and listening to Kit's increasingly frantic noises were undeniably arousing, and Devon was ready to do more than just watch his lovers. Popping open the final button on his leathers, the placket gaping to free his hardened shaft, he returned to the pleasant task of teasing up and down Jonathan's crease with lube-slicked fingers, sliding around the circumference of the thick plug just enough to stir it minutely in his sub's channel. He was pleased to see that despite the provocation, Jonathan held himself still, only a slight quiver of his thighs hinting at the effect Devon's actions were having on him.

Devon's callused but surprisingly gentle fingers circled the handle of the plug, each touch setting the thick silicone knob vibrating in Jonathan's channel. He tried to keep his muscles from clenching around it, tried to ignore the tendrils of pleasure Devon's touch sent spiraling through him. Every time Devon nudged the plug, Jonathan's cock twitched against his belly; he could feel it rubbing damply against him, knowing he was leaking and that without the cock ring to constrain him, he'd probably already have come. Focusing on the steadiness of his breathing, he sucked harder on Kit's shaft, wishing he had permission to touch so he could take Kit's balls in hand and push fingers into his hole the way Devon was driving the plug into him.

Kit wanted to beg, to plead, to do anything to move them closer to release, but the gag in his mouth silenced his words, the bonds around his limbs stilled his movements. He had only the scarf in his hand, and dropping that would end the scene entirely rather than speeding it up. Jonathan teased him with his tongue, trying to suck out Kit's orgasm through the cock ring, or at least that was how it felt. It wouldn't take much for Kit to come again despite the constriction, but he tried to hold back, wanting to come with his lovers this time.

Impressed that Jonathan was able to control his reactions even under increased provocation, Devon decided the lesson had gone far enough for this scene. The fact that his cock was throbbing against his leathers, demanding its own relief, might have played into the decision just a little. Tightening his grip on the handle of the plug, winning a smothered gasp from Jonathan as it twisted, he pulled it out quickly and positioned the head of his cock in its place. Knowing Jonathan was already well-stretched and well-lubed, he didn't hesitate to thrust in his full length with a single plunge, hissing in pleasure as the muscle contracted around him, wrapping him in a tight, hot cocoon.

Jonathan was so centered on the soft whimpers escaping from around the gag in Kit's mouth that Devon's actions took him by surprise. He couldn't hold back a gasp of shock when Devon grasped the plug and pulled it free, making Kit tremble as his mouth closed even tighter around him. When Devon's thick cock drove into him, replacing the momentary emptiness, it was so much better that Jonathan struggled not to push back against him, not to plead for Devon to fuck him hard and fast, to come inside him and to let him make Kit come.

Lifting his head as best he could, Kit tried to see what Devon was doing. The sight that met his eyes left him trembling. Devon's golden body drove into Jonathan, forcing his hungry mouth farther down Kit's cock. Kit's head fell back with another groan, every muscle in his body taut as he fought the bonds, not to end the scene, but to join in, to touch his lovers, to give back to them the pleasure they were bestowing on him. His back arched as his bollocks drew up again, pulsing hard as if to disgorge their load, the fluid held back only by the tension of the ring.

The tableau beneath Devon was so intense—Jonathan's taut arse spread wide as he pistoned in and out of it, Jonathan's mouth filled with Kit's straining cock, Kit watching them both with wide, pleading eyes—that Devon's control was evaporating fast. He tightened his grip on Jonathan's flank, reaching his other hand between them to grasp for his cock, groping blindly until he could close his fingers around the circlet constricting its base. "Take off Kit's ring," he instructed Jonathan hoarsely, fighting to hold back a few moments longer once he released the pressure of his own ring. "Let him come."

Given the permission to touch he'd been longing for, Jonathan was quick to reach for Kit, cupping his sac in one palm as he worked the catch on the ring, sliding his mouth upward as he went. The instant he reached the head, the ring popped free and Kit erupted, pumping burst after burst of creamy fluid that Jonathan tried to catch, closing around the fountaining tip and working his tongue to capture more of Kit's taste.

Kit screamed his release against the gag, the sudden cessation of pressure allowing him to climax powerfully. His body collapsed on the table as all the tension gripping him swept out through his cock. He wanted to lift his head, to watch Devon and Jonathan come, but he didn't have the strength to move.

Even after Kit's cock stopped twitching, Jonathan held the softening shaft in his mouth, lapping it gently as Kit slumped bonelessly beneath him. Without the drive to make Kit come, he could no longer distract himself from Devon's thickness moving inside him, Devon's hand on his shaft, removing his own ring. The strap slipped free of his cock, and he clenched his fists against the tabletop, fighting the need to empty his balls, wanting to feel Devon come inside him first.

Devon had expected Jonathan to come as explosively as Kit had as soon as he was freed from the restriction of the ring. That his sub was somehow managing to hold back from climaxing made the Dom in him swell with pride. "Come," he urged, rubbing his thumb over the slit of Jonathan's cock.

"You first," Jonathan managed to utter, letting Kit slide free and lifting his head, his hands clutching the side of the table. His breath came in ragged bursts as he struggled against letting his orgasm overwhelm him. "Please, Sir."

Nothing could have made Devon prouder, and nothing could have held him back after Jonathan's words. Tightening his grip, he thrust in powerful strokes until the tension coiling inside him snapped and his climax tore through him, his body shaking as he filled Jonathan's channel with hot seed. "Ah fuck," he cried, sagging forward to brace himself against the table, the change in angle just enough to rub the head of his shaft against Jonathan's prostate. With a garbled cry, Jonathan came hard, spraying over Devon's hand and Kit's belly, shuddering through each aftershock until his knees buckled and he sank onto his heels, dislodging Devon with a soft moan of loss.

The three men slumped against the table and one another in a sweaty, salty heap, their unsteady breathing the only sound for long minutes. Finally, Devon pushed back and rose carefully to his feet. He rubbed Jonathan's back and bent to kiss the nape of his neck before circling to the head of the table, unbuckling the gag, and gently removing it from Kit's mouth. As soon as it was free, he knelt to take the reddened lips in a tender kiss that grew more intense as Kit's tongue swept into his mouth.

Watching his lovers kiss and recognizing the game was over, Jonathan untied the restraints from Kit's ankles and moved forward to begin working on his wrists. The motion was enough to recall Devon's attention, and he removed the final restraint, helping Kit sit up slowly.

Letting the scarf fall from his grasp, Kit stretched a hand out to each of his lovers. "You're incredible," he told them, his voice raspy from the gag. He turned and looked at Devon. "Better now?" he asked softly.

"Only because I'm with the two of you," Devon answered, taking each of his lovers' hands and squeezing them tightly.

Rising to his feet, Jonathan tugged gently at the two hands clasping his. "I need to feel both of you against me," he urged. "Let's take this to bed."

Kit's smile lit up his face. "All in favor, say aye."

Three voices uttered "aye" in unison. Laughing, they made their way into the bedroom. They snuggled together in Devon's bed, kissing and stroking lightly, not pushing for more yet, although Kit doubted it would be long. As he lay there, spooned around Devon's back with Jonathan on the other side, he let hope bloom in his heart. They loved one another, not just in the silence of their hearts, but out loud, committed. He knew what Devon, and probably even Jonathan, would say. They'd say he was naïve for believing that love was enough to take them past the end of filming, and maybe they were right. They'd both been in committed relationships before and had those fall apart, but Kit wasn't ready to give up. The three of them had been through so much already to get where they were. The impossible had already happened. Jonathan was bisexual rather than straight, as he'd first thought, and was interested in both Kit and Devon. Devon was willing to share Jonathan and interested in Kit too. Somehow they'd managed to fall in love, all three of them, a gift beyond price. Together they'd stared down the demons from Devon's past and vanquished them. No, too much had already come right despite the odds for Kit to be anything less than optimistic. They had months still before filming was over, time to make plans and figure out a way to keep this good thing, this amazing, wonderful, out-of-this-world thing going. That wasn't naïveté—it was faith.

CHAPTER 10
PLAYING WITH FIRE

WITH A sigh, Devon settled onto the couch, flipping through the channels until he found the footie match on one of the local stations. "It's so peaceful with the youngsters gone for the weekend," he observed, propping his bare feet on the table and taking a sip of his beer. It was rare for them to have a full weekend with no filming, but their director was using the time to work on final edits for the upcoming weeks' episodes of the *Camelot* miniseries. "I miss Kit, but I don't miss the Orkney brothers dropping in unannounced and staying until all hours of the morning."

"Drinking all the beer and leaving popcorn kernels down the sofa cushions," Jonathan agreed, swallowing a mouthful of his own brew before setting the bottle next to a flickering candle on the table and sliding down to rest his head in Devon's lap. Kit had gone to London the night before for a concert with the actors who portrayed Gareth, Gawain, Gaheris, and Agravaine. Jonathan still marveled at Kit choosing two lovers more than a dozen years his senior rather than someone closer to his own age, though as far as he knew, all the Orkney actors were straight. Of course, Jonathan himself had been straight—or at least he'd never acted on his attraction toward men—before Kit and Devon seduced him. In any case, he wasn't about to question his good fortune. Lifting the hem of Devon's rugby shirt, he pressed a noisy kiss to the golden skin of his lover's abdomen before shifting half on one hip, just enough to see the television screen. He sighed, his breath warm against Devon's thigh. "Gonna be a long weekend without Kit, though."

Devon smiled ruefully, waiting for Jonathan to settle before resting a hand on his shoulder. "We could have gone with them," he offered again. "They wouldn't have turned us down."

"Oh no," Jonathan muttered. He shook his head, his stubbled cheek rubbing against the soft fabric of Devon's track pants. "I have no desire to have my eardrums blown out by that shit the Orkneys call music. I'd rather hear your orders without you having to shout them," he added with a grin.

Devon chuckled. "I wouldn't be likely to be giving orders with the Orkneys around anyway. I don't mind their knowing the three of us are together, but they don't need to know what goes on in our bedrooms," he countered, his cock starting to stir at Jonathan's movements. "Careful there, or we won't be watching much footie this evening."

"I think I'm flattered." Jonathan laughed, rubbing more deliberately over the growing bulge in Devon's crotch. "More distracting than football? Of course it's not Man U, or I'd never stand a chance."

Devon flushed a little. "A man's entitled to his vices."

"Oh, I've come to appreciate your vices," Jonathan purred, twisting until he could mouth the hard column of flesh through the soft fabric. His own cock was thickening against the zipper of his jeans, but he resisted the urge to reach down and cup himself, channeling his arousal toward heightening Devon's instead. At Devon's hands, Jonathan had not only come to terms with his bisexuality but also discovered the pleasure of occasionally submitting to his more dominant lovers. "Very, very much."

"Good to hear," Devon choked out, his hips bucking up toward the moist heat that wafted through the cloth, "although you might change your mind if you knew just how rough I can get." His fingers burrowed into Jonathan's hair, keeping him in place.

"Mmmmn… you'll have to show me." Jonathan moaned on a shortened breath before sucking harder, feeling Devon twitch through the wet cloth. In Devon he'd found a lover who shared his appreciation for a bit of rough play, though Kit's aversion to intentional pain had limited how deeply they'd explored that aspect of their relationship. Jonathan had hopes that this weekend would change that. "After I make you come," he added, biting down gently as his hands spread Devon's thighs wide to give him more room. He didn't make a move to pull the fabric away, the idea of Devon's cream soaking the already sodden cloth making him surprisingly hot. He worked his tongue along the length of the thick column, sucking hard on the way down, using his teeth again on the way back up, doing everything he could think of to drive the man beneath him crazy.

Devon bit back a curse at the sudden rough stimulation. His lovers regularly made him feel like a teenager again, with all of a teenager's lack of self-control. He started to hold back automatically, but then he changed his mind. If he came now, it would give him that much more control later, when he pounded Jonathan's fine arse into the mattress. Throwing his head back, he let his climax take him, his legs jerking as he came, one of them bumping the candle and splattering wax on the skin of his ankle.

"Oh fuck! Sorry!" Jonathan cried, righting the candle and grabbing Devon's foot, trying to brush away the cooling wax. "Did it burn you?"

"Nothing to worry about," Devon replied, an idea forming in his head. He reached for the remote and switched off the television. He didn't want any distractions for what he had in mind. "Do you trust me?"

Jonathan paused from peeling the bits of hardened wax from Devon's skin and looked up, caught by the tone of his lover's voice. Ever since Robert (or "He Who Will Not Be Named," as Kit called him— Jonathan had his own unutterable names for the bastard), they'd both done their best to rebuild Devon's confidence as a Dom. This was the first time Jonathan had heard Devon speak with the same easy assurance he'd had before his twisted former Dom had returned to torment him, and it made Jonathan's heart swell as much as it hardened his cock. Releasing Devon's foot and sliding to his knees, he looked up with love and trust shining from his eyes. "You know I do," he answered softly. "Always."

Devon's smile grew at Jonathan's reply, at the expression on his face that radiated confidence in his Dom. "Get undressed," he directed, moving everything that littered the tabletop: magazines, the week's accumulated mail, Jonathan's beer. "Lie down on the table," he added, picking up the candle, thankful that even now, the candles he bought were always safe for play.

Arousal coursing through his veins, Jonathan pulled the T-shirt over his head, letting it drop to the floor before unzipping his jeans and uttering a sigh of relief when his cock sprang free to stand erect against his stomach. He quickly kicked away the denim and bowed his head to Devon in a gesture of respect before sitting on the end of the table.

It was such a simple gesture, that inclination of the head, but it had an instant effect on Devon's libido, already revving hard from the blowjob Jonathan had just given him. "Lie back," he urged, his hand going to Jonathan's shoulder to support him on his way down.

Lifting his head to let Devon slide a small pillow from the couch beneath it, Jonathan took a deep breath and released it slowly, letting his muscles go limp as he exhaled. He shifted to align the pillow more comfortably under his neck and then stilled, looking up at Devon in quiet anticipation. He wasn't sure what in the previous moments had piqued Devon's excitement, but his nerves were already quivering beneath his calm demeanor.

Seeing Jonathan settled comfortably, Devon picked up the fat purple candle. "This will sting a little bit," he warned, tipping the candle so a droplet of wax landed on Jonathan's shoulder. He gave it a second to cool before lowering his head and tracing the edge of the wax with his tongue.

Jonathan wasn't able to hold back the flinch when the first heated drop hit his skin. It burned a little, but the pain eased quickly, especially when Devon soothed the skin around the irregular purple blotch of wax. He closed his eyes for a moment, breathing through the last of the discomfort before opening them again to find Devon's emerald gaze watching him closely. So much love was imbued in that look that his chest tightened, and he had to blink back a sudden tingle of tears. Nodding minutely, he kept his eyes on Devon's and tried to prepare himself for the next contact.

"A royal color for the King of the Britons," Devon commented as he studied Jonathan's face, his chest swelling with pride at how well Jonathan had taken the first experience. Seeing readiness there, he turned his attention to his lover's torso, trying to decide where to let the next drop fall. Tilting his wrist, he drizzled a short line of wax across the top of Jonathan's chest. Then, because the asymmetry offended him, he drew a matching line down the other side and leaned back to examine the design.

"I always thought Lancelot had the soul of an artist," Jonathan commented softly once the sting of discomfort passed. He wasn't sure if he was expected to keep quiet, but Devon hadn't forbidden him to speak. The mood felt different today, more relaxed than their previous games, not as formal. He wasn't sure if that was because it was just the two of them, or if Devon was going easy on him, or if this was one more aspect of breaking free from Robert's influence, but Jonathan decided he liked it. Of course, he liked pretty much anything that involved Devon and bodily contact. "Never been a canvas before."

"I told you I'd broaden your horizons," Devon joked, his laughter shaking the candle and spattering drops of wax across Jonathan's chest, one of them fairly sizable. He winced in sympathy. "Sorry, love," he murmured, kissing the reddening skin around the thick blob.

"Mmnn," Jonathan hummed, "'s okay." He arched slightly, wishing he could reach up to pull Devon's head back for another kiss, but some instinct told him that would be going too far. "Do that again?" he asked instead.

Surprised at the request, Devon acquiesced nonetheless, letting another large dollop of wax fall, this time onto Jonathan's stomach. Instead of kissing that flat plane, he lowered his head and captured his lover's lips, tongue slipping between them to plunder the hot cavern of Jonathan's mouth. He'd known Jonathan would make a magnificent sub, and this was just proving him right. He wondered briefly just how far he could take Jonathan without Kit's dislike of pain holding him back. Lifting his head again, he decided to find out. Aiming carefully, he let a small drop fall directly onto Jonathan's nipple.

Catching his breath in a truncated hiss, Jonathan let the pain wash through him, blinking when it suddenly stopped feeling like pain, the heat spreading through his chest, through his veins. *Endorphins*, he thought, and then he blinked again and willed himself to stop thinking, waiting for the next drop to fall.

Leaning forward, Devon licked lightly at Jonathan's other nipple, wetting it and blowing across it gently, bringing it to a tight peak before letting a slightly larger drop land on the damp flesh. He couldn't help appreciating the line of Jonathan's body as his chest arched up slightly, then settled back onto the table.

Jonathan found himself anticipating where the next drop would fall, each sensation—the burn as the wax hit his skin, the tightness as it cooled and shrank, the slight tug when movement pulled on the hairs caught in the wax—adding to the fire in his blood. He could feel his cock stirring, thickening, and wondered how long it would be before Devon noticed it. Just the thought of the wax hitting that delicate flesh was enough to make his shaft twitch against his belly.

Pausing a moment to take in his creation, Devon smiled as he noticed the bobbing cock rising from its bed of wiry curls. He didn't ask, not in words, but he let his hand hover above Jonathan's groin for several moments, drawing his attention and giving him the opportunity to use his safeword before tipping the candle to send a small drop onto Jonathan's erection. "Eager much?" he teased when Jonathan's eyes shut and his hips jerked upward.

"Shit, Devon," Jonathan hissed, waiting until he had his breathing under control again before opening his eyes. He couldn't resist glancing down to see the purple trail hardening on his reddened cock. "Fuck, that feels—" He shook his head, not finding words to describe the heady amalgam of pain and arousal. Taking a deep breath, he looked back at Devon. "More?"

"Stop me if it gets to be too much," Devon instructed, adding to the wax already decorating Jonathan's cock. When the drops became a solid line, he paused again, looking down to check how Jonathan was feeling. His eyes were closed, his face tense with anticipation but not clenched in pain. "Turn over," he directed, wanting to decorate Jonathan's arse the same way he'd done his cock.

It took Devon's words a moment to filter through the haze of sensation Jonathan was drifting in. When he realized what Devon was asking, he hummed an acknowledgment, pushing onto one elbow before rolling on his hip and settling back on the table on his stomach, all without opening his eyes. The wax flexed and tugged at him as he moved, as if dozens of tiny fingers were teasing his skin. A shiver ran through him, and he tried to find a position he could relax in, leaning on his forearms to leave enough space so his now fully hardened cock wasn't crushed beneath him.

In this position he couldn't see what Devon was going to do next, and that added another dimension to the anticipation. His hips shifted restlessly, the head of his cock brushing the tabletop, its coating of wax muting the sensation. Jonathan moaned quietly, the muscles of his ass tightening as the heat in his blood grew to a throbbing pulse of need.

Devon ran his tongue swiftly up Jonathan's crack, tasting sweat and Jonathan's unique flavor. Using one hand to part the rounded cheeks, he contemplated his next move.

CHAPTER 11
PEEP SHOW

HAVING SPENT the previous day and evening in London, Kit had found himself facing the prospect of going clubbing with the Orkneys for the rest of the weekend. Given that the alternative was coming home to Jonathan and Devon, it hadn't been much of a choice. He walked into Devon's house through the back door, dropped his bag in the kitchen, and went in search of his lovers. He reached the threshold of the living room and froze, arrested by the sight of Jonathan spread out on the table, Devon leaning over him, candle in hand.

Desire swamped him as he took in the scene: Jonathan's wiry body completely bare and open to anything Devon wanted, Devon still clothed casually, suggesting they had not planned this, but rather that it had developed spontaneously. As always when Jonathan was subbing, Kit was torn between the desire to be in his place, his pleasure totally dependent on Devon's whim, and the desire to be in Devon's place, with complete mastery over Jonathan. They were so perfectly matched, his two lovers, in age, in life experience, in size. Sometimes he wondered what they saw in a kid like him. It was subtle, the way they treated him differently, as if he was fragile. He thought they'd figured out that his scoliosis didn't slow him down anymore, that if anything, it had made him stronger than he looked, but maybe not. Kit stepped back into the kitchen so he could watch without being seen, wanting to know how the scene would play out without him. He wanted to see them together without him there, to know if the differences were all in his imagination.

Jonathan drew another of the deep, regular breaths that helped him keep from squirming in impatience. *Trust Devon*, he told himself, repeating the words with each inhalation, releasing tension with each exhalation, the mantra and the breathing settling him, freeing him from the constant noise of thoughts in his head and letting him simply be in the moment, simply feel. His skin prickled with awareness, as if unseen eyes were watching him. *Admiring him.* Hoping Devon was enjoying the picture he presented, he let the pride go too, offering everything he was to Devon in silent acquiescence to his lover's desires.

Devon could practically see the stages Jonathan passed through as he settled into his headspace, and he flushed with pride again that this magnificent man trusted him enough to submit to him. Tracing a finger down the curve of Jonathan's spine, he noted the involuntary tightening and flex of his arse muscles. "So responsive," he murmured, dipping a fingertip into the liquid wax pooled around the candlewick and on a whim tracing a small heart on one firm cheek. "So beautiful."

Kit shivered as he watched them, both from the idea of the hot wax on tender skin and from the tenderness in the gesture and Devon's voice. Then Devon's hand lifted and tilted, and a bit of wax splattered across Jonathan's arse. Jonathan's hips rose in response, his breath catching. Kit couldn't stop the reflexive wince even as Jonathan moaned, clearly asking for more. Despite his immediate reaction, though, Kit's cock swelled as he watched. He could certainly see the allure from Devon's point of view, though he couldn't quite imagine it from Jonathan's.

Frowning as the next splash of wax trickled down the crease between Jonathan's cheeks, Devon set the candle on the side table. He'd been careful to hold the flame high enough that the wax had time to cool slightly before hitting Jonathan's skin, but he wouldn't take the chance of an accidental spill burning tender flesh. Jonathan's head turned, either at the sound or the loss of Devon's attentions, and Devon took a moment to reassure him.

"I'm still here, Jon." Devon slid a finger up the shadowed cleft, tantalizing even as it confirmed the spill hadn't hurt more than it was meant to. "Going to get something from the toy box—I'll be right back."

Jonathan swallowed a moan at the erotic possibilities of Devon's statement. He thought he'd kept still enough that he didn't need to be restrained, and positioned as he was, a blindfold would serve little purpose. His nerves still quivering at Devon's brief caress, he clenched his muscles against the pinch of the cooling wax. His body ached for Devon to fill him, to claim him, but he'd learned enough of his lover's temperament to sense it was too soon for that. *Maybe a plug*, he thought hopefully—even that stretch would be welcome, as hot as he was already from this new game.

Kit held his breath as he waited to see what Devon would bring back downstairs from the wooden chest, all the while acknowledging the care the Dom was clearly taking to make sure Jonathan wasn't hurt. He reminded himself again that Devon had promised to take care of them when they played these games. His self-protective instincts still warred with that trust, though, when Devon chose painful ways to push their limits.

Kit wondered what Devon was looking for. He couldn't tell if Jonathan was wearing his cock ring, but putting it on now would surely be painful. The nipple clamps weren't really an option, either—they'd bite into the wood of the table rather than hanging loose to tantalize the sensitive points. Kit's mind raced, cataloging the other items he'd seen on the few occasions he'd glanced inside the toy box, but he hadn't even considered the small paintbrush Devon returned with. He could feel a frown creasing his forehead as he wondered what Devon intended to do.

Jonathan's anticipation flared when Devon's hands returned to spread his cheeks, and he willed himself to relax his guardian muscle. Instead of the blunt silicon head of a plug or the cool glide of lube, though, he felt the faintest, gentlest tickle, too soft even to be Devon's fingertip. The surprised muscle trembled, and he fought not to whimper in disappointment.

"You like that?" Devon's voice was smoky with lust and a trace of underlying humor.

"What—what is it?" Jonathan asked, his own voice cracking at a repeat of the teasing caress.

"Paintbrush," Devon murmured, trailing the bristles up the vertebrae of his lover's spine. "Your calling Lancelot an artist made me think of it. This will give me more control over how I decorate you."

Jonathan was more than willing to give Devon complete control, but it was hard to find his voice as he sank deeper into the space where the only thing that mattered was pleasing his lover. He hummed his agreement, following Devon's movements through touch alone as his eyelids fell closed again.

After dipping the tip of the brush in the melted well of the candle, Devon tested the temperature on his inner wrist. Satisfied it wasn't hot enough to cause undue pain, he loaded the bristles with more wax and drizzled a path across the plane of Jonathan's back. The trail reached a fading yellowed bruise on Jonathan's hip, bringing a frown to Devon's face. "Don't like having marks on your body I didn't put there," he murmured, covering the contusion with darker purple wax. "Even if you did look absolutely fuckable the day Bob gave it to you."

Kit stifled a moan. He was pretty sure he knew exactly the day Devon was talking about. The two of them had arrived at Jonathan's trailer after a day of filming, expecting to find their King Arthur ready to head home with them. Instead they'd found him outside, shirtless and covered in sweat, his torn jeans hugging tightly to the curves of his lower body as he practiced a new sword routine with the weapons master. They'd waited and watched for over an hour as Jonathan worked to memorize the intricate choreography of the battle. And when he was done and they finally got him home, their usually laid-back lover was as ferocious as Kit had ever seen him, taking control of their lovemaking as he rarely did, leaving Kit and Devon both in a panting heap when they were done. Kit shivered at the thought, wondering what it would take to provoke that side of Jonathan again. It was definitely an experience he'd be willing to repeat!

The prickle crawling down his skin made Jonathan shiver even as his cock tightened at the memory of the day Devon was referring to. He seldom felt driven to take a dominant role in their lovemaking; following the lead of his more experienced lovers was mind-blowing in itself. That afternoon, though, fired by the thrill of finally mastering the battle sequence and landing a hit on Bob for the first time, Jonathan couldn't get enough of either Devon or Kit. He'd taken them both, claimed them both, marking their bodies with sweat and dirt and come. Not for the first time, he gave silent thanks for lovers who understood him better than he did himself, who knew when he needed to take and when he needed to give. Right now, he needed exactly what Devon was offering. If only Kit were here too—Jonathan stopped that line of thought before it could continue. He wouldn't diminish his time with Devon thinking about their missing lover—and besides, there were things he'd been reading about, tempted to try, that he'd kept silent about, knowing they'd cross the line of Kit's comfort. Maybe this weekend he'd find the courage to ask.

Devon's voice was a warm rasp in Jonathan's ear, startling him. "Still with me?" his Dom asked, tasting the skin behind the whorled lobe.

"Mmnnn," Jonathan hummed, struggling for words. "Yeah. Want you."

"Not yet," Devon answered, as Jonathan had known he would. He lowered his head in acceptance and waited.

Devon skimmed the bristles over Jonathan's back, leaving the droplets in some places, dragging over the skin to broaden the line in others. Smiling at the way Jonathan arched up to meet the brush, he dipped up more wax and added to the abstract design, spiraling lower to mark his lover's taut buttocks. It would be a pure pleasure to spread those arsecheeks when he was ready to give Jonathan the fucking they both ached for!

Kit's body hummed in response, almost as if the bristles were tickling his skin instead of Jonathan's. He imagined he could feel them brush down his back, over his arse. He wasn't sure he wanted to feel the burn of the candle wax, although it didn't seem to bother Jonathan, but he longed to know what the soft bristles would do to his skin. He almost stepped forward, almost asked if he could join them, but he didn't want to intrude. He knew Devon; everything that came out of the toy box went back in. He'd get his chance with the brush, and maybe he'd work up the courage to let Devon paint him too. Jonathan was obviously enjoying the heat of the wax. Kit could feel the weight of his nerves holding him back, and he chafed against their restrictions. He either trusted Devon or he didn't. Despite saying that he did, he wondered now just how far that trust truly extended. He was going to have to work on that.

"I wish you could see yourself," Devon murmured, swirling the brush around the tattoo nestled at the base of Jonathan's spine, just above the swell of his buttocks. Dropping to one knee, he blew gently over the reddened skin and then ran his tongue across the inked mark, setting the candle aside and gripping Jonathan's hips when the other man trembled. Sliding his lips lower, Devon nuzzled the dimple that topped Jonathan's musky crease, careful not to break the wax as he parted the embellished globes. "Next time I'll plan better, have more colors ready," he added, his words ghosting over the sensitive skin, even there streaked with droplets of rich purple.

"Oh fuck, Devon," Jonathan groaned, his lover's warm breath raising goose bumps and making him clench with desire. His mind's eye could visualize the picture he made, and he let himself imagine decorating Kit and Devon's bodies the same way. He'd be sure to have his camera ready on that day. Devon's tongue, hot and wet, dragged down his cleft, and he moaned again, unashamedly. "Fuck me," he pleaded. "Need you, babe, need to feel you."

Kit slid his hand beneath the waistband of his jeans, stroking his cock in time to Jonathan's pleading. He shouldn't have been so turned on just from watching them, but this was ten times—hell, a hundred times—better than watching porn. These were his lovers in front of him, providing him with a far more intimate, erotic show than anything he'd ever seen on screen. He wanted to see this played out. And then, when they were done, he'd join them and let them provide him with the same relief they were giving each other. He'd have earned it for his patience!

Devon wanted nothing more than to give in to Jonathan's plea, but as he slid his hand beneath the waist of his track pants to grip his cock, still sticky from his earlier climax, another impulse struck him, equally strong. He pushed the damp cloth down his hips with his free hand, rose to his feet, and kicked it aside, his fist encircling his resurgent erection. "Wanna mark you," he husked, his hand shuttling over his swelling flesh. His eyes met Jonathan's when the other man twisted his head to watch him, a silent request for his lover to understand why he needed this.

Nothing else could have overridden Jonathan's desperate need to feel Devon stretching him, filling him—but the image of Devon's white come spattering over the purple wax was so compelling that Jonathan's cock surged hard against his belly. He worked a hand down his torso to grip the base of his shaft, squeezing the way Devon had taught him to keep himself from coming. "You owe me," he rasped, watching Devon's face as his lover stroked himself roughly, using the power of his words to drive him even higher. "Come on me, Devon. Mark me. Paint me with your cream."

The image Jonathan conjured with his words was so compelling that Kit had to fight not to come as well, forcing himself to release his throbbing erection and biting the heel of his hand hard to keep from groaning aloud and spoiling the moment. *Just a little longer*, he told himself. He could hold on long enough to let them finish before joining them for the second round. He'd figured out long ago that he enjoyed being watched. He was beginning to think watching was just as much of a turn-on. He couldn't remember the last time he'd been this hard without someone else's hands on him.

Devon locked eyes with Jonathan's, his lover's sinfully hoarse voice urging him on. He wasn't going to be able to hold back much longer, despite having come once already. He dragged his thumb over the head of his cock, twisting as he palmed the shaft, and his bollocks pulled up tight where he cupped them in his other hand. "Anything," he promised raggedly, "give you anything you want—everything I've got—ah, Christ—coming—Jonathan!"

The splash of Devon's climax felt nearly as hot as the wax where it sprayed over Jonathan's ass and up his back, thick white droplets pooling in hollows and weaving through the hardened purple trails. Fighting the urge to fist himself to his own release, Jonathan let his head fall to the tabletop, panting through the shudders that wracked him at each spurt of Devon's come hitting his skin.

As soon as his vision had cleared and his cock released its last drops, Devon fell to his knees beside the table, burrowing his fingers into Jonathan's shaggy hair to turn his head and claim his lips in a fierce, almost feral kiss. His tongue invaded Jonathan's mouth, fucking him as he'd begged to be fucked, shaken by the strength of his emotions at the gift Jonathan had given him.

Jonathan opened willingly to Devon's lips, leaning his weight on one elbow to clutch the back of Devon's head and drag him closer, meeting his tongue with equal hunger and the full force of his own unsatisfied need. Only the insistent throb of blood in his cock finally forced him to break the kiss, drawing air back into his lungs in deep, shaking gasps.

"You owe me," Jonathan reminded Devon, not because he was keeping score, but because a part of him was afraid, still—afraid to admit the desire that had fascinated him until it had become something of an obsession, afraid Devon might refuse. "Anything—anything I want—"

"Anything," Devon agreed, hesitating at the uneasy expression in Jonathan's changeable eyes. "You don't need my promise to ask for anything you want. You know that, don't you, Jon?" His brows rose as a faint hint of red tinged his lover's cheeks. "Jon? What the fuck do you want me to do to you?"

CHAPTER 12
HURTS SO GOOD

KIT HAD taken a step forward, eager to join his lovers and get some relief for his aching erection, when he heard Devon's question. He didn't have any more idea than Devon what Jonathan might want, but something in Devon's voice alerted him that the request might be out of the ordinary. He hesitated, wanting to hear what Jonathan would say. He suspected the two held back sometimes out of consideration for his stated aversion to pain. Certainly, he wouldn't have gone along with having hot candle wax poured or painted on his skin. Jonathan and Devon thought they were alone, free to indulge their rougher tastes without him holding them back. While he was sure they would welcome him with open arms if he made his presence known, he was also fairly sure, given the tone of the conversation, that Jonathan would stifle his request or temper it to fit Kit's tastes. And that wouldn't be fair to them. Drifting back into the shadows, he waited for Jonathan's reply.

"I've been… doing some reading," Jonathan began hesitantly. He'd thought a lot about how to broach his request to Devon, but even in his imagination, it hadn't felt this uncomfortable. "You and Kit are both a lot more—knowledgeable, experienced, than I am—hell, you know that. You both had to show me what I'd been missing…." Rolling to his side, he leaned on an elbow, grimacing at the pinch of hardening wax.

"It's not about how much experience you have," Devon broke in, reaching forward to cup Jonathan's chin and search his eyes. The hint of insecurity he found there sobered him. Had he been so caught up working through his own past that he'd ignored his lover's needs? He kissed Jonathan gently, trying to find the words to reassure him. "You know by now there are experiences I'd as soon forget. There's not a damn thing you're missing, Jon. Don't ever doubt that."

Jonathan returned the kiss avidly, threading his fingers into Devon's hair to hold him still as their tongues danced. Pulling back only enough to draw a breath, he quirked his lips in a crooked smile. "And there's no one

I want to get experience with but you and Kit," Jonathan replied. "But I thought it might help to find out a little more about—well, about what we've been doing." Devon tensed beneath his fingers, and he stroked his locks soothingly. "Because I love everything we've done, everything you've taught me. I thought maybe I could find a way to give you back some of the joy you've given me."

"You do," Devon insisted, his voice thick with emotion he wished he had the words to express.

The love shining in Devon's eyes gave Jonathan the assurance to continue. "I found some sites online, did some reading. Some of it we've already tried, some of it I'm hoping we'll try together sometime, all three of us. But this—" He exhaled, then swallowed hard, gathering his nerve. In his head, he'd composed so many ways to ask for what he wanted, but they all sounded stilted to him now. The only way to say it was to just say it. "I want you to fist me."

If either man had been looking Kit's way, they would have seen shock, then confusion cross his face. He took a step back, then another one, until he could no longer see them for the kitchen wall. He leaned against the door of the refrigerator, the metal cold against his heated skin. He couldn't get his mind around what Jonathan was asking for. Yes, he liked having his lovers' fingers inside him. He loved having either one of them fucking him, but as his gaze fell to his hand, clenched convulsively into a fist, he shuddered. There was no way in hell having that shoved up his arse could be anything short of abuse! He wanted to go in the living room and protest, insist that Devon refuse such a ridiculous request. Except Jonathan wanted it, had asked for it. If Devon had suggested it, it would have been different, been a case of protecting Jonathan from something he couldn't possibly understand or want. But Jonathan had *asked* for it. Forcing his feet to move, Kit walked slowly back to the door between the two rooms. He didn't want to watch, but this way he could interrupt if it got to be too much. His stomach churned uncomfortably, all traces of his earlier arousal gone.

Whatever Devon had expected Jonathan to ask, it wasn't that. Stunned into momentary silence, he ran his tongue over his lips, his mouth suddenly dry. "Why?" he asked, pleased that the question sounded calmer than he felt. He didn't want his own feelings to color Jonathan's response.

Letting out the breath he'd been holding, Jonathan considered his answer. Devon hadn't been shocked or rejected him out of hand—Jonathan might have grinned at the unintentional pun if he weren't still so tightly wound with desire and nerves. "I'm not sure I can explain it," he said honestly. "When you're prepping me, it always feels like it isn't enough. Not that you aren't thorough," he was quick to clarify, "but I love feeling your fingers inside me, stretching me, filling me. Even when I know you're going to fuck me, I hate that moment when you pull your fingers out. I want more, want it all—to feel you inside me, all of you, to be connected to you that intimately…." He shook his head, frustrated at the inadequacy of words to convey how strongly he wanted this.

Despite the painful memories of his own experience, Devon did understand what Jonathan was trying to say. Still…. "You have to know it's going to hurt," he responded, squeezing Jonathan's shoulder. "M'hands are so big—maybe Kit—" A quiet snort of laughter from Jonathan cut his objection short, and they shared a wry smile. "Yeah, okay, bad idea. But still…."

"I'd love to share the same connection with Kit, but you know he'd freak at the idea," Jonathan answered. "That's one reason I haven't brought it up until now. The other…." He paused, sliding his hand from Devon's hair into a matching grip of his shoulder. "I know it will hurt. I also know you would never hurt me without my consent, or more than I can stand. I trust you." He met Devon's troubled eyes with a smile that wasn't returned. "You *have* done this before, haven't you?"

The curt nod of Devon's head was answer enough to set Jonathan to cursing Robert's legacy once again. "Forget whatever happened before," he insisted, determined not to reinforce Devon's memories by asking for details. He cupped Devon's cheek in his palm, rubbing his thumb over the soft bristles of Lancelot's beard. "There's no one here but you and me, and you'll be doing this because I want you to—because I love you."

The intensity in their voices kept Kit still as he listened to them talk through Jonathan's request. Kit could understand the need to be powerfully, intimately connected to his lovers, but he couldn't understand the means Jonathan was choosing to fulfill that need. Devon said it himself—it was going to hurt. Sure, he was coming to appreciate the little smacks on the arse Devon gave him occasionally, but that was child's play compared to what Jonathan was asking.

He froze when Devon mentioned his name, wondering if he had heard him come in. He hoped not. He didn't know if he could say no to Jonathan, but he knew he couldn't do what he wanted. Kit glanced down at his fist. His hands weren't small either, even if Devon's were bigger. It wouldn't be any better, any easier, coming from him. He sagged in relief when they discarded that idea, frowning a little when he realized how much they were holding back when he was with them. Did he need to leave them alone more often so they could indulge themselves without his fears limiting their choices?

His frown deepened when he realized, probably at the same time Jonathan did, that Robert's ghost had returned to haunt them. He almost stepped forward at that point, but he couldn't help put this particular fear to rest, not as uncomfortable as he was with the subject at hand.

Devon's continued silence had nearly convinced Jonathan he was going to refuse when he crushed Jonathan to him and kissed him roughly, his tongue plunging deep and sweeping through every crevice of Jonathan's mouth demandingly, insistently. Jonathan opened himself willingly to the assault, his tongue meeting Devon's but giving him full control of the kiss. His pulse was throbbing in his veins, his cock achingly hard against his belly, his lips bruised when they finally broke apart. "I did promise you anything," Devon growled, his voice softening when he met Jonathan's eyes. "There's no one else I'd do this for, love."

"I know," Jonathan said quietly, holding his gaze.

Kit flinched as if slapped at Devon's words. He would never ask for such rough treatment, but that wasn't the point. Devon clearly didn't believe he could take it. And that was the point. *He* was the one who should be making that decision, not Devon. That was why they had safewords, wasn't it? Why they talked about things before they tried them. So that they could each make their own decision about what they wanted and didn't. His temper sparked, although he tried to tamp it down. He would bide his time and see what else Devon was keeping from him, see if there was more to this than just different tolerances for pain.

Devon let his eyes flutter closed, shaken by the unconditional trust shining from Jonathan's gaze. Drawing a deep breath, he rose to his feet, offering his hand to help Jonathan sit up. "Then let's take this up to the bedroom," he said. "I want you as comfortable as possible, and we have some prep to take care of before we get started."

"I'm clean," Jonathan said softly as they started toward the stairs, the admission bringing another rush of heat to his face. "I told you I'd been thinking about this for a while. When Kit said he'd be gone all weekend, I… well, I've been watching my diet for the last few days, and I—cleaned myself out before I came over."

Kit choked back the sob that rose to his throat, sinking down onto the kitchen floor as the other two started up the stairs toward Devon's bedroom. It was bad enough thinking this was some spur-of-the-moment decision, something that had struck Jonathan while he and Devon played, but to know he'd been planning it, had been looking forward to Kit's absence so he could get something he needed and couldn't get while Kit was there…. The churning in Kit's stomach was back, for an entirely different reason this time. He was holding Jonathan and Devon back, keeping them from exploring facets of their relationship. It tore at him to think of it, but he realized he had some serious reevaluating to do.

"You're amazing, you know that?" Devon tucked a strand of hair behind Jonathan's ear and paused on the steps to kiss him, more gently this time. "Should have known you'd done your homework." Pushing him gently toward the bed, Devon flicked on a light and dimmed it to a warm, muted glow. "Lie down and relax. I'm going to wash up and get a few things ready."

Jonathan sank onto the bed, his stomach tight with anticipation. Getting ready that morning, he wasn't sure he'd find the nerve to ask for what he wanted or that Devon wouldn't refuse; now that it was actually going to happen, he was still just as nervous. Closing his eyes, he began the routine he'd found worked best to help him relax. Letting his limbs sink into the mattress, he tensed each muscle in turn and then released it, working up from his toes, his ankles, his calves, his knees, his thighs. When he reached his chest, he began to breathe deeply, long, slow breaths that purged more of his tension with each exhalation. *You want this*, he reminded himself. *You want to give this to Devon. It's going to be good, so good….* His erection bobbed against his abdomen, all the relaxation techniques in the world useless to quell his arousal at the thought of what was to come.

Sinking fast into his headspace, Jonathan was caught by surprise at the dip of the mattress, his eyelids heavy when they fluttered open at Devon's weight settling onto the bed. Devon smiled at him, running the backs of his knuckles over the stubble on Jonathan's cheek. "God, you're beautiful," Devon murmured, bending down for a gentle kiss. "Need to take care of a couple things before you get too deep, though." Jonathan nodded, and Devon held his gaze. "Do you want me to wear a glove?"

Jonathan shook his head, then forced himself to answer out loud. "No—no glove. Want to feel you, know it's your skin touching me."

Devon nodded. He wanted that too, but he'd needed to offer Jonathan the choice. "I've trimmed all my nails nice and short, and luckily I don't have any open cuts." Given the intensity of the fight scenes during filming, that couldn't always be said. "What about the wax—want it off first?"

Jonathan shook his head again. "Leave it?" he asked, wanting to know that Devon would still see the way he'd marked him.

"Roll over," Devon urged as Jonathan turned onto his stomach. "Scoot up on your knees a bit." Jonathan settled into the new position, feeling a bit vulnerable as he presented himself and Devon spread his cheeks, examining him. *Relax*, he told himself again, breathing deeply. *Trust Devon.*

"This needs to go," Devon decided, brushing at the trails of wax that had dripped down Jonathan's crease. As much as he admired the contrast of deep purple wax against pale skin, he wouldn't risk any of it getting inside. Unfolding the thick, fluffy towel he'd brought from the bathroom onto the bed beneath them, he spread Jonathan open again. "This will hurt a bit," he warned, peeling away the first blotch of congealed wax.

The pull of hairs caught in the wax stung, but no worse than removing a Band-Aid, Jonathan decided. Catching his bottom lip between his teeth, he endured having the rest of the wax removed from his crease, humming when Devon smoothed a cool, soothing lotion over the sensitized skin.

"Lube." Devon chuckled at Jonathan's contented sigh. "Get used to it—going to be using a lot, more than you're used to, probably. And anytime you need more, tell me, all right?"

"Mmm-hmmm," Jonathan agreed, finding it hard to form words again. He let his knees slide a little farther apart, the gentle, rhythmic touch of Devon's fingers gliding down his cleft calming him, settling him. When a fingertip skittered over his entrance, he moaned softly, a tremble shaking him. "Please."

"Not yet," Devon countered, his fingers never faltering in their tender caress, his other hand reaching below Jonathan to circle his cock.

"Want you to come for me first." His lubed palm slid over the silken skin, measuring its length in steady strokes that matched the pace of his fingertips, his thumb flicking over the head each time he skated over the puckered opening that clenched at every contact.

"Want to—come—when you're—inside—me—" Jonathan protested, his voice breaking each time Devon's fingers teased him.

"You'll be much more relaxed if you come first," Devon purred into Jonathan's ear, leaning forward to lap at the salty skin of Jonathan's neck. When he felt droplets of fluid welling from the slit below his thumb, he let the tip of his finger just press inside, barely enough to stretch the guardian muscle.

Jonathan moaned louder, his hips arching into Devon's touch, but his lover refused to be rushed, keeping to the same steady, maddening pace. Each stroke sent Jonathan soaring higher and sinking deeper, until his awareness shrank down to only Devon's hands, stroking him, tantalizing him, kindling a heat that spread through his veins until it consumed him. With a hoarse cry, he stiffened under Devon's touch and came hard, his body shuddering with each pulse that erupted from him until he collapsed against the mattress, totally spent.

The strangled sound reached Kit's ears, pulling him from his self-pity. He jumped to his feet before he could consider the wisdom of it and started toward the bedroom. Yes, he knew Jonathan had asked for whatever was going on in there, and no, he didn't think Devon would abuse that trust, but he had to make sure. Still trying to move quietly, he climbed the stairs, skipping the third step with the squeaky tread. He wouldn't intrude unless he had to, but he needed to see for himself. When he arrived, though, he realized immediately that the cry he'd heard had been one of pleasure. He recognized the limp relaxation in Jonathan's pose.

Easing his hand from beneath Jonathan's damp stomach, Devon lifted his temporarily boneless lover just long enough to position a pillow underneath him. He turned his head for a moment, brushing the hair from his forehead and taking a deep breath to ready himself. Resuming the slow stroke of his fingers down Jonathan's crease, he added more lube and slid one finger inside, meeting, as he'd expected, even less than the normal resistance. He slid the finger in and out slowly, twisting it inside the clinging sheath until it moved freely, adding more lube and using several more slow, curling thrusts to distribute it before inserting a second finger. He knew Jonathan could take a third finger, even a fourth, with little more preparation, but this was as much about preparing Jonathan's mind as it was his body, and Devon wasn't about to rush either one.

Jonathan was still floating on the glow of his orgasm when Devon's finger breached him, so gently he barely felt the penetration. The unbroken rhythm kept him hovering on that blissful plateau, filling him and receding and filling him again with the inexorable consistency of waves bathing the shore. His breathing slowed and steadied, matching the ebb and flow of Devon's fingers: breathe in—fill; breathe out—withdraw; breathe in—fill and twist. A peaceful lassitude embraced him, so much that to arch his hips into Devon's touch, even to give voice to the pleasure he was feeling, would take more energy than he could muster. *Devon knows what you're feeling*, his heart told him. *Devon will give you what you need.*

When Devon could curl two fingers inside without resistance, he added more lube and slipped in a third finger, letting them rub for the first time over Jonathan's prostate. That won a moan from his blissed-out lover, and he bent down over Jonathan's back for a moment, chuckling. "Just checking you were still with me," he rumbled. Jonathan muttered something that might have been "bastard," but Devon couldn't be sure, the pillows swallowing most of the sound. He took his time stroking and twisting, only occasionally nudging Jonathan's gland with the steady motions.

Kit didn't know what he expected, but at the moment, he saw only the familiar sight of Devon fingering Jonathan's arse. Three fingers, to be sure, but Devon had done that before, to him as well. More than that, though, Kit recognized the acceptance in Jonathan's posture. He wanted this, and however uncomfortable that made Kit, it was still Jonathan's choice. Forcing himself to stay outside the room in the shadows, he continued to watch the scene playing out in the light of the dimmed chandelier.

By the time he'd eased a fourth finger past Jonathan's relaxed muscle, Devon's own erection had returned, hard and hot. This was as far as he'd ever taken Jonathan with his fingers, and his cock wanted what usually came next. Ignoring its insistent throb, he twisted his hand in the same slow rhythm, spreading the fingers as much as he could to stretch the muscle for what was coming next.

Jonathan could feel himself being stretched, but he'd been this open before—more, even, with some of the larger plugs from the toy box. With four fingers in him, Devon couldn't help but brush over his prostate with every movement, and Jonathan focused on that, the heady buzz of pleasure coming as regular as a metronome with each unvaried stroke. It was just enough to keep him on edge and too little to satisfy, and after another few thrusts he whimpered softly, trying to find his voice to ask for more.

Devon had just poured more lube over his hand, folding his thumb in between the longer fingers, when Jonathan's moan made him pause before pressing in. "Still doing all right, love?" he asked, bending close to Jonathan's face. His lover had closed his eyes when he'd come, but he hadn't given any hint of being distressed until now. Jonathan whimpered again, and Devon froze, ready to pull out completely if he needed to, when Jonathan shook his head.

"M-more," Jonathan whispered, forcing his eyes open to meet Devon's. "Please—don't stop."

Devon closed his lips over Jonathan's as he eased all five fingers in slowly, pausing when the widest part of his knuckles rested between Jonathan's cheeks. Rotating them slowly, he watched for any sign of pain, but Jonathan's moans were only ones of pleasure as Devon stroked inside him. "You're doing so well, Jon," Devon praised, spreading the furled fingers as widely as he could. "Just a little more now. Are you ready?"

"Now," Jonathan panted, willing himself not to push or clench in his need to feel Devon inside him. "Want you—all of you—"

Upending the bottle, Devon drizzled lube generously over his hand and Jonathan's crease, pressing inward as he twisted with excruciating slowness. It seemed as if he could feel himself, cell by cell, sliding inside Jonathan, the clinging slickness welcoming him, drawing him in.

Jonathan wanted to keep his eyes open, wanted to watch as Devon filled him, but as the stretch continued, he found he needed all his attention just to keep breathing, in and out, biting his lip to keep from letting any sound escape that might make Devon stop. Yes, it burned, but not more than he could bear, knowing that he was opening himself for his lover. There was a sudden moment of fierce pain, and then it was gone and Devon was sliding inside him, easily, it seemed, and Jonathan cried out in relief and sudden joy. "Devon! Oh fuck, Devon…."

Bracing himself with his free hand above Jonathan's head, Devon kissed him wetly, messily, wildly. "Love you," he whispered against Jonathan's lips, "love you so bloody much...."

"I... can feel you," Jonathan murmured, awe tingeing his voice. "Feel your pulse, your heart beating, inside me."

Kit flinched. He could hear the emotions in Jonathan's voice as clearly as if he felt them himself, and he knew that however bothered he was by everything he'd seen, Jonathan wasn't. And the love, the dedication he heard in Jonathan's voice drew him like a lodestone. He had already shifted his weight, starting to walk in and join them, when he realized what would happen if he did. They'd freeze up. Devon would withdraw quickly so he wouldn't make Kit uncomfortable, possibly hurting Jonathan in the process. Jonathan would be all apologetic about having needs Kit couldn't meet, and it would destroy the very thing he wanted to join. Better to wait until they were done, and he could deal with everything he'd learned today, about them and about himself.

Jonathan stretched to reach Devon's lips again, driving his tongue deep into Devon's mouth, wanting to fill his lover as completely as he was filled, an unbroken connection of body and spirit. If only Kit were with them—he pushed the thought away and cupped Devon's cheek in his palm, surprised to find moisture there. He brushed at the drops with his fingertips, hoping he'd managed to replace at least one of Devon's painful memories. "I love you. And I want you to make love to me."

"Be a bit of a tight fit," Devon said shakily. "Maybe I'd better pull out first and see how you feel after that, eh?"

"No!" Jonathan cried, his muscles clenching in involuntary protest around Devon's wrist. Losing Devon's fullness now would be a thousand times worse than the momentary emptiness he felt when his lover pulled out after prepping him.

Jonathan squeezing around him made Devon pause. He hadn't planned more than this, but he had to admit he wanted to feel Jonathan shuddering in bliss at his touch, feel the pressure when he made Jonathan come while still deep inside him. "As you wish," he said unsteadily, twisting his fingers with infinite gentleness until they brushed the spot that made Jonathan cry out again. Devon's other hand found Jonathan's cock, curling around it, pulling with firm strokes over the wax-embellished length.

Kit shuddered in the hallway, his cock reacting to the desperation in Jonathan's voice even as his mind recoiled at the sight of Devon's arm buried in Jonathan's arse. He couldn't reconcile the two, and he had no idea how to even try.

When Jonathan had thought about this night before finding the courage to make his request, he'd dreamed of coming with Devon deep inside him. He'd tried not to feel disappointed when Devon had made him come before they started, grateful that Devon had agreed to indulge his dark fascination at all. He certainly didn't expect to be able to come a second time in such quick succession, but Devon's hand on his cock, his hot breath against his ear, and most of all the stir of almost unbearable fullness inside him, of Devon touching him, loving him with such intimacy, set a wave of liquid heat roiling in Jonathan's core, spreading outward with each minute twist of Devon's fingers. The sense of connection was so strong he could feel his pulse beating in time with Devon's as the rapture bubbled through him and poured from him, his roughened voice calling Devon's name as he came.

Devon's cock twitched hard when Jonathan clenched around him, the rippling contraction of muscle seeming strong enough to bruise his wrist. He shunted his other hand through the hot splash of come over Jonathan's shaft, easing him through the aftershocks of his climax, his own need to come muted at the wave of love and pride he felt for Jonathan in this moment.

When Jonathan slumped in sated exhaustion, Devon began to work his hand free, nearly as slowly as he'd worked it in. They were both breathing raggedly when Devon finally slid out and wiped the lube from his hand on the bathroom towel. Jonathan rolled onto his side, wincing at the emptiness as much as the pain, then pulled Devon between his legs and into a heated kiss. Only when Jonathan worked a hand between their bodies to grasp Devon's cock did Devon draw back from the embrace, turning his head to look over his shoulder at the shadowed doorway.

"Kit?" he called. "Maybe you'd like to join us now?"

CHAPTER 13
BOTTOMING OUT

KIT FROZE, caught like a deer in headlights, when Devon called his name. His first instinct was to recoil, to deny that he'd been watching them—spying on them. He didn't figure that would pass muster, though, so he stepped into the bedroom, determined to brazen out their reactions. "I didn't want to interrupt," he said, shoulders hunched defensively.

"Kit?" Jonathan's gut clenched, his cheeks heating as he stared at their lover, his feelings in conflict. A part of him had wished Kit was with them, even at the height of his connection with Devon, but the thought that Kit had seen—or worse, heard—things Jonathan knew would disturb him was making his stomach roil. "How long have you been here?"

Kit paused to consider the question. He hadn't noticed the time, nor, he imagined, had his lovers. "I saw Devon get the paintbrush," he said finally, figuring that would give them an idea when he had arrived.

"And you didn't see fit to announce your presence?" Devon demanded, his voice sharp. He'd been aware of Kit watching from the shadows since just after the first time he'd brought Jonathan to climax. It didn't bother him that Kit had watched them—though he suspected Jonathan didn't feel the same—but that Kit hadn't respected them enough to let them know he was there angered him. "We're not a bloody peep show for you to get your rocks off watching."

"I didn't see anything to get my rocks off with!" Kit retorted sharply, forgetting how hot and bothered he had been watching Devon come over Jonathan's arse or hearing the desperation in Jonathan's voice when he pleaded with Devon to make love to him. He'd seen enough since then to kill all sense of his arousal. "As for not announcing my presence, I was obviously superfluous, and I already told you I didn't want to interrupt. I was trying to be courteous enough to let you finish."

"*Courteous* would have been to leave, if you weren't interested in joining us," Devon rejoined harshly.

"Devon, Kit, please," Jonathan interjected, trying to stave off the argument both men seemed eager to engage in. "I thought you were planning to spend all weekend in London," he said to Kit, hoping to move the discussion to a less dangerous subject, at least until everyone's tempers had a chance to cool. He might as well have saved his breath, for all the attention either of the two paid to his words.

"And leave you to do God only knows what to Jonathan?" Kit spat back. "At least if I was watching, I could make sure you didn't hurt him."

"Wait a minute," Jonathan objected, his own voice rising, shocked that Kit would make such an accusation after the weeks they'd spent rebuilding Devon's self-confidence. "Devon didn't do a damn thing I didn't ask him to do!"

"Don't bother defending me, Jon," Devon muttered, turning a frigid stare on Kit. "Obviously, all those talks about how much you both trust me were just pretty lies to make me feel better, at least as far as Kit here is concerned."

"Yeah, like all your talk about not hurting us the way Robert hurt you was any more honest." Kit glared back. "God, Jonathan, he had his fist up your arse. You can't tell me that felt good. You just can't!"

"It felt fucking incredible!" Jonathan shouted. "This is exactly why I didn't want to do this while you were around—I knew you wouldn't be able to understand. Or are you jealous?" he added, regretting the ugly words as soon as he spoke them but unable—unwilling—to call them back. "That we could enjoy something you weren't involved in?"

"Not of that," Kit ground out. "I'll just leave you to your perversions then, why don't I?"

"*Stop!*" Devon roared in a tone neither of his partners had ever heard him use before—and neither could disobey. Jonathan bit back the angry rejoinder he'd been about to make about Kit's anal beads and took a deep breath, trying to get his rampaging emotions under control. Sinking back onto the bed, he lowered his head and stared at his clenched hands, wondering how everything had gone so wrong so quickly.

"You don't have to approve of what Jonathan and I do, but you have absolutely no right to insult us for what we enjoy either," Devon told Kit, fixing him with an icy stare. "If you can't accept that, then maybe you should leave. But if you do, don't expect to come back."

"Devon—" Jonathan protested, the words drying up in his throat when Devon turned to look at him. He'd been prepared for the same angry glare Kit had received, but he could see the pain in Devon's eyes, along with an unspoken plea not to interfere. Jonathan swallowed hard and decided he needed to trust Devon a little bit longer.

"I…," Kit started, tears welling in his eyes as he looked from one man to the other, his sense of not belonging rushing back at him. "I'm sorry," he said finally, not completely sure what he was apologizing for. "I love you both, but I obviously don't belong here. I thought I could. I thought I could be adventurous enough for you, but you need things I can't give you. I'll just get my things and…."

"Dammit, no!" Jonathan jumped to his feet, throwing an apologetic glance over his shoulder at Devon. There had to be some way to keep this from tearing the three of them apart. "Kit, don't. I'm sorry, I shouldn't have gone behind your back like this—the last thing I wanted to do was hurt you."

"But it's all right for Kit to hurt you by calling you perverted?" Devon growled.

"I'm sorry," Kit said again. "I shouldn't have said that. You're right, Devon. I shouldn't have insulted either of you that way. I'm not comfortable with what you did, and I'm obviously the odd man out on that, but that doesn't give me the right to criticize either of you for it. I'll just leave you to it. You'll both be happier without me holding you back."

"Do you really believe that?" Devon asked in a quieter voice. His heart was as torn as Jonathan's at the sudden rift between the three of them, but it had laid bare what were obviously deeply felt fears. If Devon had learned anything in the past months, it was that fears had to be confronted or they would consume you from the inside out. "If you really can't accept what you saw, that's one thing, but don't try to tell yourself it's because we want you to leave. If you go, it will be your choice, not ours."

"Of course I don't want to go!" Kit exclaimed. "I love you, but…." He paused, not quite sure how to put his feelings into words. "Don't you see? You knew I couldn't be here for what you wanted today. I heard you. You need things I can't give you, and it's not fair to either of you. How long will it be before you start resenting me? Or before you start finding excuses to do things without me because I can't hurt you the way you need or take pain the way Jonathan can?"

"Yes, there are things I can give Jonathan you can't," Devon agreed. "There are things you can give him that I can't too. Don't you think I've known that from the beginning? We wouldn't have had to seduce him together if either of us alone was everything he wants. And not to give him a swelled head, Jonathan's not everything I need, either." For the first time since the argument began, Devon looked uncomfortable— anger was easier for him to express than tenderness. "I don't want you to go, Kit. I—love you too, even when you make me mad enough to chew nails."

"When you're both done disposing of me as if I wasn't here, do I get a say in any of this?" Jonathan interrupted, feeling as if an anvil had been lifted from his chest now that they weren't screaming at one another. The threat of losing either of his lovers was a physical pain in his gut, worse than anything Devon's penetration had made him feel, and he realized he'd do anything to keep the three of them from breaking apart. "I love you both, and I don't want to lose either of you. The two of you coming into my life is the best thing that's ever happened to me, and I'm not letting either of you go without fighting for you—for us."

"I guess I… overreacted," Kit said slowly, his gaze moving back and forth between the two men. He hesitated for a moment before looking back at Devon. "You really need something only I can give you?"

Shrugging uncomfortably, Devon rubbed his hand through his hair, wishing for the hundredth time that he had Jonathan's way with words. "Do you have any idea how it feels to know that someone like you— young, bloody gorgeous—wants an old man like me or Jon?" Ignoring Jonathan's relieved admonition to speak for himself about being old, Devon continued, "Jon and I, we're a lot alike, but you have so much energy, so much excitement—no matter how worn out I am at the end of filming, I just have to look at you and my exhaustion disappears. Knowing I have you and Jonathan to love when we get home, wherever that winds up being, makes me feel like the luckiest bastard on earth."

"I think I'm the lucky one," Kit disagreed. "I know I overreacted, but it did something to me to see you together, to see you sharing something I couldn't be a part of. And to know that you'd already made that decision for me made it even worse. I want so much to be with you both, to be what you need, and I wasn't today, even before I acted like such a little shit."

"But I knew you wouldn't be comfortable with it, Kit," Jonathan said, though he still felt guilty even as he tried to explain. "The last thing I wanted to do was make you feel like you had to go along with something you don't enjoy just because I wanted it."

Kit nodded. He did understand, but…. "Isn't that my choice to make, though? I know I'm just a kid, but I can make up my own mind. I don't need protecting. It makes me feel like, well, like I did earlier, like I don't belong here."

"I'm sorry, Kit," Jonathan said, taking his hand and, when it wasn't pulled away, drawing him into a full-body embrace. "You're right, I shouldn't assume I know how you're going to react. From now on I'll try to be more honest about what I want and let you make up your own mind whether you want to join in." He bent his head to kiss Kit gently, offering silent thanks that he hadn't thrown this away. "Just know how much I love you, and whether you decide to share in some of the rougher stuff or not will never change that."

"What he said," Devon murmured, moving behind Kit to wrap him in his arms, cocooning him between the two of them. "You belong right here, with both of us—don't ever let us make you feel otherwise."

Kit leaned back against Devon, curling his fingers tightly around Jonathan's hand. "I'm sorry I brought Robert up or implied that you were anything like him," he apologized softly. "I don't mean to be a snotty-nosed brat. It just seems to happen sometimes. Usually at the worst possible times. My mum despaired of breaking me of the habit; her punishments never quite seemed to do the trick."

Not knowing whether to smack Kit or kiss him in relief, Devon did both, pressing his lips to the smooth skin behind Kit's ear and at the same time giving him a playful whack on his arse. "Maybe I should have a go at it, then."

"You think you can outdo my mum?" Kit asked laughingly, leaning into the kiss and wriggling his bum at Devon. "Give it your best shot, old man."

"Be careful what you ask for, brat," Devon countered, catching Kit's hips and holding them still. Even that teasing enticement was starting to reawaken his arousal. "You just got through telling us to let you make your own choices."

"What do you think I'm trying to do?" Kit retorted. The argument had cleared the air, restoring his usual cockiness and giving him the confidence to ask, however obliquely, for something that had been playing around the edges of his mind for some time now. "I have a safeword if I need it," he added more seriously, wanting Devon to understand that he had thought about this, much as Jonathan had thought about the fisting.

Devon knew there was no chance Kit would need to use his safeword, but just the thought of how he might "punish" him sent the blood surging back to stiffen Devon's cock. "Right," he said shortly, his voice hardening into his Dom intonation. "Strip, then, and present yourself for your punishment."

Devon hadn't given Jonathan any instructions, but he moved up to the head of the bed, out of the way but able to see everything that was about to happen. He didn't think Kit had done anything that deserved punishment—he'd certainly had provocation for his initial reaction—but it was obvious the idea had Kit excited, if the healthy erection he was sporting was any indicator. Given what he'd asked Devon for himself, Jonathan was hardly in a position to protest anything Kit wanted. Leaning against the headboard, he shifted onto a hip to ease the pressure on his still-sensitive rear and settled in to see what Devon had in mind.

Breathing a sigh of mingled relief and desire, Kit dropped his trousers and boxers to the floor, toed off his shoes, and pulled his T-shirt over his head. Taking a deep breath to settle himself, he turned back to Devon, doing his best to present a meek face. "How do you want me, Sir?"

The little brat knew exactly what kind of images that question set loose in his head, Devon was sure. Sitting on the edge of the mattress, he spread his legs and patted his knees. "Right here, facedown. Maybe a good spanking will teach you not to be so mouthy."

Cock jumping in anticipation, Kit tried to figure out how to position himself as Devon had indicated without looking like a complete fool in the process. Eventually, he gave up and knelt on the floor next to Devon's feet, leaning forward across his knees, arse sticking up in the air rather awkwardly. He might have felt self-conscious were it not for the appreciative hand that ran down his back and across his bare butt. His entire body tingled eagerly, his twitching cock not the least.

"Not straining your back, is it?" Devon's palm lingered over the scar that paralleled Kit's spine. Kit had assured them that the surgery to correct his spine's curvature didn't affect his mobility, but Devon wanted the only sensation Kit felt to be Devon's hand on his backside.

"It's fine," Kit assured Devon, the concern only adding to his shame for having said such awful things about Devon earlier. He knew the spanking would sting, but he'd asked for it, just like Jonathan had asked to be fisted. Devon would give them that intentional pain, but the entire time, he was checking to make sure there wasn't any unintentional pain. "Thank you for asking, Sir."

"Such a pretty little arse," Devon commented, his voice deepening back into its dominant cadence as he allowed himself a last caress of the smooth flesh. Then, resting his left hand between Kit's shoulder blades to stabilize him, he brought his right down in a firm smack that left a rosy imprint on one cheek. "And all mine."

The thwack made Jonathan's cock jump and his ass clench instinctively as he imagined the blow on his own tender skin. Devon had given them both a whack or two on occasion, but they'd never really played at spanking before. Judging by the expression on Kit's upside-down face, though, he seemed to be enjoying it.

Kit couldn't decide which gave him more pleasure: Devon's hand on his arse or the possessive tone of the deep voice. He'd felt the blow, but it hadn't been enough to really hurt, just to warm his skin nicely. He wriggled a little, asking for more.

That wriggle was the tacit acceptance Devon had been waiting for. Splaying his hand wider over Kit's back, he laid a series of blows over his buttocks in quick succession, until the skin ripened to a uniform pink glow. Devon could feel the warmth emanating from Kit's backside when he paused to see how Kit was doing.

None of the strikes had been hard enough to hurt, but the combination left Kit's skin tingling and a warm glow suffusing his lower body. Devon hadn't told him to be quiet, so he moaned a little, letting his lover know how good it felt. Feeling the tingle start to fade, he pushed his arse up as best he could in his awkward position, asking for more. He wasn't sure Devon would go along with it, but he figured it couldn't hurt to ask, albeit silently. The motion rubbed Kit's aching cock against Devon's thigh, only adding to his arousal.

Surprisingly, Jonathan found his own erection reviving as he watched Devon's palm redden Kit's cheeks. Realizing he was anticipating the feel of that contact on his own ass, he was almost relieved when he heard Kit's moan. He was sure that would make Devon stop, and maybe he could convince him he deserved the same punishment. When

Devon drew his arm back again and landed another blow, Jonathan was surprised into protest. "Devon, isn't that enough?"

Jonathan had been so quiet that Devon had nearly forgotten he was there, but the objection made him twist his head to stare at him for the transgression. "I don't recall asking for your opinion," he snapped, his hand descending again without breaking eye contact with Jonathan. "Or giving you permission to speak." When Jonathan's head dropped in silent apology, Devon turned back to Kit, pausing for a moment to check that he wasn't in any distress. "That first bit was for spying on us," he informed Kit, hitching him a bit higher over his lap so he could angle the next blows over the unmarked bottom of his cheeks. "And these are for talking back to your Dom and insulting Jonathan." He laid another half dozen smacks over this new stretch of skin, winning a series of low moans each time his palm connected.

Kit bit his lip to keep from begging for more. He didn't want to give Devon a reason to stop, since he imagined that would be the retribution of choice if he spoke out of turn. He arched his back, pressing his buttocks into Devon's hand, hoping to convey his approval of the proceedings. His cock slid wetly along Devon's thighs each time he moved, the additional friction leaving him close to coming.

"Like that, do you?" Devon rumbled. He'd been careful not to strike too roughly, not wanting to risk damaging their fragile rapprochement, but Kit had borne the spanking like a trouper—he deserved some reward. "Jon," he called, running a gentle palm over the reddened flesh and smiling when Kit shivered beneath him, "find the lube and bring it here."

It took Jonathan a moment to find the bottle Devon had discarded at the moment of his penetration—it had fallen to the floor and he had to climb off the bed to retrieve it. He moved to Devon's side and settled onto his knees, holding out the seriously depleted container. "Here, Sir."

"Isn't he beautiful this way, Jon?" Devon observed, dragging a finger from the dip at the base of Kit's spine and just skimming the crease between his cheeks. Kit trembled again, and Devon reached for the lube, catching Jonathan's eyes before he could lower them. "Stay there and watch—and think about what punishment you deserve for speaking out of turn and questioning your Dom."

Swallowing down his response, Jonathan watched Devon squeeze the remaining lube down the cleft of Kit's ass, watched Kit flinch as the cool liquid hit his skin and relax when Devon smoothed it into the shadowed declivity with tender fingers. Jonathan's cock ached to skim that same slick channel, to find forgiveness in Kit's body, but he knew he'd have to wait to win that right again.

Whatever Kit might have said in response to Devon's question or about Jonathan's eventual disciplining, the words flew out of his head when Devon's fingers began to probe his clenching hole. He pushed up against the invading finger, wishing he had better purchase so he could move more, but he wasn't about to suggest a change of position now. He didn't want anything to interrupt what Devon was doing.

"You did fine, lad," Devon admitted, circling the puckered opening with slickened fingers before letting just one tip breach the tight muscle. "I'm sure it wasn't easy for you to keep quiet, but you did it." Easing the finger in deeper, he found the bump of nerves in the velvet channel and caressed it, pleasure to offset the pain. Kit arched up into the touch, driving the finger into firmer contact, and then he stiffened and clenched around Devon, crying out as he climaxed.

Under any other circumstances, Kit would have been embarrassed to come like a green kid at the first touch to his prostate, but after everything that had happened since he got home—watching Jonathan and Devon together, the fight, and the spanking—he was so on edge that it didn't take any more than that to push him over the edge. He peaked hard, his cock spewing cream over Devon's thighs as he collapsed bonelessly across his lap, his breath sawing in and out, only Devon's grip on him keeping him from sliding to the floor.

Jonathan had to close his eyes to keep from moving closer, to stop himself from reaching out and joining Devon's hand in soothing over Kit's back. This must have been what Kit felt like, watching him and Devon together, he realized—this hollow emptiness at being excluded from their touch. He was so focused on bringing his own longing under control that Devon's voice startled him when he spoke.

"Well, Jon, have you decided what punishment you've earned?"

CHAPTER 14
BOTTOMS UP

JONATHAN DIDN'T expect that Devon would consider letting him clean up the cream Kit had sprayed over his lap as a punishment. He also didn't think, thanks to his challenging Devon's actions, that he'd get to feel his lover's cock filling him the way he'd hoped. Swallowing regretfully, he dropped his gaze to the floor. "I think I deserve to be spanked as much as Kit did," he answered softly.

Rubbing Kit's back soothingly, Devon let the silence stretch for a moment as he searched Jonathan's lowered face, giving Jonathan the distinct feeling that he'd read both his earlier thoughts.

"Fair enough," Devon said finally. "You were arguing too. But after seeing to Percival here"—he gently nudged Kit to his feet, judging from the younger man's recovered breathing that his legs would hold him again—"m'hand's too sore to give you the thrashing you deserve." He dipped his head toward the toy box he'd left open on the floor when he'd retrieved the paintbrush earlier in the evening. "Bring me a paddle."

Kit managed to pull himself upright, but only long enough to figure out where he would fit on the bed without being in the way. Devon's voice still had its Dom cadence, so he stayed quiet, the afterglow from the spanking and the orgasm leaving him mellow enough to watch with equanimity as Jonathan went to the toy box and pulled out a wooden paddle that, except for the holes in its surface, looked like it belonged on a Ping-Pong table. Kit's arse still tingled warmly when he sat on the bed, so he stretched out on his side instead, angling his body so his belly pressed against Devon's back where he sat on the edge of the bed.

It hadn't escaped Devon's notice that Jonathan's cock was thick and swollen as he knelt before him again to present the paddle, nor had he missed the hungry look in Jonathan's eyes when he'd had Kit stretched over his lap. He'd put Jonathan through a lot already tonight, though the man had taken it all beautifully, and he obviously wanted this. The paddle sounded worse than it felt, Devon knew, the holes in its surface whistling as it swung, but the flat surface would make it easy for him to limit the impact to Jonathan's muscled cheeks and away from his undoubtedly tender hole. He curled his fingers around the oak handle, knuckles brushing Jonathan's palm before he lifted it away. "Over my lap and present yourself," he commanded, his voice steady.

Jonathan bowed his head silently and arranged himself across Devon's knees, his slightly greater height letting him use his hands and feet to steady himself against the bare wood floor. He could feel the warm slipperiness of Kit's release still coating Devon's thighs, giving him a sense of connection with both his lovers that comforted his heart. Letting his head fall forward, he pressed a kiss to the golden hair dusting Devon's calf before taking a deep breath and preparing himself for the punishment to come.

After a few experimental moves to refresh his memory of its feel in his grip, Devon brought the paddle down sharply on Jonathan's bum, leaving a bright mark on the pale flesh. Jonathan's breath caught at the impact, and he bit back a moan at the heat spreading over his backside, a different burn than the ache he still felt at being stretched to take Devon inside him.

Kit flinched reflexively at the sound the paddle made as it whistled through the air, but the dull thud reminded him too much of the feeling of Devon's hand on his backside for him to question it. He curled around Devon a little more so he could see the blows fall, could see Jonathan's reactions. Not because he doubted that Jonathan could take it, but more because he wanted to be a part of this in a way he hadn't been part of everything that had come before. He couldn't help feeling a little grateful, though, that he'd been spanked first, before Devon's hand got tired. A second blow shattered a rivulet of the wax that decorated Jonathan's cheeks, leaving a pattern of the paddle's holes in its place.

Devon landed several more thwacks with the paddle, aiming carefully until the entire expanse of Jonathan's backside colored a dusky pink. Jonathan stiffened against him at each contact, his cock a bar of hot steel burning Devon's thigh. "How many times did I spank you, lad?" he asked Kit, who was watching them both with a heated fascination.

"I didn't count," Kit admitted softly. "I didn't know I was supposed to, Sir," he apologized. "I'll do better next time."

Reaching back with his free hand, Devon stroked Kit's hip lightly in reassurance. "It's all right, lad. I didn't tell you to count them."

Kit relaxed under the gentle touch, letting the reassurance soothe him. He'd already caused enough problems tonight without making matters worse.

"A dozen, Sir," Jonathan volunteered, having felt every blow as it landed on Kit's rear. He hoped he wouldn't anger Devon by answering out of turn, but he also hoped to receive at least as many himself.

Devon's tone, when he replied, was amused rather than angry. He might have known nothing got past their eagle-eyed king. "And how many have I given you so far?"

"Six, Sir." Without his conscious awareness, Jonathan's aching muscles clenched in anticipation of another half dozen whacks.

The hunger in Jonathan's quiet answer was so palpable it spurred Devon on despite his inclination to stop. Varying his placement to spread the blows over as wide an area as he could, Devon counted out the last six strokes, dropping the paddle to the floor and squeezing Jonathan's shoulders in reassurance when he'd finished. "That's it, Jon."

Sliding to his knees, Jonathan looked up at Devon, the double burn only adding to the need already firing his blood to feel Devon claiming him completely. "Thank you, Sir," he murmured.

Devon stretched a hand to help Jonathan to his feet. "Lie down on the bed," he suggested, his voice gentling to underscore that the scene was over. "I'm going to get some lotion for the two of you. Just relax; I'll be back in a minute."

Easing himself onto the wide mattress, Jonathan rolled to his side, the air cool on his heated backside. Kit lay beside him, his brown eyes meeting Jonathan's with just enough uncertainty to send guilt spiking through him, sharper than any other pain he'd endured that night. "Can I hold you?" Jonathan asked, not wanting to take anything for granted anymore. At Kit's nod, he inched forward, his arms closing around Kit's shoulder and waist, leaning forward until his forehead rested against Kit's. "Are we all right?" he asked softly, wanting desperately to kiss Kit but needing the assurance that he hadn't damaged them beyond repair first.

"Yeah," Kit replied softly, tilting his head to kiss Jonathan quickly. "I shouldn't have said those things. I was… scared, I guess, that I'd lose you both, that you'd realize you were better off without me." He shifted closer, aligning their bodies completely, needing the contact to reassure him that he hadn't bolloxed everything up with his insensitivity. "I don't want to lose you."

His eyelids falling closed over a sudden spring of tears, Jonathan buried a hand in Kit's hair, pulling him into a deeper kiss of apology and forgiveness. "You won't lose me," he promised, his voice deep with emotion. "Not unless you push me away. I love you, love you both, so much...."

Devon watched a moment longer from the doorway as Kit and Jonathan nestled together, until the need to rejoin his lovers overcame the need to give them time to repair their own bonds. "Enough canoodling without me," he grumbled teasingly, leaning down to drop a kiss on each of their foreheads before rolling them gently apart. "On your tummies now, and let me see to your backsides." A smile warmed his face as Kit and Jonathan's hands found their way together, maintaining contact as they moved onto their stomachs.

The kiss and the clasp of Jonathan's hand reassured Kit in a way no words could ever do, enough so that he moved easily at Devon's suggestion, rolling onto his stomach and presenting his still stinging buttocks for his lover's attention.

Moving first to Kit's side, Devon poured a generous dollop of lotion into his palm, letting it absorb the warmth from his hand before leaning over to smooth it tenderly onto the reddened skin. A heartfelt sigh escaped at the soothing touch, making Devon smile, his other hand rumpling Kit's already-tousled hair. He worked the cream in gently, lingering until the heated flesh cooled and drank in the lotion completely. Dropping onto his forearm to bring his head level with Kit's, he kissed him softly, searching his eyes. "Better now, lad?" he asked, hoping Kit knew he meant more than mere physical comfort.

Kit shifted beneath the soothing caress. Knowing it was intended to ease the stinging did nothing to stop Devon's attention from having another, more salubrious effect. He pushed his hips up, asking for more attention and relieving the pressure on his rapidly renewing erection. "Yeah," he mumbled into the pillow, "but you don't have to stop."

Giving thanks for the resilience of youth, Devon grinned. "That would hardly be fair to Jonathan," he chided, stealing another kiss, "but hold that thought." Moving to the other side of the bed, he warmed another handful of lotion and rubbed his palms together to coat them both before applying the soothing balm to Jonathan's skin.

The arousal that had never fully subsided flared to renewed life at Devon's touch. The lotion's initial sting quickly eased into a cooling numbness, but each repeated brush of Devon's palms over Jonathan's skin set it on fire again. Jonathan stirred against the bedding, his cock looking for any friction to sate it, but rutting to climax against the mattress wouldn't satisfy the hunger that had been gnawing at him all night. A deep groan worked its way from his throat as Devon's fingers brushed across his crease, and he shuddered, turning his head to meet his eyes.

"Devon," Jonathan pleaded, pushing up to grasp his wrist. "Don't leave us like this." He paused, struggling for a way to admit what he needed—Devon's cock, filling him the same way his fist had—without hurting Kit by making him feel excluded again. He'd promised to be more honest about what he wanted, though, and he needed to restore his connection with Kit just as much as he wanted Devon. "I want us to make love—all three of us." Turning to Kit, he cradled his head in his hands, nipping at his lips. "I want to bury myself inside you, make us one until you'll never doubt how much I want you, love you." He reached back for Devon, one hand still holding Kit, linking the three of them together. "And I really, really need to feel you inside me, babe."

"Fuck, yeah," Kit hissed, the thought of being connected to his lovers that way bringing him to full hardness. He rolled onto his back and spread his legs eagerly.

As much as Devon longed to take Jonathan up on what he was offering—the sudden surge of his cock was proof enough of how much his body agreed with the hunger in Jonathan's words—he'd have to be the voice of reason. A Dom's highest responsibility was to ensure his subs' welfare, even when his own body was screaming for relief. "I'm sure I'm going to come off as the bad guy here, but I don't think that's a good idea just now, Jon," he said. "I think you've had enough for tonight."

In a less emotionally charged moment, Jonathan probably would have recognized the good sense in Devon's words, but with both body and spirit yearning for proof that they'd repaired the rift between the three of them, he wasn't about to back down that easily. "Shouldn't that be my decision to make, Devon? I know what I can take, and I want you—both of you."

Recognizing words were getting him nowhere, Devon ran his hand down the cleft between Jonathan's cheeks, territory he had consciously avoided since cleaning there after the fisting. Regretting the need to inflict even this small bit of unwelcome pain, he let the tip of one finger, still coated with lotion, breach the muscular opening.

The sudden hiss of Jonathan's inhalation proved his point. Sliding his finger out quickly, Devon bent to drop a soothing kiss on Jonathan's hip and then his lips. "Sorry, love. Believe me, I wish I wasn't right," he apologized. "You'll be less sensitive in a day or two, and then I promise I'll fuck you as hard as you like. In the meantime, we should probably see about getting the rest of this wax off of you. How does a shower—all three of us—sound instead?"

CHAPTER 15
CLOSE SHAVE

"AS LONG as it's all three of us," Jonathan agreed, trying to keep his disappointment at being too sore to make love out of his voice. He didn't want Devon to feel responsible for giving Jonathan what he'd asked for or reinforce that they'd excluded Kit earlier. "It will feel good to get rid of this wax—it pulls in all the wrong places."

"I think a shower sounds wonderful," Kit agreed.

"Let's go, then," Devon said, extending a hand to each of his lovers and helping them to their feet. He kept their hands clasped as he led the way to the bathroom, a wordless expression of the connection between them that had frayed but not broken. "Going to be a mite cramped," he muttered as he snapped on the light and realized how small his loo really was.

"As long as all three of us fit in the shower." Jonathan was already bending over to turn on the water, his reddened backside on unconscious display.

"It's not like we have any personal space left," Kit commented, stepping up directly behind Jonathan and pulling Devon with him. "It'll just give us a better excuse to touch each other."

"As if you ever need an excuse." Devon reached around Jonathan to turn the water a smidge warmer and snagged the bar of soap and washcloth from their recessed holder. "Now let's see what we can do about this masterpiece of modern art."

The warm water and Devon's hand working the cloth felt wonderful to Jonathan's taxed muscles, but neither did much to remove the congealed runnels of purple wax. "I didn't realize you were marking me for life, babe. I'm not sure Niall's as much of an art aficionado as you are."

"The costume'll hide most of it," Devon teased, leaning in to still Jonathan's protest with a kiss.

Wanting to help, Kit slid a chipped nail beneath one of the rivulets, peeling it away from Jonathan's skin and pulling a tuft of hair with it.

"Ow! Fuck, Kit, that hurts!" Jonathan flinched away, bumping against Devon in the restricted space of the shower cubicle.

"Sorry," Kit said, pulling his hand away automatically before he paused and said, "You weren't complaining that it hurt when Devon was putting it on."

"That was different," Jonathan answered, hesitating when he realized how important it was for Kit to recognize *why* it was different. "I'm not a masochist, Kit-Kat," he continued, sliding a hand around the younger man's wet torso to hold him close. "I'm not into random pain for its own sake. During a scene, when I'm prepared for it, expecting it"—he glanced at Devon, his free hand gripping his shoulder—"it can be incredibly arousing."

"You felt some o' that when I was spanking this lovely bum," Devon added with a playful smack. "But I don't think you'd want me to feel free to thump you that way anytime I liked."

"No, I suppose not," Kit agreed slowly, trying to work his mind around a distinction he wouldn't have imagined existed a few months ago. "So how are we going to get this off you without it hurting in a nonpleasurable way? It's all tangled up with your chest hair, not to mention all around your cock and bollocks."

"We'll have to shave him," Devon decided.

"What?" Jonathan yelped, his voice rising in surprise.

"Don't be such a nancy. I know you've shaved for roles before."

"My chest, yeah, but never my crotch!"

"You should've thought about that before you let Devon use you as a human canvas," Kit teased, running his hand over Jonathan's abdomen. "You're going to be smooth as a baby's butt. On second thought, I think I'm glad you didn't consider the repercussions first."

"See to it he doesn't try to escape while I get my razor," Devon directed, stepping out of the curtained enclosure to snap on a fresh blade and open the cabinet to extract a full can of shaving gel. He glanced longingly at the container of waterproof lube he'd picked up on his last shopping trip but turned back to the shower without it. Jonathan was still too sore, and it would hardly be right to make him watch as Devon and Kit went at it, much as they all might want to.

As Devon disappeared out of the shower, Kit playfully pinned Jonathan against the wall, kissing him torridly. "You're not going to try to escape, are you?" he asked huskily when he lifted his head. It felt so good—so right—to tease this way, the doubts and fears of the past hours melting away with the hot water and the press of Jonathan's naked body against his own. Now it only remained for Devon to return and complete them for everything to be balanced again.

Gladly ceding control of the kiss, Jonathan relaxed against the cool tiles, Kit's body sending sparks of arousal dancing up his skin everywhere their bodies touched. Sliding his arms up Kit's slick back, he drew him closer, increasing the contact and the desire until his head was reeling when Kit finally broke the kiss. "Wouldn't dream of it," he gasped when the question finally penetrated his lust-clouded brain. "Everything I want is right here," he added with a smile when Devon stepped back into the shower.

Kit turned his head to smile at Devon too, and the emotion in both expressions made Devon's heart swell until for a moment it felt as if it would choke him. He dropped his head instinctively, hiding his reaction, before he realized what he was doing and lifted it again, meeting his lovers' gazes with eyes damp with tears. "Don't know what I did to deserve the two of you," he said hoarsely, wrapping himself against Kit's back and resting his hands on Jonathan's shoulders, "but I'll be damned if I'll let us bollox it up again."

Jonathan stretched an arm to rest on Devon's hip and pressed forward over Kit's shoulder until he could reach his lips. "We have to be honest with each other," he agreed. "No more secrets, and tell each other what we want." He glanced at Devon ruefully. "Even when sometimes the answer has to be no."

Kit wriggled a little, caught between the two hard bodies of his lovers, the movement rubbing his arse provocatively against Devon's groin even as his cock bumped against Jonathan's. He'd been a bloody fool to do anything that might have jeopardized this. "And think before we speak," he added, blushing at the thought of the insults that had come out of his mouth as a result of his fear. "At least, I have to think before I speak," he amended, knowing he'd started the shouting match earlier. He looked at Jonathan and then back at Devon. "I really am sorry for what I said. It was fear talking, not my heart. You know that, right?"

"I know," Jonathan said softly, his voice rasping at the provocation of Kit's body hardening against him. "I'm sorry too."

"We all said things we wish we could unsay." Devon's voice deepened, not quite to his Dom cadence, but enough to underscore his seriousness. "I hereby declare the three of us unilaterally forgiven for all affronts, real or imagined." He kissed Kit gently, tangling a hand into Jonathan's wet hair to draw him into the three-way kiss. They were all breathing more rapidly when their lips finally separated. "No more looking backward. Only ahead."

"And the first step ahead is getting rid of this wax." Kit grinned, snagging the shaving cream out of Devon's hand and squirting it liberally over Jonathan's chest.

Jonathan jumped at the contrast of the cold gel on his warm skin. "You could have warned me first!"

"Finesse, lad. Just like lube, it helps to warm it first," Devon chided, his smile taking any sting from the words. "Now spread it out and then let me get to work on him."

Kit shook his head firmly as he worked the gel into a thick lather. "You got to put it on him. *I* get to take it off."

Laughing at Kit's territorial attitude, Devon started to whistle the theme from *The Stripper*, chuckling so much he could hardly get the notes out. "Take it off," he said with a grin, "take it all off."

Jonathan's laughter joined Devon's, echoing in the tiny enclosure. "Christ, Devon, Kit's probably not even old enough to remember that commercial."

"Be careful," Kit warned, pulling the razor from Devon's lax grasp. "I'm the one holding the razor. You don't want to end up bald." He turned over his shoulder and looked at Devon. "And I'll shave you, too, if you keep that up."

"You have to leave at least the beard, or Niall will kill us," Devon admonished. "In fact, you'd better leave a bit at the top, in case he wants a close-up of our king's manly chest. He's going to be filming scenes with Blythe next week."

"Hmmph," Kit grunted. "Camelot would be a much happier place if he never married Guinevere and just stuck with his knights."

"Much as I agree with you, even Niall can only stretch the canon material so far," Devon countered. "I don't think television is ready for an Arthurian ménage à trois."

Chuckling, Jonathan nudged Kit to continue, shivering at the careful drag of the razor over his skin. "Let's get on with it, then. I haven't shaved my chest since I read for the lead in *Wong Foo*."

Kit's grin split his face again. "And what a lovely woman you would've made too," he teased, sliding the razor carefully over Jonathan's skin, removing wax and hair in steady stripes, carefully avoiding the sensitive peaks of his nipples. When he was done, he dispensed more gel into his hand, warming it carefully this time, with a smirk over his shoulder to Devon to show that he was teachable. Dropping to his knees, he spread it carefully around the base of Jonathan's cock. "Now comes the fun part."

"Bet Patrick Swayze never put up with this," Jonathan complained, though his cock belied his grumbling by stiffening even further at the intimate caress.

"Just as well you were too young to get the part," Devon tossed in. "Given the way you go all Method to get into character, I shudder to think what you'd do to prepare for the role."

"Let somebody fuck him so he'd know what it felt like to be on the receiving end?" Kit suggested as he started shaving just below Jonathan's navel, working his way lower. "Oh, wait… he's done that."

"Not then I hadn't," Jonathan reminded him, the approaching razor and the steadying touch of Kit's hand making his voice waver. "Not sure I'm that dedicated to my craft." His voice softened as it lost its teasing tone. "I couldn't imagine doing this with anyone but the two of you."

"I'm not in any big hurry to share either," Kit admitted, working the razor carefully around the base of Jonathan's cock, "but I wouldn't say no to showing you off a little."

An idea niggled in the back of Devon's mind, but he pushed it aside, not wanting to focus on anything but the enticing tableau playing out in front of him. "Mind the wax, it's a bit heavy there," he cautioned, the melted tracks cracking and falling away in pieces as Jonathan's cock continued to thicken under Kit's attentions.

"Depends what you mean by 'showing off,'" Jonathan countered, the words slurring into a groan when Kit lifted his cock out of the way and began to draw the blade slowly over his balls. "Fuck, Kit, that feels too good."

Kit smiled, pulling the razor away for a moment to lick the tip of Jonathan's cock. "I told you before, I enjoy being watched," he said with a shrug as he returned to his task. When he'd finished, he ran his hands down Jonathan's thighs. "Did you get any wax on your legs?"

"Mmmnn," Jonathan purred, only the bits of shaving cream that still clung to him keeping him from pulling Kit's head back to his cock. "Don't think so."

"Turn round and let him finish your backside, Jon," Devon instructed, his hand going to his own cock to stroke it slowly. Jonathan groaned in protest, and Devon nudged his shoulder with his free hand. "Sooner you're done, the sooner we can get rid of sharp objects and get down to business."

Kit glanced back at Devon after he'd cleaned the patterns of wax from Jonathan's back. "I might need a little help here," he told Devon, not wanting him to feel excluded the way Kit had earlier in the day. "I can't hold him open and shave him at the same time."

"Thought you'd never ask." Devon grinned, moving closer and sinking to his knees while Jonathan groaned again at the thought of both his lovers' hands on him. He twisted awkwardly in the cramped space, hissing as his cock slapped against the still-cool shower wall.

"The two of you better hurry or I'm going—fuck!" He broke off when Devon spread a coating of foam over his still-sensitive rear, holding the cheeks spread apart.

"No fucking for you tonight," Kit joked as he swiped the razor over the lathered globes, avoiding the sensitive crease, a few more careful strokes removing the last of the wax and foam. Pushing to his feet, he kissed the nape of Jonathan's neck before biting down on the curve of his shoulder, not hard enough to break the skin, but definitely enough for Jonathan to feel it. "If you're good, though, maybe we'll let you fuck one of us."

"No fucking for any of us tonight, I think," Devon offered, still crouching at Jonathan's feet. "I tanned both your backsides fair enough that you should still be feeling it." He winked up at Kit, not wanting to single out Jonathan's greater discomfort from their earlier activity. "Surely we're creative enough to find another way to reward our king." Cocking his head to silently ask for a bit more space, Devon leaned in and ran his tongue very gently up Jonathan's crease, so lightly it was barely more than his breath soothing the swollen skin.

A deep moan sounded even louder in the bathroom's acoustics, and Jonathan's hands scrabbled at the slick tile walls. "Oh God, Devon, please don't stop, that's so—oh God, babe—" He broke off to draw a shuddering breath, pushing back into the bliss of Devon's mouth.

Wanting to be involved too, Kit dropped back to his knees and pushed on Jonathan's side. "Let me in," he requested, sliding between Jonathan's hips and the wall. When Jonathan shifted, Kit captured the bobbing cock with his lips, sucking the tip gently before sliding along the thick shaft to take the full length into his mouth.

Jonathan cried something inarticulate when Kit's mouth closed around him. Shaving had left him bare and vulnerable, exposing nerve endings that fired with sensations he'd never felt before, Kit's lips and Devon's tongue and someone's hand squeezing his balls all feeling wholly new and wonderful. He was floating—there was no way he could stay on the ground feeling this much pleasure—and he grasped to anchor himself with a hand on Kit's shoulder, the other on Devon's, to keep himself from drifting away completely. Little sounds were escaping him, raw sounds, but he couldn't help it when Devon's tongue was laving him, soothing away the last lingering pain, and Kit was alternating licking and sucking, and he was so close and he loved them both so much....

Even though he'd felt it building, his orgasm stunned him when it exploded inside him, shaking him between the twin ecstasies of his lovers' mouths, until his knees crumpled and with a wordless sigh, he slid to the floor of the shower, still clutching the two men he loved.

Kit's hands moved automatically to steady Jonathan as he collapsed, Jonathan's seed coating his tongue. He rested his forehead against Jonathan's for a moment, feeling the balance between them reassert itself. He dropped a quick kiss on the lips in front of his before lifting his head and meeting Devon's eyes, the taste of Jonathan's come alone suddenly not enough. He needed to taste his other lover as well, to reforge the bond between them that had been stretched so close to breaking. Keeping a hand on Jonathan as he moved, Kit scooted around so he was kneeling face-to-face with Devon. "Let me taste you too?"

Leaning forward, Devon met Kit's lips, his tongue slipping inside to share Jonathan's tastes, salty and dark made more delicious when blended with Kit's own flavor. "How can I say no to that?" he asked, turning to share a hint of Kit's mouth with Jonathan before helping him lean against the streaming wall of the shower and then struggling to stand up.

Waiting only until Devon was steady on his feet, Kit drew his cock into his mouth, sucking strongly, eager for a hint of Devon's unique taste. His hands closed firmly around Devon's muscled arse, urging Devon to fuck his mouth if he wanted to. He trembled at the thought of how close he had come to throwing this away. *Forward*, he reminded himself. *Look forward, not back.*

Braced into the corner of the shower stall, Devon leaned his head back and let his eyes close, his body cool against the tile and warm where the water ran down it and warmest of all where Kit was holding him, sucking him. He threaded a hand into Kit's curls and the other into Jonathan's longer locks, reforming the triangle, all three of them making love no matter whose cock was in whose mouth or up whose arse—not that he could mistake Kit's mouth for any other; the lad sucked with the same wild energy he expended in everything he enjoyed. *Well, thank God he enjoys this*, Devon thought irreverently as he pushed forward to slide deeper into the hot, wet cavity.

Devon's touch and the muffled sounds reverberating off the wall beneath his head were finally enough to refocus Jonathan's wandering senses. His eyes fluttered open to watch Kit swallowing Devon's cock, arms wrapped around Devon's buttocks to push him deeper with each dip of his head. The two of them were so beautiful together that Jonathan was content to watch in lazy enjoyment until the need to join himself to that beauty overpowered his lethargy. Pushing to his knees behind the two men, he circled his hands around the slender hips to take Kit's cock in hand, letting the silky skin slide over his palm. Bending forward, he lapped at the streams of water that flowed down Kit's back, following the ridge of his spine and pausing to press tender, openmouthed kisses over the harsh line of scar tissue that marked the perfect flesh.

Kit shivered in delight at Jonathan's hands and lips on his skin. His hips moved in time with the stroking of Jonathan's palm, finding a rhythm between the two men, determined not to come himself until he'd seen to Devon's pleasure. It wasn't pure selflessness on his part, though. Coming first would make it almost impossible to concentrate on Devon. More than that, though, feeling Devon come undone in his mouth would send him flying over the edge far more powerfully than if he came first. To that end, he slipped one hand from behind Devon to cup his bollocks, the fingers of the other hand slipping between the firm cheeks to play around the tight entrance. With no lube, he wouldn't try to work his way inside, but the outside was exquisitely sensitive too.

"Mmm, yeah," Devon rumbled, opening his eyes to look down his body at Kit kneeling before him and Jonathan behind Kit, and the image of the three of them and Kit's finger teasing over his hole was enough to break him. Garbled words that might have been both his lovers' names escaped from his lips as he rocked in short, erratic pulses in Kit's mouth, only the walls of the shower keeping him from sagging to join them on the wet floor.

Just as Kit had predicted, the explosion into his mouth and the soft moans from above him sent him flying, his cock spurting heavily onto the tile, helped by Jonathan's massaging hand. He drew deep, shuddering breaths as Devon's cock slipped from between his lips and his own trembling slowly eased. This was the way they were meant to be, wrapped around one another, loving one another. Reaching up, he urged Devon to slide down beside them in a three-way hug that might have been awkward except that such an emotion couldn't exist between them when all that mattered was caring for one another. The water beating down on them slowly turned cold, sending a shiver of a different sort through Kit. "Maybe we ought to take this somewhere more comfortable?" he suggested lazily.

"Sounds good," Jonathan agreed, pushing up from his knees and using the grab bar to lever himself to his feet before reaching a hand down to Kit and then Devon. "I can't think of anything I'd rather do than curl in bed with the two of you right now."

Devon draped a towel over each of his lovers' shoulders and snapped off the light as he followed them into the bedroom, all of them for the moment in perfect agreement.

CHAPTER 16
TWO BIRDS IN THE HAND

"YOU WANT us to what?" Ellie asked laughingly, eyes wide as she glanced back and forth between Blythe and Kit.

"Jonathan and Devon owe me," Kit explained, "and, well, I hoped you two had enough of men treating you differently just because you're women that you might be willing to help me get Jonathan and Devon back a little. I'm not going to do anything awful to them. I just want to show them what it feels like to be treated like you're made of glass."

"But Kit, what did you expect? You're such a pretty little thing," Blythe cooed, batting her lashes. "Why, I've even heard some people think that Arthur is romancing the wrong person!" She winked at Ellie, and the two of them collapsed into giggles.

Kit flushed, but he could hardly contradict Blythe's statement when he'd said the very same thing the weekend before. "Save it for tomorrow night," he suggested wryly. "That's exactly the way I want you to treat Jonathan and Devon when I'm done with them."

"That sounds ominous," Ellie drawled. "Do we want to know what you're planning to do to them?"

"Make them as pretty as I am, of course," Kit retorted with a smirk.

Ellie's eyes met Blythe's, and the two of them broke into renewed laughter. "Can I take pictures?" the blonde asked.

"Only if you give me copies," Kit replied. "Can you come to my house tomorrow around seven? I'll have dinner delivered a little after, and then the real fun starts."

"Count me in," Ellie agreed. "I wouldn't miss this for anything."

"Me too," Blythe added. "It's too bad none of our things would fit them. I have something that's just Devon's color."

"I don't want to ruin your clothes," Kit agreed, "but I could use some makeup if you'd be willing to let me borrow some stuff. All I have is stage makeup, and I don't want anything that heavy."

"How about nail polish too?" Ellie offered. "I bet Jonathan'd look pretty in pink."

Kit's grin turned gleeful. "You'll have to paint their nails for me. I don't have any experience doing that, and I wouldn't want to mess it up."

"You can leave that part to us," Blythe asserted. "I'm sure Devon will appreciate a nice French manicure."

"And even if he doesn't, we will." Ellie smiled.

"Maybe we should give them a complete facial," Kit suggested. "Or do you think that's overdoing it?"

"I don't know about you, but I'd want to see their expressions, not cover them up," Blythe considered.

"Yeah, and they might wind up enjoying it!" Ellie added.

"We wouldn't want that," Kit agreed. "So, tomorrow at seven, then?"

"It's a date!" Blythe nodded, leaning in to whisper something in Ellie's ear that set them off again in unrestrained laughter.

Kit glanced back and forth between the two of them, hoping he hadn't made a mistake by asking for their help.

"SO WHAT d'you think he has planned?" Devon asked, bouncing his leg in the passenger seat of Jonathan's Jeep.

"Who?" Jonathan asked calmly, earning a whack on the arm from his companion.

"Kit, you bastard," Devon grumbled as Jonathan hid a grin. "The lad's been too bloody cheerful all week—he's planning something. I know it."

"You should have worried about that before you agreed to let him take charge of a scene, then, shouldn't you?" Jonathan pointed out reasonably. "What are you worried about, Devon? This is Kit we're talking about. You know he'd never do anything to hurt us."

"That's what worries me," Devon admitted. "It means he's got something even worse planned."

Jonathan parked in front of Kit's bungalow, leaning over to kiss Devon tenderly and ruffle his hair before unbuckling and climbing out of the Jeep. "C'mon, tough guy, time to storm the ramparts of Castle Webster."

"I've got a bad feeling about this," Devon muttered.

Inside, Kit lay in wait for his lovers. Percival hadn't been needed in any of that day's scenes, so he'd spent the morning getting everything ready and the early afternoon pacing as he considered ways to get Devon and Jonathan to go along with his plan. In the end, he'd decided simply to take charge. As soon as the door closed behind the two men, he pounced, greeting each of them with a thorough kiss. "Now," he ordered firmly, "into the shower with you both."

"Clothes off first?" Devon asked.

"Yes," Kit replied with a little smack to Devon's arse. "Do you think you can manage that by yourself? Or do you need me to do it for you? I'd be glad to help if you're worried about breaking a nail."

"Just wanted to be sure." Devon winked at Jonathan as he rubbed his backside. "Didn't want to assume anything."

Jonathan rolled his eyes at Kit and started stripping out of his jeans and shirt.

"Wanker," Kit retorted, reaching for the buttons on Devon's shirt when the older man didn't start undressing fast enough to suit him.

"Not since I met th'two of you." Devon smirked, toeing off his shoes and letting his slacks fall to the floor. "After you, Jon." He gestured, checking out Jonathan's backside as he followed him into the bathroom, pleased to see the bruises from the weekend's paddling had faded to an anemic yellow.

Testing the temperature from the tap before turning on the spray, Jonathan returned the favor by holding the curtain aside to let Devon enter the shower first. Once they'd wet down, both men turned to Kit and waited for further instruction.

After pulling off his sweatshirt and dropping his track pants to the floor, Kit joined his lovers in the shower, running a hand down Jonathan's recently shaved chest and examining Devon critically. He picked up the razor and handed it to Jonathan. "Devon's chest is fine, but I think the rest of him is a little hairy," he said as he stepped behind Devon, as if to keep him in place. His arms circled Devon's torso, hands running over smooth skin. "Why don't you take care of that, Jonathan?"

Quirking an eyebrow, Jonathan reached for the shaving cream and then glanced back at Kit. "His beard, you mean, or…?" He trailed off at the expression on Devon's face, which, being behind him, Kit couldn't see.

"Niall would kill us all if Lancelot showed up tomorrow with no beard," Kit reminded him, probably unnecessarily. He nudged Devon to take a step forward so he could reach Jonathan, sliding his hand over the still mostly denuded skin of Jonathan's groin. "I want you to match."

Despite the warm water cascading over him, Jonathan shivered at the slip of fingers over skin that was usually shielded by hair. The idea of being able to give Devon that same erotic thrill was enough to make him harden. Sliding carefully to his knees, he sprayed a swirl of cream into his palm and spread it sensually over the golden-blond patch of hair framing Devon's cock.

Jonathan's touch was gentle, but Devon still couldn't help the tremor when his cock was lifted and the foam wisped over his bollocks. "Just remember that's not Excalibur you're slicing with," he cautioned, swallowing hard at the first touch of the razor.

Kit's grip tightened, his hands moving soothingly over Devon's abdomen. "Just relax and let him make you feel good," Kit murmured in Devon's ear. "You don't have to do a thing."

It had been a long time since Devon had consciously ceded control fully to another, but he did his best to relax into Kit's embrace, the gentle touch of Kit's hands and the enticing sight of Jonathan kneeling before him going a way toward calming him. Then Jonathan drew the razor carefully through the foam, and Devon's nerves jumped. He must have twitched without realizing it, because Jonathan paused, looking up at him in concern, and Kit's embrace tightened just a fraction. Taking a deep breath and exhaling it, Devon managed a weak smile for Jonathan, who ran a soothing hand over his thigh before returning to his task.

Hoping he wasn't about to make things worse by jumping to incorrect conclusions, Kit slid one hand up and tipped Devon's head back so it rested on his shoulder. "Close your eyes," he murmured. "Let us take care of you. Nobody here is going to hurt you." His other hand continued its soothing caress up and down Devon's stomach.

"You're going to feel so good when this is finished," Jonathan confirmed, wielding the razor with exquisite care. Leaning forward, he pressed a kiss to Devon's stomach, his cheek brushing the back of Kit's hand. "You're going to feel nerve endings you never knew you had."

"Never said I hadn't been shaved before," Devon admitted, stroking a hand through Jonathan's wet hair. He let his weight ease back against Kit, the quiet rasp of the blade baring his skin and the random kisses Jonathan peppered him with each time he rinsed the razor, not to mention

Kit's hand sliding lower with each slow caress, gradually building his arousal. "Just never enjoyed it this much."

"As long as you're enjoying it now," Kit declared, sliding his hand around the base of Devon's cock as Jonathan finished, lifting it out of the way even as he fisted it so Jonathan could get to Devon's bollocks. His own erection was swelling, prodding Devon's arse firmly.

"Beautiful," Jonathan murmured once he had carefully swiped away the last of the foam from Devon's groin, twisting to one side so the warm water could rinse away the last bits of clinging hair. Peeking up at his two lovers, both of whom had their eyes closed, he dared to run his lips over the wrinkled skin of Devon's sac, opening his mouth to take it in completely and tease the hardening balls with his tongue. The moan that wrung from Devon made Kit's eyes snap open, and Jonathan reluctantly let the heavy flesh slide from between his lips. "Is that enough, Sir, or did you wish me to shave him further?"

"His legs too," Kit instructed, not bothering to hide the thrill he felt at hearing Jonathan call him "Sir," an appellation that had previously been reserved for Devon, "and then you can switch places with him. You're getting a little stubbly too."

"M'legs?" Devon protested in shock, ignoring Jonathan's snickering promise to "take it all off."

"Yes," Kit replied archly, hands stilling, stopping Jonathan with a look as well. "You're not questioning your Dom, are you?" He didn't want Devon so uncomfortable that he couldn't enjoy the rest of their scene, but he didn't know many women who would wear a skirt with as much hair on their legs as Devon currently sported.

Jonathan had already lifted one of Devon's legs to rest on his thigh and was proceeding to lather it up before Devon grinned and shook his head. "I wouldn't dare, Sir," he answered, the picture of docility.

"I thought so," Kit teased, resuming his stroking. "I'd much rather make you feel good than have to punish somebody. Now stand still so Jonathan can finish and I can get my hands on him for a bit."

With that incentive to spur him on, Jonathan made short work of shaving Devon's rather muscular legs, rinsing them well, and passing the razor to his partner before looking up at Kit, clearly hoping he'd pleased his master.

Offering Jonathan his hand, Kit pulled him to his feet and into an embrace, kissing him thoroughly before turning him around to face

Devon. "You know what to do," he instructed, running a tender finger down Devon's cheek.

Devon leaned into the touch just a moment before moving to his knees, intent on repaying Jonathan for every teasing stroke. Jonathan's erection was bouncing against Devon's cheek by the time he finished cleaning the light scruff that had regrown around his lover's cock and stripped the softer hair from each leg. He finished with a final rinse and a kiss to each bony kneecap before kneeling back and looking to Kit for approval. "Does that meet with your satisfaction, Sir?"

"Absolutely," Kit praised, drawing Devon to stand as well and pulling him in for a kiss, Jonathan sandwiched between them. He shut off the taps and reached for the towels. "Dry off," he told them as he wrapped one piece of terrycloth around his waist, "and join me in the bedroom. I have clothes for you in there."

"See, that wasn't so bad, was it?" Jonathan said softly as he rubbed a towel over his head.

"Night's young," Devon retorted, shivering as he dried his denuded legs and crotch. Wrapping the towel around his hips, he started into the bedroom, leaving Jonathan to toss Kit's clothes in the laundry hamper—Kit hadn't asked it, but Jonathan didn't want to leave him a mess to clean up later—and follow behind. When Devon reached the doorway, he stopped short, causing Jonathan to collide suddenly against his back.

"Oh hell no," Devon growled.

"What?" Jonathan asked, though given their prep in the shower, he had a fair idea what had put Devon's hackles up. Since Devon showed no sign of taking another step into the bedroom, Jonathan wrapped his arms around his lover's chest and peeked over his shoulder at the garments arrayed on the bed—a softly flowing flowered skirt and gauzy top on one side, a slim black ensemble with a substantially shorter hemline (and lower neckline) on the other. He started to chuckle, winning an *et tu, Brute?* glare from Devon.

"No fuckin' way," Devon insisted.

"Oh c'mon, it could be fun," Jonathan coaxed, nudging Devon forward by dint of grinding his burgeoning erection into Devon's backside.

"Don't tell me you're turned on by this?" Devon protested, though his voice wavered with a hint of humor. "We'd make the ugliest fuckin' women on the planet." He turned in the doorway just enough to run a palm over Jonathan's scruffy chin. "Especially since we both still have beards."

Encouraged by the chink in his mate's armor, Jonathan caught the hand and pressed a kiss in the palm before lowering it to wrap their joined hands around Devon's cock. "Can't you imagine that tight little black number sliding over this?" he murmured, his breath ruffling the hair over Devon's ear. The shaft jumped under his touch, and Jonathan's voice deepened to a hoarse rasp. "Black silk clinging to all your curves, rubbing against you every time you move," he purred, fingers coasting over newly shaved skin.

Devon groaned, rocking into the seductive caress. "Still be… bloody ugly," he gasped when Jonathan's tongue flicked into his ear.

"Beautiful," Jonathan contradicted, pulling Devon closer against him as he continued to explore the newly bared contours. "You're always beautiful, Devon, especially when you're hard for us."

"Hey," Kit called, walking back into the main part of the room from the walk-in where he had put on his suit pants and shirt, "save it for after dinner. We're expected downstairs in—" He stopped to look at his watch. "—fifteen minutes, and you're not dressed, nor have I done your makeup."

Devon tensed again, and Jonathan's arms tightened around him. "Do this for Kit?" he murmured, quietly enough that only Devon could hear him. Without waiting for an answer, he gave a final caress to Devon's now erect cock and slid past him to the floral outfit. "Anything underneath this?" he asked, picking up the sheer blouse. At least the skirt looked like it was made of slightly more opaque material.

"Just you," Kit replied, sliding a hand over Jonathan's chest, enjoying the still mostly smooth skin. "After all, if I get the chance to get my hands on you, I want my hands on *you*, not on some fake latex tit." He picked up the black blouse and stepped behind Devon. "Let me give you a hand, luv."

Jonathan kept a watchful eye on Devon as he pulled on his own garments, but there was no protest when Kit slid the slinky black top over Devon's head, then turned him in his arms to start doing up the buttons. The highest one hit Devon midchest, guaranteeing an impressive décolletage, if only Devon had breasts. As it was, Jonathan could barely make out a hint of erect nipples under the dark silk.

Kit saw them too and pushed the silk to one side momentarily, bending his head to suck on the tight peak until Devon arched into his touch. "See what I mean?" he commented to Jonathan as he straightened, reaching for the skirt as well. He knelt to help Devon step into it, pressing a kiss to the inside of one smooth thigh, then the other as he did. Humming to show his appreciation, Kit adjusted the skirt as he fastened the zipper and hook, making sure the cut of the garment showed off Devon's arse to perfection. Finished with one of his lovers, he turned to give Jonathan a thorough once-over, pleased with his choice of outfit for him as well. "Come here, Jon."

Doing his best to affect a seductive strut, Jonathan walked toward Kit, winking at Devon over his shoulder as he passed. He wasn't sure where Kit intended to take this, but he was more than willing to play along.

"I think somebody's jealous," Kit teased, smiling at Devon. "C'mon, gorgeous, I've got enough love for both of you." He caught Jonathan's hand and kissed him thoroughly before urging him toward the bed. "You too, Devon, but just sit there on the end of the bed while I get what I need. I expect you both to still be fully clothed when I get back."

"Spoilsport," Jonathan whispered, running his bare foot up Devon's leg.

The sensation felt odd without the normal coating of hair, sending another unaccustomed shiver along Devon's nerves. Deciding turnabout was fair play, he reached over to tweak at one of the nipples clearly visible through Jonathan's sheer blouse. Jonathan hummed appreciatively, and Devon risked bending forward to mouth at the pink aureole through the filmy fabric. Jonathan's hum turned into a moan, and he tangled his hands in Devon's hair to encourage his attentions.

"Obviously I needed to be more specific," Kit commented drolly from the doorway, the borrowed makeup from Blythe and Ellie in hand. They were setting up downstairs to give Devon and Jonathan their manicures as soon as Kit finished decorating their faces. "I can't even leave you alone for a minute without you two jumping each other, can I?"

"You only said we had to be fully clothed," Jonathan pointed out, spreading a hand between them to indicate their compliance, "not that we couldn't enjoy ourselves."

"Like I said, more specific next time," Kit repeated, setting down the makeup case and flipping it open. "Now, let's see…."

"Spoilsport," Jonathan mouthed again while Kit's attention was distracted. Devon flipped him the bird, which seemed appropriate given that was what Kit was doing his best to turn them into.

"Ah, here it is," Kit exclaimed, finding the container of blush that would go perfectly with Jonathan's light-colored outfit. Picking up the foundation he'd snagged from the trailer the night before, he set to work on Jonathan's face, applying blush and eye shadow, mascara and lipstick. Only the beard spoiled the effect, but he knew better than to suggest shaving that. Nudging Jonathan's chin so he faced Devon, Kit smiled. "Isn't he beautiful?"

Devon fought breaking into laughter at the sight of their tarted-up king. "Lovely," he said solemnly, sure that making any of the comments that sprang to his lips would only incur even worse for himself.

"Close your eyes and trust me," Kit instructed Devon, digging in the makeup bag again.

"Spread your legs and think of England," Jonathan whispered, stifling an "ow" when Devon jabbed him. Schooling his face to impassivity, Devon inhaled and closed his eyes, a blank canvas for Kit to paint on.

Whereas with Jonathan, sensing his willingness to play along, Kit had used a fairly heavy hand, with Devon he used a much lighter touch, dusting just enough blush to highlight his cheekbones, only enough eye shadow to accent the set of his eyes, and only a light sheen of lip gloss to offset his mouth. "What do you think?" he asked, turning to Jonathan.

"Gilding the lily," Jonathan answered, a genuine smile crossing his face. "You've worn more makeup for filming," he reminded Devon when the other man grimaced at him. "Trust me, you don't look nearly as silly as you feel."

"You're not helping," Devon answered with a snort before turning back to Kit. "What now?" he asked, wondering if he dared hope the worst was over.

Kit reached for his lovers' battle-scraped hands. "Manicures next," he told them. "Downstairs at the kitchen table. I didn't want nail polish up here."

Shaking his head, Devon pushed to his feet, heading down the stairs followed by Jonathan and Kit. For the second time that evening,

Jonathan plowed into Devon's back when he came to a dead stop in the doorway to the kitchen. "What are *they* doing here?"

Ellie and Blythe merely smiled sweetly, their innocent expressions belied by the mischief dancing in their eyes.

"*They* are here to help me tonight," Kit explained, his hand settling gently on Devon's lower back.

"Christ, how many people know about this?" Devon complained.

"Just them," Kit replied. "Oh, and Addison."

"Addison! What th'fuck did you tell him for?"

"Clothes," Jonathan suggested, having seen their Merlin vamping it up in his own turn in drag on stage.

"And I suppose the bloody Orkneys will be here before long— why didn't you just invite the documentary crew to film us while you were at it?"

"The Orkneys weren't invited, and neither was the film crew," Kit replied with a bite in his voice, turning Devon around to face him. "Ellie and Blythe aren't going to tell anybody." He stroked Devon's face softly. "Do we need to stop? I wanted to have a little fun, not freak you out."

"It's just—" Devon took a deep breath, trying to get a handle on his own feelings before he could explain them to Kit. "You said something the other night about wanting to show us off. I'm not comfortable with that—at least, not outside people I know we can trust. I know Blythe and Ellie won't do more than take the piss with us, but if you're planning to take us in public—" He shook his head and frowned. "I won't do that. I can't."

"This is as public as it gets," Kit promised. "Dinner will be delivered. Ellie, Blythe, and I will answer the door, and the deliveryman will think I'm a lucky son of a bitch. He'll be right, but not for the reasons he thinks. We'll shut the door again and let our game play out right here where we're all safe."

Jonathan's hands settled on Devon's shoulders, rubbing them lightly, though he didn't speak. Exhaling, Devon nodded, then smiled. *This is Kit*, he reminded himself, his own advice from the previous weekend coming back to him. *Look forward, not back.* "Well then, let's get on with it," he asserted, turning his smile on the two actresses at the kitchen table. "Which one of you lovely ladies will I have the pleasure of offering my hands to?"

"Me," Blythe told him with a smile. "Come have a seat and let me pamper you to within an inch of your life. After all, a lovely thing like you wouldn't want to look anything less than your best for your date tonight, would you?"

"Not when my date's as hunky as Kit," Devon gushed, borrowing from his oldest niece's vocabulary and fluttering his lashes. "All the other girls will be so jealous!" He couldn't continue and snorted with laughter as Blythe took his hand.

"Afraid you have your work cut out for you," Jonathan apologized as he sat across the table from Ellie and displayed his hands. "My nails have taken a bit of a beating."

"Tsk, tsk," Ellie scolded, taking one of Jonathan's hands in hers. "What have you done to yourself?" She didn't wait for an answer, pulling out a tube from her manicure set and squeezing the cream onto the battered hands. "No matter, we'll get you fixed up in no time."

The doorbell rang at that moment. Kit watched Devon's shoulders stiffen before he consciously relaxed again. "I'll get it," he said to the two women, sliding a tender hand over the back of Devon's neck. He shut the door between the kitchen and the dining room to assure their privacy as he went to let in the caterers.

Blythe was chatting over the table about what she was going to do to Devon's nails, but he was giving her only half his attention, if that, the rest being stolen by the slow traverse of Jonathan's toes up his bare calf. He shot a look at his drag-mate, but Jonathan was answering one of Ellie's comments as if he didn't have a care in the world and had his nails manicured every Saturday. Shifting on the chair proved useless— Jonathan's foot followed, teasing at the bend behind Devon's knee before sliding higher to slip beneath the hem of his skirt. Devon tried to pull a hand free to swat him away, only to earn a reproof from Blythe that if he made her smudge, she'd just have to start all over.

Finished with the delivery, Kit came back to the kitchen and pulled up a chair as he watched Devon and Jonathan. It amazed him that they had agreed to this, that they loved him enough to do this. Rising again, he kissed each shaggy head. "Love you," he murmured softly.

"Now, Kit, don't muss them up," Ellie scolded, winking at Jonathan as if she had no idea what he was doing under the table. "After we've worked so hard to make them pretty."

"We should have borrowed some wigs!" Blythe exclaimed, keeping a firm grip on Devon's hand as it twitched in her grasp. "Devon would look lovely with Morgause's long blonde hair, wouldn't he? And I'd even lend some of Guinevere's extensions to Jonathan for the cause."

"They're perfect just the way they are," Kit disagreed, eyes sparkling with love and lust as he trailed his fingers along the backs of his lovers' necks. "Are their nails about done? I don't want dinner to get cold."

"All finished," Blythe asserted, taking the bottle of quick-dry topcoat from Ellie and brushing a final layer over Devon's French tips. "Now just flutter them like this for a minute or two," she illustrated, her fingers dancing in the air and reaching to encourage her partner to follow her example. Devon's grimace promised future retribution but left Blythe unfazed.

"Let me help you up so you don't bump them, sweetie," Ellie cooed, rising and crossing around the table to pull out Jonathan's chair, forcing him to quickly retrieve his foot from Devon's lap. Grinning unrepentantly, he offered Ellie his arm, only to have her lift hers and drape Jonathan's hand over it instead. Smiling at Kit while Blythe helped Devon, she patted Jonathan's forearm. "Let's get you in to dinner, beautiful."

Kit hid a smile at her condescending tone and led the way into the dining room, where his beat-up table was covered with a fine linen cloth and fancy dishes. Pulling out two chairs, he helped first Ellie, then Blythe seat his lovers. "Thank you," he mouthed in their direction as he took his own seat between the two men.

"Now you be careful with the wine. You know pretty little things like you have no head for alcohol," Blythe warned as she spotted the bottle decanting next to the table.

"Oh, I'm sure Kit will act the perfect gentleman," Jonathan sighed, blinking at Ellie. "Aren't you joining us?"

"We think Kit has his hands full as it is," Blythe answered, her voice musical with laughter. She followed Ellie to the door, waving Kit back when he would have risen. "We'll see ourselves out. You all have a good time!"

"Don't do anything we wouldn't do," Ellie added, the two women dissolving into laughter as the door closed behind them.

"Well, I'm glad they found it so diverting," Devon observed dryly.

"Now, now, don't be catty," Kit scolded teasingly. "They didn't have to come help you look your best for our date." He lifted Devon's hand to his lips and kissed the tips of the manicured fingers lightly. "And you did want to impress me tonight, didn't you?"

"You mean I don't always impress you?" Devon pouted slightly.

"Of course you do," Kit assured him, kissing him gently so as not to smear Devon's lip gloss, "but tonight is special." He began taking covers off the dishes on the table. "Avocado salad, escargots in garlic butter, coq au vin, and green beans with almonds," he enumerated as he revealed the platters. Jonathan started to reach for his plate, but Kit shooed his hand away. "Tell me what you want. I'll serve you. I wouldn't want to mess up all of Ellie's hard work."

His head tilting in consideration, Jonathan nodded. "A little of everything, please," he requested, offering a simpering smile of thanks when Kit set the plate back before him. "It all looks delicious," he added, settling his napkin demurely in his lap and waiting for Devon to be served before starting to eat.

Offering a rather gruff thanks in turn, Devon waited until their host filled his own plate before lifting his fork. Appreciating that Kit had the dinner catered rather than trying to cook it himself—the lad meant well, but his kitchen talents were rudimentary at best, unless you counted fucking against the counters—he dug in with rather more gusto than a delicately bred female would have exhibited. "So what do you have planned after dinner?"

"I thought I'd take my lovers dancing," Kit replied with a smile, enjoying the well-cooked meal. He had a whole selection of old, slow love songs programmed into the sound system in the living room, just waiting for him to hit Play. "And then we'll see what develops from there." Hopefully, the evening would end with the three of them in bed, but he would never have been so blunt on a real first date, so he held his tongue now.

"We seem to be an odd man out," Jonathan observed, patting his mouth delicately with his napkin.

"There's an understatement," Devon muttered under his breath.

"You don't think I can handle both of you?" Kit asked with a rakish grin. "I have two arms, one for each of you."

"Sounds delightful." Jonathan's smile skipped from Kit to Devon. "Dancing cheek to cheek to cheek."

"Kit leading, of course." Devon couldn't help but smile back at the image.

"Of course," Kit retorted, running his hand up their skirt-clad legs. "It is the man's job to lead."

Devon was already on edge from Jonathan's earlier teasing, and the press of Kit's hand through the clinging silk sent a surge of sensual awareness straight to his groin, the lack of hair where he rubbed against the skirt adding another layer of arousal. "Lucky we have at least one left, then."

"Lucky you, lucky me," Kit agreed. Seeing Jonathan's glass was nearly empty, he poured some more of the ruby liquid into the wineglass. "Would you like some more too?" he asked Devon.

"Plying me with drink?" Devon countered. "The other lasses warned me about you, you know. Said you only want one thing from a girl."

"Most girls don't have what you've got." Jonathan chuckled from the other side of the table.

"Do I need to get you drunk to get you in bed?" Kit countered, ignoring Jonathan. His hand slunk higher up Devon's leg, finding the slit in the skirt and taking advantage of it to find his lover's newly shaved skin.

"Ah fuck," Devon groaned, biting his lip and fighting mightily to remember he was supposed to be a lady. "I mean, sir, you take liberties! And Jonathan assured me you were a gentleman!"

"No, I said he could act like one," Jonathan corrected. "He is an actor, after all."

"Should I stop?" Kit asked, sliding his hand up until he could run his fingers over Devon's denuded sac. "Or would you rather I keep going?"

Taking pity on Devon's plight and deciding he'd been deficient in his own share of attentions, Jonathan cleared his throat. "Should I leave the two of you alone?" he offered, leaning back in his chair in a pose designed to put his chest on best display.

"I think somebody's feeling neglected," Kit told Devon in a stage whisper. Sliding his hand from between Devon's legs, he turned his attention to Jonathan instead. He traced the neckline of the silky blouse, fingers dipping beneath the cloth to tease over taut nipples. "Is that better, lover?" he purred.

"Mmmn," Jonathan rumbled, catching Kit's hand to guide it back where he wanted it. "Much better."

"Handling two at a time takes some practice," Devon advised, tossing his napkin on his plate and pushing back his chair. "C'mon, lover boy. Let's go dancing."

Kit rose immediately, keeping Jonathan's hand in his and catching Devon's as well. He led them into the living room and turned on the stereo. As Frank Sinatra's voice filled the room, Kit pulled the two men closer, one arm around each waist, chuckling as it took a moment for their bodies to begin to move in rhythm with one another.

"Nice," Jonathan murmured, sliding a leg closer between Kit's and Devon's, letting his body sway between them. It took Devon a bit longer to break the unconscious tendency to try to lead, finally simply letting his torso rest against Kit's and shuffling his feet in minute steps from side to side, an arm wrapped around each of his lovers.

The music changed, but their rhythm didn't, arms wrapped around one another as they swayed in time with the sultry beat, legs rubbing, hips bumping, slowly ratcheting up the passion between them. Eventually, Kit lifted his head. "Can I persuade you lovely ladies to join me upstairs?" he husked.

"Thought you'd never ask." Jonathan grinned.

"Just so you know, he—*she's* the easy one of the two of us," Devon added, winning a pinch on the rear from Jonathan as the three of them turned, arms still intertwined, toward the stairway.

"I'll keep it in mind," Kit replied with mock seriousness. "I wouldn't want to take you for granted." As they reached the bedroom, he pulled them close again, tilting their heads in for a three-way kiss.

Jonathan opened to both his lovers eagerly, any thought of their game forgotten as two tongues swept their way into his mouth, dancing with his the way the three of them had swayed together downstairs, to even more devastating effect. His cock filled, tenting the front of the ridiculous skirt he wore, and he pressed forward to rub against whatever he could reach, not even sure whose body he was molesting.

Kit kept track of which of his lovers he was touching by feel alone, the cotton of Jonathan's skirt contrasting with the silk of Devon's. He ran his hands over both firm arses, caressing them through the fabric until he needed more. Fumbling with buttons and zippers, he finally loosened the waistbands enough to get his hands beneath and caress flesh instead.

If he were in control of the scene, Devon would have had them all naked already, but he resisted the urge to strip Kit's slacks from him and settled for rutting against them lasciviously instead. The lad was a quick study; he'd get the message eventually. In the meantime, Devon took advantage of the convenient proximity of Jonathan's bare backside to run an appreciative hand down his flank, freezing momentarily when he bumped into another hand similarly engaged. When Kit gave no sign of resenting his presence, he carried on, running his fingers down the smooth cleft, more than pleased when a second set of fingers joined him in double-teaming their partner.

"Holy fuck," Jonathan groaned, or would have if his mouth weren't fully occupied with two tongues beside his own. He settled for arching into the dual caress, flexing his muscles in as encouraging a manner as he could muster. One of the things he'd learned over the past months was how much he loved having his ass played with, and Kit and Devon were pressing all his buttons.

"Do you like that, sweetheart?" Kit asked, breaking the kiss long enough to murmur lasciviously in Jonathan's ear. "Both of our fingers inside you, playing with you, stretching you…. You're going to be so wide open when I fuck you later."

"Fuck later, do it now," Jonathan rasped, already more than ready.

"Pushy bottom," Kit scolded, turning Jonathan toward the bed. "Let's get you out of this get-up, Devon," he added. "You can have Jonathan's mouth while I ream his arse."

Devon didn't need to be told twice, squirming his way out of the tight-fitting black garments with as much haste as the Orkneys making their way down pub row. Jonathan was already kneeling on the bed, his arse poking up and waggling, bracing himself on one arm and reaching back to pull Kit's face between his cheeks with the other. Devon plopped down onto the mattress in front of Jonathan, who all but inhaled his cock with a hunger that no woman in Devon's experience had ever exhibited.

Jonathan's eagerness was catching, and Kit rimmed him enthusiastically, his pants tightening apace as his cock swelled. He could hear twin moans, and it turned him on more than he would have imagined possible before taking up with the two men. He worked his way deeper between Jonathan's legs, sucking the smooth sac into his mouth, tonguing the hard bollocks within, fondling Jonathan's leaking cock as he did.

The slide of Kit's tongue over Jonathan's bare balls was nearly as arousing as the tang leaking from Devon's cock as it pummeled his mouth, but what he wanted more than anything at that moment was to feel Kit filling his ass. He reached up a hand to skate over Devon's sac, freeing his mouth long enough to suck in a deep breath and turn his head to plead with Kit. "Need you," he murmured, contracting as if he could already feel his lover's hard cock breaching him. "Please, Kit-Kat...."

Doing his best not to begrudge the loss (momentary, he hoped) of Jonathan's attentions, Devon occupied himself with reaching for whatever bare skin he could, diving beneath Jonathan's braced arm to pinch at his nipple, the other hand nudging Kit's shoulder. "Sooner you give him what he wants, the happier we'll all be," he suggested.

"Just a second," Kit promised, pulling away long enough to dig his cock ring out of the drawer and slip it on. He had every intention of fucking both his lovers tonight, and that meant not coming right away. Returning to his place behind Jonathan, he slicked his cock and plunged deep, groaning as the tight heat welcomed him in.

That was exactly what Jonathan had been waiting for, and with a happy moan, he turned back to Devon, wetting a finger before resuming his practice at the art of deep-throating, using the moistened digit to do some exploring of his own between Devon's newly shaved cheeks. He managed to work the finger in to the second knuckle before Kit's pounding began to steal his power of conscious thought, and he settled for twisting it in time with the thrusts splitting him until Devon's moan confirmed that he'd found his prostate. Rubbing in place and sucking up and down the hard shaft filling his mouth were about all Jonathan had the presence left to focus on as Kit set about fucking him with satisfying roughness. He pushed back into each contact, losing a little more control with each slap of Kit's balls against his, the spiraling tightness warning him he was close to coming without his cock being touched.

Devon could feel the growing wildness of Jonathan's sucking and was wise enough to pull his cock free before it was bitten down on, the finger still pressing just the right spot inside him more than enough to keep him happily buzzed. Bending forward, he pinched both of Jonathan's nipples and tugged at them roughly, adding a tinge of the pain he hoped would set Jonathan flying.

Kit could tell from the sounds emanating from his lover's throat and from the clench of muscles around his cock that Jonathan was close. Leaning closer, he encircled his straining erection, grateful for the cock ring keeping him from coming on the spot.

Devon's rough tugs on his nipples and Kit's hand pumping his cock were a double play Jonathan had no chance of withstanding. His muscles tightened, and with a garbled cry, he came hard, slumping forward onto the mattress as his release shook him. Tiny explosions continued to fire along his nerves as Kit's shaft, still satisfyingly hard thanks to the cock ring, kept rubbing in all the right spots, prolonging his shuddering climax.

Kit groaned, straining to find the release held back by the ring. He continued to thrust through the aftershocks of Jonathan's climax, letting the clenching passage caress him repeatedly until Jonathan finally lay still beneath him. Pressing a kiss to Jonathan's shoulder, he raised lustful eyes to Devon's face as he reached for his still-swollen cock. "Looks like you could use a little relief," he teased.

"Oh no," Devon retorted, knowing he wouldn't last long if Kit got his hands on him. "I expect to get as good as Jonathan got."

Kit grinned, pulling out of Jonathan gently, bestowing a tender caress on his shoulder as he did. "Turn over, then," he directed Devon. "That way, when Jonathan's back with us again, he can suck you while I fuck you. You did say you wanted as good as Jonathan got, after all."

The gentle touch was enough to recall Jonathan to his surroundings, and he rolled onto his back with a sated moan, patting the bed beside him. "C'mon back here and let me finish what I started," he rasped to Devon, his voice still husky with desire.

Swinging a leg to straddle Jonathan, Devon couldn't resist looking over his shoulder at Kit with a cheeky grin. "Hope you saved some of the good stuff for me, handsome," he flirted, batting his lashes. Jonathan recalled his attention by the simple expedient of sucking his bollocks into his mouth, and Devon braced himself on one forearm, brushing over Jonathan's beard with the knuckles of his other hand.

Kit's hand trembled with unsated lust as he prepped Devon quickly. He wanted to linger, to give Devon the consideration he deserved, but his control was near its end. "Please tell me you're ready for me," he pleaded, voice breaking as he struggled not to simply drive right in.

"More than ready," Devon assured him, his own voice wavering slightly when Jonathan let his sac slide from his mouth in favor of licking from the root of his cock to its tip. His sinful tongue teased at the slit just as Kit spread him wide and drove inside. Devon groaned his approval and pushed back onto Kit's cock, forcing Jonathan to grasp his hips so he could continue his own attentions, lapping up the beads of pearly fluid from the ruddy head of Devon's cock before closing his lips around it and slowly working his way toward its base.

Devon was just as hot and tight as Jonathan had been, squeezing Kit's cock deliciously. He shuddered in delight as the muscles worked his length, massaging every inch of him, wreaking havoc on what little remained of his control. If it hadn't been for the cock ring, this would have been over with embarrassing speed. Knowing Jonathan was already lavishing attention on Devon's cock, Kit lifted up so he could get his fingers between their bodies, circling the already stretched hole into which his cock disappeared. The shiver that went through Devon gave him ideas, and he nudged a little more firmly, curious how far the elastic muscle would give.

Feeling Devon's tremble, Jonathan drew enough concentration from lavishing pleasure on his cock to open his eyes. Devon loomed over him, Kit kneeling behind him, pounding him as roughly as even Devon could ask for. Kit's slender fingers played over the wrinkled skin that stretched to accept him, making Devon quiver again. Not letting up the fierce suction on the thick shaft that filled his mouth, Jonathan moved a hand from Devon's hip to the puckered entrance, sure the combined efforts of both he and Kit would be enough to send Devon screaming over the precipice.

A long, low groan rumbled in Devon's chest at the touch of Kit's fingers around their joining. When one of those fingers slid past the accommodating muscle, he howled, and when a thicker finger worked its way into his arsehole too, he lost it completely. Throwing back his head with a roar, his entire body spasming, he poured his juice down Jonathan's throat, slumping forward onto his chest as his bollocks emptied in time with Kit's constant thrusts.

Kit paused only long enough to pull off the cock ring before returning to pounding Devon into the mattress. Or into Jonathan, as it were. It only took seconds before his orgasm started, boiling out of him and filling Devon's hole to overflowing. The sudden cessation of sexual tension left him gasping as he collapsed forward, panting harshly.

The weight of both Devon and Kit pressing into Jonathan was a most welcome burden, and he savored it, coasting his hands over both the bodies panting against his. As their breathing slowed, so did his touches, calming and soothing them as he would Hengroen, Arthur's horse—though he had to admit this was a much more enjoyable ride. His fingers tangled into Devon's hair, and he turned his head to rest more comfortably against his chest. "Now, wasn't it worth a bit of dress-up to make Kit that happy?"

"Only for him," Devon begrudgingly admitted, nipping at a still peaked pink nub. "Who knew the lad would get so randy over seeing us in a bit o' silk and lace?" he added, knowing Kit could hear him. "Makes me wonder if he wouldn't like it even better himself."

"That wasn't the point of this exercise," Kit reminded them tartly, though he was too sated to inject much sting in his voice. "You were supposed to see what it felt like to be babied when you don't need it."

"Are we really as bad as all that?" Jonathan asked, reaching across Devon to run a hand up Kit's side.

Kit shrugged. "It just seems sometimes like you both go into 'protect Kit' mode, and I don't need it. Yes, I'm younger than you, but I *am* an adult. I can make decisions for myself, and while consideration is appreciated, coddling is not. Don't assume you know me better than I know myself."

"I've learned my lesson, believe me," Jonathan assured him.

Judging that Kit looked unconvinced, Devon rolled to one side, letting him settle in between him and Jonathan. "So what do you suggest we do to prove that to you? If tonight's little charade wasn't enough of a demonstration?"

Kit flushed a little at the thought that had been dancing around the edges of his mind for a couple of weeks, but he pushed the embarrassment aside. If Jonathan could ask for what he wanted, Kit could do the same. "I have another scenario I want to try."

CHAPTER 17
RAISING CANE

KIT KNELT on the floor, feeling at the same time incredibly silly and incredibly sexy. Jonathan was sprawled across the straight-back chair in a button-down shirt, tie loose around his neck, trousers open to reveal his ruddy cock, already hard and leaking. Kit's own attire was chosen to mimic as much as possible his schoolboy uniform, while Devon was outside somewhere, just waiting to burst into the room and catch his two "students" in a compromising situation.

Jonathan looked down at the dark head between his spread thighs, his cock twitching in anticipation. He felt a little foolish, a little insecure, which was probably in character for the schoolboy he was supposed to be. He didn't share Kit and Devon's British public school background, the uniforms and discipline unfamiliar and as a result somewhat uncomfortable, but he'd defy anyone to remain unaffected with Kit kneeling between his legs. Kit's hand closed around his own cock through his briefs, squeezing it slowly while his head lowered, tongue peeking out to lap at the tip of Jonathan's cock with a hesitance completely unlike his usual boldness. Jonathan wondered if he was seeing a hint of what Kit had been like as a youth, the thought fleeting as Kit's lips closed around the head of his shaft and he tried not to buck out of the chair.

Jonathan tasted so good on Kit's tongue. He always did, but something about this scenario made it feel fresh again. Like they hadn't done this countless times in the last few months. Kit made himself stay in character, pretending this was the first time he'd sucked another boy's cock. "You're so big," he marveled breathlessly, trying to infuse wide-eyed innocence into his words.

"I—am I?" Jonathan asked, trying to remember being that inexperienced. It had been a long time since he'd cared about how he sized up to others, but he tapped into the uncertainty he'd felt at the beginning of the relationship with Kit and Devon to color his response. "That feels really good," he added, the quaver in his voice not wholly feigned.

"It's supposed to," Kit said, not quite able to keep the smugness out of his voice. He sucked a little more of the shaft into his mouth, curling his tongue in a way guaranteed to make Jonathan moan.

It worked.

"Shhh," Kit warned. "We don't want the headmaster to hear us. He'll punish us for sure!"

"Don't stop," Jonathan pleaded, a hand hovering over Kit's head, wanting to touch but not wanting to make the younger boy feel as if he was forcing him. This had been Kit's idea, after all, not that he wasn't willing to go along, especially since Kit had promised he could go first. He curled his other hand into a fist, ready to bite down on it if the provocative feelings got too intense. "I'll be quiet, I promise."

Kit nodded and lowered his head again, licking his way down the hard length, exploring eagerly, the muffled sounds from above him making him wish they didn't have to be quiet, but he knew what the punishment would be if they were caught. They'd both feel the headmaster's cane, and rumor had it he was a right bastard when it came to certain infractions. Nobody would say exactly which ones were the worst, but Kit suspected this would count as one of them.

Jonathan's teeth sank into the fleshy part of his palm, muffling the groans that wanted to escape at the unbelievable things Kit was doing with his tongue. He should be paying attention so he could return the favor when it was his turn to suck Kit, but it was all he could do to keep from howling at the way Kit's mouth was making him feel. He shifted on the hard chair, the tightness of his muscles and the growing heat flaring in his groin making it impossible to sit still. Kit's head bobbed lower, letting the tip of Jonathan's cock graze the back of his throat, and Jonathan arched up involuntarily, his head falling back. "Ah Christ, Kit…," he wailed, both hands gripping the sides of the chair until his knuckles were white.

"What's this, then?" Devon's voice was harsh as he strode into the room, the makeshift robe they'd nicked from Wardrobe swirling around his trouser legs. "Lewd behavior again, Mr. Webster? And profanity on top of it, Mr. Braedon? That will double your punishment."

The two perpetrators stared at him in wide-eyed shock. "On your feet!" Devon ordered sharply, hiding his grin as they scrambled to stand before him. "I didn't tell you to dress, Braedon!" he added when Jonathan started to pull up his pants. "Since you found it necessary to undress to break this school's code of conduct, you can face the consequences the same way." He eyed the damp cotton of Kit's white briefs—purchased especially for today's games—and the softening but still wet length of Jonathan's cock with scorn. "What do you have to say for yourselves?"

"It's all my fault, Sir," Kit said immediately, not looking at the headmaster. "Don't punish Braedon, Sir." This hadn't been in the script they'd talked about, but Kit knew this was his fantasy they were playing out, not Jonathan's, and he wanted to give his lover one last chance to opt out. Not that he expected Jonathan to agree—or Devon, for that matter—but he needed to make the offer.

"That's not true, Sir!" Jonathan interrupted. "It wouldn't be fair to punish Kit when I—when I was the one being—being—"

"Being pleasured?" Devon drawled. "Well, I hope you enjoyed yourself, Braedon, because I doubt either of you will enjoy what I'm about to do to you."

"What are you going to do, Sir?" Kit asked in a small voice, stomach jumping at the anticipated answer. He could feel the muscles in his arse tightening already in preparation for the cane.

"You know the penalty for transgressions, Webster," Devon snapped. "Half a dozen stripes on your bare bottom." He watched the bulge at the front of the younger man's briefs thicken at his words and barely hid his smile at Kit's reaction. "Go fetch the cane from my office." He nodded toward their bedroom, where he'd left the switch he'd selected lying across the bed.

Kit resisted the urge to stick his hands in his pockets as he trudged with mock reluctance toward the "office." The thought of baring his arse and presenting it for his caning had him hardening, much as he'd done when Devon had spanked him a couple of weeks ago. "Yes, Sir."

"And you, Braedon—three stripes for you, since Webster was the instigator." Jonathan opened his mouth to protest, but Devon glared him down before he could speak. "I didn't ask you to comment, boy! And three more for the profanity you uttered. Say anything else and I'll add more."

Jonathan subsided, his expression sullen as he slouched awkwardly, his trousers bunched around his knees. Devon gave him a smart crack on his ass, making Jonathan's head snap up in shock. "Stand up straight, Braedon! In fact, go stand over there in the corner. You'll have a good view of Webster's punishment so you'll know what you can look forward to. And don't slouch, or you'll earn yourself more stripes." Jonathan shuffled away, taking the position Devon ordered as Kit returned carrying a slender length of rattan about a yard long, the handle wrapped in leather.

"Here you are, Sir," Kit said, handing the headmaster the cane, his head still bowed respectfully, hoping not to make matters worse. He snuck a glance at Jonathan standing in the corner, the tip of his cock just peeking out between his shirttails. Kit knew his own would be begging for attention the moment the headmaster ordered him to lower his pants.

Devon's fingers curled around the cane, and he took a swing that cut the air with an audible hiss. He saw Jonathan's posture stiffen where he stood to the side, but his main attention was focused on Kit, whose eyes widened. His olive complexion paled at the ominous sound—but his cock twitched noticeably, the damp spot growing on the front of his briefs. Devon paused, considering how best to position Kit to minimize the strain on his back, though the silence would only heighten Kit's tension.

The whoosh of the cane brought back memories of classmates made to suffer such punishments when he was a boy in school. Kit had always skated just shy of the line to end up in the front of the class being punished, but his classmates had generally considered the stripes as marks of pride afterward, so he figured it couldn't be too terrible an experience. His cock twitched as he waited silently for the headmaster's next order.

Eyeing the chair Jonathan had been sitting in when he entered, Devon nudged it forward with his foot until it was positioned where he wanted it. "Bend forward over that," he instructed. "Take down your trousers, hold on to the back, and don't let go until I tell you."

Kit followed the instructions to the letter, letting his trousers and briefs drop to his ankles before reaching for the back of the chair. The air in the room was cool on his bare backside, making him hyperaware of his partial nudity. He was sure that was the intention. It certainly had the effect of making his cock stand up and take notice.

Devon's eyebrows rose, and he didn't try to hide his smile as Kit shifted into place as ordered, his bare arse lifted temptingly. "This excites you, boy?" he growled, using the tip of the cane to stroke up the underside of the younger man's erect shaft. "Think you're going to enjoy it?"

"No, Sir," Kit replied automatically, even as his body made a lie of his words, his cock twitching eagerly at the currently painless touch. Devon arched an eyebrow at him. "I don't know, Sir," Kit replied more honestly, "but...."

"You needn't think I'm going to take it easy on you." Devon flexed his wrist, the movement vibrating up the supple length of wood to stir it against Kit's cock. "You think sucking cock makes you a man? Let's see if you can take your punishment like one, then."

Watching from the corner, Jonathan bit his lip to keep from asking Devon to let him take Kit's blows, or at least to let him go first. He understood that Kit wanted this; more, that Kit needed to prove, to his own satisfaction, that his lovers accepted that he didn't need to be coddled. That didn't mean it would be any easier to watch.

"I'll do my best, Sir," Kit answered hoarsely. Devon truly was a master. Each little brush of the cane, each comment, stretching the moment out, wound Kit's nerves tighter and tighter until he was all but vibrating with an odd mixture of anticipation, fear, and desire. He could feel Jonathan's gaze on him as well. He glanced back over his shoulder, seeking his lover's blue eyes. He read the concern there, even across the room, and wished he could reassure Jonathan again that he was here willingly, but he didn't want to say anything that would shatter the illusion they'd created. He settled for a tremulous smile, hoping that would fit the character and meet his goal.

Not missing the exchange of glances between the two "schoolboys," Devon twitched the cane one more time, sending Kit's cock bouncing against his belly, before drawing it back. Instead of swinging it, he brought it to rest almost tenderly against Kit's backside, letting the silence build until even Jonathan was stirring with restlessness. Then, without warning, he flexed his wrist, the length of rattan jumping up and making contact again with an audible crack.

"Oh, fu—fu—fu—fudge," Kit stuttered, trying to stop the expletive before it turned into another blow. Unable to stop himself, he reached for his stinging backside, rubbing at the smarting flesh. His erection wilted with the pain, but he was determined to see this through. And he was quite sure Devon would reward him for it later.

Gentling his swing, Devon delivered a warning rap against Kit's knuckles, just enough to sting. "Move that hand or you won't be using it for a week," he warned. Kit snatched his hand back quickly, revealing a vivid red welt across the fleshiest part of his buttocks. The corners of Devon's lips rose in the ghost of a smile; he hadn't lost his touch. "Very pretty," he purred, glancing up at Jonathan, who was watching with wide eyes. "Five more," he reminded, raising the cane again. "Count them out, Webster." The rattan whistled and a second line blossomed, parallel to the first.

"Two, Sir," Kit gasped as the second strike landed. He almost called a halt, but Devon's words echoed in his head, and for the first time, he truly understood the mentality of a sub who would accept something uncomfortable in order to please his Dom. This had started at his request, but it was more than that now. He wanted to make Devon proud of him, wanted to wear his master's marks. His head dropped as he panted slightly through the pain, waiting for the next blow to fall. To his surprise, as he let himself go, the pain faded enough to make room again for the same pleasure he had known when Devon spanked him.

Jonathan's nails bit into his palms, his fists clenching harder when the second blow fell. His cock softened as he watched, finding nothing erotic about seeing Kit suffer. If the cane were marking his own backside, maybe, but watching Kit struggle against voicing his pain was more difficult for Jonathan than taking the strokes himself. He wanted to close his eyes, but he knew he needed to keep watching, owing Kit the acceptance of his wishes even as he'd asked Kit to accept his own desire to have Devon fist him two weeks ago. At least now he better understood why Kit had reacted the way he did. Watching was completely different than experiencing.

The pause between blows gave the heat a chance to spread over Kit's arse so that the sting eased slightly. When the third blow still hadn't fallen after almost half a minute, he turned his head, seeking Devon's eyes and the reassurance that he had not somehow disappointed the schoolmaster.

Devon knew what Kit's glance was asking, but he refused to be rushed, waiting until the dark head turned away again before raising his arm. The cane whistled a third time, the evenly spaced mark a perfect mirror of its predecessors. Kit's gasp was louder this time, the pause longer before he managed a choked, "Three... Sir."

Kit's head hung between his arms as he tried to breathe through the spreading pain. He'd made it halfway. He could make it the rest of the way. He simply had to. He couldn't disappoint Devon by calling uncle halfway through the scene.

Devon paused, his hesitation this time less about ratcheting up the tension than assessing Kit's condition. The three welts would be throbbing fiercely, though he'd been careful not to strike hard enough to break the skin. He knew exactly how Kit's arse would feel—as if it were on fire, the slightest breath of air as he moved enough to fan the flame even higher. He had his doubts as to whether his lover could bear another three blows, but assuming he knew what Kit could handle was what had led them to this point in the first place. Rubbing his wrist, he glanced across the room to where Jonathan stood in the corner, eyes fixed on Kit's face, his teeth worrying his lower lip. This was nearly as hard on Jonathan as it was on either of them. Suddenly wanting the session over with, Devon flicked his wrist again, adding a fourth mark, lower this time, close to the crease where Kit's arse met his thighs.

Kit moaned when the fourth blow fell, his knees buckling slightly as the pain washed over him. He opened his mouth to try to count the blow, but he couldn't make the words come out. He took a deep breath and tried again, but he simply could not do it. "Frodo," he gasped instead, stomach churning at the thought of opting out of the scene early, but he simply could not take another blow, much less two. He looked over at Jonathan, seeing sympathy on his face, then up at Devon. "I'm sorry, Sir."

The session ending as soon as Kit uttered his safeword, Devon dropped to his knees beside the chair, the cane falling forgotten from his grasp. Knowing better than to touch the reddened backside yet, he ran a soothing hand through Kit's hair. "You've nothing to apologize for," he assured him, fingers tracing Kit's jaw, lifting his chin to meet his gaze. "Nothing—and nothing to prove. You know your limits, and you were smart enough to recognize when you reached them." He motioned Jonathan over to join them, his other hand closing over Kit's where they still gripped the back of the chair. "Jon, go fetch the jar from the dresser. It will help ease our kitten's tender backside."

Sinking to his knees, careful to keep his arse far away from his heels, Kit leaned toward Devon, needing the touch to reaffirm his Dom's encouraging words. The tender use of the most intimate of the nicknames his lovers had given him helped ease some of his fears, but the scene had left him uncertain. He'd been so confident he could handle this, and to have that confidence shaken left him in need of comfort. From both his lovers.

Devon wrapped his arms carefully around Kit and smoothed his palms up and down the trembling back. "Proud of you," he murmured, hoping Kit knew he meant more than just his ability to bear the blows. Recognizing that he couldn't assume Kit would understand, he clarified, "Proud that you trusted me enough to use your safeword."

Jonathan knelt beside them, offering the open jar of salve to Devon. He wasn't sure if it was acceptable for him to speak yet, but he let his free hand curl around Kit's where it hung at his side, offering his own silent comfort.

Not releasing his grip on Devon's waist, Kit reached for Jonathan as well. "I'm sorry you got left out," he said, remembering how he'd felt watching Devon and Jonathan together. He didn't want a repeat of that now. Not when they were finally back on track again. At least he hoped they were still on track after this fiasco.

"Don't be," Jonathan answered, stroking Kit's cheek after Devon took the jar from him. "I would have taken them for you if I could, but I'm just as happy to skip them. If Devon doesn't mind?" he added, his gaze moving from one lover to the other.

Devon shook his head, dipping up a generous portion of the balm. "I know this wasn't your scene, Jon," he said. "Not really mine either, truth be told. School couldn't have ended soon enough for me; I don't feel any special need to relive those memories." Gently, he spread the cool salve over the welts on Kit's buttocks. "That help some, sunshine?"

Kit nodded, shifting experimentally as the salve eased the burning somewhat. "I messed things up again, didn't I, asking for more than I could handle?"

Setting the jar aside, Devon shifted to kneel beside the chair, taking Kit's hand in both of his. Dealing with his sub's emotional state was often more crucial than tending to the physical aftereffects, especially when a scene ended the way this one had—the damage could be far worse if he mishandled it. "You didn't mess anything up," Devon assured him, his gaze holding Kit's, filled with love and pride. "Let's get you off this chair and into bed, and then we can talk about it. Your back and your backside will thank you for it."

Jonathan rose to his feet, one hand still holding Kit's, the other cupping his elbow to help him stand from his bent-over position. He didn't miss the wince as Kit's back straightened; his gaze flashed worriedly to Devon, who nodded in reassurance. "C'mon, Kit, bed sounds good to me too right now."

Kit let them help him into the bedroom, still too unsettled to do more than follow where they led. He wanted to believe their reassurances, but a part of him still felt like he'd failed his Dom. He stood still as Devon unbuttoned his shirt and helped him finish undressing. His back twinged and his arse ached. And his heart pounded as he waited to see if Devon or Jonathan would pull away.

As Devon dropped Kit's clothes onto a chair, Jonathan helped Kit ease down to the bed and shift onto his side. The position kept Kit's arse clear of the mattress and gave Jonathan his first close-up view of the angry red welts marking it. He bit back the instinctive words of sympathy before they could escape his lips, reminding himself that Kit had asked for this, partly to prove he was stronger than he thought Devon and Jonathan considered him. The last thing Jonathan wanted was to say anything that Kit might interpret as pity or condescension. Instead, he lay on the bed behind Kit, careful not to brush against the enflamed skin, and pressed a gentle kiss on his shoulder.

Devon joined them on the bed, facing Kit and Jonathan. He slid an arm over Kit's waist, the other hand tipping up Kit's chin to meet his eyes. "Better now?"

Kit started to nod, but Devon's piercing gaze refused to let him lie. Midmovement, he changed the nod to a shake of his head.

"You don't have to pretend to be strong for us," Devon murmured, relieved that Kit felt safe enough to give an honest answer. When Kit started to speak, he leaned in to stop the words with a soft kiss. "We need to talk this through. First of all, if you're thinking you disappointed me by safewording, don't. Do you remember when I told you about Blaine?" It still wasn't any easier for Devon to talk about that experience, but he had to put Kit's well-being above his own unease. When Kit gave a hesitant nod, Devon continued. "I knew the cutting was more than Blaine could take, but he wouldn't safeword. He was more afraid of Robert than he was of what I was doing to him." Even now, Devon's gut ached with remembered shame. "I don't ever want you to feel that way."

"I'm still a lousy excuse for a sub," Kit muttered. "I can't lose myself in our scenes the way Jonathan does."

Startled at Kit's admission, Jonathan shook his head in protest, but a concerned glance from Devon stopped him before he could speak. He squeezed Kit's shoulder instead, hoping the gentle touch could convey his loving support without words.

Devon slid a hand beneath Kit's chin, raising his head to meet his gaze. "Is Jonathan a better actor than you because he was cast as Arthur and you were cast as Percival?" When Kit didn't answer, he continued, "You're two different men, Kit. There isn't a single right way to be a sub, and it isn't a competition. Don't ever think I want you to be anyone but yourself, even—especially—during a scene. We each bring something unique into this relationship, and we each take something different from it, remember?"

Kit wanted to nod and say everything was all right and they could put this behind them, but he knew it would be a lie. "Then why do I feel like such a failure right now?"

"You are *not* a failure," Devon insisted. He was prepared to repeat that to Kit as often and as emphatically as he needed to until Kit believed it. "Can you tell me what was different between what you expected from the scene and what happened?" He didn't want to diminish Kit's concern with a facile dismissal, but he needed to understand what was driving Kit's emotions before he could try to deal with them.

"The headmaster never used the cane on me at school," Kit admitted, "but my classmates never acted like it was any big deal. I didn't expect it to hurt so much more than the spanking. I wanted to take it because you wanted me to, but it hurt so much I couldn't even stand."

"I didn't want to cane you, Kit," Devon reminded him gently. "The scene was your idea, remember? I know you don't get the same high from working through pain as Jon or I do, but if I'd stopped when I could see it was getting to be too much for you, I'd be doing just what you called us on before—going into 'protect Kit' mode." He ran his hand over Kit's jaw, his thumb caressing his cheek. "You recognized when you'd hit your limit, and you admitted it. That's exactly what you wanted to prove to us—that you can make your own decisions. Looking at it in that light, I'd say the scene was a success."

"Then why don't I feel that way?" Kit asked, though his voice had lost a little of its desperation.

Devon shook his head. "That's something you'll need to come to terms with yourself, though if anyone failed here, it was me." He ran his thumb over Kit's lips when Kit started to protest. "No, it's true. A Dom is supposed to know his sub's limits, sometimes better than the sub does himself. At a gut level, I knew it was too big a step to go from spanking to caning, but you were so determined we'd been coddling you that I didn't challenge you on it. I set you up to fail."

Kit bit back a sob. "Sometimes I don't know why you put up with me and my headstrong ways, but I'm glad you do. I'm glad you both do. Maybe someday I'll get it right."

"Ah, sunshine, I could say the same about you and Jon putting up with me." Devon brushed the moistness from Kit's lashes with a tender kiss. "Tonight isn't the time, but maybe you'd trust me enough to give us both another chance to set things right."

Kit nodded. "After my arse has a chance to heal."

Jonathan had remained silent while Kit and Devon talked, but now that Kit had recovered some of his composure, Jonathan ran a hand down Kit's hip, careful to avoid his sensitive backside. He didn't understand how Kit could possibly think he was a better sub than Kit was, and it made him feel guilty somehow, though he didn't know what he could do to make it better. Devon seemed to have reached Kit on an emotional level, though, so Jonathan decided it was time to reassure Kit on a purely physical level.

"Speaking from experience with a sore ass, it'll feel better in a day or two," Jonathan said softly, his lips nuzzling Kit's ear. "Rest for now and let us take care of you."

At Kit's nod, Devon dropped another gentle kiss on Kit's lips, then slid down on the mattress, placing kisses down the long throat, the smooth chest, the flat planes of Kit's abdomen as he went. Jonathan's hands slid around Kit's chest, caressing the warm skin, teasing gently at the tightening nipples, gliding lower to brush through Devon's hair before sliding upward again. Devon dipped his tongue into Kit's navel, causing a shiver of delight, then wove through the thin line of hair that led to Kit's cock, which was already stiffening at the sensual attentions. He closed his mouth around the head, swirling his tongue lightly as the shaft swelled and grew. Kit might not have gotten the pleasure he'd hoped from their session, but Devon was going to be sure he received it in full measure now.

If Kit's lingering doubts made him slower than usual to harden, even his worries could not defeat the seductive lure of Devon's mouth or the decadent thrill of Jonathan's hands. He thrust forward, only to hiss as his abused buttocks protested the movement. Devon caught his hips immediately in a firm grip, refusing to let him move, leaving Kit to simply lie there and enjoy the sensation. Slowly giving in to the convincing reassurance, Kit closed his eyes and drifted on the pleasure his lovers were bestowing on him. It wound higher and higher, spiraling through him until his body could no longer contain the bliss of knowing himself cherished by these two men. With a long sigh, he found his release down Devon's throat.

Jonathan watched in envy as Devon swallowed through Kit's trembling climax, then shifted upward to share a long, slow kiss. His own cock throbbed with need, and he could see Devon was in no better shape, but he knew neither of them would do anything about it at the moment. This had been for Kit, about easing his pain and showing him how much he was loved. Devon's hand met Jonathan's over Kit's chest and squeezed in silent concurrence. Spooning as best he could around Kit without pressing against his striped backside, Jonathan squeezed Devon's hand back and curled his other around Kit's hip, letting his eyes drift closed. They'd all be better for a short rest.

CHAPTER 18
FAVORITE THINGS

DEVON SMOOTHED a hand over his leathers as he considered the contents of his toy box. Kit had agreed to give Devon another chance to stretch his limits without forcing him past them. Devon knew Kit didn't see it that way; Kit thought Devon was giving him another chance to prove himself. In the end, Devon realized, it all came down to trust—Devon trusting Kit to find his limits without crossing them, and Kit trusting that Devon might by now know more about Kit than Kit did about himself in some respects. Knowing how much Kit approved whenever he wore the butter-soft black trousers, Devon wasn't above using every advantage he could to make sure this time it turned out right. He didn't usually plan a scene much in advance, preferring the freedom to adapt the play to the reactions of his sub, but after he'd bolloxed up Kit's last session so badly, he wasn't about to take any chances this time.

Since the fiasco of their last session was due to his failure to stop Kit from insisting on more than he was ready to handle, Devon was going to start tonight with all the things Kit had found especially pleasurable in their previous scenes. Devon removed anything from the box that he hadn't already used on Kit, not wanting to introduce more than one new element—a riding crop in place of the cane—to this evening. Looking over what that left in the box brought a smile to Devon's face as he remembered the sessions when they'd used the plug, the nipple clamps, the soft suede restraints. The blindfolds and gags went into the pile of items he'd discarded—Kit needed to be able to see what Devon was doing and voice his concerns, if any, though Devon was going to do his damnedest to be sure he didn't give Kit cause to protest this time.

He was still a little concerned about the role Jonathan would play during the session. Devon's first impulse had been to ask Jonathan to stay away so Devon could focus all his attention on Kit. Jonathan hadn't been willing to accept that at all.

"Don't ask me not to be there, Devon," Jonathan had pleaded. "I'll sit in a corner and not say a word if that's what you want, but don't shut me out. It was hard enough knowing I couldn't do anything to help when you and Kit were trapped by the mudslides. If I'm not there, I'll make myself crazy imagining what's going on. I promise I won't interfere with whatever you're doing, but I can't not be there."

Devon could understand that, but he could also imagine how hard it would be for Jonathan to be present but excluded from participating in the session. Still, this wasn't just about him and Kit. All three of them were in this relationship, and Jonathan needed to be a part of Kit's coming to terms with his own limits as much as Devon did.

"It's not that I don't trust you—you know that, don't you?" Jonathan radiated such sincerity and confidence that Devon had no doubts on that score. "Kit was just so shaken after he used his safeword, so sure he'd failed."

Jonathan shook his head; from his perspective, Kit didn't have a damn thing to prove, but he was enough of a rider to know that when you were thrown, you got right back on the horse. "I want him to know I'm there for him."

In the end, Devon agreed Jonathan needed to be present, though he was still debating how much of a part to let him take in the scene. Kit's perception that he wasn't the sub Jonathan was still concerned Devon. He couldn't risk turning the session into any kind of comparison between the two.

The last item he set atop the toy box was the riding crop. He'd never used it with Kit or Jonathan before. While it resembled the cane that had been Kit's undoing in their last scene, the crop was easier to control and could be far less painful. It would still make a nice audible whistle through the air, but the contact came from the leather flap at the tip, spreading the force of the blow across a wider area than the narrow, whippy rattan cane. His plan was to rebuild Kit's confidence using items he already associated with pleasure before asking him to accept the crop. Devon remembered how hard Kit had gotten off from being spanked. While the crop could deliver a more intense sensation than Devon's hand alone, he didn't think it was more than Kit could take.

He only hoped he was right. He didn't want to think about what would happen if he judged wrong again.

"YOU'RE SURE Devon didn't say anything to you about what he had planned tonight?" Kit already knew the answer. He and Jonathan had been over this twenty times if they'd been over it once, but the suspense of spending a day off knowing that when he and Jonathan went to Devon's house that night, Devon would be taking charge and trying to restore the balance they'd lost when Kit foolishly demanded more than he could handle had Kit on the edge of his seat. He almost wished Devon had decided to have this session at the end of a workday, so Kit would have had the distraction of being Percival to keep him from obsessing about tonight.

"He didn't tell me anything except to make me promise to do whatever he told me and stay quiet the rest of the time," Jonathan answered. He hesitated, wondering if it would do more harm than good to bring up the subject that had been gnawing at him ever since the night Kit had used his safeword. It was obvious Kit was on edge about what would happen tonight, and Jonathan didn't want to do anything to make that worse, but he'd promised on the night Kit had walked in on Devon fisting him that he wouldn't keep things hidden from Kit either. "You don't really think you're not as good a sub as I am, do you?" he finally asked in an uneasy voice.

"You're ten times the sub I am," Kit said with a short laugh. "I can't keep my mouth shut to save my life. I can't relax into Devon's control the way you do. I'm always pushing for more. Topping from the bottom, I think he called it once. You don't do that. You don't fight his control the way I can't seem to stop myself from doing."

"That's because I don't know what the fuck I'm doing," Jonathan protested. "You and Devon are both so much more experienced than I am. Half the time I don't know what to expect, let alone what to ask for. The rest of the time I'm coming so hard I can't think straight."

Kit snorted. "Damn good thing, since there isn't much straight about anything we've done together since the night we seduced you." Sobering a little, he sat down on the couch next to Jonathan. "You might not have much experience with gay sex, but it isn't about the sex. What we're doing with Devon as our Dom isn't a gay thing or a straight thing. I don't have any more experience with that than you do, and you've adapted to it far better than I have. I have yet to relax into a session unless I'm the one in charge or unless Devon has trussed me up so tight I can't do anything but take what he wants and come like mad."

"Maybe that's why it's easier for me to relax," Jonathan answered. "Most of the time, outside of this, I'm the one expected to take charge.

I can let go of that and trust Devon or you to take control during a scene because I know you'll take care of me. I don't think I could let myself put that much trust in anyone but the two of you."

"I'm making mountains out of molehills, aren't I?" Kit asked. "I mean, if we aren't doing anything particularly kinky, if we're just making love, everything's fine, regardless of who suggests what or what position we end up in. I need to just relax and treat the kinkier stuff the same way I treat the regular stuff." He sighed and snuggled beneath Jonathan's arm. "I wish we could go back to the beach house. Everything seemed so simple then."

Jonathan didn't contradict Kit, despite remembering his own crisis of jealousy that weekend when Devon had claimed Kit over the porch rail. "No matter where we are, I think you can trust Devon, and I hope you can trust me." Jonathan lowered his face into Kit's dark hair and kissed the top of his head. "You know we'd never do anything to consciously hurt you, and we're trying our best not to make you feel like we're overprotecting you. Don't build this up in your mind into some kind of test that you have to pass or fail. It's just going to be Devon and me, loving you. That's all it ever is, or none of this would mean anything and there wouldn't be a reason for any of it."

Kit smiled, enormously reassured by Jonathan's words. "As long as you both still love me, everything else is secondary. What time do we need to leave to join Devon?"

Jonathan glanced at his watch. "We should get going. We could explain to Devon if we were late, but I'd rather not start the session on that note." He rose to his feet, keeping his arm around Kit and drawing him up with him. "I wouldn't be surprised if he's almost as jumpy as you are."

"Not possible," Kit said, standing. "Is there anything we need to do before we leave?"

"Not unless there's anything you want to bring with you to Devon's." Jonathan's smile didn't hide the hunger underneath it. "I'm hoping none of us will be leaving until we have to report back to the set on Monday morning."

DEVON PACED the floor, catching himself when he started to glance at his watch for the third time in five minutes. Realizing he was working himself into a state that would hardly be conducive to overseeing a scene, especially one as important as this, he halted in the middle of the room. Taking a deep breath, he focused on his anxiety, breathing smoothly and deeply until the knot of tension began to unravel and his innate self-confidence returned to the fore. *You can do this*, he told himself. *This is Kit, not a stranger. You know what gives him pleasure, and you know how far you can take him to make it that much better.* He wouldn't be alone either. Jonathan would be there too, grounding them both with his quiet strength and unquestioning love.

The sound of a car door closing broke him out of his reverie. After a final glance around the room to be sure everything was ready, he walked out of the bedroom to open the door for his lovers.

Kit was surprised when Devon met them at the door rather than letting them use their keys to come inside, but it reassured him in a way as well. Maybe Devon *was* as nervous about this as he was. As counterintuitive as that seemed, it helped settle his nerves to the point that he could walk into Devon's embrace, seeking shelter and safety. Devon's arms closed around him immediately. Kit inhaled deeply, smelling musk and man and the amazing, earthy smell of Devon's leathers. "I love you."

"And I love you, sunshine." Kit had never deserved the nickname more, Devon thought, just his smile and the surety of his love enough to banish the last dark tendrils of doubt from Devon's mind. He looked up and held out a hand to Jonathan, drawing him into the circle of their embrace. "And you no less."

Jonathan wove an arm around Kit's waist, the other around Devon's shoulders. How far they'd come—how far *he'd* come—from that moment at the beach cottage when he thought Devon's claim on Kit was excluding him. He had no doubts now; his lovers had shown him time and again that their hearts—all three of their hearts—had room for more than one love.

Kit turned his head to kiss Jonathan, not wanting him to feel excluded. He knew the focus of the next hour would be primarily on him, and he didn't want that to make Jonathan question his place in their lives again. "Love you," he murmured with a quick nip to the lush lower lip before turning his gaze back to Devon. When emerald eyes met his, he lowered his lashes, consciously trying to put himself in a place of submission. "What do you want me to do, Sir?"

"Into the bedroom with you," Devon said, easing his embrace so Kit could slip free. "Strip and put on your cock ring. There's one on the bed if you don't have yours with you."

"I brought mine, Sir. I wanted to be prepared for whatever you wanted." He glanced up from beneath his lashes, hoping the initiative would please his Dom.

"Good lad." Devon smiled and sent Kit on his way with a pat to his delectable arse, then turned to Jonathan. "I'd like you to be there for Kit," he said, then kissed him in this moment before he settled fully into his Dom role. Still wary of Kit's perception that Jonathan was a better sub than he was, Devon had decided not to ask Jonathan to take a more active role, not wanting Kit to feel he was treating either of them any differently than a normal session. "Don't speak unless I ask you a question, and I'll expect you to follow my instructions just like any other scene, but stay in his line of vision, even if you're not a part of what's happening at the time. Just seeing you will help keep him centered and remind him of how strong he is."

"How strong we are together," Jonathan replied, pulling Devon into his arms. "You're as much a part of that strength as I am, and you'll give Kit just what he needs. Love you—Sir." With a final smile over his shoulder, Jonathan followed Kit into the bedroom, slipping buttons free as he went.

Kit had let his clothes drop to the floor as he stripped, but the careful organization of the bedroom drew him up short. He went back and picked up his discarded garments, folded them, and set them carefully out of the way on the chest. Taking inventory of the items on the bed, he fastened the cock ring around the base of his burgeoning erection, the kiss in the hall and the anticipation of what was to come enough to have him already partially worked up. He smiled at the sight of the nipple clamps, the chain with the weights sitting next to it this time, and the medium-sized butt plug, the one that filled him but left him tight enough that he still felt Devon's girth when he fucked Kit later. The restraints were familiar as well, but the last item brought him up short. He'd watched the horse trainers on set use crops on their mounts. He wasn't quite sure how he felt about seeing one on the bed. Before his nerves could get the better of him, though, Jonathan's arms closed around him from behind, his lips nuzzling Kit's neck.

"Looks like Devon picked all your favorite toys," Jonathan murmured. "Those clamps are going to look so good on you, kitten." His erection nudged against Kit's cheeks, but he resisted the urge to rut against the firm ass. Jonathan suspected he wouldn't get off during the session; he could take care of his arousal, or one of his lovers would help him with it, once they were finished.

Kit pushed back against Jonathan, the thought of the clamps pinching his nipples stoking his need. Without thinking that Devon might object, he drew Jonathan's fingers to his chest, asking silently for the stimulation his mind already anticipated.

Leaning forward so he could kiss Kit's cheek, Jonathan plucked at the pebbled nubs on Kit's chest. He didn't expect to be able to touch Kit once the scene started, so he'd take advantage of the short time he had now. "Love you," he murmured. "Devon's going to make you feel so good."

"Seems someone's started without me," Devon remarked from the doorway, though the humor in his voice made it clear he wasn't really upset.

"What do you expect when you leave us alone?" Jonathan smiled unrepentantly, stepping back to finish undressing. He set his clothes beside Kit's, retrieved his own cock ring from his pocket, and fastened it around himself before sinking gracefully to his knees.

Kit took a deep breath and moved in front of Devon, mimicking Jonathan's pose. He wanted to speak, to offer himself to Devon again, but he needed this scene to go well, and so he schooled himself to silence, not wanting to break one of the earliest rules Devon had given them before the scene even began. Instead, he pressed his cheek against Devon's thigh and made himself wait for whatever came next.

Devon let a hand settle on Kit's hair, standing silent for a moment in thanks for these two exceptional men. Then he turned his head to look at Jonathan. "Bring me the cuffs."

As Jonathan rose to do his bidding, Devon stroked soothingly through Kit's hair. He could feel the slight tremble shaking Kit's frame, but he judged it was anticipation, not fear. When Jonathan knelt before him, offering the suede-lined restraints, Devon took them and pointed Jonathan to move to the foot of the bed. "Arms behind you," he directed Kit, unfastening the cuffs.

Kit crossed his wrists behind his back, unable to stop a shiver of delight when the soft restraints fastened, immobilizing his arms.

"Does that strain your back?" Devon asked, running a fingertip up the line of scar tissue from Kit's scoliosis surgery.

Kit smiled, gratitude surging through him at the care Devon had always shown for the limitations of his condition. "No, it's fine, Sir." Another time he might have said more, might have thanked Devon for his concern, but he was trying hard to be a model sub.

"Good. Tell me if it starts to bother you." Devon moved in front of Kit, mindful not to block his view of Jonathan. Kit's expression gave no sign of objecting to the reminder, which to Devon's mind wasn't coddling—he'd be as cautious with Jonathan if the other man had injured himself during filming, but he hadn't been sure Kit would take it the same way. Devon reached down to finger a nipple already tightened from Jonathan's attentions. "Bring me the clamps, Jon."

Jonathan retrieved the clamps and the weighted chain from the duvet. Though he kept his head down, he couldn't resist an oblique glance at Kit, who presented a picture of submissive acceptance, his posture erect, head bowed. Jonathan presented the items to Devon and moved back to his place without being told, though his eyes remained on Kit.

"You seemed to enjoy these the last time we used them," Devon said, holding his hand low enough that the clamps and accessories were clearly visible in his palm. "Since you did so well then, I thought we'd add the chain between them this time."

Kit refrained from speaking or even from nodding eagerly, but he couldn't stop from pushing his chest forward in invitation.

"Eager much?" Devon chuckled, giving the other nubbin a firm tweak.

"Very much so," Kit replied, flashing a grin at Jonathan. Devon *had* asked him a question, after all.

Jonathan didn't try to stop his grin in reply. Kit might never become a model sub, but his cheekiness was part of his charm, and he and Devon would never want that to change.

Devon merely shook his head, unable to rebuke Kit since he'd given the lad the opening to respond. "Cheeky brat," he murmured affectionately as he slid the bead up the first clamp, spreading its tweezer-like teeth. Dropping to one knee, he caught the nipple he'd pinched between his lips, tugging and dampening it until it stood hard and erect. Then he fitted the clamp over the nub, adjusting the tension to hold firmly but without pain.

Kit's breath caught in his throat when the constant pressure of the clamp replaced the wet heat of Devon's mouth. Catching his lower lip between his teeth, he waited impatiently for Devon to adorn the other side.

Even the slight hitch of Kit's breath was enough to start Devon hardening beneath his leathers. There was nothing as arousing as a responsive lover, and both of his were exceptional in that regard. Devon shifted to tease at Kit's other nipple, already thrust out for his attentions. He nipped it a little harder than the first one, fastened the clamp, and then sat back on his heels to admire the effect.

Kit bit his lip harder to hold back the flow of pleas that wanted to escape. Devon had merely touched him and he already wanted to beg. He had no idea how he'd make it through the rest of the session without breaking at least that rule.

Devon removed the individual weights from the chain and ran the links between his fingers. "I'm going to fasten this to the two clamps first and then add the weights." That would allow him to judge the point past which pleasurable awareness became pain. The chain itself was heavy enough to add a definite tug when he clipped it to the rings at the end of each clamp.

Kit moaned softly at the additional weight, every breath setting the chain swinging. He swayed as shivers of delight ran down his spine.

"You're doing fine," Devon praised, catching the arc of chain on his forefinger and tugging it just enough to pull the clamps taut on Kit's chest. He smiled at Kit's blissful hiss, selected one of the small weights, and fastened it to the center of the chain before letting it dangle free again. The rhythmic swing caught the light on the clamps' crystal beads, setting them sparkling. Watching Kit's face, Devon added a second weight to one side of the chain, then balanced it with a third on the opposite side, pausing when he caught a fleeting wince cross Kit's face. "That's enough, I think," he murmured, skimming beneath the links to caress Kit's skin with his fingertip. "Doesn't he look beautiful, Jonathan?"

"Beautiful," Jonathan agreed. He wished he'd been able to keep eye contact with Kit as Devon added the weights, but Kit had kept his eyes down, though from what Jonathan could see of his expression, it didn't look like the discomfort was more than Kit could take. "Always."

"Only for you, Sir," Kit said, smiling at Devon before darting a glance at Jonathan.

Once Jonathan might have felt excluded by Kit's comment, but the love in Kit's gaze was so clear he had no doubt the statement included him as well as Devon. He smiled in response before turning his eyes to their Dom, hoping Kit's speaking out of turn wouldn't earn him a reprimand.

"Never going to break you of talking when you're meant to be silent, am I?" Devon asked. "What am I going to do with you, sunshine?"

"Keep me, I hope?" Kit replied meekly. He had noticed the absence of gags on the bed and hoped that meant Devon didn't really intend to deprive him of speech.

"No doubt of that," Devon answered with a wry smile. "But I can hardly let you get away with flaunting the most basic rule." He rose to his feet and turned to Jonathan. "Bring me the chair from the desk, Jon."

Kit tensed at the mention of the chair they had used in their aborted session, but just as there had been no gags on the bed, the cane was equally absent. Whatever Devon intended, *that* was not it.

Jonathan set the chair at Kit's side, letting his arm brush against Kit's as he did so. It might earn him a rebuke in turn if Devon noticed it, but Devon had told Jonathan to be there for Kit, and he hoped the contact would remind Kit that he had Jonathan's support in whatever happened next.

Devon let Jonathan's touch pass without comment, glad he had found a way to remind Kit of his presence. He had plans to involve Jonathan even more, but he had Kit's intransigence to deal with first. Grasping Kit's shoulder, he helped him rise to his feet, and then turned him around to unfasten the chain that held the suede cuffs together. That this left Kit facing the chair on which he'd safeworded during the caning wasn't lost on Devon. He rubbed Kit's back in reassurance, hoping Kit's trust in him would get him past the bitter memory. "Can you hold on to the chair and not let go, or should I refasten the chain between the slats?"

"I won't let go," Kit promised, grasping the top rail of the chair. He had no idea what Devon intended, but whatever it was, Kit didn't want to be chained in place.

Kit's position, leaning forward over the straight-backed chair, put his arse within tempting reach. Resisting for the moment, Devon ran his palm down the path of Kit's spine, stopping before he reached his buttocks. He reached his other hand around Kit to give a light tug to the nipple chain, setting it swinging again. Only when the tightness in Kit's muscles eased did Devon bring his hand down in two swift swats, one to each of Kit's cheeks. "That's for the first time you talked out of turn."

Kit jumped in surprise at the love taps that stung slightly but didn't really hurt. His movement caused the weights on the chain between the clamps to bounce lightly, adding a second sharp jolt of sensation. Then the import of Devon's word penetrated. "First time? But the other times, you asked me questions!"

"That makes four," Devon retorted. "You know a rhetorical question when you hear one." Wrapping an arm around Kit's chest to brace him (and incidentally setting the weighted chain to rocking wildly) he rained six more slaps to Kit's backside, three to each cheek, turning them a lovely shade of blushing pink. Though judging by Kit's wriggling reaction, he'd have been happy for Devon to continue, the spurious reasoning behind the spanking had been satisfied. Devon let the arm around Kit's chest slide lower, grinning to himself when it bumped against a healthy erection. No doubt there that Kit was enjoying this! "Bring me the plug from the bed," he directed Jonathan, giving Kit's cock a quick tug before turning to open a drawer in his dresser.

Kit moaned happily at the thought of being filled, even if he would have preferred one of his lovers rather than a plug. He widened his stance to facilitate his penetration.

Jonathan returned with the butt plug just as Devon turned back with an obviously depleted tube of lube. He winked at Jonathan before holding the tube low enough to be in Kit's line of vision. "We seem to have a slight problem here," he drawled, dangling the empty tube. "What do you think we should do about it, Jonathan?"

"Let me rim him," Jonathan answered promptly, all but slavering at the prospect of being allowed to take an active part in the scene. "Sir," he added belatedly, recognizing that Devon's obsessive preparation would never have overlooked something as essential as having enough lube on hand.

"Go ahead, then," Devon agreed, ruffling Jonathan's hair as he dropped to his knees behind Kit.

Shifting his hands to the side of the chair, Kit let his palms slide down until they rested against the seat. The new position pushed his arse out directly into Jonathan's face.

"I didn't say you could move," Devon objected, swatting Kit's upraised bum. "I don't like the strain that will put on your back either. Stand up again."

Kit moved back into position, but even the reprimand couldn't temper his anticipation when Jonathan's hands parted his cheeks. Devon was a genius, Kit decided as Jonathan grasped his tingling backside. Jonathan's touch was no firmer than usual, but Kit's skin was ultrasensitive thanks to the spanking Devon had given him. He knew better than to expect Jonathan to dive right in, but it didn't make waiting any easier. By the time Jonathan's tongue finally made contact, Kit was mewling with rapture.

Despite his own eagerness, Jonathan started slowly, drawing his tongue along Kit's crease, wetting it thoroughly before focusing his attention on the quavering rosette. He traced its circumference, lapping over it without penetrating until he could feel Kit trembling against his palms. Before Kit could draw Devon's ire again by speaking, Jonathan curled his tongue and pierced the ringed muscle, experience having taught him the cadence that would drive Kit wild.

Jonathan was glad he'd had the foresight to put on his cock ring before they'd gotten started. The moaning and gasping sounds Kit made while Jonathan's tongue wet and spread him went straight to Jonathan's groin, hardening him almost painfully. If he hadn't needed both hands to keep Kit's cheeks apart, he'd be hard-pressed to keep from stroking himself to climax. As it was, he channeled all that need into delving as deep into Kit as his tongue could reach, inching his thumbs closer until he could work them in to spread the passage even wider in preparation for the thickness of the plug.

Devon remembered from the days they'd spent trapped by the mudslides how much Kit loved being rimmed. Watching the joy with which Jonathan tongue-fucked Kit now was nearly as arousing as if Devon had been doing it himself. He popped open a button on his leathers to ease the growing pressure on his cock as Kit's lewd noises increased in volume and intensity. The lad was close, without question. There was little doubt Jonathan was about to bring him there.

Nearly wild with the need to climax, Kit lifted his head to meet Devon's eyes. "Please, Sir, I need to come."

Noting that Kit had again spoken out of turn, which would play nicely into the next stage of Devon's plans, he simply answered, "Go ahead and come, then. But I'm not taking off your ring."

Now that he had Devon's permission to make Kit come, Jonathan decided that was tacit approval for more than just rimming. Besides, this scene was all about Kit—Devon wouldn't want to sidetrack things by stopping to discipline Jonathan. Not that Jonathan would care either way, as long as he could bring Kit to climax first. Flicking his tongue back and forth in the constricting channel, he eased one of his hands down until he could cup Kit's heavy sac, massaging the balls with his fingers, hoping the extra attention would be enough to push Kit over the edge.

The added provocation of Jonathan's hand started Kit's orgasm tingling at the base of his spine. The cock ring held it back to some extent, but it didn't take long before nothing could stop him from coming. His cock twitched dryly as all the sensations spread outward through his limbs, leaving his knees weak and his muscles trembling.

Jonathan remembered the muffled intensity of coming through his cock ring, and he did all he could to prolong the sensations, his tongue stroking as much of the quivering passage as it could reach while he rolled Kit's still-full balls in his palm. When Kit's hips finally buckled, the sagging posture pulling his ass away from Jonathan's face, he dared a gentle caress of Kit's cock, capturing the single pearl of liquid at its tip, before sitting back to wait for Devon's next command. Devon nodded him silently back to his previous spot beside the bed, turning his attention, as he should, back to Kit. Jonathan raised his fingers to his lips and savored the taste of Kit's bliss.

Devon ran a gentle hand up and down Kit's back until the worst trembling stopped, coming to rest just at the top curve of his buttocks. "Did Jon open you well enough to take the plug?" he asked. "Or do I need to send him off to find some more lube?"

Devon had asked Kit that question once before, at the beach cottage, but Kit's reaction this time was completely different. "Yes, Sir, I can take it," Kit said breathlessly. The last thing he wanted was for Jonathan to leave the room.

The first time Devon had asked Kit that question, it was early days in their relationship, and he'd never used a plug on him before. They'd played with enough plugs of varying sizes since then that Devon had no doubt Kit could take this one easily, or he'd have retrieved the full tube of lube from his drawer without even asking Kit the question. Still, it stoked his pride when Kit answered without hesitation. Devon dipped two fingers inside Kit's moist passage, spreading them easily, more proof if he'd needed it of the efficacy of Jonathan's efforts. Keeping his fingers in place, he slotted the tapered head of the plug between them, easing it inside slowly enough to minimize any remaining discomfort when the resilient ring stretched to accept the wider base. "Good lad," he praised when Kit had taken it all.

Kit squirmed a little as the plug came to rest directly against his prostate. Every little movement would drive him wild. Hoping to provoke at least a few more swats, Kit turned to look at Devon over his shoulder. "Feels good, Sir, but not as good as your cock."

Devon had to laugh at Kit's comment—the lad was playing so perfectly into his plans, Devon could almost believe he'd read the script. "You're just asking for another spanking, aren't you?"

"Is that another rhetorical question, Sir?"

Even Jonathan laughed at Kit's pert response. "Right, then, but you're not getting away with a few love pats this time," Devon growled. He helped Kit straighten from his position over the chair and sat down in it, patting his knees. "Over m'lap with you, sunshine."

Kit all but dove into place, the deep rasp of Devon's voice doing unspeakable things to his already overactive libido. The inverted position caused the clamps to pull in the opposite direction on his pinched nipples, adding yet another layer of sensation. Squirming to get comfortable, he slid his hand around Devon's ankle.

"Hands off!" Devon chided, pulling his ankle free of Kit's grasp. "Jonathan, get over here and hold our boy's hands still so he won't be grabbing me with them."

Jonathan responded with alacrity, crouching beside the chair and taking Kit's hands into his. He intertwined their fingers, squeezing gently, wishing he dared to bend forward and press a kiss to Kit's lips, though in Kit's current position, Jonathan would have to be lying beneath him on the floor to reach Kit's mouth. Even with Devon's relaxed restrictions, Jonathan doubted he'd be able to get away with that.

Kit returned the squeeze, waiting with bated breath for the promised spanking.

"Count them out," Devon said, wrapping one hand around Kit's chest to brace him. "How many did I give you the last time?"

"Twelve, Sir," Kit replied immediately.

"We'll have that many again, then." Devon flexed his wrist, letting the anticipation build before bringing his palm down on Kit's cheek. The blow was harder than his earlier swats, and with the added stimulation of the butt plug, it was enough to set Kit undulating beneath him before he responded with a husky, "One."

"One, Sir," Devon prompted, adding a second whack to Kit's other cheek.

"Two, Sir," Kit answered, sounding a little breathless.

The appropriate appellation won Kit a slight caress of his reddened backside before Devon landed the third blow, a little lower than before.

"Three, Sir." Kit's voice cracked on the number. Devon paused, flicking the nipple clamp he could reach with the hand around Kit's chest. Kit whimpered softly, and Devon rubbed his back with his other hand until he felt the muscles relax.

They made it to seven before Kit's voice cracked again. Devon paused longer this time, reaching between Kit's legs to play with his bollocks until he had Kit breathless for a different reason. He spaced the next four blows so they hit spots he hadn't struck before—the uppermost curve of Kit's buttocks, the tops of his thighs—until Kit's voice broke again and he struggled to choke out a garbled "Eleven. Sir."

This time Devon focused his attentions on the butt plug. Each blow had already stirred it in its channel, but Devon worked it in earnest, rubbing the head against Kit's prostate until he judged Kit was nearly ready to come a second time before he stopped. Caressing Kit's back in a loving massage, he delivered the last blow firmly across the center of Kit's arse, driving the plug as deep as it could go with the force of the blow.

"Twelve, Sir," Kit said with a gasp of relief, shoulders sagging as he relaxed. His entire body throbbed, his chest from the pull of the weights when each blow made the chains swing, his backside from the swats, his erection from the pressure of the plug against his prostate. When Devon didn't immediately give him another order, he wondered if the session was over. He rather hoped it wasn't.

"You did well, lad, very well," Devon said, rubbing his tingling palm. It was a good thing he had something else in mind for what came next. "Jonathan, help Kit stand up."

Jonathan had held on to Kit's hands throughout the spanking, his grasp tightening reflexively at each blow. He'd been on the receiving end of Devon's spankings before, but never while wearing a plug, and imagining what it would feel like to have Devon's swats pressing against it made his own ass clench and his cock twitch in reaction. While he didn't want to lose contact with Kit by letting go of his hands, it would be too awkward to help him up that way, so he braced Kit's hands against his thighs and gently lifted Kit's shoulders instead, easing him back onto his feet. As soon as Kit was upright, he stood himself and stepped around the chair, wrapping Kit in his arms. "I'm so proud of you," he murmured, giving in to the temptation to kiss his lover. "You took all twelve and didn't make a sound except to count them."

Devon let Kit lean into Jonathan's embrace without protest, knowing Kit would need the support to stand steady, at least for a few minutes. Watching his two lovers together gave him an idea, and he rapidly adjusted his plans for the rest of the session. While Jonathan whispered praise into Kit's ear, Devon moved the chair aside and picked up the crop from the bed, tucking it into the back waistband of his leather pants.

"Enough of that, now," Devon said, working a hand between Jonathan and Kit to tug on the weighted nipple chain. "I expect you'd both be more comfortable without these poking and pulling." He turned Kit in Jonathan's arms until they stood back to chest. Resting his thumbs on the ends of the nipple clamps, he slid the adjusting beads down with his fingers, releasing the pressure and removing both clamps at the same time.

Kit let out a hoarse shout as the blood rushed back into his nipples, sending a flash of pain and pleasure along his nerves. His head fell back against Jonathan's shoulder, making him grateful for the support. Panting, he opened eyes that had fallen closed and met Devon's glittering gaze. He couldn't stop another groan as his Dom lowered his head and licked each swollen bud thoroughly.

Jonathan slid his arms to Kit's hips, holding him stable as Devon laved his chest. He would have gladly assisted Devon in that cause, but it was almost as good to feel Kit leaning back against him. Jonathan's cock rested awkwardly against Kit's ass, the crease it would have nestled into obstructed by the base of the butt plug. The reddened flesh was warm against Jonathan's, making him wonder how much Devon would object if he slid down to soothe the marks of Devon's hand in the same way Devon was easing the sting of Kit's pinched nipples. Now that he had Kit in his arms, Jonathan couldn't bear the thought of being relegated back to the role of mere observer for whatever else Devon had in store for Kit.

As if he could read Jonathan's thoughts, Devon raised his head, meeting Jonathan's gaze. Taking a step back, he turned Kit in Jonathan's arms again, putting them face-to-face. Kit's face lifted to Jonathan's and their lips met, as naturally as their bodies fit together, chest to chest, hip to hip, thigh to thigh. Devon enjoyed the picture the two made a moment more and then tapped Jonathan on the shoulder, reclaiming his attention.

"Hold Kit just like that," he instructed Jonathan. Having Jonathan's strength to lean on, literally as well as figuratively, would ground Kit far more securely than any restraints—enough, Devon hoped, to get them through this last stretch of Kit's limits. "But keep your hands above his waist or I won't be responsible for the consequences."

Kit didn't even think to look back at Devon to see what he had planned. He'd seen the riding crop on the bed earlier, the only implement Devon hadn't used on him yet, so he figured that was next. At the moment, though, it could have been the cane in Devon's hand and he didn't think he'd be worried. Not with Jonathan holding him so securely and Devon touching him so tenderly. He tilted his head up for another kiss as Jonathan's hands splayed across his shoulder blades, rubbing his distended nipples through Jonathan's chest hair. Kit barely even jumped when the leather slapper nipped the upper curve of his arse.

The last tightness in Devon's chest eased when Kit scarcely flinched at the slap of the crop. He hadn't talked with Kit about it first, hoping his lover trusted him enough to accept that the unfamiliar instrument would not be more than he could endure. That Kit had let him continue without protest filled him with pride and love.

Jonathan raised his head from the kiss to look over Kit's shoulder at Devon. The impact of the crop had barely stirred Kit against him, and Kit hadn't reacted in pain, but Devon had never used the crop on either of them before, so Jonathan had nothing to compare it with. It looked intimidating, but it didn't seem as painful as the wooden paddle Devon had spanked him with before. Mindful of Devon's warning, Jonathan let one hand slide down Kit's back to rest on the swell of his ass. He had no doubts that Devon would not use anything that could actually hurt Kit; he was just curious what the crop would feel like.

Holding back a smile, Devon aimed the next stroke higher, letting the edge of the slapper catch Jonathan's hand. He knew from experience it wouldn't give more than a slight sting; though Jonathan's hand wasn't as sensitive as Kit's backside, especially after the spanking, Devon wasn't wielding the crop hard enough to truly hurt either of them. "Are you asking me to use this on you next?" he asked, raising an eyebrow at Jonathan.

"Whatever would please you most, Sir," Jonathan answered softly. He hadn't meant to turn Devon's focus away from Kit, so he raised his arm back to Kit's shoulder blade, meeting Kit's questioning gaze with a smile and another lingering kiss.

The exchange between the two penetrated Kit's consciousness, but it wasn't enough to rouse him from the plane of euphoria where he was drifting, endorphins and passion mixing together to leave his heart pounding and his head spinning. As long as one or both of them kept touching him, he didn't care what they did to each other. He just needed their hands or their lips on him. Since Jonathan seemed perfectly happy to oblige, Kit lost himself in their kiss, each little bite of the crop causing his hips to rock against Jonathan's cock until he was rutting against him like a cat in heat, moaning into the kiss and almost as desperate to come as he had been when Jonathan was rimming him.

After a dozen strikes of the crop, Devon realized Kit was beyond feeling the blows unless he was willing to use far more force. That wasn't the purpose of this exercise. He'd wanted to show Kit that he could face a challenge that pushed him beyond his comfort zone, to erase the perception of failure that colored their previous scene, and he'd succeeded beyond his hopes. Devon let the crop fall to his side. Kit didn't seem to notice the cessation any more than he had the blows, so lost was he in Jonathan's embrace and kisses. Suddenly, the arousal Devon had forced himself to ignore as he saw to Kit refused to be repressed any longer. Unfastening the remaining buttons on his leather trousers, he let his cock spring free, wanting nothing more than to bury it deep in Kit's arse.

Well, why not?

Devon spared only a moment to pull a fresh tube of lube from his dresser drawer. He might have let Jonathan open Kit for the butt plug with nothing but spit, but after Kit had stood up to everything Devon had thrown at him, he wasn't about to risk hurting him now by fucking him dry. After spreading a generous coating of lube on his insistent erection, Devon tossed the tube on the bed next to the crop and stepped behind Kit. He pulled the plug out, smeared the gel left on his fingers around Kit's hole, and thrust inside, one hand gripping Kit's hip, the other grasping Jonathan's shoulder for leverage as he claimed Kit in the most primal of ways.

Kit cried out as Devon filled him, his body rocking hard against Jonathan. Jonathan pushed back with equal force, providing an erotic frottage that left Kit incoherent with need. His lovers set such a hard pace that he could not find a balance to move between them. He could only stand there locked in their embrace and let them ravish him. Kit thought that was the finest idea he had heard in a month of Sundays.

His head fell back against Devon's shoulder as a particularly powerful thrust nearly lifted him off the ground. Someone's hands, Devon's, he thought, worked their way between Kit's and Jonathan's chests to pinch his nipples, tearing another cry from his throat. He was soaring so high he thought he'd never come down, surrounded by his two lovers, driven out of his mind by their attentions, their love and faith in him. His body shuddered, fighting for the release the cock ring held back. He tried to let it go as he had the first time, climaxing despite the barrier, but he couldn't find the focus to release the tension. His bollocks drew up tight, his cock twitched with every brush of Jonathan's shaft against his, his nipples ached, and his entire body tingled. "Please!" he begged. "Let me come!"

When Devon's first thrust had slammed Kit against Jonathan, the only way Jonathan could keep on his feet was to push back just as forcefully. That this had the side effect of dragging his engorged cock firmly against Kit's was an unexpected bonus. Jonathan's grip on Kit's shoulder tightened, his other hand reaching farther to grab hold of Devon, needing the contact with both his lovers as much as the added stability. Every snap of Devon's hips pressed Kit against him, until it almost felt as if Devon was fucking them both. Every pump of Jonathan's hips in return increased the friction of cock against cock, setting sparks flaring through Jonathan's nerves. Kit's cry, echoing the chant growing in his own mind, was the match that set him off.

A nod from Devon granting him permission, Jonathan dropped his hand from Kit's shoulder between their bodies, fumbling blindly until he found the clasp of Kit's cock ring. As soon as he'd snapped it free, he groped for his own, shaking so hard he could barely work the release. Devon slammed into Kit again, making Kit's cock jump against Jonathan's as he came. The spurt of hot fluid between their bodies, easing the friction and letting them slide more freely against each other, was enough to trigger Jonathan's orgasm. Suddenly it was Devon holding them up as Jonathan shuddered in the throes of a climax that burned through his blood to every cell in his body.

The weight of both his lovers trembling against him was all Devon needed to spark his own release. With a guttural cry, he froze against Kit's back, his arms tightening around Kit and Jonathan, tears springing to his eyes as he shook with the ecstasy that flooded him. Luckily, Jonathan's support was enough to keep them all from sagging to the floor in a sated heap.

"Bed," Kit croaked, his balance nonexistent after everything Devon and Jonathan had made him feel. Fortunately, they seemed to agree with him, shuffling toward the wide expanse of Devon's bed and collapsing across it, Kit still caught firmly between them. He sighed with disappointment as the movement jostled Devon's cock from his passage, but he could feel the stickiness between his cheeks, and Devon was still pressed up against his back, Jonathan nestled against his chest, prolonging the sense of being precious to them both. "Thank you," he murmured after a while.

"Still feel like a failure?" Devon asked with a lazy smile.

Kit chuckled huskily. "No. Do you?"

Devon shook his head. "I feel like the luckiest bastard in the world."

"I think that makes three of us," Jonathan said, stretching his arm to enclose Kit and Devon both.

CHAPTER 19
THE SEND-OFF

"I THINK today might well have been the most intense scene between Arthur and Lancelot yet," Kit said as they drove home from the day's filming. "I couldn't decide whether Arthur felt more betrayed because Lancelot slept with Guinevere or because Lancelot didn't sleep with him."

"And given that Jon shagged me six ways from Sunday not six hours before, he deserves an Oscar nomination for his performance." Devon rubbed a hand over his arse with a grin. "M'backside's still feeling it."

"Don't think there's a category for 'Best Performance Boffing Your Costar.'" Jonathan turned the corner and pulled up in front of Devon's rental house. "Besides, miniseries aren't eligible for Oscars. Not that it wouldn't be quite an acceptance speech," he added with a chuckle.

Kit laughed. "I can see it now. 'Well, you see, Niall had all these ideas about highlighting the homoerotic tension between the knights, and Lancelot was such a stud, and I just couldn't help myself.' Something like that, Jon?" he teased, trailing his fingers over the backs of both his lovers' necks from his place in the back seat.

"I was thinking about recognizing the competition from my fellow nominees," Jonathan countered, capturing Kit's wandering hand and pressing a kiss to the teasing fingertips. "You and Devon would both get my vote."

"Can you imagine Niall filming a 'For Your Consideration' teaser for that award?" Devon's voice was shaking with laughter as they got out of the car. "At least he seemed happy with today's take. He shouldn't need Lancelot on set for the next couple of weeks."

Jonathan's grin wavered at the reminder of Devon's upcoming absence as they entered the house. "You're still planning to fly to LA during your break?"

"Might as well take advantage of the time," Devon agreed, hoping he sounded more positive than he felt. "The solicitors have most of the terms worked through, finally. Just a few more details to iron out and we should be able to sign the papers to finalize the divorce."

"You could wait until you're sure they're ready," Kit said, not wanting to beg, but he didn't want Devon gone for weeks. He could hardly stand it when they were apart for hours. It was why he'd come home from London early and gotten an eyeful a couple of weeks earlier. That had been traumatic, but it had made them stronger in the end.

Devon shook his head. "I'm ready to have it done." Not that he was looking forward to having to face the reality of his failed marriage, but his relationship with Marcy had been over for almost a year, and in trouble long before that. "I won't enjoy being gone—or the bloody long flights there and back—but at least I'll have coming back to both of you to look forward to."

"You can spend the time on the planes thinking up all sorts of devilish things to do to us when you get home," Kit proposed, rubbing the tense muscles in Devon's neck. "That will distract you from where you are."

"I don't know," Jonathan countered. "He might give his seatmate quite an eyeful. He'd have to keep a blanket over his lap the whole flight."

"And those airplane loos are too cramped for a proper wank," Devon agreed. "Those Viagra commercials warn about an erection lasting four hours—I don't even want to think about having to deal with one for eleven."

"There is that," Kit said with a laugh. "Well, you're not gone yet, so we can take care of your erection a few more times before you leave. When is your flight?"

"Friday morning. I wasn't sure how long it would take Niall to get the scenes he wanted."

"Then you have another full day before you have to leave." Jonathan wrapped his arms around Devon from behind, offering his silent support. His own divorce had been amicable, but that didn't mean he couldn't understand what Devon was going through. "And two more nights for us to take care of you before then."

"And we promise to take very, very good care of you," Kit said, moving in front of Devon so that he and Jonathan caught him between them. He matched his lips with Devon's, taking his time brushing their mouths together in a slow, sensual rhythm. They had all night and all of tomorrow night, and a day off tomorrow. They didn't need to rush.

"Since you always take such good care of us," Jonathan added, sliding his hands up Devon's chest to tweak his nipples, lips nuzzling at the back of Devon's neck. He could feel the tightness of the muscles beneath his fingers and mouth. Most nights, between Kit and himself, their combined attentions would have Devon melting between them—or taking command of the situation, to their unanimous pleasure. That he did neither, still carrying the stress-induced tension in his muscles as he leaned into the embrace and returned Kit's gentle kisses, told Jonathan that the upcoming trip had Devon tied up in knots even more strongly than he'd admitted to them. Devon's claustrophobia made him a poor flyer at the best of times—which these definitely weren't. There was no way Jonathan was letting Devon step on a plane in this condition. Raising his head, he caught Kit's eyes over Devon's shoulder. As sensitive as Kit was to his lovers' moods, he had to be sensing the same thing Jonathan was.

When Devon made no move to take control of his kiss, indeed barely responded to it at all, Kit pulled back, studying his face. He could see the lines of tension around Devon's mouth that usually faded as they left the set and went home together. Devon could joke all he wanted about the trip to LA giving him something to do while Lancelot was banished; he was taking it far more seriously than that. Glancing over Devon's shoulder, he saw a matching concern on Jonathan's face. "You all right there, luv?"

Devon forced his mind from the rut it seemed to be stuck in back to where it belonged—with his lovers. He'd deal with the divorce when he got to LA—he couldn't let it steal the time he had with Kit and Jonathan now, especially when it might be weeks before he could return. "Just not sure I can take care of m'self at the moment, let alone the two of you," he admitted wryly.

Kit grinned. "We already told you we were going to take care of you, remember?" He glanced at Jonathan with a raised eyebrow, offering him the opportunity to take charge if he wanted to.

Jonathan grinned back at the devilish sparkle in Kit's eyes but shook his head. As much as he loved giving in to either or both of his lovers, he seldom felt the desire to take control himself. Maybe it was selfish of him, but he relished being able to lose himself in their lovemaking without being responsible for anything more than pleasing Devon and Kit in return.

Kit had expected Jonathan's response, but now that he had it, he felt the weight of the responsibility for their evening fall heavily on him. Taking a deep breath and reminding himself that he didn't have to impress either of his lovers by being a perfect Dom, he nudged Devon toward the stairs. "Jonathan, take Devon upstairs to the bathroom and get him undressed. We'll help him relax a little, and then we'll see how wild we can make him before we let him come." He caught Devon's chin in his hand. "You're ours for tonight."

"Only tonight?" Trying for a humorous tone, Devon hoped the comment didn't sound as needy to the others as it did to him.

"Always," Jonathan assured him, turning Devon's head to press his own kiss to the sculpted lips before slapping his lover on his equally sculpted ass. He remembered how vulnerable he'd felt after splitting from Jean, wondering if he'd ever make a relationship work again, but he wasn't going to let Devon wallow in that same insecurity. "And knowing Kit, I suspect he's planning to prove it to you in ways you'll feel longer than just tonight. Now get a move on upstairs before I have to sling you over my shoulder and carry you there."

"In your dreams," Devon countered, twisting to swat Jonathan in return. Before he could make contact, Jonathan let out a whoop and caught Devon around the knees, bent and lifted, and the next thing Devon knew, he was dangling upside down over Jonathan's back as his lover bounded up the stairs with more energy than any man should have after a full day of filming. Jonathan worked in another good grope of Devon's backside before dumping him on the bed with enough force that he bounced before settling onto the mattress.

Kit shook his head even as he marveled at the perfect ploy on Jonathan's part to break the somewhat somber mood. Yes, Devon was leaving, but only for a short time, and he'd be back completely free of his ex-wife. They should be celebrating. "Bathroom," he reminded them as he walked into the bedroom behind them and found Jonathan pinning Devon to the bed.

"Can't I undress him here?" Jonathan countered, working his hands under the back of Devon's shirt. He shifted his hips to rub his erection more firmly against Devon's, the two layers of denim between them no barrier to the heat sparking at the contact. "He's much easier to keep in line this way."

Devon growled and tried to break free of the press of Jonathan's body against his, but though he might outweigh Jonathan, he wasn't going to get out from under him without a fight. Not that Devon was really interested in getting free—Jonathan felt too good moving against him for that—but a man had his pride, after all. Jonathan tugged the shirt over his head without bothering to open any of the buttons, sending at least one of them dancing across the carpet. "Oi! I plan to wear this shirt again someday, you lunatic."

"Then stop fighting him and do what your Dom tells you," Kit retorted, joining them on the bed and tweaking Devon's nipple roughly, the way Devon liked. "I promise it'll be worth it."

Jonathan bent forward, closed his teeth around the other nipple, and tugged until his busy hands had unfastened Devon's belt. "I wouldn't piss off your Dom if I were you," he agreed, sliding the waistband past Devon's hips once he'd loosened the buttons. His palms lingered over the strong globes of Devon's ass, one fingertip teasing into the crevice between them. He might have hesitated once to say anything that could remind Devon of his time with Robert, if Devon hadn't made it clear he'd put those memories firmly behind him. "I've heard he can be a right bastard if you cross him."

"You'd better believe it," Kit agreed. "Now, I think I said something about getting Devon in the bathtub. Can you two handle that on your own, or do I need to pull out the big guns?" He wriggled his fingers suggestively.

"Is that a Magnum in your pocket, or are you just anticipating getting at Devon's ass?" Jonathan countered, pinching a cheek before sliding down Devon's legs, dragging the jeans with him as he went. He tossed them to the floor and stripped off Devon's socks, then leaned back on his heels, admiring the thick cock that curved up from the golden curls at Devon's groin, grown back since he'd shaved them for Kit's "dinner party." He was tempted to forget about the bathtub and just take that delicious erection in his mouth, but that wouldn't set a very good example for Devon on proper submissive behavior. "You going to come along to the bathroom peacefully, or do I need to get physical again?"

"I'm counting on it," Devon answered with a grin.

"Getting physical or coming?" Jonathan retorted. "Because it's Kit's call either way."

"Bathroom!" Kit exclaimed, his exasperation clear in his voice. "Now! Or neither of you will be coming tonight." Kit knew that was an empty threat—he'd never be able to resist either of them long enough to carry it out—but he hoped it would at least get their attention.

"That's it!" Jonathan exclaimed, pulling Devon back into a fireman's carry before crossing the floor to the bathroom. He set him down on the lip of the tub and then settled onto his knees in the submissive posture Devon himself had taught him. "I don't know about you, but I don't plan to be left wearing my cock ring all night long."

Devon snorted, but since Kit hadn't given them any other directions, he sank to his knees as well. "It was only the once, and you deserved it," he muttered, clasping his hands behind him as Kit strode into the room.

"Jonathan, run a hot bath for us. Devon, find the waterproof lube. I haven't decided exactly what I'm going to do to you two yet, but I want to be ready for anything. When you've found it, get in the tub, both of you, but don't start without me. Don't start *anything* without me," Kit ordered, turning back toward the bedroom. "I'll be back in a few minutes."

Inching over to the tub, Jonathan turned the taps, feeling the water until it reached the perfect temperature. "Front or back?" he asked when Devon returned from the medicine cabinet with the lube Kit had requested.

Devon pretended to think about it, but Jonathan had gotten his own way too often already this evening. In the mood Jonathan was in, there was no way to tell if his current obedience to Kit's commands would last, and Devon wasn't about to open himself to more of whatever devilry Jonathan had in mind by sitting in front of him. "Back," he answered firmly, stepping into the tub and sighing as he stretched his legs into the warm water.

"Killjoy," Jonathan murmured without rancor as he eased into the tub in front of Devon. Judging by the way the water lapped the edge of the porcelain, there was imminent danger of it splashing onto the floor, so he leaned forward to close the taps and then wriggled backward until Devon's cock nestled against his ass. Devon slid his arms around him, whether to hold him in place or to keep him from squirming further, Jonathan wasn't sure, but in either case they felt so good that he leaned back and twisted his head until he could reach Devon's lips in a welcoming kiss.

Devon supposed he could have given Jonathan back some of his own again, but just as his arms had closed around his lover in an instinctive embrace when Jonathan leaned against him, his mouth opened just as readily to the touch of Jonathan's lips.

Keeping an ear out for any suspicious noises, Kit pulled Devon's toy box out from under the nightstand where it had taken up permanent residence. He had been the willing recipient of a good number of the items inside, but tonight he was thinking about wielding them, a different question entirely. He immediately set aside the paddle and flogger, knowing he wouldn't be able to use them properly even if he dared. The nipple clamps, on the other hand, required little to no expertise and offered a lovely sensation. Kit's nipples tingled at the mere thought of the times Devon had used them on him.

Digging a little deeper, he found the spreader bar Devon had used on Jonathan when they'd gone to the beach. Kit smiled. That would be perfect. He didn't have a rail to bend Devon over, but the spreader bar and a little creativity would leave Devon equally as helpless. He pulled out a dildo, starting to set it aside until he realized the end contained a carefully concealed battery pack. Turning it on, he listened to the buzzing sound and grinned. *Oh hell, yes.* Devon wouldn't know what hit him. Setting that on the bed next to the spreader bar and nipple clamps, Kit added a pair of supple suede cuffs before putting everything else back inside the toy box, and then walked back into the bathroom to enjoy his lovers' company—only to find them snogging with a single-minded dedication that left them oblivious to anything else.

Not even the sudden burst of humming from the next room, quickly cut off, had been able to distract Devon while Jonathan's tongue was busy tangling with his. Only when Kit announced his return by loudly clearing his throat did Devon pull back guiltily, though Jonathan merely smiled with a smugness uncharacteristic of his usual sub behavior.

"What did I tell you two about starting without me?" Kit scolded, reaching for the washcloth and tossing it at Devon. "Get cleaned up. I was going to linger in the tub with you, but since you can't listen, we'll move on to other things."

"Would have been a tight fit," Devon muttered, reaching over Jonathan for the soap.

"Just the way you like it," Jonathan returned under his breath, arching his back so that Devon's cock slid more firmly between his cheeks.

"Smart-arses, both of you," Kit said with a roll of his eyes. "Do I need to get a ball gag or two? I saw them in the toy box." He had other plans for their mouths, but they didn't need to know that. Not yet, anyway.

"No, Sir," Jonathan answered demurely, folding his hands between his knees and sitting quietly, the picture of innocence. Devon "accidentally" elbowed him as he finished his quick cleaning and passed the washcloth to his tubmate, then rose at a nod from Kit.

Kit shook his head at their antics and grabbed a towel to run over Devon cursorily. He had assumed Devon had initiated their kiss, being unused to following directions, but now he wondered if Jonathan had been the one responsible. It didn't actually matter. Devon was the one in need of their attention tonight. "Go in the bedroom and stand by the bed. Jon, finish up and join us as quickly as you can."

With no reason to linger once Devon stepped out of the tub, Jonathan made short work of washing up, opening the stopper to let the water drain, and hanging their towels to dry. When he returned to the bedroom, Devon was standing at the foot of the bed, eyes downcast, feet spread the perfect distance apart to square with his shoulders. Even from across the room, Jonathan could see that the tension had eased from Devon's stance. Whether it was his teasing or the prospect of Kit's mastery, their actions were working. Jonathan hoped Kit wouldn't be too hard on him for acting out, because if it helped Devon relax, he'd be happy to demonstrate how far from a perfect sub he could be.

Devon was a little surprised at how easily he slipped into a sub's posture, a sub's mind-set. Settling into that headspace had never been easy for him after leaving Robert, but he felt none of the anxiety or guilt that had stopped him from truly giving control to anyone else in the years since. The frisson of awareness that prickled along his nerves was anticipation, not fear. His lovers had shown without question that they accepted him with all his flaws. Whatever Kit had in store for him and Jonathan, Devon had no doubt that while it might have him begging for release, that release would ultimately be granted. More than granted—it would be shattering, and when his world came back into clarity again, Kit and Jonathan would be there to hold him together.

Kit had no real idea what he was doing, but he wanted Devon to understand that, no matter what else happened, this was about them being together, them being in love. He picked up the spreader bar and showed it to Devon. "I want you as much at our disposal as you had Jonathan at yours when we were at the beach," he said. "I want you to be the center of our world for the next few hours."

The spreader bar was a surprise, but Devon inclined his head in acceptance, tightening the grip of his clasped hands to mask his reaction. "As you wish," he answered. Kit had taken control of scenes before this, but they usually involved role-play and had been more playful than intense. He'd never rummaged through Devon's toy chest beforehand, never set as formal a tone as this. Devon wasn't sure if Kit wanted to be addressed as "Sir" or even if he expected Devon to remain silent unless he asked a direct question. Deciding a basic protocol was best, he didn't add anything more, waiting to see if Kit would give him clearer instructions.

At the sight of the spreader bar, Jonathan's memory flashed back to the afternoon at the beach house and the first time Devon had shown him how high he could soar when he let himself go in complete trust. Even knowing the constraint was intended for Devon, not him, it set a roil of arousal curling in his belly. His cock stiffened as he fell into a posture mirroring Devon's, but he couldn't force his eyes to the ground, drawn by the change in roles between his lovers.

Kit fastened the spreader bar carefully around Devon's ankles, fiddling with the restraints for several moments, trying to get them positioned for maximum effect. Devon had slapped them on Jonathan like finding the right placement was a piece of cake, but Kit wasn't satisfied. He glanced at Jonathan for help, even knowing he had no more experience with employing the kinky restraints than he did. "The damn things fit you right. Why don't they fit Devon?"

God, Devon looks beautiful like that, Jonathan thought, imagining sliding his hands up those long, strong legs, feeling them quiver at his touch. Taking Kit's question as permission, he sank to his knees before Devon, running his palms over the fine golden hairs that limned his lover's calves. "Maybe bind him higher," he suggested, his touch lingering at Devon's knees before boldly gliding upward, stopping just short of the crease where thighs merged into torso. "If you move the bar here"—his touch returned to Devon's knees—"it will give us better access here."

Running his thumbs up the inside of Devon's legs, Jonathan spread his fingers when they met beneath Devon's balls, framing his erection.

"Aye," Devon rasped, already aching for more of Jonathan's touch. His gaze lifted to Kit's face as he fought the urge to unclasp his hands and grab Jonathan's head to guide it to his cock. "Fasten them at m'knees."

Kit saw no reason to ignore his lovers' advice and affixed the restraints directly above Devon's knees, forcing his legs far enough apart that his arse opened for their attention and his bollocks hung free of any impediment. "Perfect," he said with a smile of thanks. He ran his hand up Devon's widespread thighs, stopping to tousle Jonathan's hair in passing, before closing his fingers around Devon's cock, stroking it twice. "Jon, he needs his cock ring. Can you find that?"

Rising reluctantly, Jonathan retrieved the slim leather band from the top of Devon's dresser. They no longer kept their rings in the toy box, since they saw far more use than any of the other toys. There were days, when they'd been working on particularly intimate scenes, that he was sure he'd never have made it through filming without jumping one or both of his lovers if he hadn't been wearing his ring. Returning to where Kit and Devon stood at the end of the bed, Jonathan slid gracefully to his knees again. "May I put it on him?" he asked Kit, wondering if he ought to ask for his own as well. He wasn't sure how long he'd be able to last without it, given the visual temptation of Devon in restraints and at their mercy. Well, at Kit's mercy, to be precise, but Jonathan had every intention of adding his own touches to Kit's sweet torment.

"Go ahead," Kit allowed. "And while you're doing that, I'll see how else we can decorate him." He picked up the nipple clamps from the bed. "You all right with these?" He knew how much he enjoyed them, and he couldn't imagine Devon doing something to either Jonathan or Kit that he didn't enjoy himself, but he wanted to check anyway.

"Fuck, yeah." Devon's voice sounded harsh to his ears, but that was because he was having trouble breathing when all the blood in his body was rushing to the places that anticipated Kit's touch. His cock jumped when Jonathan's fingers resumed their teasing meander up his thighs, skating over the most sensitive spots, seeming in no hurry to reach their ultimate goal. Knowing he wasn't supposed to speak, he tried to glare at Jonathan to urge him to speed things up, but Jonathan just flashed him a wicked grin that made it clear the snail's pace was deliberate. By the time those wandering fingers finally reached his bollocks and wove into the thatch of hair above them, Devon's cock was jutting upward in its own silent plea for attention.

Jonathan wasn't immune to Devon's predicament, but he'd been the recipient of enough of the same teasing attentions to know how much more intense delayed gratification could be. Not that Devon wasn't providing his own form of torment, even if it was unintentional—it was all Jonathan could do not to swipe his tongue over the swollen crown of Devon's cock, bouncing only inches from his face. "Don't threaten me with that thing when you aren't going to be able to use it," he muttered, fitting the ring around the base of the thick shaft and adjusting the strap to the perfect degree of tightness.

Kit frowned at Jonathan's comment. It wasn't like him to act this way in the middle of a scene, at least not when Devon was their Dom. That was usually Kit's role, one he took a great deal of pleasure in because Devon always "punished" him so delightfully. Kit wasn't comfortable in that role, though. He had no qualms about trussing Devon up and ratcheting the pleasure so high that he couldn't do anything but beg and moan and come, but the thought of having to discipline a recalcitrant sub made his stomach queasy. He sent Jonathan a quelling look, hoping he'd get the message, and turned his attention to fastening the nipple clamps to Devon's chest.

Devon's nipples were already taut, but Kit wanted the pleasure of teasing Devon a little before affixing the clamps, so he tweaked one, then the other, firmly, even twisting a little to add the tiny bite of pain Devon loved. As expected, Devon's eyes closed immediately, a soft gasp escaping. Kit smiled and did it again. "Open your eyes," he said. "I want to see how good I'm making you feel."

Devon's eyes opened slowly, the emerald gaze hazy with desire. Kit smiled and kissed Devon quickly. "Beautiful. And all ours."

Kit pulled away too quickly for Devon to return the fleeting kiss, leaving his mouth open in a gasp of pleasure that deepened into a groan when Kit fixed one of the clamps to his nipple. They were among the first toys he'd come to crave as a sub, their bite teaching him the riches to be found skating the boundary between pleasure and pain. Devon wished Kit had picked one of the butterfly clamps instead, preferring their tighter grip, but since he'd never used them on Kit, the lad wouldn't know the difference. "Tighter," he moaned when Kit slid the adjusting bead to a stop about halfway down the legs of the clamp.

"Anything you want," Kit replied, pushing the bead higher. "Tell me if it gets to be too much. You have to talk to me, Devon, okay? You know I have no real idea what I'm doing."

"Doing… fine," Devon managed to rasp out between breaths as he let the bite of the clamp's teeth wash over him, sending him deeper into the subspace he hadn't been sure he'd ever reach again. "Want… the other."

Jonathan watched from his vantage point at Devon's feet, his own nipples tightening as if Kit were fastening the clamps to his chest instead of Devon's. It felt awkward, wanting to feel Kit's hands on him, wanting to touch Devon, but having to wait for Kit to remember to include him. That he hadn't wanted to take charge of the scene himself didn't make taking a passive role any easier. He drew in a breath and released it slowly, trying to find the headspace Devon seemed to be able to put him in without effort.

Kit bent his head and bit Devon's unclamped nipple sharply before licking over it, enjoying the way Devon's back arched in response. He glanced down at Jonathan and smiled. "I think he liked that. I think you should bite him again. You always manage to bite him harder than I do."

Sending Kit a grateful glance, Jonathan pushed up on one foot until he could reach Devon's chest. Wrapping an arm around Devon's hips to brace himself, he tongued around the swollen nipple, imagining he could taste a trace of Kit's saliva overlaying the flavor of Devon's skin. He tried to catch Devon's gaze, but his eyes were soft and unfocused. Jonathan knew that feeling well, of being lost in a place where every sensation seemed amplified and it was too much effort to do more than respond to his Dom's demands. He bit into the pebbled flesh, sucking it between his teeth, relishing the sounds he wrung from Devon's lips since he didn't know how much more of a part Kit would allow him to take in Devon's ravishment.

Devon wasn't sure what sounds he was making, but he didn't try to hold them back. Kit had asked him what he wanted, but at the moment he couldn't think of anything he wanted more than this: to be wholly at Kit's command, feeling Jonathan's hands and teeth on him, knowing his lovers would give him what he needed.

Kit stroked Jonathan's hair as he paid homage to Devon's chest. Leaving them for a moment, he went back to the bed to get the weights that clipped onto the clamps. Devon had used three on him, but he suspected he could take—indeed, would want—more than that. Returning to Devon's side, he tapped Jonathan's head lightly. "Enough now. Let me finish decorating him, and then we can play."

Jonathan couldn't stop the moan of protest at Kit's command, though he was pleased to see he'd left Devon's nipple swollen and red when he released it. Sinking back to his knees, he nipped Devon's flat abdomen on the way down, grinning when the muscles rippled in reaction.

Kit frowned again as Jonathan took liberties with his command, but he decided simply to ignore it. It hadn't upset Devon, nor had it kept Kit from doing something he had intended to do. Turning his attention to Devon again, he pinched the swollen nipple once more, holding it ready for the clamp. After tightening the bead until both sides matched, he slipped the chain into the hooks and tugged on it lightly. "How many weights can you take? Or should I just add them until you tell me it's enough?"

"Whatever… you want." Devon had to concentrate on forming the words, every time Kit asked him a question pulling him out of the place he wanted to stay in, where he could forget everything that was waiting for him in the States and focus only on what Kit and Jonathan were making him feel. "Doms… don't ask."

"You do," Kit said softly, remembering how many times a simple question had settled his nerves because Devon cared enough to check in with him.

"He does because he's Devon." Jonathan knew he was talking out of turn, but helping Kit understand was more important than his teasing disobedience. "Every time you ask him a question, it forces him out of his headspace. He trusts you, kitten. We both do. Just trust yourself. You'll know if it gets to be more than he can take."

Kit marveled once more at his lovers' ability to find that headspace Jonathan referred to. He wasn't sure he ever had. Perhaps for a moment before the caning went wrong or in the later scene when Devon used the riding crop on him, but even then, he hadn't been able to hold on to it. Taking a deep breath, he nodded. Tonight was supposed to be about giving Devon what he needed. If what he needed was for Kit to be decisive, then that's what Kit would do. "Okay then." He added a weight to each side of the chain, watching Devon's face closely for any sign of unwelcome pain. When Devon's body swayed toward him rather than away, clearly begging for more, Kit gave it, adding two more weights, still balanced on either side.

Admiring the sway of silver chain against Devon's broad chest, Jonathan wished they were using the silver cock rings he'd bought the first time they'd visited the adult novelty store, back when Devon and Kit had first seduced him. He understood that leather rings were safer than the unyielding metal bands, but the balance of jeweled clamps, joined by a silver chain, and a silver ring on Devon's golden torso was an image he'd love to photograph. Not that he'd share the pictures with anyone but his lovers. That would have to wait for some other time, though. Judging by the bliss on Devon's face that he was enjoying the pull of the weights, Jonathan reached up to touch one, setting the chain swinging gently. Devon's groan was reward enough to offset any chastisement from Kit at acting without permission.

"I was planning on using the restraints on Devon's hands," Kit said to Jonathan in exasperation, "but now I'm wondering if I need to use them on you instead. Are you trying to make this difficult for me?"

"You don't need to ask Devon what to do, but you do have to tell me," Jonathan answered softly, being careful not to sound critical or complaining. He realized he wasn't going to be able to sink into the same headspace Devon had clearly found, and he was okay with that; tonight was about loving Devon well and truly enough that he could make it through the weeks of separation. "I thought my acting out a bit seemed to help Devon relax, though he's probably too deep to notice it now. But I need to be a part of this, Kit. Tell me what to do or let me do it on my own, but don't shut me out." He swallowed, surprised at the sudden sting of tears burning his eyes. Devon wasn't the only one who was finding his imminent departure hard to face. "I need this as much as he does."

Kit nodded, heart aching at the depth of feeling in Jonathan's voice. His own voice was hoarse when he spoke. "I'm sorry. This is all new to me. I'll try to do better." Casting around for a task to give Jonathan, his eyes settled on the swell of Devon's arse, more pronounced than usual because of his forcibly widened stance. "All spread out like he is, he's just begging to be rimmed. Get him nice and wet for what's next."

Jonathan stood, but before he stepped around Devon, he took Kit in his arms. He knew it was breaking all kinds of D/s protocol, but at the moment Kit was his lover, not his Dom, and his lover needed reassurance. "You're doing fine," he told Kit, kissing him gently. "Don't worry about me. Just let us take care of Devon together." Releasing Kit with another soft kiss, Jonathan knelt behind Devon, tracing the skin above the cuffs of the spreader bar. Just as he'd teased the front of Devon's thighs earlier, he now explored the back, ruffling the fine coating of hairs, following the lines of muscle, inching his way toward the firm globes that were his ultimate destination.

Devon had vaguely registered the quiet discussion between Kit and Jonathan, but it didn't really penetrate his consciousness the way the lack of their hands and mouths on his body did. He sighed in relief when Jonathan knelt behind him, even though he seemed determined to draw out his anticipation even further. He could hardly complain when Jonathan touched him so lovingly, when Kit added a final weight to the center of the chain, sending curls of fiery sensation coursing from his chest through his limbs, setting him trembling.

Kit kissed Devon again, lingering this time to enjoy the press of the nipple clamps against his own chest as he rubbed against Devon's body. He let his hands wander over Devon's golden skin, across his back and the upper curve of his arse, around to his belly and the treasure trail that led downward to the hard shaft confined in its ring. All the while, he kept his lips moving against Devon's, his tongue claiming every inch of the hot cavern as his own.

There was something so right about the two of them loving Devon this way, Jonathan thought as his touch slowly worked its way upward and Kit's hands roamed downward, claiming the magnificent body they shared. Devon began to tremble between them, and his own cock swelled in reaction to Devon's responsiveness. Suddenly touch wasn't enough. Jonathan needed to taste Devon, dark and deep on his tongue. Running his palms over the toned globes, Jonathan parted them, inhaling the musky scent of sweat and desire and Devon before leaning forward, letting his tongue trace up the shadowed crease.

Devon gasped against Kit's lips at the first swipe of Jonathan's tongue. Not that Kit's mouth against his wasn't enough to steal his breath, but paired with Jonathan's facile tongue working its way inside him, the combined sensations were enough to make breathing nearly impossible. Though he could do without breathing himself when each of Kit's breaths intensified the bite of the clamps against his nipples, when each of Jonathan's breaths added to the heat of his tongue as it delved inside him, slick and wet and probing. The rush of sensations, spreading from everywhere their bodies touched, flowed to Devon's limbs, stealing his strength as they built toward a climax throbbing in his bollocks behind the constraint of the ring.

Devon trembled again, swaying unsteadily, breaking Kit from the kiss.

"Jon, Devon's going to fall if we aren't careful. Help me get him onto his knees," Kit directed.

Kit's voice recalled Jonathan from his single-minded focus on Devon's ass. He loved rimming almost as much as he loved being rimmed, but he remembered how unsteady he'd felt the first time Devon had used the spreader bar on him and knew Kit was right. With a final kiss to the now well-wet pucker, Jonathan stood and moved to Devon's side, holding his shoulder and helping Kit ease him down to his knees. He couldn't resist leaning in to claim a kiss, sharing the intimate taste that lingered on his tongue with Devon himself.

There was no mistaking Jonathan's kiss for Kit's, Devon thought as he opened willingly to the insistent press of his lips. Kit probed and claimed, but Jonathan tangled with him in a silent war of dominance, fighting for mastery in this arena when he wouldn't in any other. Devon lifted a hand to pull him closer when Jonathan would have drawn away, savoring the muskiness in Jonathan's mouth.

Kit grinned as Devon and Jonathan kissed. He loved watching them together almost as much as he loved being with them. The movement of Devon's hand, the first since the scene had begun, gave Kit the opening he'd been waiting for. "Hands behind your back, Devon. Since you can't keep them to yourself, I'll have to take care of them for you."

Kit grabbed the suede restraints from the bed and reached for Devon's arm to draw it behind his back.

The sudden movement put Devon off-balance, but that wasn't what made his muscles tense in fear. Just for a moment, he was back in Robert's crawl space, restrained on his knees, his arms cuffed behind his back, helpless. He shook his head, freeing himself from the vision. He wasn't there anymore, wasn't that man anymore. These were his lovers—he'd trust them with his life—but that didn't make the irrational reaction any less powerful. "Not behind my back," he asked quietly, ashamed of the weakness that made him ask but not willing to taint a moment of this time with those memories.

The combination of clarity and fear in Devon's voice struck Kit to the core. Releasing Devon's wrist, he knelt next to him, running a soothing hand up and down Devon's back. He still liked the idea of restraining Devon's hands, but not if it would bring back bad memories. The rings on the outside of the spreader bar caught his attention. "What about against your knees, then?" he asked, touched and reassured beyond measure that Devon had limits he could not cross the same as Kit did.

Jonathan's knuckles brushed Devon's cheek, his other hand grasping Devon's shoulder in wordless reassurance. Devon had to swallow against the tightness in his chest as his lovers once again proved their acceptance of the worst days of Devon's past. "Aye," he managed to force out, moving his hands to his knees. "Front is fine."

"That's likely to leave him a little unsteady, Jon," Kit warned. "You won't let him fall, will you?" Kit remembered with perfect clarity the feeling of leaning against Jonathan's steadying warmth as Devon flogged him and then fucked him a few weeks earlier. Having that support for his body had let his mind go flying. He hoped it would have the same effect for Devon.

"Never," Jonathan promised, hoping Devon knew he meant that in far more than their present circumstances. He scooted in front of Devon until their knees met and then leaned forward until their foreheads touched, clasping Devon's shoulders. In that position, there was no way he could resist claiming Devon's lips in another kiss.

Devon didn't even register Kit fastening the soft cuffs around his wrists or securing them to the outer edges of the spreader bar. The tenseness was gone, washed away in the unconditional love from Kit and Jonathan. He let Jonathan's strength brace him, losing himself in the kiss until Kit nudged him forward, off his heels. The shift in position pushed him against Jonathan's shoulders and set the weighted chain between his nipples swinging. The pull of the clamps was so exquisite that he didn't realize the move had exposed his arse to Kit's ministrations until a loving swat recalled his attention.

"Are you paying attention to your Dom?" Kit teased from behind Devon, fingering his arse to see how wet and open Jonathan had gotten it in the limited time he'd had. The snug heat was so enticing, Kit modified his plans slightly, reaching for the lube to coat his fingers so he could give Devon a thorough prostate massage before starting in with the dildo.

"Always," Devon groaned, more at the enticing touch of Kit's fingers around the skin already sensitized by Jonathan's tongue than by the swat. Twisting his head to try to see what Kit was doing behind him was too awkward in his current position, so he settled his head against Jonathan's shoulder, trying to focus on the warmth beneath his cheek instead of the anticipation building in his groin at the thought of what Kit might do next.

Devon's new position meant Jonathan couldn't kiss him again, but that didn't mean Jonathan had to sit idle. He ran a palm over Devon's hair, smoothing the golden strands, then slipped his hands between their bodies, roving blindly until his fingers found the nipple clamps. Tugging them gently away from Devon's chest, he set the weighted chain swinging, anything to add to the sensations of whatever it was Kit was doing behind them.

Kit took his time finding Devon's prostate and pressing against it, then drawing his fingers away for a moment, only to plunge back inside and repeat the firm pressure. Devon caught the rhythm, rocking back to meet his fingers, hips following in protest at each withdrawal. Kit grinned and gave Devon's arse another playful swat. "None of that, now. If I want to pull out, I will."

"Mmnnn," Devon moaned in protest, though he tried to still his hips. "Feels too good."

"Maybe I can help," Jonathan murmured, letting his hands slide lower to grip Devon's hips. Of course that put them in much closer proximity to Devon's cock, hard and leaking between his thigh and stomach. Giving in to temptation, Jonathan worked a hand between their bodies, caught the glimmer of fluid that welled at the tip, and raised it to his lips.

"Just don't make him come," Kit warned Jonathan. "I'm not done with him yet."

Devon groaned at the promise in those words, making Kit suddenly eager to see how he would react to the dildo. He grabbed it from the bed and coated it with lube, then pressed it against Devon's hole. Devon rocked back against it, already a satisfying response. With a grin, Kit hit the On button, starting the vibrations.

"Bloody fuck!" Devon cursed as Jonathan's hand wrapped around his cock at the same instant Kit hit the power on the dildo. The buzzing he vaguely remembered hearing when he and Jonathan were in the bathtub made sense now, not that Devon could spare the brain cells to focus on anything but the mind-blowing sensations of Jonathan's palm caressing his cock and the blasted dildo vibrating in his arse. Kit was wielding it like a master, too, not allowing more than the most fleeting of buzzes against his gland before pulling it out, keeping him dancing on the knife's edge of climax.

Kit turned up the vibrator as he pressed the tip directly against Devon's sweet spot, a thrill going through him at the howl that escaped Devon's mouth. With his free hand, he plucked at the button on his trousers, getting it open and the zip lowered enough that he could pull his cock free of his boxers. He wouldn't make it to naked, but at this point, he didn't care. Tugging the vibrator free, he pressed the tip against Devon's bollocks as he plunged his aching cock into Devon's arse. "Take his ring off and make him come," Kit told Jonathan, "but hold back if you can just a little longer."

It was probably a good thing their positions wouldn't allow him to take Devon's cock into his mouth, Jonathan thought. As much as he'd love to suck Devon off, he wouldn't be able to keep from coming himself once the first spurt of hot, salty seed hit his palate. Promising them both that pleasure before Devon had to leave, he settled for giving Devon the best hand job he could, adding to the vibrations transmitting from the dildo against Devon's balls with long, steady strokes of his hand, twisting as he reached the head and swiping his thumb over the oozing tip. "Come for us, babe," he crooned into Devon's ear, following the words with the moist rasp of his tongue over the outer shell. His other hand worked at the cock ring, finding it harder to unfasten with one hand and blind than he'd expected. At last the release popped free, and Devon's cock surged in his palm. "That's it. Come for us now, come on...."

Jonathan's sinful voice exhorting him was the last straw to send Devon over the edge. Crying out hoarsely, he came hard, spattering Jonathan's hand and clenching around Kit's pumping cock, instinct taking over as he rocked between the two stimuli mindlessly, intent on extending the ecstasy as long as he could.

Once Devon came, Kit gave in as well, knowing he wouldn't be able to hold back without a cock ring, as much as he might wish he could fuck Jonathan too. There would be time for him and Jonathan to be together while Devon was in LA. Dropping the vibrator, he grabbed

Devon's hips with both hands, holding him steady as he pounded into the upturned arse, drawing out their climaxes as long as possible. When his cock had nothing left to give, he released his grip and reached for Jonathan, stroking his cheek tenderly. "Help me get Devon free and on the bed, and then I promise I'll take care of you too."

Before Jonathan could answer, Devon shook his head. "Want to… make him come," he managed between heaving breaths.

"Oh hell, yeah." Jonathan already had his free hand squeezing the base of his cock to hold back his orgasm; he wasn't about to argue with Devon over that. He'd love to feel Devon fuck him to climax, but the cock in question was already softening in his other hand, and he didn't want to wait for Devon to recover enough to get hard again. "Kit?" he asked, remembering Kit was nominally in charge of the session.

Whatever nebulous plans Kit might have had went right out the window with Devon's request. The whole point of the evening's activities had been to show Devon how much they loved and would miss him. Kit wasn't about to deny a perfectly reasonable request. "He can't very well get you off trussed up like a Christmas goose. Help me get him loose and on the bed so we can take care of you." He started unfastening one of Devon's wrists as he spoke.

"Yes, I can," Devon insisted, not questioning why he was loath for the scene to end. He knew the answer—it would mean he was that much closer to having to board the plane that would take him away from these two incredible men. "Just undo m'hands. Jon, love, stand up." With his hands free, Devon didn't feel he was fighting for balance, and he could give Jonathan's neglected cock the attention it deserved. Bracing a hand on the floor, the other around Jonathan's hips, Devon took him in, drawing his teeth down the straining shaft until Jonathan's pubic hair tickled his nose.

Jonathan grabbed Devon's shoulders and held on for dear life. He was so close already, two strokes in and out of Devon's mouth and he was coming like a teenager getting his first blowjob. Devon didn't seem to care, swallowing every drop and lapping at Jonathan's balls as if asking for more. His knees buckling, Jonathan slid to the floor and took Devon's mouth in a hungry kiss, needing that contact, that reassurance of the love between them as much as he'd needed to come. When he finally had to break the kiss to draw a breath, he glanced over at Kit, extending a hand to pull him close. "Now we can go to bed and start this all over again."

Kit released the buckles on the spreader bar, freeing Devon completely, and moved into his lovers' embrace. "I can't wait."

CHAPTER 20
TO KINK OR NOT TO KINK

KIT SAT at the table in the kitchen of his house and stared at the riding crop in his hand. Devon had used it on him to devastating effect. Kit could feel his backside tingling just from the memories of the thorough spanking followed by the bite of the crop, the combination of sensations enough to have sent Kit flying, the one time he had truly found the headspace of a sub. Kit knew Jonathan had been curious about the feeling of the soft leather slapper. He just wished he felt a little more confident about using it.

Jonathan let himself in the back door of Kit's house, finding him sitting at the kitchen table, a forlorn expression on his face. He was about to ask what was wrong when he saw what Kit held in his hand. "Were you planning to use that on me, or are you going riding when we're finished?"

Kit looked up, flushing in surprise since he hadn't heard Jonathan come in. "I went to get it because I was missing Devon and thinking we hadn't done any kinky stuff since he's been gone, but I don't know…. It just doesn't feel right without him here."

Jonathan pulled out a chair to straddle and sat facing Kit. "It's not just you, Kit-Kat. If you'd really wanted to use that on me, I'm not sure I would have gone along." Concerned that Kit might misunderstand, he was quick to assure him. "It's not because I don't trust you as a Dom. It's just that…." Jonathan shrugged. "I miss Devon enough as it is. Doing D/s without him here… having the memories of him without having him with us would be ten times worse."

Kit nodded, relieved Jonathan understood. "Exactly! I was sitting here remembering him using this on me and how incredible it felt to be held in your arms the whole time and then to have him fuck me right into you." Kit shivered. "I'm hard just thinking about it, but if I tried to use it on you, I'd spend the entire time worrying I wasn't doing it right or that I'd hurt you accidentally or… or I don't know what. Just that it wouldn't be right without him here. Will it always be like this if he isn't with us? Not that sex with you in any form is anything less than incredible, but… well, I like the kinky stuff we get up to with Devon."

"Honestly, I'm not sure," Jonathan said. "I've tried to avoid dwelling on it, but filming is going to end in a few more months. We're going to have to start thinking about what will happen when we're not all together every day." His heart ached just at the thought, but it was a reality they were going to have to deal with eventually. "The likelihood is that it will be easier for two of us to get together than all three of us, most of the time. I know you and Devon did okay when you were trapped together by the mudslides—"

"We made love plenty of times, but we didn't do anything kinky," Kit said. "We didn't have any toys or anything with us. They were all in your suitcase. I didn't miss it then because I was so worried I wouldn't be enough for Devon by myself, and it was only a couple of days. Devon's been gone nearly three weeks."

"Not that Devon needs his toy box to get kinky," Jonathan interjected with a grin. "I swear he could do a MacGyver and turn kitchen gadgets and rubber bands into sex toys if he put his mind to it."

"I'm sure he could, but they weren't his kitchen gadgets and rubber bands," Kit reminded Jonathan. "We felt bad enough about breaking into the house to begin with. We weren't going to abuse their belongings any more than necessary." He didn't mention Devon rimming him until he came on the kitchen table. They'd cleaned up after themselves and left a note for the owners offering to compensate them for the unexpected use of their cabin. "It's more than that, though. When the three of us are together, it's so easy, so natural to slip into that mode, but it didn't happen then without you, and it hasn't happened between us since Devon's been gone. It makes me worry about how things will be after filming ends. Our games have been such a part of our relationship. What's going to happen, with me, anyway, since you and Devon seemed to have no problem when I went to London for the weekend, if we can't have that when we aren't all together?"

There was no criticism in Kit's voice, but the reminder of the weekend when he'd walked in on Jonathan and Devon engaged in a kink they knew was outside Kit's comfort zone still made Jonathan feel guilty for the inadvertent pain he'd caused Kit. He reached out to cover Kit's hands with his. "First of all, I'm not going to stop wanting you because

Devon's not around—these last few weeks should be proof enough of that." There certainly hadn't been any reduction in the number of times they made love, even if the sex was pure vanilla by BDSM standards. "I think the key is what you said, though—it has to be natural. Right now, we're both worried about Devon, so doing something we associate so closely with him is going to feel wrong if he's not a part of it. After filming ends...." Jonathan swallowed, hoping it would get easier to contemplate, let alone deal with. "It's hard to imagine, but we'll have to get used to being apart. I think by then, anytime we can be together, in any combination, will be special enough, whether we bring kink into it or not. If it feels right, we can, and if it doesn't, that's fine too." He frowned, a distinction forming in his thoughts. "Besides, I think there's a difference between kink and D/s," he said slowly, thinking it through out loud. "I don't know that I'd ever feel comfortable trying to Dom you or Devon, but that doesn't mean I might not want to play with some toys. That dildo you bought the first time we went toy shopping, for example—I could see myself using that on you." He could see it so clearly in his mind's eye, in fact, that he was getting hard at the mental image of sliding the purple latex into Kit's tight ass.

"It's in my bedroom," Kit offered with a flirtatious grin. "I think you're right, though. The problem is that I went to get this because I felt like I should, not because I particularly wanted to or because something you said or did made me think you wanted me to." He tossed the crop toward his backpack so he'd remember to take it back to Devon's later. He turned his palms upward so his fingers entwined with Jonathan's and squeezed gently, leaning forward and kissing his lover. "I do, however, want to do this, and I have reason to suspect you might want me to as well."

"Do what?" Jonathan asked, his eyes sparkling. "Kiss me? You can do that anytime, kitten."

"Anytime?" Kit teased. "I'm not sure you're ready for me to walk up to you on the red carpet and lay one on you."

"Don't be too sure," Jonathan retorted. "I may never be happy about strangers speculating over my private life, but I'm not ashamed of being with you and Devon. And even if we try to be discreet, people will be bound to notice if we keep turning up in the same places together."

"I guess it depends on how high profile we become in our careers. I know you and Devon keep saying you're not big Hollywood names, but you're certainly not unknowns," Kit said. "Before this, nobody cared what I did or who I was seen with because I wasn't that big. If we keep getting the attention we have so far, though, that could change, for all of us." He sighed. "Can we just pretend filming won't ever end and we can all stay here in our little corner of Glastonbury and go on exactly as we are now? Well, not quite exactly, since Devon's stuck in LA, but you know what I meant."

"That's what I've been doing ever since we got together, but we can't pretend forever," Jonathan said softly. "We're going to have to start talking about this, Kit. We can't make any decisions until Devon's back, but we have to start thinking about how we want things to be when we're apart."

"Speaking of Devon, he hasn't called yet today," Kit said, glancing at the clock. "I know it's only noon there, but he usually calls earlier than this so he doesn't keep us up late, with the eight-hour time difference and all. Do you think we should call him and make sure everything is all right?"

"Eventually," Jonathan agreed, leaning forward to brush his lips over Kit's. Not that he didn't want to talk with Devon, but their conversation had strengthened his need for the lover he could still feel and touch. His mouth brushed Kit's again and again, each pass lingering a bit longer, pressing a bit harder, desire swelling as Kit's lips parted beneath his, welcoming him in. "Need you now, Kit."

"I'm yours," Kit replied immediately, "and the bedroom's just through that door. Or there's lube in the drawer beneath the phone if you can't wait that long."

"Bedroom," Jonathan declared, rising to his feet and tugging Kit with him. "Bring the lube along—and while you're at it, find that purple dildo."

Kit didn't bother getting the lube out of the kitchen drawer; he had a tube in the bedroom as well. The purple dildo required a little more thought. He hadn't needed it in so long that he had to remember where he'd put it. He found it, after a minimum of searching, in the back of his underwear drawer. He offered it to Jonathan with a sly grin. "Unless, of course, you wanted me to use it on you."

"Oh no," Jonathan growled, pulling his shirt over his head and stalking forward, unfastening his jeans as he went. "Your ass is mine tonight." He kicked off the denim and eyed Kit's clothes, his gaze darkening. "You going to take those off, or do you want me to do it for you?"

"Oh, I definitely want you to do it for me," Kit drawled, eyes fixed on Jonathan's now bare skin. If Jonathan was in the mood to take charge, Kit was going to give in for all he was worth!

"Your choice." Jonathan lunged forward, tackling Kit onto the bed. His cock, already hard, stiffened even more at the rasp of Kit's jeans against the sensitive skin. Hitching his hips to keep Kit pinned—not that Kit was making any move to get away, but Jonathan wasn't about to give him a chance—he slid his hands under Kit's sweater, palms gliding up and back down the warm, smooth flesh before grasping the hem and tugging the garment over Kit's head. As soon as the tousled curls popped free of the sweater's neckline, Jonathan leaned down to reclaim Kit's lips in a kiss that was no longer tentative, imbued with all the passion driven by the thought that their time together was drawing toward its end.

Kit returned the kiss eagerly, forcing his hands to remain passive on the bed next to him. He knew his control wouldn't last, but for as long as he could, he would give Jonathan complete control. He shifted as much as he could, enjoying the sensation of Jonathan's light mat of chest hair brushing against his nipples.

Rubbing up against Kit's bare chest wasn't enough. Jonathan needed to feel, touch, taste every inch of Kit's body. Breaking the kiss, he pushed up enough to get his hands to Kit's waist, opened his jeans, and shoved them as far down his legs as they'd go. Begrudging even the momentary loss of contact, he rolled to one side and tossed the jeans to the floor. As soon as they were out of the way, he rolled back atop Kit, legs spreading wide to straddle his thighs, hips pushing against Kit in a primal need to feel skin against skin.

Kit bucked up against Jonathan immediately, the rub of cock against cock sending an electric charge through him. He had no idea why Jonathan thought they could take the time to play with the dildo when he was already this needy. He slid his hands down Jonathan's back, cupping the globes of his arse and squeezing, urging him to pick up the pace of their frottage.

It would be so easy to rut against Kit until they both came, but Jonathan intended to be deep inside Kit's ass when he climaxed. And he planned to make Kit come a time or two before he got there. After rolling his hips one more time to drag his cock against Kit's, he pulled back, reaching for the lube Kit had dropped on the mattress when he'd tackled him.

Once he'd squirted some of the clear gel over his fingers, Jonathan reached between them, trailing over Kit's balls until he reached the rosette behind them. His fingers played over the ring of muscle, spreading the lube around it, dipping inside just enough to stretch the resilient opening before pulling out again.

"Don't stop!" Kit protested, pushing at Jonathan's hips until he could get his legs free of his weight. He pulled them up to his chest, holding them wide open for Jonathan's attention.

"I was just getting started, but if you think you can do it better, go ahead." Jonathan squeezed a healthy dollop of lube down Kit's crease, hiding a smile when Kit squealed at the cold gel hitting his skin. It would be no hardship to watch Kit open himself, Jonathan thought, sitting back on his heels to enjoy the show.

Kit mewled in protest at the sudden absence of Jonathan's hands on his body. "I didn't say that," he said quickly, his lower lip pushing out in a pout. "I'll beg if I have to. Just don't stop touching me."

"I don't plan to stop touching you," Jonathan said, feeling the loss of contact with Kit himself. Grasping Kit's shoulders, he swung him around until Kit was leaning against his chest. Jonathan's fingers found the dusky disks of Kit's nipples, teasing them with the gentle touch Kit loved. "Now, if you expect to feel anything inside you, you'd better get busy." It was an empty threat—Jonathan was going to fill Kit one way or another—but he wanted to see Kit's long fingers stretching himself for his lover's pleasure.

Kit thought about protesting again, but he certainly didn't want to be left high and dry. If Jonathan wanted a show, Kit would give it to him. He slid his palm over his cock, lingering for a moment at the head to catch the fluid already leaking from the tip, letting that act as lubricant as he stroked himself a few times. Craning his head to the side to look at Jonathan, he smiled at the rapt attention on his face. While his own fingers inside him wouldn't be nearly as satisfying as Jonathan's, his body ached to be filled, the teasing touch of Jonathan's fingers on his skin enough to raise that expectation. He worked his index finger past the guardian muscle, swiftly followed by his middle finger as well, stroking in and out to stretch himself. He avoided his prostate, though. He wanted all of that attention to come from Jonathan.

Watching Kit stretch himself was as arousing as Jonathan had known it would be. His cock swelled against the small of Kit's back where he leaned against it, but Jonathan ignored its demand for the moment. Not taking his eyes from the enticing image of Kit's fingers sliding in and out of himself, he groped around the bedding with one hand, the other roaming over Kit's chest, tweaking and rubbing. When his fingers found the dildo and closed around it, he lowered his head to nip at the side of Kit's neck. "Add another finger," he murmured against the skin, lips and teeth moving down the curve of Kit's shoulder.

Kit wanted to protest again, since his own fingers were not nearly satisfying enough, but he did as Jonathan directed, adding his ring finger but keeping the penetration shallow so the entrance stretched but the rest of his passage stayed tight in anticipation of Jonathan's fingers or, preferably, Jonathan's cock.

When Kit breached himself with a third finger, Jonathan's cock jumped, but as hungry as he was to take the place of those probing fingers, there was something else he wanted to fill Kit with first. "That's enough," he rumbled, holding the dildo in front of them and coating the flexible shaft with more lube. He wiped the excess on Kit's thigh, pulling the leg over his own to open Kit even wider. "Christ, you've got me so hot," he growled, rubbing the rounded head over Kit's entrance. "So fucking hot like this, kitten…." Lowering his head to press his mouth against any skin he could reach, he slid the dildo in until his knuckles brushed against Kit's balls.

"Then fuck me already," Kit insisted, his breath catching as the dildo slid far deeper into his arse than his fingers had done. He braced his feet on the bed and lifted his hips, wordlessly asking for more. The length of latex couldn't compare to Jonathan's cock filling him, but knowing it was wielded by Jonathan's hand made it a marked improvement over Kit's own fingers. "Please!"

That was a request Jonathan fully intended to grant—eventually. In the meantime, he slid the dildo out until just the head was stretching Kit's opening, then slowly pushed it in again, twisting it when it was as far in as it could go. The moan this wrung from Kit told Jonathan the dildo was hitting its target. Remembering how Kit had used the toy on himself the night they'd bought it, he set a slow, steady rhythm, rubbing Kit's prostate with every inward thrust, his other hand massaging Kit's balls. Kit's head leaned back against Jonathan's shoulder, eyes closed, lips parting with each gasping breath. "So beautiful," Jonathan murmured, nuzzling Kit's temple. "Letting me love you this way... let me see what I'm making you feel, kitten."

A soft sob escaped Kit's throat as Jonathan teased him exactly the way he liked. He wanted to tell Jonathan how perfectly Jonathan was loving him, how wild Jonathan's attentions were making him, but words were beyond him. He stroked Jonathan's knee next to his, trying to convey his emotions nonverbally. He had no idea if he succeeded, but Jonathan did not pause in his slow, steady teasing.

Jonathan's arousal surged with each new sound of pleasure he won from Kit, each time Kit pushed his hips up to meet him as he twisted the dildo. "Want you to come for me," he said, sliding the hand teasing Kit's balls up to encircle his shaft. Jonathan's fingers were already slick with lube, aided by the cloudy fluid leaking from the slit as he rubbed them over the crown of Kit's cock. "Come on, kitten. Come for me so I can make you come again, with me inside you."

"Yes," Kit groaned, eyes closing as his head fell back and his body gave in to Jonathan's demands. He shivered in his lover's embrace, his seed spilling over Jonathan's hand and his own belly as waves of pleasure washed through him. His entire body went limp with his climax, every muscle pliant and willing for whatever Jonathan wanted to do to him next. Blindly he turned his head, seeking Jonathan's lips for a kiss.

Kit's lips were tender against Jonathan's, but the moment they parted beneath him, the hunger he'd held at bay demanded more. Discarding the restraint he'd used with the dildo, Jonathan delved deep into Kit's mouth, probing and insistent. Unable to get as close as he needed to be in their current position, he pulled the dildo free and tossed it aside, then turned Kit in his arms until they were face-to-face. Kit's legs spread to circle his waist, and Jonathan lifted him up, the head of his cock rubbing against Kit's slippery entrance. "Need you," Jonathan husked, his lips finding Kit's again as the ring of muscle pulsed against him, resisting his ingress. His hands spanned Kit's ribs, thumbs stroking his tightened nipples. "Need to be in you, loving you...."

"Take me, then," Kit said, pushing down against Jonathan's cock. The head popped past his ring, and the rest was a long, slow slide in. When he hit bottom, he stayed there for a moment, reveling in the feeling of being filled not by a piece of latex, but by Jonathan's living warmth.

Jonathan pushed up, trying to sink himself deeper in Kit's tight heat. His hands slid down Kit's sides to grasp his hips, lifting him up and pulling him down again, groaning as the rippling contractions massaged his length. Head falling back, his normal veneer of control cracked and shattered beneath his overwhelming need. His fingers tightened over Kit's pelvic bones, hitching him closer, his own hips pumping in a fierce beat that slammed their bodies together with every thrust. A tight knot coiled in his groin, pulling tauter with every stroke, every heartbeat that pounded in his chest, but it still wasn't enough. Lifting his head, he sought Kit's mouth, lips slipping and sliding apart with each shuddering thrust. "Kit," he groaned, trying to capture and hold the fleeting contact. "Fuck, Kit, so good, so close."

"Then come," Kit urged, the constant prodding of Jonathan's cock against his prostate keeping him on edge despite his earlier climax. He caressed the strong chest in front of him, fingers lingering on Jonathan's pert nipples. He wanted to bend and take them in his mouth, but that would have dislodged him from his current seat, and the last thing he wanted was to lose the intimate contact. "Come and take me with you." He squeezed his inner muscles tight, hoping to push Jonathan over the edge.

The inciting words had Jonathan aching to feel Kit spasm around him as they came together, but as hard as he thrust, he couldn't get deep enough, powerful enough. Tensing his thighs, he rolled forward, carrying Kit along until he had his lover pinned beneath him. Planting one hand on the mattress next to Kit's shoulder, he used the other to work Kit's cock as his hips snapped with all his strength, filling Kit as far, as deep, as fully as he could join them. His mouth closed over Kit's, chest heaving as the knot in his gut coiled tighter and tighter and then exploded, flooding his senses. He vaguely registered the hot splash of Kit's come over his hand, but he couldn't stop, pumping into the clenching channel until the waves of sensation finally faded. His muscles giving out, he collapsed atop Kit in a sweaty heap.

Kit cried out as he came a second time, his release tossing him about like a rag doll as he shivered through his climax. He gasped Jonathan's name as the pounding went on and on, extending his orgasm beyond what he would have thought possible. The sudden press of Jonathan's weight left him perfectly replete. He circled Jonathan's neck, brushing a tender kiss to sweaty skin. "Love you."

"Love you too." Jonathan rolled to one side, Kit's arms still clasped around his neck, and pressed his own kiss to the hair tangled at Kit's temple. "Sorry for going all caveman on you there at the end."

"I don't remember complaining," Kit replied lazily. "In fact, I rather enjoyed it. I'm feeling thoroughly ravished."

"Have enough strength left to talk with Devon?"

"Always," Kit said. "I'll always have enough strength to talk to either of you. I think my phone is still in the kitchen, though."

"I'll get it," Jonathan volunteered, groaning as he pushed to his feet. "Fuck, I used muscles I'd forgotten I had."

Kit let Jonathan go, taking advantage of the opportunity to ogle his arse as he retreated across the room. Damn, he was a lucky bloke! Jonathan came back a few minutes later, giving Kit the chance to appreciate the front view as well. He couldn't help the low wolf whistle at the sight of Jonathan's half-hard cock. "That excited about calling Devon?" he teased.

"Maybe I have more plans for you after we talk with Devon," Jonathan retorted, handing the phone to Kit. "Can you put it on speaker so we can both talk with him at the same time?"

"Yeah, I'll do that," Kit said, hitting Devon's number on speed dial. "And you can make all the plans for me you want." He reached for Jonathan, pulling him back onto the bed and snuggling close as they listened to the phone ring on the other end.

"Aldridge," Devon's voice snapped when the line stopped ringing.

Are things that bad? Jonathan thought, exchanging a concerned glance with Kit. "It's Jon and Kit, babe. How are you holding up?"

A disgusted grunt sounded over the phone. "Bleeding solicitors— excuse me, *attorneys*," he corrected himself in a flat American drawl, "are dragging everything out. Even things I thought were settled before I left England are suddenly up in the air again." Jonathan shook his head. He and his ex-wife had been able to work things out amicably, but even so, the process had been far from enjoyable; he could only imagine what Devon was going through. "I'd hoped to be able to finalize things in a week, ten days tops. It's been three weeks, and it doesn't look like we're any closer to wrapping this up."

"I'm sorry this has been so difficult for you," Kit said, not really knowing what else to say. He didn't have any experience with the kind of negotiations Devon was going through and had no advice to offer. "Just remember that when it's all over, you get to come back here to people who love you."

"That's the only thing keeping me sane," Devon admitted, the tone of his voice tearing at Kit's heart.

"What can we do to help?" Kit asked immediately. "Anything we can do. You know that, right?"

Devon did know it, but there was a limit to what his lovers could do at such a distance, especially when what he really wanted was to feel their arms around him. "I don't know that there's anything you can do."

"We could try to distract you for a bit," Jonathan offered.

"What kind of distraction did you have in mind?" Devon asked warily, having learned by experience that Jonathan's offers weren't always as straightforward as they seemed.

"Are you someplace private?" Jonathan asked, his voice turning husky.

"So you mean *that* kind of distraction, do you?" Devon asked.

"What other kind of distraction is there?" Kit asked, hoping Devon could hear his grin through the phone.

The mischievous tone in Kit's voice was enough to bring a smile to Devon's face. "Trust me, sunshine, I much prefer your distractions to the ones I have here." He shifted the phone to his other ear, stretching out on the couch in the hotel suite's working area. "I'm waiting for a call back from my solicitor. Hers and mine are negotiating terms again. I might hear something in an hour, and I might not hear from them until tomorrow." He worked an arm under his head and sighed. "I hate this bloody waiting. I'm half tempted to let her have her way just to make it end, but I don't want to give her the satisfaction of thinking she's won."

"That's what her attorneys are counting on," Jonathan said. "Doesn't make it any easier to take, I know."

"And all the more reason to let us help you relieve a little stress," Kit purred. "We don't want you making a rash decision because you're tense and frustrated, now do we?"

"I think the frustration's a given until I get back to you two," Devon answered. "You're welcome to do something about the tension, though."

"Why don't you lie down and get comfortable?" Jonathan suggested. "Kick your shoes off, and any other clothing you feel like removing while you're at it."

"Want to imagine me starkers, do you?" Devon laughed, starting to free the buttons of his shirt.

"Well, we are a little ahead of you in that respect," Jonathan admitted.

"Besides, you like being starkers with us," Kit reminded him. "And we can get up to far more fun if we can get at you more easily." He winked at Jonathan and reached for a rosy nipple, flicking the tip with the end of his finger. "Let us know when you're comfortable. We wouldn't want to get any farther ahead of you than we already are."

"I suspect you're already a fuck or two ahead of me," Devon countered, stripping out of his shirt before easing down the zipper of his trousers. Just hearing his lovers' voices had him half-hard beneath his boxers. "That always makes you cheekier than usual."

"Not that I'm complaining, but I'm doing double duty here until you get back." Jonathan rubbed his thumbs over Kit's darker nipples in return, adding a gentle tweak.

"It's not my fault I'm twenty-two and perpetually horny," Kit said, not able to stifle the moan that rose at the touch of Jonathan's fingers on his nipples. They didn't have the nipple clamps here, but maybe Jonathan would play with them for a while as they teased and pleasured Devon. "There is a reason I need two of you to keep me satisfied."

"It takes two thirty-year-olds to satisfy one twenty-year-old? Something's wrong with that math," Devon complained, slipping off his pants and stretching out naked on the couch. "We should have three twentysomethings catering to us, don't you think, Jon?"

"Christ, I can barely keep up with one," Jonathan retorted, leaning over to swipe a tongue down the middle of Kit's chest. "I think three would kill me."

"And what makes you think I'd be willing to share with two other twenty-year-olds?" Kit demanded, or tried to anyway. It was a little hard to be demanding when Jonathan's tongue was doing wicked things to his chest.

"Well, send one of those other twenty-year-olds over here to take care of me," Devon suggested. "Don't think I can't tell the two of you are getting up to something." He didn't begrudge Kit and Jonathan their time together; he just wished the hell he could get back there to share it before filming ended and all three of them would have to go their separate ways. That thought was even more depressing than the divorce procrastination, and he pushed it from his mind. "At least tell me what you're doing so I can get a little vicarious zing."

"We're at my place," Kit began, mindful of Devon's lessons about phone sex and building anticipation from when they were trapped in the cabin and only had the phone to stay in touch with Jonathan. "In my bedroom. I'm leaning back on the pillows and Jon is leaning over me." His eyes closed momentarily as Jonathan's tongue moved from the middle of his chest toward one pert nipple, skating around it without ever touching. "He's got his mouth on my chest. I keep hoping he'll suck my nipples, but he seems determined to suck everything else instead."

"The young these days have no patience," Jonathan commented, in between drawing his tongue to the other side of Kit's chest and circling the other nipple. Their earlier lovemaking had restored his accustomed control, and he'd gladly spend as long as it took to help Devon unwind while giving Kit the slow, sweet loving he deserved. "I'm planning to taste every bit of your skin before I think about sucking anything."

Wetting his fingertips with saliva, Devon drew them over his chest, circling his nipples the way Kit described Jonathan doing to him. "I'd normally say something about anticipation making your release more intense, but I'm feeling a bit short of patience m'self lately."

"See?" Kit said to Jonathan, grabbing his lover's head and trying to hold it still as he moved beneath Jonathan's mouth. Jonathan squirmed away, much to Kit's frustration. "Devon doesn't want slow and drawn out. He wants hard and fast and blow your mind, right, Devon?"

"Thought I just gave you that," Jonathan countered, moving down Kit's torso to repeat the teasing circumnavigation of his navel. "Any harder and you'd be too sore to ride tomorrow."

"Besides, it isn't easy to do 'hard and fast and blow your mind' on your own." Devon was getting ahead of Kit and Jonathan, but he flicked his fingers over his nipples anyway, tugging at the hardened nubs even though it never felt as good as Jonathan's teeth closing over them.

"I'll just tell Niall my back's bothering me," Kit retorted with a glare for Jonathan. "As for you, Devon, if you can't do 'hard and fast and blow your mind' over the phone, then tell us what you want us to do. You know we can follow directions."

"One of you can, anyway." Devon snorted. His fingers tightened around his nipples as he remembered how beautiful Kit had looked the first time Devon used the clamps on him. Which had been as a result of

Kit acting out during a session, now that he thought of it. Continuing to tug at a nipple with one hand, he let his other drift lower, ghosting over the skin of his abdomen lazily, in no hurry to move things along too quickly and lose this moment of intimacy, even if it was over nothing more than a cell phone connection. "Seems to me Jonathan's got the right idea. If I were there"—his throat tightened for a moment, and he cleared it, then went on—"I'd want to take my time with you m'self."

"I'm glad one of you thinks I know what I'm doing," Jonathan said, sliding lower to drag his tongue across the valley that ran from Kit's hip bones to the crease of his thighs.

"So what would you do to me if you were here?" Kit asked, his voice growing hoarse at Jonathan's continued teasing. "Tell us and Jon will do it for you. I'm spread out on the bed, completely naked, Jonathan's spunk running down my legs, just waiting for you to take me. Tell us what you'd do, taking your time."

Devon's cock jumped at the provocative image, but he refused to acknowledge it for the moment. He closed his eyes, picturing Jonathan crouched between Kit's spread knees, his tawny head dipping to taste Kit's olive skin. "I'd kiss my way down your legs," Devon rasped, his hand slipping lower to lightly skim the flesh of his thighs. The urge to taste Jonathan's seed leaking from Kit gnawed at him, but even if he was there with them he'd wait, driving Kit's arousal and his own higher by licking and nipping his way down and back up Kit's long legs first.

"We're sharing a brain, babe." Jonathan's mouth was already moving over the olive skin of Kit's inner thighs. With a nudge to prompt Kit to bend his knees, he ran his tongue over the back of the joint, winning a shiver from Kit. "I think we just discovered a new ticklish spot behind his knee."

Kit could hardly deny the ticklish spot when his entire leg had jerked at the sensation of Jonathan's tongue stimulating the smooth skin. He ordered his muscles to relax, but the constant scratch of Jonathan's beard made it hard to resist the urge to pull away.

"I'll remember that for sometime when we want to tease him." Devon chuckled. Running his fingers over the back of his own knee didn't create the same reaction, but then he seemed to remember reading somewhere that it wasn't possible to tickle yourself. "Right now I just want to keep tasting him."

Soothing the tender skin with his tongue, Jonathan moved lower, tracing the tensed muscles of Kit's calf, lingering at his ankle, gliding over the arch and across and between Kit's toes, trying to keep the pressure firm enough not to tickle. Kit's skin tasted slightly salty, not surprising given the sweat they'd worked up earlier. Licking his lips, Jonathan shifted and started on Kit's other foot, slowly working his way upward with the same loving attentions.

"Toes," Kit pleaded when Jonathan's mouth skated across the instep of his foot without moving lower. "Please." He had no idea what it was about having a lover suck his toes that turned him on, but since Jonathan was intent on tasting him everywhere, Kit was glad he'd taken a shower before he went to Devon's to get the riding crop. He could ask for what he wanted without worrying about it being repulsive.

"You're determined to have me suck on something, aren't you?" Jonathan teased, though his reluctance was wholly feigned. He had every intention of sucking on more than just Kit's toes before their call with Devon ended. In the meantime, he retraced his path over Kit's foot, taking the smallest digit into his mouth, swirling his tongue around it, then hollowing his cheeks and sucking firmly. He hoped Devon could hear the sounds Kit was making over the phone line, and that they were turning him on as much as they were arousing Jonathan.

"Ah fuck, whatever you're doing, do it again," Devon insisted. Kit's groan had gone straight to his cock, his bollocks tightening at the lascivious tone in the inarticulate cry.

"Fuck, yes!" Kit begged, his entire leg trembling with the jolts of pleasure at the sensation and the sight of Jonathan sucking on his toes. His lover's fingers slid between the stubby digits, separating them so each one could receive its due share of attention. "Feels so good."

Jonathan took his time laving each of Kit's toes in turn, moving back and forth between one foot and the other. Glancing up, he could see Kit's cock, swollen and red, a pool of silvery liquid forming where it dripped against his stomach. "You should see him, Devon. I don't know how we didn't figure out before this how much of a slut he is for having his toes sucked."

Devon's best intentions of taking things slowly couldn't stand against growing heat in his belly at Jonathan's words and Kit's moans. Wrapping a hand around his cock, he stroked it slowly, letting his own precome lubricate his palm. "Can't blame him, love—what you do with that mouth of yours is pretty hard to resist, no matter what you're sucking."

"I'd be flattered, but you know I learned it all from you and Kit." With a final nip to Kit's smallest toe, Jonathan started upward again, hungry to fill his mouth with something more substantial. His attentions to Kit's knee were more perfunctory on this side, but Kit wasn't complaining, spreading his legs wider to facilitate Jonathan's path over his thigh.

"Then show us what you've learned already," Kit demanded, impatient with the slow pace. "My toes aren't the only appendage in need of your attention."

"I ought to flip you over—there's a whole 'nother side I haven't even started on yet." Jonathan paused, his breath ruffling the dusky hair that curled at the base of Kit's cock. "What do you think, Devon?"

"I think Kit will have your bollocks if you try." Devon laughed. He didn't need to see Kit's expression to know he would be all but frothing at the mouth by now with the need to come. His hand moved faster over his own cock in anticipation of what he was sure Jonathan was about to do next.

"I think you're right," Kit said, spreading his legs wider and running his fingers into Jonathan's hair. "So are you going to stare at it all night or are you going to suck it?"

"Maybe I'll turn it into an all-night sucker." Jonathan chuckled. His tongue darted out, still not homing in on the target as Kit demanded but laving the sac that hung heavy beneath it instead, wetting the testes well before taking them, one at a time, into his mouth and sucking gently. When he let them slide from between his lips, his tongue skated backward, over the smooth skin of Kit's perineum to gather a taste of himself from their earlier lovemaking. "Wish I could share this with you, Devon," he whispered, too softly for their missing lover to hear, before finally licking up the vein of Kit's long-neglected cock.

Kit's moan resonated through the room as Jonathan finally gave him the attention he had been craving. "So good," he said huskily. "So fuckin' amazing, what you do with your mouth." He tried not to buck up into Jonathan's throat, but he doubted he'd manage for long.

The conversation stopped after that, but Devon had no trouble imagining what was happening from the sighs and moans and gasping breaths that sounded as clearly as if Kit and Jonathan were across the room from him rather than across a continent and an ocean. He licked his palm and stroked himself more roughly, the saliva a poor substitute for the heat of Jonathan's mouth, his own fingers tugging at his nipple a pale echo of the attentions Kit would pay them, but the sudden cry as Jonathan must have brought Kit to climax was enough to drag Devon along with them. His groan as he came was lost in the loving murmurs, too low for him to make out specific words, between Kit and Jonathan as he imagined their embrace.

Kit shivered through his release, not trying to stifle his sounds but no longer consciously aware of projecting them into the phone for Devon. "What about you, Jon?" he asked when he could focus enough to form a coherent sentence.

"I'm good," Jonathan replied lazily, licking at his palm where he'd stroked himself to release, the salty flavor mingling with Kit's in his mouth. "You okay, Devon?"

"Be better if I was there with you, but I think I can make it through the afternoon now without murdering Marcy's attorney," Devon answered. "Making this go away is sounding better and better."

"Don't do anything rash," Kit warned again. "Stick to your guns and get it worked out right. We'll be here when you get back. A few extra days won't change anything."

"Except make me miss you even more," Devon replied.

CHAPTER 21
DOUBLE YOUR FUN

KIT LOOKED at his watch for the fiftieth time. "What time did Devon say he was going to be home?" he asked Jonathan. It had been five weeks since Devon had left for Los Angeles, and Kit was ready to have him return. He pushed aside the thought that filming would be ending soon and that their careers could separate them for far longer than that. Devon was due in from the airport any moment now, and Kit wanted to focus on welcoming Devon back where he belonged.

"He isn't going to get here any sooner for your worrying about him." Jonathan halted Kit's pacing by the simple expedient of stepping behind him and wrapping his arms around him. He could all but feel Kit vibrating with excitement and anticipation. "I'm anxious to see him too, but he'll get here when he gets here, Kit-Kat." Jonathan decided Kit needed something to take his mind off checking his wristwatch every two minutes. Easing a hand under Kit's chin, he tilted his head backward, nuzzling a trail of kisses down the smooth cheek. Just as he neared his destination of Kit's mouth, a car door slammed outside. Kit's head snapped up, his forehead connecting with Jonathan's chin with an audible crack.

Devon unlocked his front door to find his lovers standing in the middle of his living room, Jonathan rubbing his chin and Kit holding his forehead, both of them laughing. "Damn, that's a sound I've missed hearing," he said, dropping his bag and opening his arms.

"Devon!" Kit flew across the room, arms going around Devon as he pressed kisses to every part of Devon's face he could reach. "We missed you!"

Jonathan enclosed both Devon and Kit in his arms, letting Kit work off some of his excitement before leaning over his shoulder and capturing Devon's mouth in a slower if no less impassioned kiss. "It's good to have you home, babe."

Returning the kisses in equal measure, Devon could feel the weight of the past five weeks rolling off him as he relaxed into their embrace, recognizing the appropriateness of Jonathan's greeting. He'd left the house he'd be selling as part of the divorce settlement behind him in LA, but this rental cottage in the Glastonbury hills was his home, as much as the cabin he'd been stranded in with Kit or the hotel they'd stayed in during location shooting on the Isle of Skye. They might be, would be, separated once filming ended, but whenever they could be together, he'd be home. "I missed you too," he answered when their kisses eventually slowed. The words were wholly inadequate, but he didn't doubt Kit and Jonathan understood the emotions behind them.

Needing more than a welcome-home kiss, Kit slid to one side so that Devon was caught between Jonathan and himself, working his hands under layers of clothes until he found smooth skin. "Missed your kisses, your touch, your smell, everything about you, but I especially missed having you inside me," he murmured as he started undressing Devon, intent on recreating all the moments they'd had to share over the phone while Devon was gone. Today, if possible.

"How exhausted are you?" Jonathan asked, moving his hands to Devon's shoulders to rub at the corded muscles. "Not that I'm not as eager to get you into bed as Kit is, but unless you were able to rest on the plane, you might actually need to sleep." As long as he got to hold Devon while he slept, Jonathan would live with that, even if it meant enduring eight hours of blue balls until Devon was awake enough to do something about them.

"I dozed a bit," Devon admitted, arching his head to give Jonathan better access to the muscles of his neck, which were loosening under the kneading massage. Kit's fingers, busily pushing his shirt upward, found and pinched his nipples, starting another part of Devon's body hardening just as rapidly. "I'm sure the two of you can find some way to manage to keep me awake."

Kit hesitated in his rediscovery of Devon's body. "Are you sure? I want you, but I want you to be awake enough to enjoy it." Devon's hand closed over Kit's, urging it to move again, so Kit took that as an affirmative answer and returned to undressing Devon as quickly as possible, adding his lips to his fingers as soon as bare skin came into view.

Devon's appreciative moan was all the convincing Jonathan needed to start nudging them toward the stairs to the bedroom, peeling

Devon's shirt over his head as they went. As soon as it hit the floor, his lips replaced his fingers on Devon's neck, freeing his hands to start working at the buckle of Devon's belt.

"Careful not to trip me," Devon protested as his trousers slid to his knees. His aborted half step made him stumble against Kit, Jonathan's arms tightening to steady him. The position had its benefits, but he'd rather be horizontal to feel the press of his lovers' cocks against him— and he'd infinitely prefer to feel bare skin against his. "The last thing I need is to wind up in a cast."

"Then let's take this upstairs," Kit proposed, dropping to his knees to help Devon step out of his jeans. He took advantage of the position to lick a stripe up the underside of Devon's cock. "We'll all be more comfortable on the bed."

Devon kicked off his shoes and stripped his socks before offering Kit a hand back up. "Then the rest of you'd better get naked on the way. I've been imagining being free and in bed with you for five bloody weeks, and I can tell you there were no clothes involved."

"As if Kit would ever complain about getting naked," Jonathan chuckled, pulling his own shirt over his head without bothering with the buttons before starting on his jeans.

Laughing, Kit stripped, leaving a trail of clothes behind him as he scampered up the stairs. "Last one to the top—" He didn't even get the words out before Devon tackled him to the ground. "Did you have something else in mind?"

"Beyond getting into bed with the two of you?" Devon paused, wriggling a bit to settle his cock more closely against the curve of Kit's arse. He wasn't sure how he'd choose which of the many fantasies he'd consoled himself with while he was gone to indulge in first. Topping Kit, topping Jonathan, being taken by either of them—that sparked an idea, something Kit had brought up one of the first times they were all together. But they needed to be in bed first. "I'm sure something will come to me."

Jonathan snorted and prodded Devon's backside with his knee. "I'm sure *something will come* to all of us, but in the meantime, you're blocking the stairway. Get your lazy free ass up in bed."

Devon grinned as he pushed to his feet, offering Kit another hand up as well. He did feel free, in a way that had little to do with his divorce finally being official. "Get there yourself and I'll show you how lazy I am," he retorted. "I haven't been fucking Kit blind for the last five weeks like you."

"What makes you think he's been fucking me and not the other way around?" Kit asked, taking Devon's hand and pulling him toward the bedroom. "You know what a slutty bottom Jon is."

"And proud of it," Jonathan agreed, groping Devon's ass as he helped him along from the rear. "With either of you, anytime. Not that we kept track, but we both did our share of topping. Didn't keep us from missing you, babe. It's just not the same when you're not with us."

Ah hell. He would *not* cry, Devon insisted to himself. Their reunion was a time for celebration, not tears. And that they'd have to deal with an even longer separation all too soon was not going to be allowed to cast a pall over this night. "You had the toy box to keep me in mind."

Kit chuckled wryly. "Whole hell of a lot of good it did us," he said. "We couldn't even make ourselves open it without you. Apparently kinky sex is only really good with you involved."

The admission made Devon vaguely uneasy, as if that was all he brought to the relationship. He knew that wasn't how Kit meant it, knew that wasn't how either of them felt, but it strengthened his resolve about what he wanted to ask them for. "Well, I hope you won't be disappointed, but I wasn't planning to use anything from it tonight."

"God, Devon, you could never open it again and I'd be okay with that as long as you were here with us!" Kit froze in his tracks, spinning around to catch Devon in his arms. "Jon and I talked quite a bit about it, actually, and we realized it doesn't matter whether we're kinky or not as long as it feels natural. We just want to be together, however that looks, whatever that means. Yes, the games are fun, but only because they feel right with you, not because we need them to love you."

"Bed," Jonathan reminded them with a nudge. Yes, they needed to share what they'd discussed with Devon and start talking about how they'd cope once *Camelot* ended, but they didn't need to do it tonight. "Whatever we do, I need to feel Devon in my arms, and I need it now."

"No argument from me," Devon agreed, pulling back the duvet and climbing into bed. He patted the sheets on either side of him in invitation. "I want to feel both of you next to me."

Kit hurried around to the far side of the bed and slid beneath the sheets to press against the length of Devon's body. "Fuck, it feels good to have you between us again. We missed you, luv. Don't ever doubt that."

He wrapped his arms around Devon's torso, snuggling as close as he could possibly get, draping his thigh over Devon's as well, as if to keep him in place.

Jonathan slid against Devon's other side, marveling as he always did how perfectly the three of them fit together, no matter which of them was in the middle. Reaching up to run a hand through Devon's hair, he turned his head until their mouths met, the gentle kiss of welcome turning heated as soon as their tongues slipped together. He delved into Devon's mouth, relishing the taste of mint and scotch and pure, undiluted Devon.

A blissful groan erupted from Devon's throat at the intensity of the kiss. Fuck, he'd missed this. His own hand could bring him off, and had while they were apart, but it was this connection he'd missed, this loving that didn't hide the hunger beneath it but was so much more than just lust and need. He broke the kiss with a final nip to Jonathan's lips and turned his head to capture Kit's mouth with the same fierce tenderness.

Kit gave in to the kiss completely, offering Devon his mouth as he did his best to climb inside Devon's skin. He needed to eradicate all distance between them, as if he could somehow erase the last five weeks of separation. He tugged on Devon's hips until he rolled onto his side so their cocks bumped. Kit bucked against him suggestively, realizing fleetingly that he could come right now if Devon let him. He sucked harder on Devon's tongue, hoping Devon would order him to suck something else before long.

Jonathan watched Devon and Kit kiss with a smile on his face before leaning up on an elbow and bending over them, his tongue darting out to lick at their joined lips. Three-way kisses were always messy, but he didn't care; almost nothing else made him feel the unity between them as strongly.

Devon opened his mouth to Jonathan's, three tongues tangling in an intricate, unchoreographed dance. His cock bumped against Kit's, Jonathan's grinding into his thigh as they kissed. They could easily come just from this needy frottage, but Devon wanted more than that. There was no way he could decide which of his two lovers he wanted first, no way he would willingly cede the decadent connection to the two men who owned his heart.

Easing back from the kiss, he ran a hand over each of his lovers' heads, tawny and dark strands slipping through his fingers. "Want you to make love to me," he said, the moment too fraught with emotion for him to use the crude word *fuck*. "Both of you. Together."

"Jon's already behind you," Kit said, slithering down the front of Devon's body. "If you stay right like you are, he'll have access to your arse while I suck you off from this side."

"That's not what I meant, sunshine." Devon grasped Kit's shoulder and tugged him back upward, knowing he'd never last once Kit got his mouth on his cock.

"Both of us?" Jonathan's eyes darkened as the meaning of Devon's words sank in. "Fuck, Devon, I'll need to get my ring. I'd come as soon as I'm inside you, let alone with Kit rubbing against me."

"Get mine while you're at it," Kit said hoarsely, trembling at the thought of what Devon had proposed. He pressed against the length of Devon's body, remembering a comment Devon had made soon after the three of them had gotten together about making love this way. The thought had turned his insides to mush then, and it had the same effect now. He would never have suggested it, but now that Devon had, he ached with the wanting of it, but he had to ask. "You sure about this?"

"As sure as I am about how much I love you both," Devon answered. "No rings, though," he told Jonathan, who raised an eyebrow but didn't protest further. "If you come, you come, but I want to feel both of you without anything between us, even the rings. No toys, no kink. Just the three of us."

"You are at least planning to let us use lube, I hope?" Jonathan remembered how slowly and thoroughly Devon had prepped him the night he'd asked to be fisted. Having two cocks inside him would stretch Devon nearly as widely, and Jonathan was going to be sure Devon was as well prepared as both he and Kit could make him before either of them breached him. He also fully intended to ask for the same kind of loving at some time in the very near future.

"I'm not a masochist." Devon grinned and reached toward the bedside table to extract a full tube from the drawer. "But this is all I want between you and Kit and me."

"So how do we do this?" Kit asked seriously, taking the tube from Devon's hand and squirting a generous dollop in his palm to warm. He wasn't about to have Devon accuse him of rushing. "I'm having trouble imagining everything in the right places."

"Before we do anything, Devon's lying back and letting us prep him," Jonathan interjected in a voice that would brook no argument. Nudging Devon to the mattress, he raised one of his knees and moved between his legs, leaning forward until he could lick the skin behind Devon's cock.

"Ah Christ, Jon," Devon groaned, bending his other knee and spreading his legs wider to open himself more completely to Jonathan's attentions. He wrapped his hand around his cock, squeezing the base to keep himself from coming in Jonathan's face. He wasn't going to come until he had both Jonathan and Kit inside him.

"I knew that," Kit muttered, pushing Devon's leg toward his chest so he could slide beneath it to get his mouth on any part of Devon he could reach. He bumped heads with Jonathan, chuckling a little and nuzzling him as Jonathan lifted Devon's other leg to make room for them. "You get his hole; I'll play with his balls," Kit proposed, "or vice versa. Whichever you prefer."

"Leave m'bollocks alone or I won't last long enough for this to happen," Devon complained.

"Didn't you tell me once I'd be more relaxed if I came first?" Jonathan replied before sliding his tongue along the smooth skin of Devon's perineum.

"You did say that," Kit agreed, pushing Devon's leg out of the way so he could take Devon's cock into his mouth and down his throat in one smooth motion.

"Bloody—" Devon's response was cut off as his muscles seized and he came hard down Kit's throat, pulse after seemingly endless pulse. He could feel Kit swallowing around him, feel Jonathan licking at his balls as they emptied, his body shuddering with pent-up release. When he finally stopped trembling enough to move, he cuffed Kit's head, Kit grinning up at him unrepentantly. "Bastard," he groused, though it was hard to complain when his body felt so deliciously sated. "I didn't mean to come like that."

"You can punish me for it later," Kit promised. "For now, though, we have some prep work to do." He looked down at the dollop of gel he had smeared all over his hand. "Although I think maybe I'd better start over with the lube." He grabbed the tube, squeezing some more into his palm before offering it to Jonathan. "He wants both our cocks, so maybe we'd better start with both our fingers?"

"I had something else in mind before our fingers." Jonathan glanced up at Devon, his eyes sparkling. "Didn't you tell us that being multiorgasmic was a state of mind? Well, prepare to have your mind blown, babe." Lifting Devon's knee, he bent between his legs again, his tongue sliding wetly over Devon's hole.

Devon's legs fell open without prompting, his heels digging into the sheets as Jonathan's tongue traced over the tight ring of muscle. It clenched in anticipation of the probing tongue breaching him, but Jonathan seemed determined to restoke his arousal lick by teasing lick. He buried a hand in Jonathan's hair, holding him in place, willing the wet tongue to work its way inside him.

Since he loved rimming his lovers nearly as much as he enjoyed being on the receiving end of their attentions, it was no hardship for Jonathan to take his time. It was harder to ignore his own growing arousal at the grunts and growls and flat-out whimpers as he teased Devon. He could only think of one thing that would make it better, and he glanced to the side as the tip of his tongue pushed against Devon's entrance, not yet pressing inside. He met Kit's gaze and tilted his head, silently inviting Kit to join him.

Kit hitched Devon's hips higher, bending him nearly double to make room for his head as well, his tongue darting out to join Jonathan's against the puckered hole. He could taste the sweat from Devon's travel as he helped Jonathan rim their prodigal lover. He didn't know how long they could maintain the position they had Devon in, but he'd enjoy the musky flavor for as long as he could.

Devon grasped his knees to hold them out of the way, opening himself as wide as his legs would spread. His thigh muscles would probably ache tomorrow, but since he already anticipated aching in a much more pleasurable way, it was the least of his concerns. Raising his head, he watched Jonathan and Kit turn toward each other, their tongues meeting in a kiss over his dampened flesh, the sight almost as arousing as when those tongues were sliding against him.

After plundering Devon's smoky flavor from Kit's mouth, Jonathan's tongue finally delved into the furled entrance for a taste of his own. Kit's tongue followed his, the slick muscles sliding together in a foretaste of the contact to come that made Jonathan groan from deep in his chest. Together they probed as deeply into Devon as they could reach, stretching and wetting him, though Jonathan knew that wouldn't be enough. After lingering as long as he could, he reached for Kit's hand, gathering some of the warmed lube he still held in his palm.

Giving Devon's arse one last lick, Kit pulled back, his fingers rubbing against Jonathan's as they smeared the lube over their hands. Keeping their hands entwined, he extended one slick finger and circled Devon's dampened hole. "Ready for more?"

Taking Devon's groan for an affirmative, Kit pushed his finger in as far as the first knuckle, waiting for Jonathan to join him before going deeper. Their fingers rubbed together as they opened Devon, the sensation markedly different than when Kit had two of his own fingers in either Jonathan's or Devon's arse. He could only imagine the same slip and slide when they got their cocks inside Devon. The thought made him so hard it hurt.

Given the number of times Devon's lovers had put two fingers—or more than two fingers—inside him, the sensation shouldn't have been this arousing, especially when he'd already come once. But knowing that one of the fingers was Kit's and one was Jonathan's, and that they'd be replacing those fingers soon with their cocks, had Devon hardening again with each slide back and forth past his slackening ring. When one of the fingertips—he couldn't tell whose—brushed his prostate, he cried out, his resurgent cock slapping his stomach as he bucked into the touch.

They could probably make Devon come again like this, Jonathan thought, holding back a smirk as he rubbed against his lover's gland a second time. He wasn't sure his own control could hold out that long, though, each time Devon pushed against their fingers making his cock swell with need. Deciding Devon needed to be stretched wider, he worked a second finger inside, holding still while Kit followed suit and Devon released the gasp of breath he'd been holding.

Kit was tempted to lower his head and lick at Devon's bollocks again, but he restrained himself, focusing instead on stretching Devon as thoroughly as possible. When their four fingers slid in and out easily, Kit looked questioningly at Jonathan, who nodded his agreement. Folding his ring finger beneath the other two, Kit pressed the tips against Devon's entrance, studying his lover's face to make sure they were not hurting him. A moment later, he felt Jonathan do the same. Slowly, they pushed in together, feeling the slackened muscle give even more, surprising Kit with its flexibility. "You're amazing," he whispered, kissing Devon's knee tenderly. "Letting us love you this way."

"Going to be... even more amazing," Devon answered hoarsely. His chest was already tight, his breath rough and uneven, as he willed himself to relax into the alternating glide and retreat of his lovers' fingers. When the next deep push pressed against his prostate again, his heels slid to the sheets. "Enough. Want you inside me now."

"How do you want us?" Jonathan asked, spreading his fingers before sliding them out, trying to judge if they'd stretched Devon enough to accept them both. He had personal experience in how much a sphincter could accommodate, but he didn't want this experience to be tinged with pain, for any of them. "What will work best for you, babe?"

"One of you underneath me and one on top." Devon had to fight not to clench against the fingers sliding out of him. For the first time he understood Jonathan's comment about how empty he felt in the moments between fingers sliding out and his lover's cock sliding in. "I'll straddle the one on the bed, and then the other one can slide in from behind me."

"Best if it's me on the bottom, then," Jonathan volunteered. "It might be too much of a strain on Kit's back to have both of us on top of him." Not to mention that the thought of both Devon and Kit's weight pressing him into the mattress would be the next best thing to both of them fucking him.

"It wouldn't be the first time you've both been on top of me," Kit reminded them, "but I'm game to drive." He offered Devon a hand. "Up with you, then, so Jon can lie down and get ready for you."

The moment Jonathan stretched out on the bed, Kit ran a hand up his cock, slicking it and then holding it upright for Devon to mount. Jonathan placed his hand over Kit's at the base of his cock, his control too tenuous to let Kit keep stroking him.

Devon braced a knee on either side of Jonathan's waist and lowered himself onto the erect shaft, opened enough from his lovers' ministrations that Jonathan slid in easily, the silken flesh rubbing him in all the right places. "Fuck, Jon, feels so good," he groaned, leaning forward to capture Jonathan's mouth, pushing his tongue inside the way Jonathan was pressed into him.

Jonathan's moan was swallowed by Devon's mouth as he struggled against coming as soon as he was sheathed in the clenching heat. Devon had ridden him before, and he'd always found it wildly arousing to watch as Devon took his pleasure from Jonathan's willing body, but knowing that Kit would be pushing in beside him, the friction of his skin against Jonathan's adding to the constricting pressure, was almost enough to make him come from the image alone. He wrapped his arms around Devon's back, keeping him from moving until he could gather together the tatters of his self-control.

Kit took their stillness as an invitation and pushed at Jonathan's legs until they parted to make room for him between them. Applying more lube to his fingers, he probed the place where his lovers were joined, adding a finger on either side of Jonathan's cock to make sure Devon was stretched well enough to take him too. The muscle gave easily, reassuring him that this could work without hurting any of them. "Ready?" he asked Devon. "Or do you need me to stretch you a little more?"

Jonathan let his head drop back to the mattress, freeing Devon's mouth to reply. Devon flexed his thighs, pushing upward on Jonathan's cock and then sinking again, the stretch and play of muscles and nerves exquisitely sensitive but not painful. His eyes met Jonathan's loving gaze before he twisted his head to meet Kit's eyes. "Ready," he answered, leaning forward against Jonathan's chest to offer himself to Kit's cock.

Taking a deep breath, Kit moved closer, slipping his fingers from Devon's body. He smeared the remaining lube over his cock. "Pull out to the tip," he told Jonathan, "so we can push in together. I think it'll be easier that way."

Jonathan did as Kit suggested, and Kit lined up their shafts, pushing hard to get inside. Devon's guardian muscle gave suddenly, and both of them popped in. "Oh fuck," Kit groaned, the always exquisite tightness doubled by the increase in bulk inside Devon. "I'm going to come before we ever start." He pinched the base of his cock tightly, trying to stave off his climax.

"Just hold still for a minute," Jonathan ground out, biting his lip. Kit's cock against his was provocative enough before they'd pressed inside; Devon's hot channel squeezing them both together was exquisite torment. "Let Devon adjust to us."

Devon's eyes had drifted closed against the brief instant of pain, but it was fading quickly, replaced by the incomparable fullness of taking both his lovers inside him. He could feel the pulse pounding through his stretched tissue, taking on the rhythm of Jonathan's heartbeat below him, of Kit's breathing where his chest rose and fell against Devon's back. "This… just like this," he whispered, reaching for Jonathan's arms as Kit's hands closed around his hips, joining them in one pulsing, loving entity.

Jonathan's lips met Devon's tenderly, the wonder of the moment even stronger than his need for release. His hands covered Kit's on Devon's hips, twining their fingers together. The only drawback of their current position was that he couldn't kiss Kit the way he could Devon, but he squeezed Kit's fingers, knowing the fullness of his emotions was strong enough for Kit to feel through even that tentative contact.

When the burn of the initial stretch faded, Devon turned his head, Jonathan's lips continuing to nuzzle his cheek as Kit's lowered to meet Devon's. Wrapped in their arms, surrounded, filled by their bodies and their love, was a feeling he never wanted to end, and even though he knew that as on edge as they all were, it couldn't last long once they started to move, he needed to feel more. "Now," he murmured against Kit's lips, squeezing Jonathan's arms. "Love me."

"Always," Kit promised, beginning to thrust slowly into Devon's body, trying to find the balance that would let him and Jonathan move, together or in counterpoint, to give everyone the most pleasure. After a moment's fumbling, they settled on moving in counterpoint so one of them was always filling Devon and their cocks rubbed against each other with constant friction. Kit's heart swelled as the love he felt for Devon and Jonathan rose up within him, threatening to bubble over and out of him. "Not gonna last long," he warned them, his climax beginning to tingle in his balls.

"Me either," Jonathan agreed hoarsely. He loved every and any way they made love, but this, the slick glide of Kit's cock against his and the tight clench of Devon's channel around them both, connected them in a way that filled his heart as much as it fanned his arousal. He worked a hand between his hip and Devon's, sweat and the precome leaking from the head of Devon's cock easing the slide as he wrapped his fingers around the stiff shaft. The way it jumped in his palm told him Devon wasn't far behind. "Take what you need," he told Devon, shifting his legs to give him a little more room to move. "And take us with you."

"You—were," Devon gasped, rocking into Jonathan's grasp, chasing the final touch that would send him flying. "With me." Kit's lips closed around his shoulder, sucking at the muscle, and he groaned, throwing back his head to increase the contact. "Always."

The erotic frottage was too much for Kit's control. He thrust forcefully against Devon, his entire body jerking as he climaxed hard, the continued movement of Jonathan's cock against his own prolonging his release. He started to pull back, but Devon's voice stopped him.

"Don't." Devon clenched to hold Kit in, drawing a hiss from Jonathan, who bucked up beneath him. "Want you—both—inside me—when I—come—"

The wetness of Kit's come let Jonathan slide just a little bit easier, a little bit deeper, and when Devon clenched around them, his panting voice taking on the deep-timbred accent Jonathan only heard in their most intimate moments, his own orgasm overwhelmed him. His fist tightened around Devon as he froze, every muscle and nerve and cell in his body caught in the rush of pleasure welling through him.

Devon teetered on the brink. He was so, so close.... If only Jonathan's hand hadn't stopped moving.... He hitched between the two bodies surrounding him, straining for just that fraction more.

Realizing Devon hadn't come a second time, Kit slid his hands around Devon's chest, seeking his nipples. He wished he could reach for Devon's bollocks, but their current position didn't allow for that. He would have to settle for pinching the sensitive peaks and hoping that was enough to push Devon over the edge.

Blinking out of the haze of his climax, Jonathan wove his free hand into Devon's hair, pulling his head down for a kiss, sliding his other hand up Devon's still-hard cock. When he reached the tip, he rubbed his thumb over the slit, sliding his tongue deep into Devon's mouth at the same moment.

Devon gave himself up to his lovers' hands, letting their touch set him flying. He should have felt trapped between them as he shuddered and shook with the force of his second climax, but the press of their bodies, the damp glide of their skin against his, their fullness as the waves of his orgasm rippled around them, grounded him and at the same time set him free. He had bared his soul to these men, and they had accepted it, accepted him and loved him, and whether they were together or apart, nothing would change that.

Even though Kit had softened somewhat, the spasms of Devon's climax squeezed him hard enough to send new tremors running through his body. He pressed as close to Devon as he could get, wanting to stay joined with his lovers for as long as possible. Eventually, though, his cock slipped free. He rolled to the side, urging Devon and Jonathan to turn with him so they still had Devon sandwiched between them, just without crushing Jonathan beneath their weight.

Jonathan almost missed the burden of both their bodies pressing him into the mattress when they rolled away. He wrapped himself against Devon, stretching an arm across to reach for Kit, not willing to lose contact with either of them. "Wow," he exhaled, catching his breath. "Not that I didn't hate it when you were gone, but that was some homecoming."

Kit grinned. "If it weren't for the separation that led up to it, I wouldn't complain about that kind of homecoming more often," Kit agreed, squeezing Jonathan's hand and pressing a kiss to Devon's sweaty shoulder. He snuggled in closer, if that were possible. "Although I think we still have some catching up to do."

Sated by two climaxes in short succession after a twelve-hour flight, Devon felt his eyes drifting shut. "Mnnn," he agreed sleepily. "T'morrow… your arses are mine." Yawning widely, he curled into his lovers' warmth and slipped into the first decent sleep he'd had in six bloody weeks.

CHAPTER 22
THE GIFT THAT KEEPS ON COMING

"HEY, DEVON," Kit called from the room Devon had turned into a sort of office. He'd been checking his email on Devon's computer and started surfing once he finished. "Come look at this."

Devon pulled his head from inside the refrigerator, along with the last two bottles of beer from the bottom shelf. It was a good thing Jonathan had volunteered to stop for groceries after finishing the run-through of Arthur's upcoming fight scene with Mordred. After popping the tops, Devon carried the sweating bottles through the small dining area into the den and offered one to Kit. "Make yourself at home," he said dryly, taking a draw from his own bottle. "Mind you don't disturb any of the porn."

"I still don't know why you think you need porn with Jonathan and me around," Kit retorted, reaching back to squeeze Devon's half-hard cock. "Look at this." He pointed to the picture on the computer screen of a piece of modern furniture, the length of a couch but with one end higher than the other, a long, elegant curve of smooth leather. "I thought Jonathan might like one for his birthday."

"Where do you think I find my ideas?" Devon retorted with a chuckle, dropping a kiss on Kit's head and moving his hand back to his own tackle with an answering squeeze. He bent closer to the computer screen, peering over Kit's shoulder at the display. The sinuous lines of the loveseat-like bench might appeal to Jonathan's artistic sensibilities, he supposed, but it seemed an odd choice for Kit to suggest. "What makes you think Jonathan wants more furniture? He's barely at his place often enough to use what he has." And he'd have to find a way to get it home to the States after filming ended in a few more weeks, but Devon wasn't going to ruin the mood of the afternoon by bringing that up.

"Ah," Kit said, clicking a link, "but this isn't just furniture. This is Tantric furniture." The image on the screen changed to one of a couple intertwined, clearly using the chair as a prop for their lovemaking. He clicked to the next picture, the woman lying back across the upper portion of the couch so that her hips were at just the right height for sex. "Just think of all the interesting positions we could get into with this to help us out."

A spark kindled in Devon's eyes. Leaning forward, he covered Kit's on the mouse with his own, clicking between screens that illustrated a variety of positions: the man reclining over the chair's curves with the woman on top of him, her back to his chest; the woman seated in the lower arc as the man sprawled over the upper one, at the perfect height for her to fellate him; the woman lying on the lower end with her legs draped over the man's shoulders as he knelt on the floor before her, his face between her legs. "I like that one," he said, pausing at a scene of the two partners lying with their heads at opposite ends of the chair, the curve in the center supporting the man entering the woman from behind. "Looks like it would give good support for your back."

Kit turned his head and kissed Devon deeply, touched by his lover's concern for his well-being. "Love you," he said when their lips parted. "So what do you think? Shall we get it for Jonathan? If we order it now, it should be here in time for his birthday."

Already imagining a third member joining the scenarios, Devon nodded distractedly. "Look at this one." He pointed, his voice deepening as his mind's eye replaced the woman with his two most definitely masculine lovers. "The one at the head end would be able to suck off a man standing right there while his lover took him from behind like that...." He adjusted the hardening shaft beneath his track pants, trying to decide which position of the imaginary threesome he'd want to find himself in most.

"I like this one best," Kit admitted, skipping ahead a few to one with the woman lying on the lower end of the chair with the man kneeling on the floor as he entered her. "One of us where she is, Jonathan where the guy is, and the other one of us behind him so that he's the filling in our sandwich." He shifted on the seat. "He better get home soon or I'm going to end up jumping you without him."

"You'd better find something else for us to look at or he'll wonder what the hell got us so worked up before he got here," Devon retorted. Spinning the chair, he knelt and pulled Kit into a deep kiss, letting his hands roam over the warm skin under his T-shirt. Kit's legs wrapped around his back, pulling him closer, and Devon found it hard to remember there was ever a time that he'd only seen Kit as a rival for Jonathan's attention. They didn't break apart until the sound of a car door slamming outside caught their attention. With a click of the mouse, Devon changed the display on the computer screen, winking at Kit. "Told you that porn comes in handy," he murmured before leaning in to claim his lips again.

Since Devon had stolen the words right out of his mouth, Kit simply enjoyed the kiss and waited for Jonathan to join them. He'd order the chair in the morning, when Jonathan left for early call.

"I come bearing beer—and food," Jonathan announced loudly, dropping his bags on the kitchen counter and walking into the house. "And this is the thanks I get," he complained, pausing in the doorway to enjoy the sight of the two most important men in his life wrapped in a torrid kiss. "Starting without me again, I see."

"You're welcome to join us," Devon beckoned with a grin. "Just bring some fresh beers, will you?"

"Beer?" Kit protested, pulling Devon's head back toward his. "What do you want with beer when you can have me… and Jonathan?"

Jonathan enjoyed watching Kit and Devon kiss a moment longer— the only thing more arousing than seeing the two of them together was knowing they wanted him to join them. However much he missed home and Josh, however long and exhausting the day's filming, knowing he had this to come home to made it all bearable. Pushing away the intrusive thought that filming was going to be ending in a few short weeks, he turned back to grab the necks of three beers, leaving the rest of the groceries for later. "Beer to cool off so he can last longer," Jonathan teased, pressing a cold bottle to each man's neck. "The two of us might be too much for him otherwise."

"Bring it on," Devon retorted, catching Jonathan's arm and pulling him to his knees and into a welcoming kiss every bit as ardent as the one he'd just shared with Kit.

Jonathan moaned into the kiss, the taste of beer and Kit and Devon himself setting the spark to his desire. "God, I love it when I come home and you're already worked up," Jonathan gasped, pulling away just long enough to speak before diving back into the kiss. And anything else his lovers had in store for him.

JONATHAN WAS practically vibrating with anticipation by the time Devon pulled the car to the curb in front of his house. It wasn't a sensation he'd been accustomed to before becoming intimate with his two lovers, and he wondered idly if Kit was rubbing off on him, before the young man in question opened his door, grabbed him by the arm, and dragged him to his feet.

"C'mon, birthday boy, now the real celebration can begin."

Devon grinned as he climbed out of the driver's seat. "And don't pretend you weren't thinking about this during the cast party—I saw how you were squirming in your seat while everyone sang 'Happy Birthday' to you."

"It was the only thing that got me through, between the bad jokes and that ridiculous hat they made me wear," Jonathan groused, though Kit leaning over his back whispering filthy suggestions in his ear and the gleam in Devon's eyes as he smiled at him from across the table had played their part in his eagerness to abandon the cast party for their own, more private festivities.

"Awww, poor baby," Kit teased as they walked up the sidewalk to Jonathan's house. "We'll make it up to you, I promise." Opening the door, he led Jonathan inside. "Now close your eyes while we get your present ready."

"I thought you two were going to be my present," Jonathan answered, tugging Kit into his arms and stretching out a hand for Devon, who was just closing the door behind them. "I've been looking forward to it all afternoon."

"Oh, we are your present," Kit promised, returning the embrace, "just with a little… shall we say, extra dressing today."

"More interested in undressing," Jonathan murmured, burrowing under Kit's T-shirt to the warm skin underneath. "Devon?" he asked, lifting his head from Kit's neck when Devon hadn't joined them. While he'd never complain about an armful of Kit, Jonathan was greedy on his birthday—he wanted to celebrate with both his lovers. "What's that?" he asked, locating Devon lounging against a cloth-covered lump in the corner of his living room.

"Your present," Devon drawled, running a hand over the mound the way Jonathan had seen him caress Kit's bare flank. "Aren't you a little bit curious what it is?"

Glancing down at Kit, who flashed him a mischievous grin and pushed him toward Devon, Jonathan stepped forward. He couldn't imagine what could possibly be concealed beneath the oddly shaped drape. With

Devon's amatory gaze encouraging him, he caught the corner of the cloth and pulled it away, revealing an equally oddly shaped couch or lounge of some kind. "It's—nice," he said, at bit at a loss, running a hand over the butter-soft saddle-tan leather. "Very... nice."

"Don't you even want to know what it's for?" Kit asked, draping himself provocatively along the upper curve. He stayed horizontal for the moment rather than letting his head drop down, grinning as he watched Jonathan's expression. "Of course, the effect would probably be better if I was naked."

"Not that I'd ever complain about your being naked," Jonathan agreed, eyeing the couch with a little more interest, "but that can't really be what this is for, is it?"

"Oh, but it is," Devon assured him. "It's a Tantric chair—specifically designed to support an endless variety of sexual positions. There's quite a helpful video if you run out of ideas on your own."

"Leave it to the two of you to come up with something like this." Jonathan tilted his head, his gaze losing focus as he imagined some of the possibilities of the chair's sensuous curves. "Where on earth did you find this, anyway?"

"The internet, where else?" Devon chuckled. "You'll have to thank our randy Percival for the idea, but it was actually manufactured just for you to our own exacting specifications."

"So, do you want to try it out?" Kit purred, reaching for the hem of his T-shirt and pulling it over his head as he leaned back, letting his body mold provocatively to the curve of the chaise. "Just look," he added. "I'm at the perfect height for you to fuck me while I suck Devon off. Or vice versa if you prefer."

Jonathan's cock made its opinion of either option known, pressing insistently against the placket of his jeans, while at the same time his photographer's eye admired the contrast of the smooth leather against Kit's olive skin. He was just reaching to pop open the first button on his fly when a raucous pounding on the front door startled him. "You didn't," he growled ominously, his gaze jumping from Kit to Devon and back again.

"Bloody right we didn't," Devon agreed. "This was meant to be a private party."

"Get rid of them," Kit suggested, sitting up, though he did pull his shirt back on for the moment, in case Jonathan wasn't successful. "I've had enough of Orkneys and Mordred's knights for the day. I want my king and my Grail companion and nobody else."

Before Jonathan could retort that Kit obviously had an inflated idea of his ability to dissuade the Orkneys in search of a party, the door opened and said Orkneys tumbled inside, followed by the rest of the *Camelot* principal cast. "About time we found you," Colm complained, flopping onto the cooler he'd dragged in with Warwick's help. "We checked Kit's and Devon's places, but there was nobody there."

"Maybe because we were planning a private party?" Kit snarked, less than impressed with the invasion. "You know, just the three of us?"

"What fun would that be?" Colm demanded. "You can't have a real party without Orkneys. Everyone knows that."

Behind Colm, Glynn eyed the seat where Kit still perched with a speculative gaze. "Nice chair."

Maybe it was his imagination, but Jonathan had a feeling that Glynn knew exactly what the damn chair was designed for. "Thanks. Birthday present," he added, biting back a flare of jealousy when Glynn took a seat on the lower end of the curve.

"Don't be selfish." Rhodri grinned, popping open a beer and handing it to Kit. "You can have the king to yourself later, but we're not passing up a perfect excuse for a party."

"We even brought refreshments this time," Bevan added amiably. "Since Devon's always bitching we drink all the beer." He tossed a bottle to Devon, who caught it before it could hit Jonathan in the head.

"Careful where you throw those things," Kit scolded sharply. "Niall would hardly appreciate Arthur showing up with a black eye on set tomorrow."

"Who pissed in your cornflakes this morning?" Colm asked. "I haven't seen you in this bad a mood in months."

Kit rolled his eyes. "If I have to explain it to you, you won't get it anyway." He slid down the chair to sit in the dip next to Glynn, a definite pout on his face.

Addison carried a beer over to Jonathan, a twinkle in his eyes as he examined the new piece of furniture. "Looks very… comfortable," he murmured, lifting his own bottle in a silent toast. "Don't worry, dear boy, we won't let them stay up too far past their bedtime."

Jonathan accepted the beer with a rueful grin. He was truly fortunate to have made so many good friends among the cast; it would be churlish to wish they'd all disappear just so he could try out his new birthday present. After taking a sip, he smiled back at Addison and asked about his plans for the coming weekend.

Glynn smiled at Kit and leaned his arm over the rising curve of the lounge. "Best just to let them have their fun," he advised, the chair's contours pressing them together. "You know arguing with them only makes them more stubborn."

Kit muttered under his breath, but he had to admit the other man was right. He wouldn't get rid of the Orkneys any faster by arguing with them. He'd just had fantasies of spending the evening in far more intimate activities. After a moment, Glynn rose from the seat, grinning down at Kit. "Don't worry, a chair like this never wears out. You can still enjoy it after we're gone."

Kit's eyes grew wide as he realized that Glynn knew what the underlying purpose of the chair was, but he wisely kept his mouth shut. No reason to confirm the man's hypothesis.

Devon eyed Glynn warily as the dark-haired man joined him and Éamon where they chatted about the upcoming scenes of the battle with Mordred. For all that Glynn and Éamon were practically married, the Welshman had seemed to be quite comfortable in Kit's personal space, though in fairness, the chair's contours made it next to impossible not to throw its occupants into intimate closeness. That's what it was designed for, after all. Swallowing his irritation at the delay in exploring everything else the chair was designed for, Devon nodded at Glynn and slid over to make room for him at the kitchen counter.

"That's quite a gift Jonathan's got," Glynn said, slipping an arm around Éamon as he joined the two men. "He's a lucky man to have you and Kit to take care of him."

"I'd say we're the lucky ones," Devon replied, hoping his expression didn't give too much away as his gaze moved to his castmate.

Glynn smiled. "Glad to see you realize what you've got in him." He turned to Éamon. "Let's see if we can get the Orkneys moving. I think our hosts would rather celebrate alone. Your 'brother' can owe us one later."

"Let 'em finish their beers, at least," Devon relented, though the look he turned on Glynn was pure gratitude. "But if you can clear 'em out after that, we really will owe you one."

Glynn grinned, gesturing for Éamon to start rounding up the others. "We like to watch," he whispered before joining Éamon and herding the rest of the cast toward the door in far less time than Devon would have believed possible.

Devon was fairly sure that Glynn was just taking the piss with him, but he wasn't about to complain when the last of the Orkneys trailed out the door not a quarter of an hour later. Glynn clapped Jonathan on the shoulder and wished him many happy returns of the day, his hazel eyes meeting Devon's with a wink as he and Éamon left together.

"Not that I'm complaining," Kit began, locking the door behind their departing friends, "but what put such a fire under Glynn and Éamon to get everyone out?"

"Who cares?" Jonathan turned back to the parlor, fingers already working at the button fly of his jeans. "They're gone, and the two of you can demonstrate all the special features of my birthday present for me now."

Not particularly anxious to admit that he wasn't exactly sure what he'd agreed to, Devon kept quiet in favor of shedding his own clothes as quickly as possible. "There's a video guide to positions," he offered instead, "though it's only two partners, and one of them is a bird. Still, if you can get past that, it's not half inspirational."

"Do you really think we need help figuring out how to have sex?" Kit teased, pulling his shirt off again and returning to his earlier position on the upper end of the couch. "Unless you really want to watch it, Jonathan."

"Right now, I'm not interested in anything that doesn't involve the two of you touching me somehow," Jonathan admitted, kicking the denim from his legs and dropping his shirt on the floor. Devon promptly stepped up behind him, molding his chest to Jonathan's back, one hand on his hip so he could slot his cock along the crease between Jonathan's cheeks, the other moving to turn Jonathan's head into his kiss. For a moment, Jonathan forgot everything in the pleasure of losing himself to Devon's kiss and the heat of the hard body pressed against his.

Watching Jonathan and Devon kiss quickly made Kit's jeans too tight. He stood up and stripped off rapidly to join his two lovers, pressing along Jonathan's chest the way Devon was pressed along his back. He lifted up onto his toes so he could join his mouth to theirs, a wet, sloppy three-way kiss that was absolutely perfect.

Sandwiched between Kit's lean grace and Devon's innate strength was exactly where Jonathan wanted to be, and for long moments he was content to simply sate himself on their touch and taste, kisses moving languidly from one mouth to another, fingertips grazing over any skin he could reach. Eventually, though, his curiosity—and the possibilities running rampant through his fertile imagination—won out, and he shifted so they were facing the sinuous leather chair. "So who's going to demonstrate how this thing works?" he murmured.

"What's your pleasure tonight?" Kit asked breathlessly. "Top, bottom, middle? The possibilities are endless."

"It's like being at an all-you-can-eat smorgasbord." Jonathan chuckled. "I could never decide what I wanted to try first. Since this was your discovery, I'm sure you've checked out all the suggested positions. Pick one—I'm sure I'll enjoy it, whatever it is." He dropped a kiss on each of his lovers' lips. "As long as it involves both of you, how could I not?"

"Devon?" Kit asked, wanting to give both of them the option of making a suggestion before he took over, but Devon just shook his head. "In that case," Kit continued with a huge grin, "I'm going to go with my earlier suggestion." He leaned back over the higher end of the chair, his feet lifting off the ground as his head fell back, leaving his hips at the perfect height for Jonathan to enter him and his lips at the perfect height to suck Devon. "There's lube in the drawer over there."

"Is it gift-wrapped too?" Jonathan teased, retrieving the tube but dropping it onto the leather below Kit's head. "I want to enjoy this part of my gift first," he added, bending to run his lips over the alluring expanse of Kit's torso, spread out for his delectation.

"You won't mind sharing, will you, Jon?" Devon asked, kneeling in the chair's lower curve. Leaning forward, he caught Kit's lips in an upside-down kiss, lifting a hand to tangle into Jonathan's hair where he lingered at a coffee-colored nipple.

"Some things are even better when shared," Kit gasped into Devon's mouth. His blood was rushing to his head, leaving him wonderfully giddy as his lovers lavished attention on him.

Devon's touch reawakening the need for both his lovers, Jonathan caught his chin and lifted him into a kiss, his other hand continuing to tease at Kit's nipple. Breaking the kiss, he guided Devon's head to replace his fingers and moved to the opposite side of Kit's chest so they could pleasure him in tandem. The sudden gasp and arch of Kit's back into their touch betrayed just how much he enjoyed the dual attentions. Easing him back against the supportive surface, Jonathan let his mouth drift over quivering abdominal muscles until he was nuzzling into dark pubic curls.

"Please," Kit husked, the teasing caresses hitting all his sensitive spots and driving him wild. When Jonathan made his way to the base of Kit's cock but didn't immediately give the aching appendage the attention it desired, he resorted to begging. "God, Jonathan, please suck me!"

Dropping to one knee, Jonathan inhaled deeply, the musky scent whetting his need to taste. He let his tongue dart through the dusky curls, lapping over the tightened sac before painting a wide swath up the underside of the rigid shaft. A pearl of fluid trembled at the tip, and Jonathan caught it on his tongue, rolling the salty flavor over his palate before taking the head into his mouth. Kit pushed up, wordlessly begging for more, but Jonathan straightened, nudging at Devon's cheek until he looked up from tracing the outline of the birthmark on Kit's hip and sharing the taste with him in a deep kiss.

Kit groaned as his lovers kissed above his head. He could see their tongues twining together and imagined Devon stealing a taste of Kit's essence off Jonathan's tongue. The image was enough to make him harden even more. "Fuck, you two are gorgeous."

"No more than you, lad." Devon reached for the container of lube on the curve beside him and passed it to Jonathan. "Watching Jon prep you will like come near to getting me off—next time I think we'll need to wear our rings so we can last longer." He pushed upward enough to steal his own taste from the tip of Kit's bobbing cock, prompting Kit to do the same to Devon's erection, which was all but hitting him in the face.

Jonathan paused from slicking his fingers with the cool gel, the image of Kit taking Devon in his mouth as Jonathan took him with his cock sending a tremor of pure desire flaring in his gut. "Scoot up, Devon," he instructed, his voice husked with passion. Anointing Kit's crease with the lube, he slipped two fingers inside, knowing Kit would be as eager as he was by this point. "Let me watch Kit-Kat suck you."

Kit didn't bother replying with words. He simply let Devon's cock work its way farther into his throat. With his head tipped back this way, he could take Devon deeper and with greater ease than usual, truly allowing him to fuck his mouth. Devon was still careful not to choke him, but Kit was pretty sure sucking dick had never been easier. Then Jonathan's fingers pressed past his entrance and Kit moaned eagerly, wrapping his legs around Jonathan's hips and drawing him closer. His hands went around Devon's hips, not guiding but definitely encouraging the continued movements as he felt himself filled from both ends.

Seeing how easily Kit all but swallowed Devon's cock made Jonathan's own shaft throb with need. He prepped Kit with more speed than usual, but judging by the wanton way Kit pushed onto his fingers, it was enough. Slicking himself with an ample squeeze of lube, he slid into the yielding passage, the chair's angle putting him at the perfect alignment to thrust deeply. "Oh fuck, kitten," he moaned, looking down at the dual sight of his and Devon's cocks filling their lover. Scrambling for control, he tore his gaze away, only to find himself nearly eye-to-eye with Devon, who pulled him into a kiss. Jonathan wrapped an arm around Devon's back, loving the way the position opened both his lovers' bodies to him as his palms coasted over pale and olive skin and his hips pulsed in an instinctive rhythm.

Kit wouldn't have needed much more to come untouched, but when Devon's hand closed around his bobbing cock, that was all it took. His body clenched in release, hot fluid shooting from his shaft all the way down to his chin. He shuddered and shook with the power of his orgasm, going limp in satiation.

The reflexive clench of Kit's muscles around his, coupled with the look of ecstasy on his face, were enough to send Jonathan crashing over the precipice of his own climax. Blinking his vision back into focus, he reached down to help Devon bring himself off, the splash of his come mingling with Kit's on his chest. They sagged against each other, foreheads resting together, until their panting breaths slowed to a calmer rate.

"Best… birthday… present… ever," Jonathan rasped between inhalations.

"For all of us," Devon drawled in agreement, leaning back on his heels. "I can see we'll be breaking this in right and proper."

"The only drawback I can see is that we have to get up to go snuggle in bed," Kit added, pushing up to sitting again slowly, letting the blood rush back out of his head. "But I think that's a small price to pay if the sex is always this good."

"We'll have to try it again tomorrow." Jonathan grinned, offering Kit a hand to rise to his feet and reaching for Devon with the other. "You said something about an instructional video?"

CHAPTER 23
EYES ON THE PRIZE

JONATHAN AND Kit were already seated in the catering tent, well into their lunches, when Devon arrived. He hadn't been filming any scenes that morning, but he needed a fitting for his armor for the upcoming battle scene and had hung around afterward hoping to share an hour with his lovers during their lunch break. That was before Glynn had bumped into him leaving the armor workshop. Still searching for a way to explain the fix he'd gotten them into to his partners, Devon walked past their table before Kit's shout called him back.

"Too good to have lunch with us?" Kit teased when Devon joined them. "Be careful. We'll start thinking you prefer Kay and Bors to us."

Not missing the slight uncharacteristic flush of Devon's cheeks, Jonathan glanced around the mostly empty tables nearby, his voice lowering. "Is something wrong, Devon?" He gave Kit's teasing suggestion the credence it deserved, which was none, but he wondered if Glynn or Éamon might have inadvertently said something to bring back memories Jonathan hoped were finally behind them all.

"No!" Devon answered, too quickly. "Just thinking whether we had any plans for this weekend. I, uh, kind of invited Glynn—and Éamon—over to your place Saturday night."

Surprised by the odd hesitancy in Devon's usually confident voice but relieved that he didn't seem upset, Jonathan raised an eyebrow. "Mi casa es su casa, Devon, but any reason why you didn't invite them to your place? It's usually neater than mine."

This time Devon definitely blushed. "I—er—I told them they could come back. On your birthday. When they cleared the Orkneys out for us?"

"Come back for what?" Kit asked suspiciously. Something about Devon's behavior didn't compute. "I mean, they're welcome anytime, but you're not stuttering because they want to come to dinner. What's going on?"

"Something you'll likely enjoy, even if Jon and I don't," Devon muttered.

"Devon, just tell us," Jonathan insisted. "It can't be as bad as you think it is."

"And what makes you think I'd enjoy something you and Jonathan don't?" Kit asked. "Even if I like the idea of something, I'm not going to enjoy myself if you two are uncomfortable. We've been through that already, remember?"

"That night—your birthday?" Jonathan nodded and Devon swallowed before continuing. "Glynn knew what your gift was. He said they—he and Éamon—they like to watch."

Jonathan chuckled. "I'll be happy to lend them the instructional video, then."

Devon shook his head. "I told them we'd owe them if they could get the Orkneys to leave. That's what Glynn wants in return—to watch. Us."

Kit shivered, the thought of two pairs of eyes on him as his lovers made him scream or vice versa a serious turn-on. "I'm in," he said immediately. "I'm hard just thinking about it."

Jonathan was slower to answer. He'd filmed enough nude scenes in his career to be able to detach himself from the surroundings and ignore the cameras and crew, but this wasn't a movie. This was letting someone else watch the most intimate moments between himself and the men he loved. He'd gotten to know Glynn and Éamon well enough that he didn't suspect there was anything more to the request than prurient interest, but he still wasn't wholly comfortable with it. "There would have to be conditions."

"I've already told them no cameras and no touching. They'd sit on the other side of the room and watch, that's all. But Glynn insisted we use the couch—that's why I had to ask them to your place, Jon."

"And they don't have any say in the action—they can watch, but they don't get to direct. We get enough of that on set." Despite himself, Jonathan grinned. "I can understand why they'd want to watch, but this is a pretty hefty payback for rousting a couple of drunk Orkneys. What's in it for us?"

"We get their eyes on us," Kit replied, grin widening as he imagined what Saturday night might bring. "We get to tease them with everything we have and they don't. Every time I touch one of you, they'll wish they could too. And every time you touch me, it'll be the same. It's the ultimate playing to an audience because it's so incredibly intimate but at the same time separate because they can't touch, can't direct. All they can do is watch and wish they were in our shoes."

"And we'll make them ache for it," Devon agreed, free of the anxiety he'd felt at broaching the idea to his lovers. He really was the luckiest bastard alive. "They'll be going home with the bluest bollocks in the British Isles."

Kit chortled. "Unless they come just from watching us."

"This is awkward," Jonathan complained, taking a swig of his beer as they waited for Glynn and Éamon to arrive. "Should we be naked already so we can get started as soon as they get here? Or do we sit around first, have another beer, make a little small talk before we get it on?"

"If you're not comfortable, we'll call it off, Jon," Devon assured him. "I'll tell Glynn we were just taking the piss with him." And deal with any fallout the other man might direct his way for going back on his word, but that was his issue to resolve, not Jonathan's.

"No, I agreed and I'll go through with it. I just wish they'd get here already." Jonathan rose and lifted the curtain to look outside, but the street was still empty.

"Would it help you feel better if we talk about what we want to do ahead of time so that doesn't cause any awkwardness?" Kit suggested. "And to answer your question, we do exactly what makes you feel most comfortable. If that's already naked and in the middle of the action, then we do that. If you'd rather ease into it, then we do that. There isn't a right or a wrong way for this any more than there is to any other way we make love."

"We have to use the chair," Devon reminded them. "Beyond that, it's up to us. We can use a position we've already tried if that will make things easier, or go for something new." He crossed to the computer, pulling up the bookmarked link to positions they'd found so inspiring thus far. "What do you say, Jon, Kit? Anything take your fancy?"

"That one," Jonathan decided when Devon had clicked through a few screens. "One of us lying at the bottom, another sitting on the floor sucking him off. And the other could lie facedown over the top and let the one in the middle suck him or rim him."

"Works for me," Devon agreed readily, happy to go along with anything that would ease Jonathan's discomfort.

"The guy on the floor isn't getting any," Kit pointed out immediately.

"That can be Devon, then, for getting us into this in the first place." Jonathan softened the dictate with a kiss for Devon at the computer. "I promise we'll take care of you later, babe."

"I have no fears on that score." Devon pulled Jonathan's head down for a deeper kiss, his cock already stirring with interest. If Glynn and Éamon didn't get here soon, he wasn't sure how long he'd be willing to wait. "So which of you want the other two places?"

"If Jonathan doesn't mind, he can have the middle and I'll take the top," Kit replied immediately. "That way he'll be distracted on both ends and I can work the crowd, so to speak."

"When have I ever protested being in the middle of you two?" Jonathan answered, breaking into his first grin of the evening. "Putting yourself on display, hmm?" His lips twitched as he imagined Kit sprawled over the upper arch of the chair, watching their guests watching them. At least, between Kit and Devon, Jonathan would be kept busy enough to drive their audience's presence from his thoughts. He hoped.

"Then let's get you there," Kit proposed, pulling Jonathan into his arms and kissing him thoroughly. "Come on," he urged when he realized Devon was still sitting at the computer. "Jonathan needs distracting."

Devon powered off the monitor, then rose and wrapped himself around Jonathan from behind, coasting his hands over as many of his erogenous zones as he could reach. "Fuck Glynn, if he doesn't get his sodding arse here soon, it won't be my fault if he misses the show."

Jonathan returned Kit's kiss with interest, pressing back against Devon's hard cock prodding his crease and snaking an arm behind him to pull Devon even closer. He couldn't agree more.

A knock at the door interrupted the kiss. "You invited them. You get the door," Kit muttered, pulling away from Jonathan's mouth long enough to speak. Not bothering to see if Devon listened, he dove back into the kiss, sliding his hands beneath the hem of Jonathan's T-shirt to work it up his back and chest.

With a final nip to the side of Jonathan's throat, Devon pulled away, hitching his track pants over his erection as he walked to the door. It would be too much to expect Glynn or Éamon not to notice, but then that's what they were there for, after all. "Thought maybe you'd changed your mind," he grumbled as the two came inside.

"Not a chance," Éamon drawled. "We've been watching you three from afar since we got here. We're not about to miss the chance to see you up close. Although it looks like we've missed the beginning of the action if that tent in your pants is any indication."

"It's more of a permanent condition around these two." Devon led the way into the living room, where Jonathan and Kit were still wrapped around each other, Jonathan's T-shirt half off and caught on one arm, his hands cupped around Kit's arse as they did their best to wedge their tongues down each other's throats.

A stifled moan that didn't come from him or Kit caught Jonathan's ear. He broke out of the kiss, drawing a heaving breath before glancing over his shoulder at Glynn and Éamon. "Make yourself at home. Beer in the fridge—" His words cut off as Kit yanked him back down and reclaimed his mouth.

Glynn and Éamon looked at each other, back at Jonathan and Kit, and then at Devon. "We'll just sit over there on the couch, shall we?" Glynn said. "We wouldn't want to miss anything, since they don't look to be slowing down anytime soon."

"No, I don't expect they are," Devon admitted with a grin. "And if you don't mind, I'm going to rejoin them." Not waiting for an answer, he crossed back to his lovers, stripping his shirt over his head and dropping it on the floor along the way.

"Look at that," Éamon murmured to Glynn. "How long have you wanted to see that chest in person?"

"Since I saw *Perfect Lover*," Glynn replied honestly. "And I'm hoping we'll get to see more than his chest, gorgeous as it is."

Devon flipped them both the bird without turning his head, focusing his attention instead on insinuating himself back into the tangle of his two lovers' limbs. Once he'd freed the remaining arm of Jonathan's T-shirt, he tossed it aside and half turned Jonathan until he could latch on to one of his rosy nipples. Jonathan arched back beautifully, letting Devon work a hand between them to fondle Kit intimately.

Kit released Jonathan's lips in favor of the curve of his neck as he leaned back, a moan escaping him when Devon's hand found his cock. Feeling the two sets of eyes on him, he angled his hips a little so Glynn and Éamon could get a better look at the big hand stroking him so perfectly. He glanced at them quickly, making sure he had their full attention before he lowered his head and licked lasciviously up Jonathan's chest to his other nipple, tonguing it repeatedly until Jonathan let out a long moan, echoed by one across the room.

"Fuck!" Éamon muttered. "He's good with that tongue."

Kit smirked at the comment and went back to proving exactly how talented his tongue was.

Having both his lovers lick and bite at his nipples soon had Jonathan's knees trembling and his cock aching for more. Weaving his hands into dark and light hair, he tugged until they both looked up at him. "Glynn wanted the chair," he murmured, twisting to press a kiss to each set of lips. "Let's give him what he wants." Glynn was just damn lucky their desires coincided with his.

"You need to get naked first." Dropping to one knee, Devon made short work of stripping Jonathan's jeans down his legs, wondering if their audience would notice the lack of anything underneath. "Your throne awaits, my king," he proclaimed, dropping his own pants as Jonathan sat at the foot of the wave-shaped chair.

Not wanting to be left behind, Kit stripped as well, bending to remove his track shoes and give Glynn and Éamon a good view of his arse, grinning at the twin moans that escaped at the sight of three naked, aroused men.

"This is even better than I'd imagined it could be," Glynn groaned. "Their movies didn't do them justice."

"They weren't hard in their movies," Éamon replied.

"Bet they were, though," Devon murmured quietly enough for only Jonathan to hear. Returning Jonathan's grin, he nudged him back, tweaking his tightened nipples, until Jonathan was reclining on the curved surface. Devon arranged himself at the chair's foot, lifting Jonathan's legs over his shoulders, opening him to his touch, his mouth.

Just the feel of Devon's fingers parting his thighs, draping his legs over his strong torso, sent Jonathan's arousal spiraling. The only thing missing was— "Kit." He stretched out a hand, fingertips brushing up his shin. "C'mon. Thought you were the one who wanted them to watch."

"I'm here," Kit promised, straddling Jonathan's chest and kissing him softly. "But there's no reason not to give them a show at the same time. Now, what's your pleasure, lover? My cock in your mouth or your tongue up my arse?"

The moans from across the room made Kit grin. He winked at Jonathan as he stroked his cock with one hand, reaching the other behind him to part the cheeks of his arse.

"I have to choose?" Jonathan stretched to pinch the offered cheek, his tongue sating itself on the last it would taste of Kit's mouth for the moment. The nip of Devon's lips, and occasionally teeth, moving up the inside of his thigh pulled him out of the kiss. "Scoot up and I'll bet I can reach them both."

"Yeah, move it." Devon added a nip of his own to a smooth olive globe before turning his attention to Jonathan's other thigh. "Some of us are working down here."

"Work, is it?" Jonathan's chuckle turned into a gasp when Devon's mouth ghosted over his sac. "Lucky for me you're so damn good at your job."

"Doesn't look like work from where I'm sitting," Glynn commented.

Kit glanced over at him, grinning at the sight of Glynn's hand inside his shorts. Arching deliberately to push his arse out more, he brushed his cock across Jonathan's lips, offering himself to his recumbent lover. "It isn't," he replied. "Jonathan tastes too good for it to be work. Devon just likes to complain."

That comment elicited more moans from their audience, much to Kit's delight.

"That's just mean," Glynn grumbled, "since you won't share him with us."

"Sorry, boys." Kit shrugged, his breath rushing out as Jonathan's mouth opened around his cock. "You only get to watch tonight."

"So what else are we going to get to see?" Éamon asked, practically drooling as he watched Devon go down on Jonathan.

"Yeah, maybe some real sex," Glynn added, voice husky with desire.

The constant comments starting to distract him, Jonathan let Kit's cock slide from his lips. "Define sex," he challenged, turning to stare at Glynn and Éamon. "If a blowjob is sex enough to impeach Clinton, it's enough for you. It's all you're going to see, anyway, so keep it down. It's like trying to make love on *MST 3000*." Turning back to Kit, he resolved to ignore any further remarks in favor of driving Kit wild instead. To that end, he raised a hand to part the smooth cheeks and lap up the crease between them, moaning at the smoky flavor tantalizing his palate.

He succeeded. Kit writhed and moaned beneath the lash of his tongue, perhaps a bit more theatrically than usual, but unlike Jonathan, he didn't want to forget their audience was there. He wanted their audience so wound up they couldn't contain themselves, so he wriggled and groaned a little harder than usual, trying to stay just this side of ridiculous.

A quick glance at Glynn and Éamon proved he was managing. Their eyes were glazed, both their hands in their pants now, stroking in time with Devon's bobbing head and Jonathan's talented tongue. Kit smirked at them, silently goading them with the fact that he was getting rimmed while they could only watch.

Devon had briefly considered adding his own retort to Jonathan's, but that would have meant letting Jonathan's cock out of his mouth, and berating Glynn and Éamon just wasn't worth it. Not when he could win more of the delicious full-body moans that had to be tickling Kit's arse. Devon glanced up the quivering planes of Jonathan's torso, past the shaggy head buried between a pair of wide-flung legs, over Kit's heaving torso. Kit's head was flung back, his back arched in passion, his eyes fixed on Éamon and Glynn before glancing over his shoulder to meet Devon's gaze. In that moment, Devon felt the connection between them as surely as if it were Kit's cock straining against the back of his throat.

Jonathan had forgotten Glynn and Éamon were there the moment Devon's mouth moved from his balls up the length of his shaft to envelop him. He'd never known anyone who could give head as well as Devon, except maybe Kit, who might not have Devon's skills but made up for it in enthusiasm. Devon swallowed around the head of Jonathan's cock, and Jonathan spread the love by working his tongue as far as he could up Kit's hot, tight channel. The currents of pleasure surged along his nerves from both ends, meeting in a molten charge deep in his gut. He clutched at Devon's shoulder with one hand and gripped Kit's thigh with the other, forging a conduit of pure sensation that fused the three of them together.

"Damn," Glynn muttered, making sure he didn't speak loudly enough for Jonathan to hear. "I don't think I could watch them fuck. I'm about to go off just from this."

Éamon leaned closer and blew lightly in Glynn's ear. "So come," he said. "Let yourself go when they do."

Devon couldn't hear what Éamon and Glynn were saying to each other, but they were obviously getting off on what they saw. Not that there was any surprise there. Hell, Devon was damn close to popping himself, just from watching Jonathan and Kit. Jonathan's fingers were digging into his shoulder hard enough to leave bruises, his hips undulating in an effort to work just a little deeper into Devon's throat. The chair really did put him at a perfect angle. Sliding a hand under one hip, he shifted Jonathan just a fraction, then slipped two fingers from his other hand into his mouth beneath Jonathan's cock. Jonathan's legs slid off his shoulders, spreading himself even wider when Devon worked the two wet digits up the crease of Jonathan's arse. Two heels dug into the small of his back, a rumbling groan urging him to press inside.

The moment Devon's fingers breached him, Jonathan lost it, his entire body spasming as wave after wave of ecstasy surged through him. His grip tightened on both his lovers, grounding himself in their union, their oneness.

"Hey, no fair," Glynn protested as Jonathan came down Devon's throat. "We didn't get a come shot!"

Swallowing the flood of seed before easing Jonathan's cock from his mouth, Devon glared at Glynn with all the strength of his own unsatisfied arousal. "You want a bloody come shot? How's this?" he growled. Kneeling up, he moved his hand quickly over his throbbing shaft. It didn't take more than a few strokes before he was painting Jonathan's belly with ropes of thick white semen.

Kit reared back as well, his cock spurting energetically all over the leather as he stroked himself to climax. He collapsed back onto his heels, his arse connecting with Jonathan's chest as he panted harshly, trying to keep his wits about him. Two low moans drew his attention back to their audience in time to watch tremors shake both bodies. He grinned to himself. *Mission accomplished.*

CHAPTER 24
MANFLESH

"LANCELOT IS the greatest knight the Round Table has ever seen," Percival said hotly, defending his Grail companion against Bors's slurs. "With him at our side, we will defeat Mordred easily. Without him, I fear for our chances."

"He betrayed Arthur once before," Bors insisted. "We cannot trust that he will stand at the king's side now."

If Kit hadn't been worried about blowing another take—they were on their fourth already—he'd have made a comment about Arthur and Lancelot not being lovers then. As it was, he forced himself to stick to the script. "He departed on the quest for the Holy Grail to prove his repentance. He deserves our forgiveness."

"Cut," Niall called, and Kit let Percival slip away for a moment, catching his breath and admiring the sight of Glynn in character. He'd thought Glynn was a good-looking man from the moment he first saw the other actor, but he hadn't been prepared for the power of Glynn as Bors. Out of character, he was charming, sexy in a boy-next-door kind of way. In character, he was compelling, easily a match for Arthur or Lancelot. Easily a match for Devon and Jonathan, and committed to his lovers or not, Kit felt his body responding to the presence of an alpha male. He tamped down on the reaction and turned his thoughts to improving his performance for the next take. Maybe he could channel his reaction into Percival's anger. And hope Devon and Jonathan didn't notice.

Leaning against an off-camera outcrop of rock, Devon watched the interplay with bemused interest. Niall had played up the sensual tension between Percival and Lancelot during the Grail quest, even if the sacredness of their mission had prevented them from acting on it. At least on camera. Niall might have been intending Percival's reaction to Bors's words as protective anger, but Devon hadn't missed the spark in Kit's eyes. He'd seen that glance directed at himself and Jonathan often enough to recognize that Kit was feeling randy.

Apparently satisfied with the take, Niall called for the next scene, and Jonathan strode toward the two men, Arthur's attention having been captured by the raised voices of the two knights. Judging by the way

Arthur's arm moved to Percival's in a silent show of possessiveness, even as he spoke the scripted words to calm Bors, Devon suspected Kit's arousal hadn't been lost on Jonathan either.

"Damn," Éamon murmured, coming up beside Devon. "Glynn looks even better in costume than he does normally. So do Kit and Jonathan, for that matter. You're one lucky bastard, Devon. Unless, of course, you'd be interested in sharing? Just think about all that manflesh rolling around in one bed."

"Are you including Niall in that invitation?" Devon cocked an eyebrow at Éamon, grateful that the jeans he wore since he wasn't filming hid the stirrings of his own reaction to the image of Glynn, Jonathan, and Kit together. Not that Éamon was any hardship to look at either. The redhead's slender build might suggest he was the bottom of the twosome, but his blunt speech and the glitter in his eyes as he turned them back toward Glynn made Devon doubt he was as dutifully submissive as the character he portrayed on screen.

Éamon mimed a shudder at the thought of Niall anywhere near his bed and draped his arm around Devon's shoulders. "Glynn and I would love to have the three of you join us. It's an open-ended offer. So, do we have any chance of coaxing you to come play with us sometime?"

"I can't speak for the others without talking to them first." Devon watched appreciatively as Bors argued with Arthur. He might not feel the need for anyone but Kit and Jonathan in his bed, but he sure wouldn't kick either Glynn or Éamon out. "But I'll pass the offer on to them."

"No rush," Éamon assured him. "After the show you three put on the other night, we decided you're worth the wait. And that's not something we think very often."

"Niall cast some fine-looking men," Devon allowed with a grin. "Makes me wonder whether he was only trying to make his wife happy."

"He sure made me happy." Éamon laughed softly. "It looks like filming's over for the day. I'm going to reclaim my husband. Enjoy your evening, and think about our offer." After clapping Devon on the shoulder one last time, Éamon set an intercept course for Glynn, falling into step beside the other man as they walked toward their trailer.

"SCENES LOOKED good today," Devon commented as he pulled a trio of beers from the refrigerator, Jonathan having corrupted them with his preference for chilled brew. "Glynn makes quite a powerful Bors."

"He certainly does," Kit agreed, a little breathlessly. "Niall did a fabulous job with the casting."

Well aware that his own presence in England was due to Niall's casting decisions, Jonathan didn't respond to Kit's comment, turning to Devon instead. "That what you and Éamon were discussing so intently?"

"Éamon was there today?" Kit asked in surprise. "I didn't see him."

"Not surprising," Devon answered with a roll of his eyes toward Jonathan. The hint of tightness in Jonathan's expression told him he wasn't the only one who'd noticed. "You didn't have eyes for anyone but Glynn."

Kit flushed, unable to deny the accusation. "Just because I'm in love with you two doesn't mean I'm blind," he said defensively. "It was a little hard not to notice him, since he's the one I was trading lines with all day."

"Glynn's a good-looking guy," Jonathan admitted, forcing back the niggle of jealousy that had been threatening to erupt all day. "He and Éamon make a striking couple."

"They've got nothing on the couple of men in my bed," Kit insisted, the odd note in Jonathan's voice making him want to reassure his lover.

"That's apparently what Éamon thinks too." Devon ran a hand through his hair, wishing not for the first time that he had Jonathan's skill with words. He didn't know any other way to present Éamon's offer than to come right out and say it. "He suggested that he and Glynn would like to join us sometime, if we're interested."

"That wasn't the deal," Kit said immediately, the stunned look on Jonathan's face enough to put him off the idea entirely. "It was a onetime offer to watch; that's all."

"But you liked being watched, didn't you?" Jonathan knew Kit had made adjustments for him and Devon, accommodating their occasional taste for a bit of rough in their lovemaking Kit didn't share. If this was something Kit and Devon wanted, he ought to be willing to consider it, even if the idea made him uneasy. It was too much of a reminder of what he'd have to face when filming ended—the thought of either of the men he'd come to love in someone else's bed.

"Of course I liked being watched," Kit replied, "but that's because while they were watching, you and Devon were touching me. They're undeniably attractive men, but that isn't enough for me to be willing to put what we have at risk in any way, and that's what we'd be doing if we aren't all completely comfortable with the idea."

"But you would be?" Jonathan glanced up, including Devon in the question. "Willing to have them join us? Not just willing," he clarified. "Is that something you'd want?"

"I don't know," Kit replied honestly. "It isn't something I've thought about. Not really, I mean. It's one thing to look and think they're attractive, but that doesn't mean I'd want to act on it. We have so little time left before filming ends already. I don't want to do something that would cause problems now, when we might not have time to work them out before we leave."

Jonathan's eyes flicked back to Devon. "I'd not kick them out," Devon answered the unspoken question, echoing what he'd admitted to himself when Éamon first posed the offer. Jonathan and Kit deserved an honest response. "But only if both of you agreed. Kit's right; it isn't worth risking us to satisfy a passing itch." Not when he was beginning to believe that what they'd found together might last even when filming was over—at least for him.

"I can't say they aren't both attractive." Jonathan shook his head, pushing back the lock of hair that fell forward, refusing to hide behind its concealment. "Just the kind of men I wouldn't let myself notice, before the two of you. But I don't think...." He trailed off. "You have to remember, until a few months ago I'd never had even one man in my bed, let alone two. Now you're asking me to think about five of us?"

"What kind of timeline did they give us for making a decision?" Kit interrupted, sensing Jonathan's indecision. If they had to decide tonight, he'd put the brakes on the discussion for good. If they had a little more time to let Jonathan get used to the idea, they'd see where things went.

"I told them I couldn't speak for all of us, and we left it at that. Though Éamon did say it was an open-ended offer." Devon set his beer on the counter and squeezed Jonathan's shoulder. "If you don't like the idea, I'll tell him no, and that'll be the end of it."

"If it really is open-ended, then we don't have to decide now either," Kit interjected. "We can take some time, think about it and what it would mean to us, and then decide tomorrow or next week or never, although I suppose the end of filming in a month is probably the outer limit."

"Don't tell him no," Jonathan said slowly. He still suspected that if not for his hesitance, Kit and Devon would have taken the other two up on the offer immediately. Between them, they'd opened his eyes to so much about himself already. More than that, Kit had accepted that he and Devon could enjoy a level of pain mixed with their pleasure that Kit himself would never be comfortable with. They deserved more than to have him reject this out of hand just because it stretched his own comfort zone. "Where would I be if I'd said no to the two of you when you first approached me? Just give me some time to think about the idea."

"As much time as you need," Devon assured him. "And if at the end of it the answer's still no, that's fine too." He glanced at Kit, who nodded his agreement. "In the meantime, let's make a simpler decision. What's for dinner?"

JONATHAN LEANED against the bar, the noise of the music and conversations around him a welcome distraction as he waited for their drinks. It wasn't that the past week of filming had been more grueling than any of the others—not that the Orkneys in particular needed that excuse or any other for partying—but it had seemed longer than usual to him. The reasons why were a few hundred feet away from him, moving on the dance floor along with a crowd of other dancers. In the mass of bodies, it was nearly impossible to pair off any two as partners, but he'd seen the touch of hands or brush of hips that linked Glynn and Éamon together. There had been an undercurrent of awareness in all Arthur's scenes with Bors this past week—despite himself, Jonathan couldn't help but think of Éamon's offer every time he faced Glynn. He'd been aware of Glynn watching him too, and Kit when Percival was a part of the action.

It was true, as he'd admitted to Kit, that Glynn and Éamon were just the type he'd have fantasized about, back when he was still resisting his attraction to men. Except now he had two exceptional men in his life and in his bed. He didn't need to risk that by welcoming in any others. Did he? His decision might be easier if he wasn't aware that his lovers didn't share his hesitation. Maybe he was being selfish by not agreeing to something Devon and Kit obviously wanted?

The bartender interrupted his uneasy musings by setting their drinks in front of him. Jonathan picked up the tumbler of Jameson he'd ordered with his beer and tossed it back. Drinking heavily was starting to sound like a viable option.

"Hey, Jonathan," Glynn said, sliding onto the stool next to him. "I don't suppose you'd share a drink with a thirsty mate."

Startled that he'd been so lost in thought he hadn't noticed the object of those thoughts sitting next to him, Jonathan slid a beer over to Glynn. "Help yourself—I was going to order another for myself anyway."

"You're drinking heavy tonight, mate," Glynn commented. "You didn't have a bust-up with Devon and Kit, did you?"

Jonathan waved to the bartender to bring him another round, Glynn's words cutting too close to his fears for him to answer immediately. Moving the two remaining beers closer, he shook his head. "Nothing like that—they're just over there, waiting for me to bring them their drinks." The booth he nodded toward was empty, though; it took him a minute's searching to find his lovers on the dance floor, where Éamon was still moving to the beat, sweat making his shirt cling to his chest. "Surprised you could tear yourself away."

Glynn followed Jonathan's gaze and grinned. "He'll still be there when I get back, waiting for me with open arms," Glynn drawled. "But he's not the only good-looking man in the room." He bumped Jonathan's thigh with his from his perch on the stool. "And neither of us is averse to sharing occasionally."

"So I've heard," Jonathan answered dryly, his gaze still following Devon and Kit. He'd hoped one of them would look up and see him watching them, but they were too caught up in each other. Shaking his head, he turned his attention back to the man beside him. "Why?" he asked softly, honestly trying to understand. "Isn't he enough for you?"

Glynn spluttered into his beer. "Oh God, Jonathan, you have no idea. He's more than enough for me. It's not that at all. Nothing shakes that foundation. Nothing. But occasionally someone will catch our eye—our eye, mind you. We don't do this if we don't agree on the other or others we want to add. It's fun. It adds a little spice to things now and again. And we both get to act on our occasional crushes without it damaging our relationship because it's festering between us."

"How long have you been together?" Jonathan didn't feel the need for any additional spice in his relationship, but maybe Devon and Kit didn't feel the same.

"Three years," Glynn replied immediately. "Three wonderful years. And I'm hoping for many, many more."

Rubbing the back of his neck, Jonathan considered Glynn's response. He and Éamon had managed to make a relationship work for years; of course, they were much closer geographically than he and Devon and Kit would be after filming ended, but the thought gave him a bit more hope. "And bringing others in really doesn't threaten that?"

"It might," Glynn admitted, "if we weren't so strict about how we bring others in. If Éamon weren't here, I never would've approached you three. That would be cheating. When we swing, we swing together or not at all. Some people would say that makes us pretty poor swingers, but it works for us."

Not giving Jonathan a chance to reply, Glynn leaned forward and brushed his lips over Jonathan's. "Give us a chance," he murmured before kissing him again, with more enthusiasm.

Jonathan meant to pull away after the first touch of Glynn's lips, but the gentle kiss was surprisingly compelling. He couldn't deny to himself that he'd been imagining something like this for most of the week's filming. Knowing his lovers would probably encourage him, he let Glynn deepen the kiss, slipping his tongue out to swipe against the darker man's lips.

The moment Glynn felt the touch of Jonathan's tongue, he lifted his hand to tangle in the shaggy hair, holding Jonathan in place as he plundered the willing mouth, claiming that new territory with the same ferocity he demonstrated in fighting Mordred's knights.

"Have you persuaded him yet?" Éamon asked, interrupting them.

"I think I'm making progress," Glynn replied, lifting his head but not moving his hand.

Eyes sparkling, Jonathan smiled at Éamon. "I haven't quite decided," he murmured before lifting his own hand to pull Glynn back into the kiss.

"I take it that's a yes, then?" Devon's arm was wrapped around Kit's waist as they squeezed their way up to the bar, his eyes kindling as they took in Jonathan and Glynn leaning together. "If that's decided, how about passing me a beer, Éamon?"

"Forget the beer," Kit protested. "We need to figure out who has the biggest bed." He tried to adjust himself discreetly as he watched Glynn and Jonathan kiss. "We need to take this somewhere private, and fast."

"That would be me, like," Devon offered, his own cock thickening at the thought of what was to come. He had no idea what size bed Éamon or Glynn had, but he knew Jonathan was already making enough of an adjustment. He'd be more comfortable in familiar surroundings.

"Then what are we waiting for?" Glynn asked, letting go of Jonathan's mouth only long enough to answer. "We'll meet you and Kit there. We're taking Jonathan with us."

Seeing only eager acceptance in both his lovers' expressions, Jonathan acceded, letting Glynn lead him out to his car. Éamon slid into the driver's seat, Glynn pulling Jonathan into the back and into another kiss as the redhead followed Devon out of the lot. Doing his best to ignore his lingering doubts, Jonathan returned Glynn's kiss, focusing on his body's physical reaction as a hand slid down his back to cup his ass in a large palm.

"God, you taste good," Glynn mumbled against Jonathan's lips, his hands squeezing and caressing through the loose clothing. "Can't wait to get you in bed."

Delving between Glynn's open lips, Jonathan did some exploring of his own. It felt strange, after the few months he'd been with Kit and Devon, to taste another man's mouth, to feel another man's torso beneath his hands, even if Glynn's chest was every bit as toned as Bors's appearance had promised.

Glynn released his grip on Jonathan's backside long enough to unbutton the blue cotton shirt he was wearing, giving Jonathan easier access to his skin. When he was done, he slipped his hands under Jonathan's T-shirt, running his palms over strong muscles before teasing along the waistband of Jonathan's jeans.

Glynn's skin was warm beneath Jonathan's palms, with a light coat of hair tickling his skin. Jonathan was surprised to find his body reacting to Glynn's answering touch, his cock pressing up toward the promise of the other man's fingertips when they slid beneath the soft denim of his jeans. He inhaled sharply, the muscles of his abdomen quivering, as Éamon pulled to the curb behind Devon's car.

"Did they take good care of you?" Kit asked Jonathan as they tumbled out of Éamon's car, though he thought he knew the answer to that from the glazed look in Jonathan's eyes.

Not sure how to answer, Jonathan hooked an arm around both Glynn and Éamon, steering them up the steps as Devon opened the front door. He couldn't resist reaching out for a quick touch to both Devon and Kit, grounding himself with their presence before turning to Glynn, already sliding his opened shirt off his shoulders, and Éamon, who wasn't far behind him. "How do we do this?"

"Bedroom's upstairs." Devon nodded in the general direction of the stairs, his eyes roaming appreciatively over the flesh their guests were baring. "Unless you'd rather have at it right here."

"The couch is barely big enough for the three of us," Kit interjected. "The bed is definitely the better option." He pulled his T-shirt over his head and grabbed Jonathan with one hand and Éamon with the other. Jonathan didn't need directions, but Kit rather thought he might need the reassurance. "This way."

That left Glynn to Devon for the moment, which was fine with him. Moving behind the darker man, he slid his arms under Glynn's, tweaking his nipples. He canted his hips to nudge his erection against Glynn's crease while he nipped at an earlobe. "Best not let them get too far ahead of us," he murmured.

"Eager, are they?" Glynn asked, leaning back into Devon's caress, rubbing provocatively against the hard cock. "I like that in a man."

"Yeah, well, they'll start without us if we don't get up there, and that's not something I plan to miss. So move that gorgeous arse." Stepping back, Devon landed a swat on the arse in question before grabbing Glynn's hand and starting up the stairs.

Glynn followed willingly, crowding Devon all the way up the stairs and into the bedroom.

True to Devon's prediction, all three men in the bedroom were already out of their shirts, and Kit's jeans flew past their heads as they came through the door. "You weren't kidding," Glynn observed, dropping trou as well as he pounced on Kit to strip away his boxers.

Kit jumped at the unexpected touch but settled again quickly and turned in Glynn's arms, attacking his lips as he returned the favor, stripping Glynn completely. He met Devon's eyes over Glynn's shoulder and winked lasciviously as he grabbed a handful of firm butt and squeezed.

Éamon had backed Jonathan against a wall and was kissing him with enthusiasm, his hands working at Jonathan's belt. Jonathan grasped Éamon's shoulders, his eyes closed until one of the busy hands slid behind his zipper to palm his cock. His lids snapping open, he found himself watching Kit and Devon strip the last of Glynn's clothing and tackle him to the bed. Well aware of how it felt to be the focus of their combined attentions, he twisted his head to nip Éamon's ear. "Let's join the others," he suggested, kicking his jeans off when Éamon moved away enough to do the same.

Éamon followed Jonathan's lead, joining Devon, Kit, and Glynn on the king-size bed. He paused to kiss his lover lingeringly before nudging his way into Glynn's place between Devon and Kit. "I want a taste too," he requested, licking his way up Kit's chest to his nipples.

"He's all yours," Glynn offered, turning his full attention on Devon instead.

Kit moaned as Éamon sucked his nipples, but he caught sight of Jonathan, not involved with either of their guests, and reached out a hand toward him. "Come here," he purred. "I want a kiss."

Kneeling alongside Kit, Jonathan bent to capture his mouth, watching beneath lowered lids as Éamon worked his way down the smooth torso. The Irishman seemed just as fascinated by Kit's birthmark as Jonathan was himself, and Kit arched beneath the teasing nibbles.

A groan from the other side of the bed caught Jonathan's attention. Devon had straddled Glynn's hips, dragging their cocks together as he tugged at Glynn's nipples. Draping his thighs over Devon's calves, Glynn cupped Devon's arse and rocked him forward, increasing the friction between them.

Kit stroked Jonathan's cheek, drawing his attention again. "Go over there and rim Devon if you want. You know he'll enjoy it." He started to say more, to encourage Jonathan to participate in whatever way was comfortable for him, but Éamon's mouth on his cock distracted him, leaving him gasping and squirming as his shaft slid down the Irishman's throat.

Since Éamon had Kit well in hand—or rather, in mouth—Jonathan moved over them with care to crouch behind Devon. "Lean forward," he murmured, turning Devon's head enough to claim a deep kiss before nudging him downward. Glynn pulled Devon down the rest of the way, covering his mouth. Jonathan's palms slid over the planes of Devon's back, covering Glynn's, which were still cradling Devon's cheeks. He nudged them gently to the sides, leaning in to swipe his tongue down Devon's crease. Instead of slipping away, Glynn's fingers tangled with his, the combined touch inviting Devon to push his hips into Jonathan's questing tongue and lips.

The combination of Éamon's mouth and the erotic tableau presented by the other three men was enough to have Kit begging. "Somebody has got to fuck me," he pleaded. "Now!"

"That's an offer I've been waiting weeks to hear," Glynn said, wriggling out from under Devon. "Point me in the direction of the condoms and the lube and I'm your man."

Kit jerked open the drawer, finding the lube immediately and a few stray condoms in the back after another moment. He tossed them in Glynn's direction. The other man caught them deftly and moved between Kit's widespread thighs, leaning down to mouth at the tendon connecting his thigh to his hip as he coated his fingers and began stretching Kit's entrance.

Éamon slid into the space Glynn vacated, watching for a moment as Devon pulled Jonathan up into a kiss. As soon as they came up for air, he ran a hand up each torso, pulling at the fine hair dusting Jonathan's chest. "I hope you're willing to share," he murmured with a smile to Devon before urging Jonathan down into a kiss. "Fuck me, Jonathan?"

Before Jonathan could draw breath to answer, Devon had retrieved another condom from the drawer. Taking the lube from where Glynn had dropped it, he pressed them both into Jonathan's hand. "Go ahead, Jon," he urged. "And once you're inside him, I'll fuck you."

"Oh hell." Devon's voice had fallen into the husky register that was nearly enough to get Jonathan off just listening to it. Squeezing some lube over his fingers, he did his best to focus on opening Éamon while Devon helpfully rolled the condom onto his cock.

"Fuck, yeah," Éamon gasped, planting his heels on the mattress to press onto Jonathan's fingers. "Now, Jonathan. Do it." Slicking himself generously, Jonathan moved into position between Éamon's legs and pushed slowly against the tight ring of muscle. Two of Devon's fingers slid inside Jonathan, pressing with intimate knowledge against his sweet spot, at the same moment Éamon relaxed enough for Jonathan to slip inside. Resisting the urge to rock back against Devon's twisting fingers, Jonathan slid deeper by slow degrees, leaning forward to nuzzle Éamon's neck and make it easier for Devon to move into place behind him.

Kit groaned when Glynn added a third finger, stretching him urgently. "Enough," he rasped. Glynn took him at his word, withdrawing his fingers and lining his cock up at the glistening entrance, surging forward with the same force of will that had shone in Bors's eyes as they argued over Lancelot. Kit gasped and shifted, eyes rolling back in his head as his body reacted to the stimulation. Blinking rapidly, he turned his head so he could see his lovers, Devon driving into Jonathan as Jonathan thrust into Éamon. Needing that connection with them, he reached out, his hand resting lightly on Jonathan's knee as he arched into the pummeling Glynn was giving him.

The touch to his leg drew Jonathan's attention from the dual sensations assailing him. Even though he knew Devon was behind him, filling him, he blinked to see a dark head rather than a blond one bending forward to plunder Kit's lips. Reaching out to thread his fingers between Kit's, Jonathan threw his head back as the heat around and inside him grew and welled. Leaning back into the pressure of Devon's chest, he closed his other hand around Éamon's cock, fisting it with short, choppy strokes until his climax erupted, Éamon spilling through his fingers seconds later.

The touch of Jonathan's hand did what all Glynn's skill could not, tipping Kit over the edge of his release, his body clenching around the invading member as his cock disgorged its load. He forced his eyes open to fix on Jonathan and Devon, maintaining the connection with his lovers.

Devon felt Jonathan clench and tremble around him, heard Éamon's and Glynn's groans as they found their release, but not until he met Kit's eyes and watched his face tense and slack with the force of his climax did he allow himself to let go. Pulling Jonathan upright and turning his head into a kiss, he shuddered through his own fierce orgasm, not releasing Jonathan's lips until the last aftershocks died away.

Five bodies collapsed on the bed, Éamon and Glynn gravitating together at the same time Kit moved toward Jonathan and Devon. As physically satisfying as the sex had been, Kit needed the emotional connection he only had with his lovers. They pulled him against them, clearly sharing his need, arms encircling him and each other to reestablish the bond between them. Lust sated, Kit trembled at the thought that they might have inadvertently damaged this link, and his embrace tightened as if he could stave off any threat if only he could cling hard enough.

Wrapping his arms around his lovers, Jonathan glanced at Glynn and Éamon, who were trading their own warm kisses. He shifted uneasily, feeling an awkwardness he hadn't experienced since his earliest relationships. Would they want to spend the night? He'd rather be alone with Kit and Devon, but there was no way to suggest that without sounding crassly rude. He realized he wasn't even at his own house, but among the three of them it had stopped mattering whose bed they wound up in—it was always theirs. Except now it was apparently Glynn's and Éamon's too. Jonathan bit back a wry chuckle at trying to navigate the etiquette of a five-way fuck.

After a few moments, Glynn and Éamon rose from the bed. "Thanks, guys. It's been fun," Glynn said with a grin. "We'll see you on set tomorrow."

He grabbed his clothes and started getting dressed. "Don't get up," Éamon added. "We'll see ourselves out. And obviously, as far as anyone outside the room is concerned, this never happened."

"I'll see you down." Devon disentangled himself and pulled on a pair of boxers, hoping they were his. Maybe it was strange to worry about covering up after what they'd just shared, but while his ingrained courtesy wouldn't let him lie in bed while their guests left, he didn't feel like parading in front of them starkers. Glancing over his shoulder at Jonathan and Kit, who made muffled goodbye-sounding noises, he escorted Éamon and Glynn downstairs and saw them out.

Turning back as he started down the porch steps, Éamon met Devon's eyes. "I probably should have said this before, but tonight caught me a little off guard. Glynn and I have a rule: we don't ever invite the same outsider—or outsiders, in this case—into our bed a second time. I hope there won't be any hard feelings."

Surprised at the surge of relief that swept through him, Devon smiled. "No hard feelings. It was good, though."

"It was," Éamon agreed with a grin. "If anyone could make us reconsider our rule, it would be you three, but to tell the truth, I can only share him for so long before I need him to myself again, so I know it's better this way. Enjoy the rest of your night." He waved once more as he walked out to the car and joined Glynn, pulling his lover's head down for another kiss before backing out of the driveway and disappearing into the night.

Jonathan was curled around Kit when Devon reentered the bedroom, the younger man's head pillowed on his chest. The unusual position was clue enough that the experience had thrown his lovers off-kilter; his own reaction to Éamon's caveat was equally telling. Sitting on the edge of the mattress, he reached out to touch, sliding a hand into each man's hair. "Still okay?" he asked softly.

Kit looked up at Devon, reaching for him and pulling him back down. "Yeah," he said slowly, "but I have to admit, I'm not in any hurry to do it again. I... I missed you. The sex was fine, but I've gotten spoiled, making love with you two all the time."

"That's just it, I think," Jonathan added slowly. "It felt good, but something was missing when I couldn't feel that connection with the two of you. Just good sex isn't good enough anymore. Not when you've shown me how much more there can be."

"It isn't an option again anyway." Devon lowered himself to spoon against Jonathan's side, wrapping an arm over his chest to touch Kit. "It seems they have a rule never to do anyone more than once."

"That makes things easier where they're concerned," Kit agreed. "We don't have to worry about hard feelings spilling over onto the set. But what about later? If someone else approaches one or more of us?"

Though his gut insisted he'd had enough of sharing his lovers, Jonathan knew it wasn't a reasonable reaction. They were going to go their separate ways after filming, and even though he was convinced they'd find a way to keep their relationship going after *Camelot* ended, he couldn't expect Devon and Kit to go months or more without someone else catching their eye. Could he? "It's sure to happen," he said quietly. "Maybe not while we're still together, but later...."

Kit shuddered. "I don't even want to think about later, but I know we have to. I'll be honest. I was never very good at sharing, and that's even truer than usual where you two are concerned. It would have to be someone utterly amazing for me to even consider risking what we have by bringing someone else into our bed again. And the thought of doing it without you there at all is totally unappealing. At least if you're there, I have some connection to you."

"'Later' will get here sooner than any of us wants to think about." Devon tried to keep the sting of that thought out of his voice. "And I have to admit I have no desire to think about any of us with anyone else. If nothing else, because going back to using condoms again is a bloody pain."

"What about this?" Jonathan suggested. "We have to expect that once we're apart, any of us might find someone who appeals to us. But we all have to agree before anyone acts on it."

"And we all have to be there," Devon added.

"Are you sure?" Not that his heart didn't agree, but Jonathan was afraid that rule would prove easier said than done. "It may be hard for even two of us to get together once filming ends, let alone all three of us."

"At the moment, I'm having trouble picturing someone special enough to want to share you with at all," Kit insisted, "but I can't imagine what it would do to me to know you two were together and with a third who *wasn't* me. That would be… like having my heart ripped out of my chest. I don't know that I could handle it. And if I can't handle it, I don't want to expect either of you to have to go through it either."

"Tonight was proof enough for me that I don't want anyone but the two of you," Jonathan asserted. "But would you do that? Give up being with anyone else for the few times we might be able to be together?"

Kit cuffed Jonathan lightly on the back of the head, the odd angle keeping the blow from doing any damage. "I already told you I love you, you prat. I don't want anyone else but you and Devon. I haven't since the moment I laid eyes on you, tonight notwithstanding. I'm not naïve. I know it won't be easy, but I'm not going to make it more difficult by adding infidelity to the distance we'll have to figure out how to span."

"My track record in relationships may not be very good, but it's never been because of infidelity." Devon rubbed Jonathan's head where Kit had bopped it, then rubbed over Kit's curls for good measure. "I'll make do until my hand falls off before I risk what we have for some meaningless fuck."

"Why make do with your own hand when you can have mine?" Kit joked.

Devon grinned and flopped onto his back. "What are you waiting for then, boy? Service me!"

"Who made you king?" Jonathan laughed with sudden joy before leaning down to pull both his lovers into a kiss. He still wasn't sure how, but he finally believed they'd make this amazing relationship last even when filming was ended.

CHAPTER 25
MAKING THEIR MARK

KIT SHIFTED nervously on the stool at the tattoo parlor, itching to reach for Devon's hand in comfort as the buzz of the tattooist's gun got louder. That Jonathan looked sublimely unconcerned as the needle pierced the skin of his inner thigh repeatedly did not have any effect on Kit's edginess. He had never liked needles, even before his back surgery, so being here, agreeing to this, was a real test of courage on his part.

They had decided on tattoos as a way to commemorate their relationship in a permanent but discreet manner. Kit grinned still to think of Devon's reaction to his first suggestion, since obviously they could not wear rings. "Nobody would notice another charm on my necklace," Kit had proposed, liking the idea of having some outward mark of their commitment to one another.

Devon had glared at him as if the very idea offended his masculinity. "If I turned up sporting a necklace, I can guarantee someone would comment on it."

"I've gotten tattoos to commemorate the special events in my life," Jonathan had interjected, heading off Kit's incipient protest that there was nothing inappropriate about his charm necklace. "I've been trying to decide what kind of design to get for this, because the role that brought me the two of you is definitely something I want to mark that way. I know Devon doesn't have a problem with tattoos either, but is that something you might consider, Kit?"

It wasn't something Kit had ever really thought about before, but beyond the thought that it would hurt—other than the occasional spanking, he really wasn't into pain; he'd had enough of that with his back—he didn't have a reason to say no.

"It's looking good," Devon commented, leaning in for a closer look when the tattooist paused to reload his ink gun. "You did a great job with the design, Jon." The outline of the stylized Grail cup was already visible, in preparation for the Celtic scrollwork design that would fill it.

"I think it will look good when it's finished," Jonathan agreed. "I couldn't think of a better symbol for what this time has meant to me than the Holy Grail." He smiled at Devon and Kit, knowing they'd understand the deeper meaning behind his words. The tattoo shop they'd selected had a private room for work on intimate areas—which he appreciated, since he'd had to strip down to his boxers to bare the inside of his right thigh for the inking—but he was still trying to be discreet about what he said in front of the tattoo artist.

"Are you doing all right?" Kit asked Jonathan. He knew the other man had gotten tattoos before, but this was the first time Kit had watched it.

"Doing fine," Jonathan assured him. He could tell Kit was still a bit apprehensive, though he'd insisted he wanted to do this. "The skin has more give here than it does over bone, like when I had the first one done on the small of my back. It really doesn't hurt—more like little pinpricks." He hoped that would hold true for Kit as well, though everyone's pain tolerance was different. "Nothing compared to some of the things you've been through," he added with a wink toward Devon.

Devon chuckled at the color that bloomed in Kit's cheeks. "Compared to the surgery on your spine, this will be nothing," he added, though he was sure that wasn't what Jonathan had been referring to.

Kit could feel the flush staining his cheeks as he thought about all the different positions he'd found himself in with his lovers over the months of filming. He certainly wouldn't have believed he'd enjoy being spanked or having a crop taken to his backside, but Devon had made both of those things incredible experiences. His arse still tingled from the playful swats Devon had given him last night when he couldn't keep his mouth shut.

He'd been pushing and he knew it, but filming was ending in less than a week, and Jonathan would be returning to LA to see his son and Devon would be heading for Prague almost immediately to begin filming his next role. Kit had no idea what he'd do without them there all the time. He'd gotten a couple of offers, but he hadn't accepted them, hoping to take one that would put him near either Jonathan or Devon. That might have worked if they weren't going to be on opposite sides of the globe.

He reached for Devon's hand when the impulse took him this time, the need for contact too great to deny. They had a matter of days left. Blythe and James Sinclair, the actor who had played Mordred, were already done. They'd had the send-off party the same night he and his lovers had decided to get tattoos. Addison would be leaving tomorrow, and everyone else this weekend. Even with the tattoos, Kit felt like something precious was slipping through his fingers. He bit his lip against asking for reassurance where the tattooist could hear him. It was this very fear that had led to their decision to get tattoos in the first place.

They'd walked to Kit's after the farewell party for Blythe and James, since it was closest to the pub and they'd been drinking enough that none of them felt safe to drive. "I didn't have the chance to get to know James very well, but I'm going to miss Blythe. I couldn't have asked for a better Guinevere," Jonathan had said with a mournful tone in his voice. "She promised to keep in touch, but I know how hard that can be. You start out with good intentions, but then you get caught up in the next role, and the one after that...."

"You think that's what's going to happen to us, don't you? You think we're going to drift apart when we aren't living in each other's pockets anymore," Kit had said sadly. The final scene between Arthur and Guinevere had been as powerful as anyone could have hoped—regret, contrition, and an enduring love coming across so powerfully Kit would have sworn the emotions were real if Jonathan hadn't left the set and come home to Kit's and Devon's arms. If that kind of connection could fade, what hope did the three of them have?

"I didn't mean us, Kit," Jonathan had insisted, pulling Kit into his arms. "It's the reality for most of the friendships that form during filming, though sometimes you can make them last. But this—what we have, the three of us—this isn't some casual acquaintance that's going to wear off just because we aren't seeing each other every day. We proved that while Devon was gone. Besides, even after I go back"— Jonathan's voice had caught in his throat, despite how much Kit knew he was looking forward to spending time with Josh again—"you'll still have Devon."

"Not for long," Devon had interjected. "I signed on for *The Handler* while I was in LA. It starts filming in Prague next month." Looking a bit guilty, he'd shrugged. "At the time, I thought staying busy would help keep me from missing you both so much. Now I'm wishing I hadn't been so quick to jump into something else right away."

Shaking his head to push the memories aside, Kit focused back on the tattoo artist as he finished the scrollwork on Jonathan's tattoo. He shifted a little in his seat, imagining running his lips over the new mark… and from there up to more intimate locations. The tattooist wiped the area clean, slathered it in Aquaphor, and covered it with a gauze pad. "Leave that on for about an hour," he instructed, "and then you can take it off and wash it gently with soap and your hands. Don't rub it with a washcloth or anything."

Nodding his agreement, Jonathan levered himself carefully from the chair, patting Devon on the shoulder and sliding onto the stool next to Kit as soon as Devon vacated it. "Drop trou there, Devon. You're next."

"Same place?" the tattooist asked, stretching while Devon removed his slacks and positioned himself in the chair.

"Same place," Devon agreed, winking at Kit as he spread his knees so the tattoo artist could move between his legs. "I don't expect this is the oddest spot you've ever had to ink."

"You'd be amazed where some people want a tattoo," the artist agreed, looking up from his needle. "You're the actors from *Camelot*, aren't you? I thought I recognized you when you made the appointment, and the design fits with that."

"We wanted something to remember the filming by," Kit said quickly, hoping the man wouldn't read more into the tattoo than that. It was one of the reasons they'd decided on the Grail in the first place. It gave them credible deniability if anyone ever asked them about it.

The artist picked up a marker and copied the design from his stencil onto Devon's skin the same way he had done Jonathan's before he began, making Kit squirm in his seat as he imagined the felt tip tickling his skin.

Jonathan draped an arm around Kit's shoulders, hoping it would look like nothing more than one friend reassuring another. "And we decided on someplace where we wouldn't always have to hide it with makeup." He wasn't sure the tattooist would buy that, though it was certainly true. "Not like that fanboy emblem on Devon's shoulder."

"Just because some directors can't appreciate the glory of Man U—"

It turned out the tattooist was also a fan, and before long he and Devon were engaged in a fervent discussion of this year's team and their chances in the upcoming match against Chelsea. Jonathan took the opportunity of their distraction to nuzzle Kit's ear. "You're going to look so beautiful in that chair. I'm going to be hard just watching you."

Jonathan's comment was enough to have Kit hardening in his track pants. "Not a good idea when you're still just wearing your boxers," he whispered back. "We're trying to keep this guy from finding out about us, not advertising our relationship to him, remember?" He couldn't help but appreciate Jonathan's effort to put him at ease, though. Knowing Jonathan was watching him, thinking lusty thoughts about him, would help distract him from the needle against his leg.

"Just imagine what it will feel like once it's healed enough for me to trace it with my tongue." Jonathan shifted on the stool, the image affecting him just as powerfully as he intended it would Kit.

Kit only hoped the buzzing of the needle hid the moan that escaped his lips at the decadent image evoked by Jonathan's words. "If you get me hard before I get in the chair, he's going to notice for sure," Kit hissed, "and somehow I don't think he'll buy that I get off on the experience, since I've never done this before to know."

"Sorry." Jonathan grinned, leaning back to put some space between them. He'd started to suggest Kit flirt with the tattooist and maybe the man would think the arousal was for him, but the words died on his lips. He didn't want to think about Kit flirting with anyone but him or Devon, even when it was just playing a role. "Did you like any of the scripts your agent sent you?" he asked instead, steering the conversation to a safer topic.

"There was one that looked fun," Kit replied, appreciating the diversion. *The Romany Affair*. It's a thriller. They're looking at me for the role of the Romany prince who's torn between helping his brother escape from prison and the agent he's falling in love with."

"Sounds perfect for you." Jonathan had no doubt that Kit would prove as convincing a prince as Devon would the lethal bodyguard he'd signed on to play in his next film. He glanced at Devon in the chair, any discomfort overshadowed by the passion with which he was decrying the officiating in the Reds' last match against Newcastle. "Vidic was screwed—Smith should have been tossed after that hit," Devon was saying, the tattooist nodding in agreement as he refilled his ink. Jonathan grinned as he caught Devon's eye, remembering the equal passion Devon had brought to their bed the night before. He'd miss that energy as much as Kit's still unbridled enthusiasm…. Blinking, he turned his attention back to Kit. "Who are they looking at for your love interest?"

"I haven't heard," Kit replied. "It's not a sure thing. I'd still have to go to an audition, but they asked me to come, so I figure that's a good sign." Kit paused and looked up at Jonathan from beneath his lashes. "You could audition for the role of the love interest."

"Are they casting a male as the agent?" Jonathan asked in surprise before the twinkle in Kit's eyes let him in on the joke. "You're the only one who thinks I look good in drag, Kit-Kat."

"But I'd give a much more convincing performance if I was falling in love with you than if it's some girl," Kit said. "I have to admit I'm a little nervous about the sex scene toward the end. It fades to black before it gets too explicit, but I don't know what to do with a girl."

"You're an actor; you act." Jonathan ached to drop a reassuring kiss on Kit's lips, but he settled for running a hand through the dark hair, letting it rest at the base of Kit's neck. "I've filmed enough love scenes, some with women I wouldn't share the time of day with if I had the choice, that I've learned to recast my partner in my head when I have to." He rubbed his thumb over the ridge of Kit's spine, the warm skin beneath his making him harden again in anticipation of stripping the short, tight T-shirt from Kit's body once they were all finished. "Besides, I seem to remember you handling two 'girls' and not leaving either of them complaining."

Kit couldn't stop the chuckle at the memory of Jonathan and Devon in drag, bearded faces and all. "But that's because I love you," he said, careful to keep his voice low. He paused for a second before adding, "I guess that's what I have to keep in mind when I'm filming. I have to let what I feel for you show on my face when I'm looking at her, whoever she is. Or I could try to convince the director that the film would get a whole lot more attention with a male agent."

"You might get an independent director on a smaller film to consider that, but with a blockbuster like *Romany*, that isn't the kind of attention the studio would accept." Jonathan had been giving serious thought to what might happen to his career if his relationship with Kit and Devon became widely known. He'd done well enough that he didn't have to take roles just to pay the bills anymore; if the major studios had a problem with his personal life, he was pretty sure he'd still be able to find parts. Maybe in smaller films with more avant-garde directors, but he wasn't sure that would even be a sacrifice at this point, if it meant more time to spend with

Devon and Kit. "Anyway, the director must think you're enough of an actor to carry it off, since he's inviting you to audition."

Kit nodded. "I know. I'm just nervous. This will be my first big film audition. I did *Around Every Corner*, and I've done a couple of indie things, but this is in a totally different league." He glanced toward Devon, where the tattoo artist was applying a thin coating of gel and a gauze pad to Devon's thigh. "Looks like it's my turn."

"You'll do fine, Kit." Devon clasped Kit's shoulder, the touch enough for him to tell Kit was anxious about more than just the upcoming audition. Letting his voice lower in tone as well as volume, he added, "Just watch Jon and me watching you. It'll be finished before you know it."

Kit couldn't stop the butterflies in his stomach as he took off his track pants and settled in the chair, the leather warm from Devon's body. He glanced around the room, trying to find something safe to look at as the tattoo artist started tracing the stencil of the Grail onto his leg. The pen tickled, making it hard to stay still. "Don't move," the man said. "It's not that big a deal if I mess up with the pen, but if I mess up with the gun, it's a lot harder to fix."

Kit nodded, his eyes pleading with Jonathan and Devon for help.

"Would it be okay with you if we hold his hands?" Devon asked, hoping it sounded casual. "The lad's a tattoo virgin. Maybe we can hold him down and keep him from jumping on you."

"We'll stay out of your way," Jonathan added, dragging the wheeled stool he'd been sitting on to a spot at the other side of Kit's chair.

"Sure, lots of people are nervous their first time." The tattooist looked up at Kit and smiled. "I promise to be gentle, and if your friends here are any guide, you'll be coming back for more."

"They've certainly convinced me to come back for more of other things," Kit said, gamely summoning a smile as the tattooist picked up the gun. The first prick of the needle startled him, and he jumped a little despite the steadying hands, but it didn't hurt as much as he'd expected. He was able to relax a little, although the steady bites of pain killed what remained of his hard-on from flirting with Jonathan earlier. It was probably just as well, given the way his legs were splayed. The openings of his boxers were loose, and one side was pushed up to give the tattooist access to the skin he was inking. If he looked right, he'd probably get an eyeful. Fortunately he seemed too focused on what he was doing to ogle Kit's package.

Devon had no such distraction, and he rolled his stool a few inches to give him a clear view inside Kit's boxers. "Looking good, sunshine," he said in a jovial voice that belied the anticipation of getting more than his eyes on Kit's body.

Jonathan rolled his eyes, though he knew Devon was just trying to get Kit to relax. "From here too," he said softly, watching the Grail's outline take form under the tattooist's steady hand.

Kit scowled at Devon for using the nickname in front of the tattooist, but at least he hadn't called Kit "kitten." He supposed he should be grateful for small mercies. Despite the nearness of the needle, he could feel his body reacting to Devon's gaze. He glanced at Jonathan for help or distraction or both.

Constrained by the tattooist's presence, Jonathan traced the lifeline on Kit's palm with his thumb, his gaze holding Kit's eyes. He'd been struck by their dark intensity the first time they'd met, but now, watching the pupils dilate and the ring of golden highlight that rimmed the iris brightening, he could tell without having to share Devon's view that Kit was getting aroused. Leaning down, he murmured in a voice that would carry no farther than Kit's ear, "Are you getting hard, kitten? Giving Devon a show, watching your cock fill up?" His own balls were tightening, and he knew he was playing with fire by teasing Kit this way, but he couldn't help himself—not when they had so little time left.

Devon couldn't hear what Jonathan was whispering to Kit, but he could make a good guess, based on the way the younger man's cock was starting to bob beneath the thin veil of cotton. Bending down, he nudged the shell of Kit's ear with his nose. "Is Jon being naughty? Maybe we should discipline him when we get home."

"Now who's being naughty?" Kit hissed as the thought of playing out a discipline scene with Jonathan only added to his arousal. It wouldn't be long before he had a wet spot on the front of his boxers if they kept this up. "Can I spank him this time?"

If the tattooist heard the sibilant comment, he kept his head down, his focus on the intricate knotwork design. Devon glanced across the chair at Jonathan, but he couldn't tell if their lover had heard the remark either—Jonathan was whispering something else to Kit, his tongue flicking out to trace the whorl of Kit's ear when it was clear the tattooist wasn't watching them.

Between Jonathan's whisperings about what he'd do to Kit as soon as they got home, most of which involved his mouth on Kit's dripping cock, and Devon's silent agreement to let Kit be the one to spank Jonathan if they punished him for his forwardness, Kit hoped the tattooist was either woefully clueless or incredibly discreet, because there was no hope of willing away his erection. They'd be lucky if he managed not to turn his head and kiss Jonathan within an inch of his life just to stop the sinful murmurings.

The whir of the needle fell silent, but only Devon noticed, Kit and Jonathan still lost in whispered conversation. The tattooist set down his gun and raised his head to meet Devon's gaze with a lifted eyebrow. Devon winked, and the corners of the tattooist's lips tilted up in a smile. The man slid his stool back and cleared his throat. Kit's head snapped up as the artist smoothed a coating of cool gel over his heated skin and covered the image with a taped-down square of gauze.

"Leave it covered for at least an hour to let the inflammation go down," the tattooist reminded him, stripping off his latex gloves. "After that, you can take off the gauze."

"Will it hurt to get them wet?" Kit asked, thinking about all the things he wanted to do to his lovers.

"Showers are fine, but try to stay out of tubs or pools for about a month. Wash with a gentle soap and only use your hands—don't use a washcloth or rub too hard." His lips twitched again, as if he was holding back another comment. "A little flaking is normal for the first few weeks, but use a lotion to keep the skin moist and supple. If you have any problems, you can always give us a call or stop in. I'll be happy to take a look."

"None of us will be around after next week," Jonathan said softly, sliding his stool from Kit's side but not standing—he didn't need to make his erection any more obvious than it already felt. "This is the last week of filming, and after that we're all going on to new projects." Resisting the urge to glance down and see how badly his boxers were tented, he offered his hand to the tattoo artist. "Thanks—you do great work."

Already pulling on his slacks, Devon took several bills from his wallet and handed them to the tattooist as he shook his hand. "We appreciate your accommodating us this way. It's been a pleasure."

"Anytime you want to add to your ink, I'd be happy to work on you." The artist nodded to them all and turned toward the door. "Take your time getting dressed," he added over his shoulder. "We don't have anything else booked for the room until tomorrow."

"You two are lucky I don't jump you right here," Kit fussed, getting up from the chair gingerly, the tape from the gauze pulling at the skin of his leg. "I thought we were going for discretion!"

"I was discreet!" Devon protested. "You were the one flaunting your assets once Jon started getting you all wound up."

"It took your mind off the needle, didn't it?" Jonathan countered, easing his jeans up his legs with care. "You didn't jump once after Devon and I started distracting you."

"Fine," Kit huffed, "but I'm still taking it out of your arses when we get home. Whose house are we going to?"

"Jon's is closest," Devon observed, frowning when Kit pulled his loose pants over his boxers, then cheering up when he realized he'd have the pleasure of removing them again in just a few minutes.

"Works for me." Jonathan would agree to anything that would get them all naked as quickly as possible. "We'll work out whose ass belongs to who when we get there."

THE MUSIC blared loudly as the remaining cast of *Camelot* gathered to say goodbye. Kit had lost count of how many drinks he'd consumed since arriving at the wrap party, but he was pretty sure it was well over what was wise. He couldn't seem to help himself, though. The thought of the idyllic months he'd spent in Glastonbury with Jonathan and Devon ending had him more than a little out of control. Bouncing across the room, he flopped down on Addison's lap and planted a hearty kiss on the older man's mouth.

"I'd be flattered if I didn't suspect that owes more to Jose Cuervo than to my personal charm," Addison said. "You're going to regret this tomorrow, Kit."

Addison was probably right, Kit had to admit, but it didn't seem to matter now. "So tell me how to stop," he said, his voice slurred. "At least it doesn't hurt as much right now."

"Ah, youth." Addison shook his head. "You make me feel positively ancient. Kit, trust me when I say I know this is difficult, but you'll have opportunities to see them again. If *Camelot* isn't nominated for several BAFTAs, I'll turn in my membership card, and I suspect both Arthur and Lancelot will stand among the nominees. Niall will be sure to invite the principal cast to attend."

Kit nodded. "Jonathan said he thought it would get the attention of the Emmys too, since it's being broadcast in the US. It's just so uncertain. Jonathan's going to LA, Devon's off to Prague or Budapest or somewhere in Eastern Europe, and I'm going to be stuck in London alone."

"I predict you won't be stuck in London for long," Addison retorted. "If your agent is worth his or her salt, you have a stack of scripts waiting for you to choose from. Self-pity doesn't become you, lad. Go find your partners and celebrate the time you have left."

Kit rose to his feet unsteadily, looking around for Devon or Jonathan. He caught sight of them near the bar and started their direction before getting waylaid by the Orkneys, nearly as drunk and unsteady as he was. He tried to extricate himself from their clutches, but the four young actors seemed nearly as dejected by the end of filming as he was and insisted on dragging him with them onto the dance floor. The beat from the music was seductive, and Kit found himself giving in to it, losing himself in gyrating in time to the pulses of sound and the movements of Colm, Bevan, Warwick, and Rhodri around him. Suddenly hot, he pulled his T-shirt off and tucked it into his waistband.

"Bloody hell," Devon cursed, his beer splashing the counter of the bar as he set it down. "The lad's going to be the death of me."

"But what a way to go," Jonathan said, watching the gleam of light play on the trickles of sweat down Kit's torso as he moved with sinuous grace to the driving beat. Finishing his own brew in one long swallow, he clapped Devon on the shoulder. "Take your vitamins and come join us," he invited before wending his way through the press of bodies on the dance floor.

Kit barely registered the hands that settled on his hips until they drew him backward against a hard body. A hard cock. Eyes opening, he turned his head to see Jonathan behind him. Heedless of their audience— the cast all knew about them anyway, right?—he parted his lips, inviting a kiss as he ground back against Jonathan's groin, determined to get his lover as worked up as he was.

Before Jonathan's lips could close over his, a hand grasped Kit's jaw and an equally hard body pressed against his chest. Devon pinched Kit's lower lip, his hips moving in time to the music, brushing against Kit's in a tantalizingly inconsistent rhythm.

Sandwiched between his lovers again, Kit felt the world tilt alarmingly for a moment before everything fell back into its proper place. He leaned back against Jonathan, his head resting on his shoulder as he pressed his hips forward, seeking Devon's body as well. When the contact he sought remained elusive, he lowered his hands, grabbing Devon's hips to pull him against his own.

"Easy," Jonathan breathed into Kit's ear. "Just because everyone here knows about us doesn't mean we have to give them an exhibition."

Kit whined in protest, but he subsided, letting Jonathan and Devon guide his movements. He had the fleeting thought that it apparently took being halfway to sloshed before he could truly let go and give in to his lovers.

Devon's eyes moved between Kit's and Jonathan's as he let his body's instinctive response to the music move him, storing away the sensory memories: the citrusy scent of Kit's shampoo and the clean musk of his sweat; the warmth of heated skin as their movements brushed Jonathan's or Kit's arm against his; the thump of the bass in his chest and the echoing pulse speeding to match it; the colored lights waking the shine in Jonathan's tawny hair as it mingled with Kit's darker locks. He'd pull these memories out when he was alone in some anonymous hotel room in Prague to remind himself that this was all real.

Jonathan moved back just enough that the brush of his hips against Kit's, his arm against Devon's, could be rationalized as random touches. Not that he honestly thought they were fooling anyone. Certainly not Éamon and Glynn, who were on the dance floor too, watching them with rueful empathy in their eyes. Niall had rented the pub for the wrap party and closed it to all but the *Camelot* cast and crew, so they didn't have to worry about photos showing up in the next day's papers, but Jonathan had enough professionalism and respect for his coworkers to remember discretion. Barely—though if Kit kept rocking his ass against Jonathan's thigh the way he was, Jonathan wasn't sure how much longer that professionalism would last.

The alcohol, the music, the press of his lovers' bodies, but most of all the knowledge that they would say goodbye to their friends tonight and to one another tomorrow combined to leave Kit suddenly desperate. "Please," he whispered, not even sure he could articulate what he needed. His lovers had always known before. He only hoped they would understand now.

Devon glanced at Jonathan over Kit's shoulder, recognizing the wordless agreement in the blue eyes. Taking Kit's hand, he steered him off the dance floor and toward the restrooms, Jonathan wrapping an arm around Kit's waist to steady him as they walked.

As soon as the bathroom door closed behind them, Jonathan set his back to it and pulled Kit into his arms. "I think you were asking for this earlier," he murmured, his lips closing over Kit's in a deep, claiming kiss.

Kit moaned into Jonathan's mouth, giving himself over to the kiss, needing to be claimed. He reached blindly for Devon, wanting both his lovers touching him. He thought briefly about asking them to mark him, but they had already gotten their tattoos to demonstrate their commitment. Instead he pressed closer to Jonathan, as if he could climb inside his skin and never leave.

Devon closed his mouth on Kit's neck as he reached between Kit and Jonathan—no easy task, that, given the way Kit seemed determined to fuse their very atoms together—to work at the buckle of Kit's belt. He'd normally be more cautious about leaving a bruise where it could be seen, but they no longer had to worry about filming tomorrow, and Kit would have enough time for it to heal before starting his next role that for once Devon could forget the need to be circumspect. Closing his teeth over the muscle where neck met shoulder, he sucked with just the degree of pressure Kit loved while he inched down the zipper to free Kit's heavy cock.

Feeling Devon opening his jeans, Kit arched his hips backward, pressing up against Devon instead to abet his disrobing. The pinch of teeth on his shoulder wrung a cry from him that even Jonathan's tongue in his mouth couldn't completely muffle. He was flying, high on alcohol and fear, and only his lovers' hands kept him grounded.

Breaking the kiss when Kit's cry into his mouth recalled his attention to what Devon was doing, Jonathan grinned. "You always have the best ideas, babe," he acknowledged, sinking to his knees. He lapped up the pearl of fluid trembling at the slit of Kit's cock. Moaning at the musky-sweet flavor, he grasped Kit's hip, opening his mouth to slide over the silken head and envelop the shaft in moist heat.

Kit bit down on the heel of his hand to stop the scream that wanted to escape at the feeling of Jonathan's mouth closing over his cock. He hated to muffle the sound, but he didn't want their castmates coming to investigate and interrupting them. It wouldn't take long for him to come, as worked up as he was, but even so, he wanted to savor it.

Devon watched the erotic tableau of Jonathan swallowing Kit's cock for a few moments, thinking as he always did how perfectly their light and dark coloring complemented each other, until the need to join in grew insistent. He slid Kit's slacks as far down his narrow hips as he could until they bumped into Jonathan's hands.

Jonathan glanced up, grazing a palm over bare skin as Devon worked the slacks down Kit's legs, letting them pool at his ankles. Jonathan wrapped his other hand around the base of Kit's cock, gliding up the saliva-slicked skin as it slipped from his mouth. Ignoring Kit's mewl of protest, he moved his lips over the delicate crinkled flesh of Kit's balls, stirring them with his tongue, his free hand caressing Kit's thigh as it drifted downward. Kit sighed and Jonathan's mouth followed his hand's descending path, pausing just before it reached the patch of dark ink adorning Kit's inner thigh. "So beautiful," Jonathan breathed, his words warming the skin before he closed his lips reverently over the stylized Grail.

Kit's protest died when Jonathan's lips brushed his new tattoo, still incredibly sensitive only a week after they'd gotten them done. "For you," he said huskily. "Only for you and Devon. For everyone else, it's just for show."

The words made Devon swell with pride at the knowledge that only he and Jonathan would ever see Kit this way. Grateful that Kit had already removed his shirt, he ran a hand up the smooth chest to catch a tightened nipple with thumb and forefinger, rolling the sensitive bud between the pads. That wrung a groan from Kit and made Devon determined to win more of them. Kneeling, he traced his other forefinger down the crease between Kit's cheeks, his tongue following a moment later.

"Please!" Kit babbled, hips bucking back against Devon's mouth. The pinch and pull on his nipples felt wonderful, but nothing except

Devon's or Jonathan's cock inside him felt as good as being rimmed. "Oh fuck, Devon, rim me, please!"

Well pleased to give Kit exactly what he was begging for, Devon curled his tongue and drove it past the ring of pink muscle, wetting the hot channel as far as he could reach. Kit cried out, his hand scrabbling for contact before clenching around a handful of Jonathan's hair.

Pressing a final soft kiss to the inked chalice, Jonathan teased at Kit's cock, lips tracing along the veined underside, then pushing back the foreskin as his tongue swirled around the exposed head. Kit's fingers tightened as Jonathan bobbed his head, sliding the foreskin up and down as he went.

If he'd been sober, Kit might have been embarrassed by how quickly he came once Jonathan's mouth returned to his cock, but he was drunk and desperate, and Jonathan was sucking him, Devon was rimming him, and someone—he had lost track of hands—was playing with his nipples. Three of his four favorite things. He had no hope of holding back and no desire to do so. "Coming," he warned Jonathan, though he doubted Jonathan needed the notice.

If Kit hadn't said a word, Devon would have known the instant Jonathan pushed him over the edge by the way the tight channel squeezed around his tongue. Consoling himself with the thought that he'd be able to feel that sensation on his cock before the night was over, Devon drove his tongue in and out in a foretaste of things to come, doing his best to prolong Kit's climax.

As soon as Kit's cock stopped twitching in his mouth, Jonathan pulled away, his hand cupping the softening shaft. Leaning to the side, he caught Devon's head with his other hand, pulling him forward to share a kiss redolent with Kit's tastes on both their tongues.

Looking down at the sudden cessation of sensation, Kit groaned as he watched Jonathan and Devon share a messy kiss. He slid to his knees, wrapping his arms around his lovers, joining them in the kiss as best he could. "Now what can I do for you?" he asked, keenly aware of how selfish he had been.

Jonathan shook his head. "That was for you, kitten."

"You were going to explode if we didn't do something to drain off that energy," Devon added, pushing to his feet. "You can make it up to us later."

Rising himself, Jonathan offered Kit a hand to help him stand. "We've got another day to spend together, but only a few more hours to spend with our friends."

"Let's go gather some more blackmail material on the Orkneys—they're even more pissed than you were." Devon adjusted himself discreetly before backing away enough to let Jonathan open the door.

CHAPTER 26
FOREVER FAMILY

"STOP FIDGETING." Devon tightened his arm around Jonathan's chest, holding his lover firmly against his side. His other hand stroked through the tawny hair pillowed against his shoulder, the gentle touch offsetting the insistence of his voice. "It's only been five minutes since the last time you looked at the clock. You're getting as bad as Kit."

"He should have been here by now." Jonathan would have chided his son Josh for the pout he heard in his voice, but he was past caring. Kit was supposed to have joined them a day ago, returning to London at about the same time Jonathan had arrived from LA, but bad weather at the location where he was filming had delayed him while the director shot the final scenes. It had happened to Jonathan often enough in his own career, but being on the opposite side of the delay for a change didn't make it any easier to take.

"You know he'll get here as soon as he can." Devon's hand followed the curve of Jonathan's cheek to his chin, turning his head for a kiss. "He's missed you as much as I did."

"At least you got to see him when he came to spend that weekend with you in Prague, and then you got to visit him in Budapest. I haven't seen either of you since *Camelot* wrapped." Jonathan shifted in Devon's arms so he could reach the blond head and pull it back down to his. He had three months of missed kisses and empty beds to make up for, and while he and Devon had made the most of the past day and night, it wouldn't be perfect until Kit was there to join them.

"And if you decide to accept one of the roles you're here to read for, you'll get to spend more time with both of us," Devon pointed out. The inevitable separation when the miniseries ended hadn't been any easier on him, but he and Kit had both been kept busy with new roles almost immediately, while Jonathan had headed back to the States to spend some time with his son. Devon and Kit had managed a few weekends together, but Jonathan hadn't had anything but some admittedly incendiary phone sex to hold him over in the three months since.

The sound of the front door opening caught their attention. Before they could do more than sit up, Kit came barging into the bedroom, coat falling to the floor as he pulled his sweater over his head. "Starting without me again?" he teased, his brown eyes sparkling with happiness at being reunited with his lovers. "What have I told you about that?"

"You honestly expected me to keep my hands off him after three months until you could get your skinny arse here?" Devon grinned. "I've just taken the edge off him for you—he still has plenty left for both of us."

"Hold that thought," Jonathan told Devon, standing to pull Kit into his arms, then capture his lips in a long, slow kiss. Only when the damp chill from Kit's clothes started to seep into his skin did he raise his head. "You're freezing!" he exclaimed, reaching up to ruffle Kit's wet curls.

"It's fucking sleeting out there," Kit said, leaning into Jonathan's warmth for a moment before pulling back to finish undressing. Both his lovers were naked, and he wanted to join them. Yesterday. "Let me get rid of these wet clothes before I kill every lustful thought in your head. And Devon, I don't care what you did while you were waiting for my skinny arse to get here as long as you're planning on doing that arse now that it *is* here."

"Sunshine, it'd take a sight more than a little sleet to cool either one of us down. I was about ready to tie Jon to the bed if you didn't get here soon, he was that impatient." Devon grinned, scooting over to make room for Kit.

"You should have," Kit said, snuggling into the warm spot Jonathan had just vacated and reaching out to pull his other lover down behind him. "You know he likes it when you do."

"Maybe later." Jonathan slipped into bed beside Kit, cocooning around him. "Once I get enough of being able to hold you again—like in another three months or so." His lips found Kit's once more, opening to the demand of Kit's tongue before meeting it and delving deep into the warmth of Kit's mouth in turn, drinking in the sweetness after three months of thirst.

Kit returned the kiss ardently even as he arched into Devon's body, relishing the warmth against his chilled skin. He broke the kiss momentarily to gasp, "Nothing feels like this. Nothing compares to being here with the two of you, surrounded by you. Nothing." He didn't wait for them to answer, turning to kiss Devon as he had kissed Jonathan, needing to reconnect to both of them, to the reality of the three of them being together. A moment later, he felt Jonathan lean over him to join the kiss, and he groaned again. He was going to come just from kissing them if they weren't careful.

Devon's hands roamed Kit's smooth skin, bumping into Jonathan performing a similar exploration. Since he'd been with Kit more recently than Jonathan had, he ceded the territory, scooting down on the mattress just enough to let his lips close around one of Kit's nipples. The gasp of approval this won prompted him to bite down gently, well aware of just how much pressure to use.

Jonathan smiled into the kiss when his hands brushed Devon's. He hadn't been able to get enough of touching and kissing Devon's fair skin when they'd fallen into bed together, and he was just as hungry for the touch and taste of Kit's olive flesh. His mouth followed along Kit's jaw to the curve of his neck, lingering over the rapid pulse in the hollow of his throat before moving lower, mirroring Devon's nibbling attentions to Kit's chest and the dark, stiff nub crowning it.

"Fu-uck," Kit groaned as Devon and Jonathan attacked his chest, one on each side. His body ached already, and they had barely gotten started. He slid his hand down, squeezing tightly around the base of his shaft, not wanting to come yet. He wanted their reunion to last longer than this! His other hand clenched in Jonathan's hair, not guiding but simply touching, needing the affirmation that they were all together again, that Jonathan was there with them after the three-month separation. He didn't know what the future would bring, but he knew one thing for certain. Three months was way too long to spend without his lovers.

Meeting Devon's eyes over the expanse of Kit's torso, Jonathan paused to claim the tempting lips so close to his own, burrowing one hand in his hair while his other drifted lower, maintaining the connection with Kit. Having Devon to himself for twenty-four hours had been wonderful, but nothing was better than all three of them together, the bond between them even stronger for the absence they'd endured.

Devon leaned into Jonathan's kiss, rubbing the swollen bud of Kit's nipple to let the younger man know he hadn't abandoned him. He'd had several chances after Jonathan returned to America to rediscover how responsive Kit was, but it never failed to swell his pride—and his cock—

when Kit arched up into his touch, moaning. Devon slid the fingers of his other hand down the taut plane of Kit's abdomen, his lips quirking into a smile against Jonathan's when he met Kit's hand clutching the base of his shaft.

"Eager much?" The warmth in Devon's voice took the sting from his words once Jonathan freed his mouth in favor of kissing his own languid path down Kit's torso.

"How many times have we been over this?" Kit gasped. "I'm twenty-two and perpetually horny. And it's been far too long since I was last in bed with both of you. Somebody'd better hurry up and fuck me or I'm not going to last until you get inside me." He wanted to. He wanted to have the control to hold back and draw out their lovemaking, but he'd waited too long for this, and he needed them too much. There would be time later for slow and tender. Right now, he needed hard and fast.

Jonathan chuckled against Kit's belly button, the answering quiver of muscles beneath his lips stoking his own arousal. He could understand Kit's impatience—he hadn't been able to wait for Devon's preparations either the first time, needing the stretch of that long, hard cock inside him too badly to care about niceties like lube—but he was enjoying himself too much to let this first time with Kit pass by quickly. He also knew how much harder they could make Kit come if they made him wait for it. Contenting himself with a single lick to the crown of Kit's cock to savor the droplet of fluid trembling there, he slid lower, pulling on Kit's thigh to open him wider so he could follow the crease of skin where leg and pelvis met.

"You don't have an exclusive on being perpetually horny," Devon countered. "It seems to be a permanent condition whenever I'm around either of you. And when I'm blessed enough to have you both together"— he dragged his tongue across Kit's groin, teeth closing around the ridge of bone hard enough to leave a mark—"I feel like I'm twenty-two again m'self."

"You say that," Kit protested, "but you're not inside me yet. Fuck me already!"

"Nothing's going to break you of being a bossy bottom, is it?" Devon rolled back to reach for the lube from the bedside table, letting Jonathan's head slide between Kit's splayed legs. The dark outline of the Grail tattoo on Kit's inner thigh caught Jonathan's attention, and he leaned in toward it, flicking his tongue out to trace the intricate design with loving licks.

The brush of Jonathan's hair over Kit's sac and the sensation of his tongue over the now healed tattoo were too much for Kit's control. He shivered as his cock twitched despite his restraining hand. He cried out sharply, his lovers' names coming out as garbled nonsense.

Turning back at Kit's cry, Devon let the now unneeded lube fall to the mattress and bent back over Kit, his lips closed around the still-twitching shaft, claiming a taste of the creamy fluid and prolonging the tremors of Kit's climax. Jonathan peeled Kit's hand from around the base of his cock, letting Devon take the full length into his mouth while Jonathan lovingly cleaned the seed clinging to Kit's fingers. When he'd lapped up every drop, he pillowed his head on Kit's shoulder, turning Kit's head for a deep, slow kiss.

"I warned you," Kit said hoarsely, his body still trembling as Devon and Jonathan did everything they could to extend his release. "This is what three months of not seeing my lovers does to me. Don't let it happen again."

"Don't let you come again?" Jonathan asked, his eyes twinkling as Devon turned Kit's head to claim his own welcome-home kiss. "Sorry, kitten, but I think you'll have to deal with it a few more times," he added, nestling closer to let his own resurgent erection prod the swell of Kit's cheek.

"Wanker," Kit grumbled, though he was feeling far too good to put any force into the insult. "No more three-month separations."

"Now that I can agree with." Devon was just as hard against Kit's other side, his arm wrapping around to rest on Jonathan's hip. "I don't want to wait that long to be together with both of you either. We have to do a better job of making our schedules fit together."

"Well, if one of the offers I came here to talk about works out, I'll be around more," Jonathan said. "Assuming that one or both of you aren't going to be off on location somewhere."

"We've got at least a month of studio work here in London to wrap up *The Romany Affair*," Kit said. "I'll have to be on set during the day, but I'll be home every night, just like when we were filming *Camelot*. What about you, Devon? Are you in town for a while?"

"I'm looking at some scripts, but I haven't signed on for anything new just yet." Devon shifted so he could see both Kit and Jonathan.

"I don't think you realize how popular *Camelot* has made you, at least here in the UK," he told Jonathan. "Directors are going to be scrambling for the chance to cast you. You'll be able to take your pick of any role you like."

"That's what my agent seems to think," Jonathan agreed. "If the offers I have now are any indication, I could probably split my time between London and LA. That way, I can spend time with Josh and with both of you."

"Really?" Kit asked, eyes lighting up at the prospect. "You'd do that? I mean, I know Josh has to be your first responsibility, but I've been beating my head against the wall trying to figure out how to spend more time in LA. If you were here some of the time…." He paused a moment, not wanting to bring up the media and speculation, but he'd kept an eye on the fan sites he'd found soon after filming started. "You know the more time you spend here in London, the more you're opening yourself up to speculation. Devon and I are from here originally, already have homes here, but even if you're working, people are going to talk."

Jonathan shrugged. "I had a lot of time to think while I was missing you in LA. I still don't see that who I choose to sleep with should be anybody's business but my own, and I'm not going to make a point of flaunting what we have, but if someone finds out, I'm not going to deny it."

"I've never cared a rat's arse what they print about me," Devon said, squeezing Jonathan's hip. "Any publicity's good publicity, right? And anyone who'd have a problem casting me because of the two of you isn't someone I'd want to work with anyway."

"Exactly," Jonathan agreed. "I'm past the place where I have to take any role that's offered to me, and I've honestly never had the ambition to be a blockbuster leading man. I'm more likely to be interested in playing the kinds of characters in smaller indie productions anyway, and those directors are less likely to care about what I do in my personal life, as long as it doesn't interfere with filming." He found Kit's and Devon's hands and linked their fingers together. "My only real concern was that Josh was okay with this, and he is. He loved the time he spent with us during his school break, and I don't think he'd have any problems spending his summers here. In fact, he wanted me to ask both of you if you'd consider coming to LA during the holidays so he could see you again."

"I'll be done filming by then," Kit said, a grin spreading at the thought of spending the holidays with his lovers. "We'd be, like, a real family. Josh's mom wouldn't mind sharing him with us?" He squeezed their joined hands. "I'd already decided not to sign on for another project until I'd talked to you two, hoping to find something that would let us be closer together, or at least apart for a shorter time. If we're going to work around Josh's holidays too, maybe I should start a calendar for us, where we can all record our various dates so we can actually make plans like a real family instead of each of us deciding on his own what we're doing next. I mean, if that isn't too clingy. I know nobody's going to let all three of us get married, but that doesn't mean we can't think like a couple. Right?"

"Like a threesome," Devon corrected. "I'd love to spend the holidays with you and Josh in LA, Jon. I'll just let my agent know I don't want to start anything new until after the first of the year."

"Like a family," Jonathan insisted. "The three of us and Josh. He'll be so excited about being able to have both of you there, I could probably not get him anything else for Christmas and he'd be happy." Not that he'd do that—in fact, he'd have to be sure the three of them together didn't spoil Josh silly. Luckily, his son had a good head on his shoulders. "The calendar is a good idea, Kit-Kat," he added. "When Jean and I were married, I'd always talk over my offers with her before accepting anything, especially if it meant leaving LA for location filming. It'll be a little more tricky juggling three schedules instead of two, but we can make it work."

"Like a family," Kit agreed. "That's what I meant, even if I didn't say it very well. It won't take but a minute or two to get it set up online. I can do that no—"

"Don't even think about moving," Devon growled, hauling Kit back between him and Jonathan when he pushed on an elbow to get up.

"None of us are signing any contracts this minute." Jonathan threw a leg over Kit's, pinning him to the bed. "There'll be plenty of time to set that up later. Besides, I haven't even met with any of the directors I supposedly came here to talk with yet."

Kit relaxed back between them, squirming a little. "So if I'm not getting out of bed, does that mean I can have my turn at Jon's arse, since I'm sure you've already had your turn?" Kit asked Devon with a cheeky grin.

"If you hadn't taken your sweet time getting here, Jon would have been the one who'd been away the longest," Devon retorted, swinging a leg over Jonathan's to aid in holding Kit in place. "And that would have made him most in need of our combined attentions. But since he got here almost a day before you did, that honor falls to you."

"I like that idea," Jonathan chimed in, a wicked grin spreading across his face. "Whoever's gone the longest gets to be in the middle." He grinned at Devon, already imagining how he'd welcome Kit home—because no matter how long they were apart or what continent they were on, when the three of them were together, they were home. "Heads or tails, babe?"

"He gets heads," Kit declared, "because while I've been gone the longest, I've seen him since I've seen you." He squirmed around beneath their confining legs so he could rub his backside against Jonathan's cock. He tugged on Devon's hips, urging him to slide up so he could get his mouth on Devon's cock. "Unless you have a better suggestion?"

"Works for me," Devon agreed, his eyes rolling back as the heat of Kit's mouth enveloped him. He'd never complain about submitting to Kit's enthusiastic oral prowess. "Just means I… get your arse next time."

"Suits me fine," Jonathan added. Deciding to take "tails" literally, he grasped Kit's hips and slid down until he could drag his tongue down the length of Kit's crease. He might have been able to bring himself off with his own hand while he was apart from his lovers, but Lord, he'd missed a good rimming. And if Kit came before Jonathan had opened him up enough to fuck him, well, he'd just have to deal with coming again. Somehow Jonathan didn't think Kit would mind too much.

Kit moaned in delight at the taste of Devon's cock and the feel of Jonathan's tongue forging inside him. All the phone sex, all the visits with one lover or the other couldn't even come close to competing with the joy of having both his lovers touching him, loving him. They'd still have days and weeks when they weren't together, but if they could stick to their current plan, those times would be few and far between. He was pretty sure Dorothy had it right after all. There was no place like home.

Growing up in Chicago, NICKI BENNETT spent every Saturday at the central library, losing herself in the world of books. A voracious reader, she eventually found it difficult to find enough of the kind of stories she liked to read and decided to start writing them herself.

Facebook: www.facebook.com/100011754789784

When ARIEL TACHNA was twelve years old, she discovered two things: the French language and romance novels. Those two loves have defined her ever since. By the time she finished high school, she'd written four novels, none of which anyone would want to read now, featuring a young woman who was—you guessed it—bilingual. That girl was everything Ariel wanted to be at age twelve and wasn't.

She now lives on the outskirts of Houston with her husband (who also speaks French), her kids (who understand French even when they're too lazy to speak it back), and their two dogs (who steadfastly refuse to answer any French commands). The cat pretends they're all beneath her, no matter what language they're speaking.

Visit Ariel:
Website: www.arieltachna.com
Facebook: www.facebook.com/ArielTachna
Email: arieltachna@gmail.com

EXPLORING

Exploring Limits: Book One

LIMITS

NICKI BENNETT
ARIEL TACHNA

Exploring Limits: Book One

We could always share him....

After failing to capture the attention of their bicurious costar singlehandedly, Kit and Devon team up to seduce Jonathan, who plays King Arthur in the new miniseries *Camelot*.

The chemistry between the three actors is off the charts, and it brings out the adventurous side in all of them. Things heat up in the bedroom as the trio explores the pleasures of dominance, submission, bondage, toys, and anything else they can find to get the most out of their secret time together.

But a gay ménage presents problems without easy solutions—especially as they work closely together on set. For their threesome to survive and evolve into a true committed relationship, they'll all have to test their physical and emotional limits.

This volume includes newly edited and expanded versions of the novellas:

Exploring Limits
Stretching Limits
Refining Limits

www.dreampsinnerpress.com

www.ingramcontent.com/pod-product-compliance
Lightning Source LLC
Chambersburg PA
CBHW070046030726
47506CB00002B/377